NIGHTMARE CITY

Also By Nick Oldham

A Time for Justice

NIGHTMARE CITY

Nick Oldham

HEADLINE
FEATURE

First published in Great Britain in 1997 by
HEADLINE BOOK PUBLISHING

A HEADLINE FEATURE hardback

10 9 8 7 6 5 4 3 2 1

British Library Cataloguing in Publication Data

Oldham, Nick
Nightmare city
1. Thrillers
I. Title
823.9'14[F]

ISBN 0 7472 1780 7

Typeset by Avon Dataset Ltd, Bidford-on-Avon, Warks

Printed and bound in Great Britain by
Mackays of Chatham PLC, Chatham, Kent

HEADLINE BOOK PUBLISHING
A division of Hodder Headline PLC
338 Euston Road
London NW1 3BH

To Sarah and Philip

Chapter One

It had been a hectic afternoon and looked set to become a bloody night. The custody office at Blackpool Central police station, always busy even at the quietest of times, was full to bursting. Since noon, over sixty prisoners had lurched through the door. Usually fighting, either between themselves or with their arresting officers, the majority were drunk and often covered in blood, vomit, snot or beer or a combination of all four. They were all males with an age range between sixteen and twenty-four. And all of them were connected with the football match which had taken place that afternoon between Blackpool and Bolton Wanderers at the Bloomfield Road ground.

What had started as a trickle of prisoners before the match became a raging torrent when the visiting side went ahead and won convincingly. Miffed, the home supporters reacted in the only positive way they knew. With violence.

When the final whistle blew, the crowd surged out of the ground and a series of running battles between opposing fans broke out, culminating in a massive head to head confrontation on a large car park adjacent to the football ground. This was only broken up when officers in riot gear waded in and got the message across; the police were not taking any shit today.

Despite numerous arrests from that one incident, the fighting continued unabated. This was because Blackpool, unlike most other towns, has countless attractions which make visitors reluctant to leave until at least a few have been sampled. Thus the Bolton supporters would not be departing until the early hours of Sunday when the night clubs kicked out; it also meant that Blackpool fans would harry them until they went.

All in all, a recipe for trouble.

The fighting gravitated away from the Ground into the town centre pubs and cafés. The police, even though reinforced from across the country, were stretched to their limits.

In the custody office, Acting Detective Inspector Henry Christie was up to his eyeballs in prisoners. He and a team of three Detective Constables had been assigned to help process and interview any prisoners suspected of committing more serious offences.

The majority of youths had been arrested for run-of-the-mill matters such as minor assaults, public order offences and drunkenness. Henry and his team could therefore have spent a relatively stress-free afternoon had he so wished; however he was uncomfortable when it became apparent that the large number of prisoners were keeping uniformed officers off the streets where their presence was desperately needed.

Eventually, after listening to the personal radio going berserk without respite, Henry made an unpopular decision. He volunteered his detectives to assist with any prisoner, no matter how trivial the reason for arrest. This would speed up the process and release uniforms back outside as quickly as possible.

His DCs were disgruntled by the gesture.

'Not our fuckin' job,' one of them moaned bitterly, 'bein' a fuckin' gaoler.'

'Just do it,' Henry said shortly, 'and I'm sure it'll reflect in your next appraisal.'

Henry took his jacket off, rolled up his sleeves and knuckled down to the task. When his reluctant team saw this, they also got down to it without further dissent.

Two hours later, without having had the opportunity to finish a cup of tea, he'd taken so many sets of fingerprints and mug-shots, charged so many prisoners and flung so many bodies into cells, that he'd lost count.

He'd had his fill of skin-headed, foul-mouthed, smelly, lager-bloated youths who wanted to hit him or spit at him. In fact, he was surprised he hadn't decked several of them already. He was proud of his remarkable, but waning, self-control.

He began to hope that the few football supporters who were still at large would do something horrendously bad – like machete each other to pieces – so that he and his team could be liberated.

Anything to get out of this hell hole.

Prior to hitting the shop they cruised the dark January streets in a stolen Alfa Romeo 164 3.0 Super, scouring the area for any signs of blue uniforms. They also had a scanner tuned into the local police frequency.

Nothing seemed untoward. The meagre resources of law and order were concentrated on rampaging football supporters, making the chance of a stray PC drifting by virtually nil; it would also mean that the response time to incidents would be vastly increased when the alarm went up. Which it would. Very shortly.

They were feeling good, hyped-up and buzzing. Adrenalin and speed coursed through their veins and sinuses like white water, pushing them up to a high plâteau from which they felt they could take on the world.

As in the past – and their Modus Operandi detailed this – all four of them were expensively and identically dressed in Dolce & Gabbana casuals: white tennis tops with black collars and cuffs, the letters *DG* clearly visible on their left breasts, grey slacks and two-tone (black and white) shoes. On their wrists they wore identical Dunhill watches.

2

The weapons they carried, and had shown they were prepared to fire, were a frightening combination which seemed to have been purposely chosen to complement their designer clothes. Each carried a semi-automatic 9mm 'Baby Eagle' pistol in a shoulder holster; the three who would actually do the business had an Italian SPAS 12 sawn-off shotgun and two mini-Uzis between them.

Whilst driving around they handed a carton of Lucozade to each other which was tossed out of the window when empty. They had found that the bubbles assisted the speedy percolation of the amphetamines into their bodies.

It was 7.27 p.m. Saturday evening. The perfect time.

They were ready to roll.

'We know what we have to do,' the man in the front passenger seat said, whipping up enthusiasm. 'Let's get it done.'

'Yeah, let's fuckin' do it,' voiced one of the others.

They all fitted their white porkpie hats onto their heads and pulled on surgical face masks, including the driver.

The Alfa pulled up unspectacularly outside the newsagents.

The shop was owned by a couple of middle-aged gay men, formerly actors who had bought it between them when they came to the sad conclusion that if they weren't careful they would spend the rest of their thespian days as soap-opera extras. They had been running the shop about four years, building it up from nothing into a thriving, profitable business.

Since the advent of the National Lottery, trade had boomed as they were the only Lottery retailer in that particular area of Blackpool. Like other newsagents they had taken to staying open late on Saturday evenings in order to catch as many last-minute players as possible.

Today the shop had taken in nearly two thousand pounds of extra revenue, as a treble rollover and a forty million pound jackpot had brought out punters in ever-hopeful droves.

Three men stepped casually out of the Alfa, leaving the driver sitting at the wheel. They trotted without undue haste across the pavement and filed into the shop.

Inside, two people were queued up at the till, eagerly hoping to get their lottery slips through the machine before the 7.30 p.m. deadline. Another customer was browsing idly through a woman's magazine in the rack by the door. She looked up unconcerned when the first of the men came through the door. It took a second for her eyes to register with her brain that he was carrying a shotgun. Her mouth popped open. She began to scream.

With an absolute cold lack of compassion the lead man nonchalantly pulled the trigger back and blasted the left side of her face off – cheek, eye and ear. She spun backwards into the magazine rack, toppled over to one side and, in an instinctive gesture, reached out and grabbed a card stand which overturned as she fell to the floor, covering her with rude birthday cards.

By this time all three men were in the shop, facing the remaining customers and owners.

With a burst of low fire from an Uzi, the two customers who were standing side by side at the till were virtually sliced in half. As the bullets punched them full of holes, their writhing torsos, spitting and gushing blood, were thrown together against the counter. From there they quivered to the floor, where for a few moments they appeared to be fighting each other in a grisly conflict which was actually their death throes.

The owners had not moved. Terror, like a vice, gripped them, constricted their throats and held their hearts in a claw-like embrace.

The cacophony of bullets echoed away, leaving silence.

Three violent men faced two gentle men.

No one spoke until the man holding the shotgun stepped forwards. He brought the weapon up and pumped the action. He aimed it straight into the face of one of the owners, less than two inches away from his nose.

'Get that bastard in the back out here now,' he said quietly. The sound of his voice was muffled by the face mask, making it more sinister and deadly. 'Otherwise you're next.'

He was smiling behind the mask.

He spun the barrel of the gun towards the other man. 'You go and get him – *now!*' His aim returned to the first man. 'Or I'll kill this fucker.'

At 7.40 p.m. Henry slumped wearily back against the cell corridor wall. He was completely shattered. The prisoners kept coming. All the cells now contained a minimum of three and it was proving a logistical nightmare to ensure that opposing fans didn't end up in cells with each other. It was likely that by the end of the night there would be five in every cell.

'C'mon Shane,' Henry urged the sallow youth who was washing the fingerprint ink off his hands in a wash basin. He had been arrested early in the day (and had missed the match) for slashing a Bolton fan across the face with a Stanley knife. He had been completely uncooperative throughout his period of detention. 'I haven't got all night,' Henry geed him up.

'Why don't you just fuck off,' responded Shane, speaking into the basin. He pulled the plug. The dirty water belched away.

Henry bridled. The temptation was to smash Shane's shaven head against the wall and say the young man had attacked him without provocation. There was no one else in the corridor, no one else to see them, one word against the other. Henry's patience was so paper-thin that, for a fleeting moment, this was a realistic option.

Then he shrugged it away. 'Suit yourself,' he said with a wicked smile, 'but I'll lay odds that remark has completely ballsed-up any chance you had of bail. Looks like court on Monday for you.'

4

With his back still towards Henry, Shane stood upright. With the exception of his red Doc Marten boots which had been removed and were outside his cell door, Shane was dressed exactly as he'd arrived in the custody office: in a pair of loose-fitting jeans and nothing else. He'd lost his jacket and T-shirt long before his arrest.

He was a thin boy, no muscle, and the lily-white skin of his back was streaked with scratches and grazes where he'd been rolling around on the ground, fighting. He'd also been drinking heavily, but having been in custody for almost seven hours, he'd sobered up somewhat. The process had left him with a bad head and a mean disposition. Henry's remark about bail rankled him.

Still facing away from the detective, he appeared to pull his jeans up, fiddling with the button and the fly for an inordinate length of time.

Henry tutted and raised his eyes.

Just then Shane spun quickly round, catching Henry unawares. In his hand was a slim flick-knife which had been concealed in the waistband of his jeans.

The silver blade shot out, locked into position.

He lunged at Henry.

At the very last moment Henry saw him coming. With a curse on his lips he pivoted out of the way. The knife plunged into thin air. Shane stumbled clumsily, slashing wildly with the blade.

Henry didn't have time to think, only react.

The lack of any alcohol in his system was the only thing that saved him. It meant he could move quicker and with better coordination than Shane. And his six foot two, fourteen stone body (slightly overweight, but modestly fit) gave him the edge as regards power and strength.

For a brief instant, Shane was at right angles to Henry, who punched the young man on the side of the head, just below the ear.

Shane staggered away, but recovered quickly. He turned and charged at Henry, running the knife at him as though he was holding a bayonet, screaming, 'You're dead, you cunt!'

But the move was telegraphed, giving Henry ample time to sidestep again, like a matador. Had he wanted he could have allowed Shane to run past him, put a boot up his backside and sent him sprawling like the stupid lad he was.

But the 'red mist' – the police officers' worst enemy – slotted down over his eyes like a visor.

He knew he shouldn't. Knew it was wrong. But he'd been so wound up that afternoon that he shrugged the angel off his left shoulder and nodded conspiratorially to the devil on his right.

He parried the knife to one side with the palm of his hand, grabbed Shane's wrist and twisted. A yelp of pain shot out of Shane's mouth, his fingers opened, and the knife clattered harmlessly to the floor. Henry continued to apply the pressure, twisting until he was almost at the point of breaking the wrist, then he yanked Shane towards him so they were nearly face to face.

Shane's breath reeked of stale alcohol and vomit.

Henry gave a hard, dry smile, pulled down on the wrist like he was pulling on a toilet chain and at the same time drove his right knee up into the young man's testicles. An animal-like howl of agonising pain burst up from the deepest recesses of Shane's abdomen and exited via his mouth.

Henry let go.

Clutching his privates with both hands, Shane collapsed weeping to the floor. Moaning. Crying.

Henry picked up the knife. He touched the release catch with his thumb and the blade slid harmlessly back into the handle.

The 'red mist' lifted. He hoped – belatedly – he hadn't done too much damage.

The Custody Sergeant, Eric Taylor, appeared in the corridor.

'Henry! What the fuck's going on here?'

'Nothing I can't handle . . . but whoever searched this prisoner wants their balls chewing off.' He handed the flick-knife to Taylor who looked at it, then at the writhing body on the floor.

'Make sure you put an entry on the custody record to cover it, will you? For your own safety. Then go up and see comms. There's a big robbery come in, firearms job – somebody shot, I think. They want you to turn out to it.'

'With respect, Eric, as much as I've enjoyed myself today in the dungeons – thank God for that!' He walked off down the corridor, stopped and turned back. 'Oh, and by the way, don't give him bail. He got me really mad.'

The first officer on the scene had done all the right things. She had quickly checked for any signs of life, found none, but requested comms to call an ambulance anyway, just to be on the safe side. She retraced her steps carefully to the front door of the shop, bundled several gawping members of the public away, stepped outside and closed the door behind her. The scene was effectively sealed off.

Onlookers had already begun to gather. She ordered them back. Then as calmly as she could, after taking a deep quavering breath, she relayed a situation report over her PR and asked for help. *Quickly, please*.

Henry Christie and a Detective Constable called Derek Luton were the next officers on the scene, arriving before the ambulance.

Before going in, Henry got the story from the female officer.

With trepidation, and not a little disbelief, he opened the door, ensuring he didn't spoil or leave any fingerprints on the gloss-painted wood.

One of the first things he'd been taught as a young copper was that there was only one occasion when it was acceptable for a police officer to be seen by the public with hands in pockets. That occasion was at the scene of a crime. It was OK because it prevented an officer touching and possibly tainting evidence which is all too easy to do.

Let your eyes do the walking, he'd been told. Take it all in for a few minutes, then take your hands out.

It was a piece of advice which had stood him in good stead for many years. Apart from anything else, it was a way of preventing panic rising at a particularly violent or messy crime. Like this one.

He stood just inside the door of the newsagents. Luton was one pace behind him.

'Christ!' breathed the young detective into Henry's ear.

Henry pursed his lips and gave a silent whistle. It was an effort to keep his hands pushed in his pockets. He wanted to rub his eyes because they could not believe what they were looking at.

'Do you see what I see, Degsy?' he asked Luton.

'Er – yep, think so,' he replied unsurely.

'You stay here and don't move,' Henry told him. 'And make sure no one else comes through that door.'

'You got it.'

Taking care not to step in the blood – difficult because there appeared to be gallons of the stuff – he moved around the body of the female shopper covered in birthday cards. He took a couple of long strides to the counter where he squatted down briefly to look at the bodies of the two customers. Both still clutched their lottery slips. Some jackpot, Henry thought.

He stood up, walked behind the counter.

The bodies of the two shopkeepers were lying in an untidy pile, one on top of the other. They seemed to be clinging to each other in a final embrace. Both had massive head wounds. They had obviously been blasted against the shelves behind the counter and the contents had tipped over them. Packets of cigarettes, cigars, matches, were scattered everywhere.

At first Henry did not spot the other body lying in the semi-gloom of the hallway which connected the shop to the living area beyond.

Carefully he stepped over the shopkeepers and went to inspect what he truly hoped was the last body.

Once again he thought his eyes were playing tricks on him.

He found a light switch, turning it on by pressing it with his thumbnail. Fluorescent lights pinged on, flooding the hallway with eerie brightness.

He saw the police firearms cap.

He saw the body armour with the word *Police* stamped across the chest.

He saw the 9mm Sig next to the body.

And the face blown away beyond recognition.

In that instant Henry knew that, as bad as it had been to begin with, this whole crime had taken on a much darker, murkier complexion.

He blinked.

Somewhere in the distance, getting closer, was the wail of an ambulance siren.

Not much point in you coming, he thought bitterly.

Henry stood on the pavement outside the shop, watching the uniformed cops push the public back and begin to string out a cordon.

'Right back,' he shouted, confirming his words with a sweeping gesture of his hands. 'Right back. That's it.'

Derek Luton appeared by his side.

'What've you got so far then, Degsy?' Henry knew Luton had been asking questions.

Luton consulted the scrap of paper he'd used to write on. 'Two witnesses saw three big guys leaving the shop armed to the back teeth. Got their names and addresses here . . .'

'Oh good, let's go and arrest them.'

Luton looked at Henry slightly nonplussed for a second. 'No, no . . . I mean the witnesses' names and addresses.' He didn't quite see the joke and carried on. 'All wearing white hats, masks, T-shirts. They piled into a car which could've been a Peugeot 405 or Cavalier, something like that, colour uncertain. Drove off without undue haste. Cool bastards. Sounds like the crew who've been hitting the newsagents for the last couple of months.'

Luton was referring to a vicious armed gang who had robbed six newsagents in the last nine weeks, all in the Fylde area of Lancashire. They were getting to be a real headache for the police who had warned that it was only matter of time before someone got killed.

'Mmm, sounds like,' Henry agreed.

'And apparently it looks like they blagged another shop in Fleetwood before doing this one.'

'Oh?' Henry perked up. 'Where did you hear that?'

Luton cocked his thumb at the female officer who'd been first on the scene. 'Just came over the PR when I was chatting to her.'

'Any details?'

'Round about seven-ten, seven-fifteen. A newsagents. Discharged a shotgun, but no one got shot. Helped themselves to the contents of the till, seven hundred quid or so. Usual MO. Usual dress. Same lot, I'd say.'

'Then they've been busy,' commented Henry. He considered what Luton had told him. His eyes narrowed while his brain chewed it over. 'Hang on . . . like normal, they rob a shop and fire the shotgun, like they've done on every job, then they tear-arse eight miles down the road like shit off a shovel to do this one? They steal money from up there, like they normally do, yet murder everybody in sight here – and apparently leave all the cash in the till. Fucking odd, if you ask me. And if that guy in the body armour really is a cop, what the fuck was *he* up to?' Henry shook his head. 'I'm not saying it's not possible, Degsy, but . . .'

Several cars were pulling up outside. Henry's boss, a Detective Chief Inspector, got out of one; the others disgorged a mixture of policemen including Detective Chief Superintendent Robert Fanshaw-Bayley, known colloquially as FB, Head of Lancashire CID, and Brian Warner, Assistant Chief Constable (Operations).

Henry's gaze returned to Luton. 'Looks like the circus has arrived and here come the clowns. Let's give 'em what we've got and retire with good grace. I doubt if I'll be involved in this investigation, which is a shame. Looks like being a juicy one. But you might get a shot. I'll see what I can do.'

Chapter Two

Henry and Luton spent another two hours at the scene before finally handing everything over and returning to Blackpool Central to book off duty.

Henry was correct: he would not be forming part of the team assembled to investigate the murders. He'd been told by FB to continue with the reactive CID work which was his normal job. This was no surprise. Someone had to hold the fort. Other crimes did not stop being committed and they had to be dealt with. In truth he did not mind too much. As Acting DI he had the responsibility for running the CID office whilst the real DI was off sick. Henry intended to apply for promotion later in the year; his proven ability to manage a busy department was something positive to tell the Board.

Luton, however, was told he would be going on the squad. Henry smiled when he saw the young detective's reaction. Although he had been involved in a couple of domestic murders and one night-club stabbing, this was Luton's first major enquiry. Henry was pleased for him. It would be invaluable experience.

Henry patted him on the back and congratulated him. Inside he was envious. Having been on many major murder enquiries himself, he knew what a real buzz it was to be part of such a team.

In the car on the way back to the office, Henry asked Luton to keep him abreast of all developments. Luton promised he would.

Back at Blackpool, Henry declined Luton's offer of a quick drink in the club on the top floor. He wanted to get home, shower, put his feet up and watch *Match of the Day* with the assistance of a large Jack Daniel's and his wife, Kate.

Luton waved good night and left. Henry was alone in the deserted office. He sat down at his desk and quickly shuffled through the mountain of paperwork and scanned the array of yellow post-it stickers which desecrated his desk top. There was nothing that couldn't wait.

Yawning, stretching, he stood up to go. The phone rang shrilly.

It was Eric Taylor, the Custody Sergeant.

'Glad I caught you, Henry. Thought I'd better let you know: that lad, the one with the flick-knife?'

'Shane Mulcahy,' said Henry.

'You really should've written something on the custody record, like I told you to.'

Henry mouthed a swearword. An empty, achy feeling spread through his stomach. He hadn't written anything in the record because he'd been so eager to get out to the robbery; it had completely slipped his mind. 'Problem?' he asked cautiously, knowing there would be, otherwise Taylor wouldn't be phoning.

'You could say that. We had to get an ambulance out to take him to hospital – and he's still there. Looks like he might have to have a testicle removed. If they can find it, that is. Apparently it's somewhere up in his throat.' Taylor chuckled.

Henry groaned. He slumped back into his chair, closed his eyes despairingly and slapped his forehead with the palm of his hand.

'And there's nothing on the custody record which covers what happened between you and him. I booked him out into your care so you could document him, then came along twenty minutes later to see him squirming on the floor, clutching his bollocks. And you gave me that knife and that's all I know. I've had to write down what I saw and it doesn't look good, Henry. Sorry.'

'Couldn't you have left a line or two for me to write something?'

'Yeah, right, Henry. You know damn well I couldn't do that. I asked you to write something and you didn't. Now he's in hospital with a double Adam's apple. If he makes a complaint – and he's just the sort of little shit to do so – you've got a lot of explaining to do. Sorry, pal.'

Jack Daniel's did not help Henry to get to sleep. His mind kept spinning from the sight of all that death, right round to his complete stupidity in not carrying out such a fundamental task as writing up an entry in a custody record. Bread and butter stuff. It was so easy not to do it, and detectives had a poor history where custody records were concerned. They were seen as something that got in the way of detection, some bureaucratic tool to be treated with contempt. But not by Henry Christie. Normally so diligent, careful . . . professional. He fully understood the possible legal ramifications of not being meticulous and recording everything. And he always stressed the importance of custody records to his detectives. They protected both officer and prisoner.

He tried to make excuses for himself.

He'd been busy. He was turning out to a multiple killing.

But if he were honest and critical, they were thin, paltry excuses.

Now he faced the possibility of an assault complaint, followed by a tedious investigation and maybe – he grimaced at the thought – a court appearance facing a criminal charge.

All because he hadn't covered himself.

The thought appalled him, but it was the worst case scenario, he assured himself. He'd be very unlucky if it came to that.

His wife Kate turned over and draped an arm across his chest.

She smelled wonderful, having dabbed herself sparingly with Allure by Chanel after her bath. He stroked her arm with the tips of his fingers. She smiled and uttered a sigh of pleasure. She loved to be stroked. Like a cat.

'I forgot to tell you,' she murmured dreamily. 'We won ten pounds on the lottery.'

'Aren't we the lucky ones?'

He purged all thoughts of death and prosecution from his mind, snuggled down into the bed, took gentle hold of Kate and felt himself harden against her belly.

Chapter Three

A t ten o'clock the following morning, Sunday, John Rider emerged unsteadily through the front door of his basement flat situated in the South Shore area of Blackpool.

He walked stiffly up the steps to pavement level, then turned and surveyed the building which towered above his flat.

In its better days it had been an hotel, but over the past thirty years had undergone a series of changes – to guest-house, back to hotel, to private flats, back to guest-house . . . until in the early 1980s it had been completely abandoned, quickly becoming derelict. By the time Rider saw it advertised for sale, deterioration through damp and vandalism had set in and the building was nothing more than a shell. He bought it for almost nothing and set about refurbishment with as little outlay as possible. He turned it into a complex of twelve tiny bedsits and, after getting a Fire & Safety certificate, filled the rooms with unemployed people drawing dole who needed accommodation and breakfasts, but who always paid the rent. Or to be exact, had the rent paid for them by the Department of Social Security.

So, in colloquial parlance, the newest metamorphosis of the building was a 'DSS doss-house'.

This had marked the beginning of a new and lucrative career for Rider, who had subsequently bought three similar properties and converted them into little gold mines.

Though he had done well out of the business, the lifestyle was nowhere near as exciting as the one he used to have. But it was safe and divorced from his past. The most difficult things he had to deal with these days were the damage to his property, caused usually during drunken squabbles between his tenants, or drug-taking by the same people – a pastime he abhorred and clamped down on firmly, sometimes violently.

Looking up at his property that morning he was pleased to see that there didn't seem to be any windows broken, the usual for Saturday night.

Glad about this, Rider walked across to the only remnant he possessed of his previous life. It was a maroon-coloured Jaguar XJ12, bought new in 1976. A real gangster's car which had seen much better days.

He and the car complemented each other. Both were slightly tatty, worn at the edges – ravaged, even – with a rather cynical air about them and an aura of aloofness which had a sinister undertone of danger and power.

And both of them smoked and drank too much and took a long time to get going first thing in the morning.

The engine fired up after a prolonged turn of the ignition. The twelve cylinders rumbled unevenly into life, coughing and spluttering until they caught fire and settled into a steady, burbling rhythm.

Rider let the car warm up for a few minutes. Realising he had forgotten to bring his cigarettes, he slid the ashtray open and poked distastefully through its overflowing contents until he found a dog-end which contained at least one lungful of smoke in it. He lit it with the electric lighter and took a sweet, deep drag.

He pressed the button on the console and the driver's window creaked open, jamming halfway down as always. He blew out the smoke from inside his chest, flicked the fag-end out onto the pavement and set off.

He drove down onto the Promenade, turned right, heading north. It was one of those clear, crisp January mornings with a fine blue sky, no clouds and a silver sea.

The Promenade was quiet. A few grimy locals meandered around. Traffic was light. A council truck lumbered down the inner promenade, emptying dog-shit bins.

He turned off at Talbot Square and headed inland, picking up the signs for the zoo, where he'd arranged to meet Conroy.

It was actually Conroy who wanted the meet. He who suggested the zoo. More informal, more natural and convivial, he'd said. And he hadn't been to a zoo since he was a kid.

Rider, out of curiosity more than anything, had agreed.

It had been a long time since he'd seen Conroy and although he'd no wish to re-open old wounds, he was intrigued.

He wondered exactly how 'convivial' the man would be. To the best of his memory, conviviality was not one of Ronnie Conroy's strongest points.

Henry arrived for work at 8 a.m. that morning. He immediately went to check Shane Mulcahy's custody record. With a bitter twist on his lips he read it and saw there was nowhere for him to add an entry.

He also learned that Shane was still in hospital and was being operated on later to remove a severely damaged testicle which had apparently split like a plum.

So that was the situation. Nothing he could do about it but wait, cross his fingers and pray. No point thinking If only . . . Too damn late for that.

Disgusted with himself he tried to put it to the back of his mind and concentrate on the day ahead.

The screen on the custody office computer – coupled with screams and shouts from the cell complex – told him the cells were full. He was relieved to be informed that there was only one overnight prisoner for the CID to deal with, although he would not be fit until he sobered up – conservative estimate being midday. Sounded like a good job for the detectives coming on at two.

He left the custody office and drifted up to the communications room where he read the message pad which logged all incoming calls and deployments. It had been a busy night in Blackpool. Henry was glad his days as a patrol officer were long gone. It was a dog's life at the sharp end.

After this he had a quick cup of tea and a piece of toast in the canteen before descending to the CID office and his cluttered desk, where he began to draft out a careful statement regarding his interaction with Shane while it was fresh in his memory.

Throughout the morning he was disturbed by a stream of detectives who had been brought on duty to form the murder squad. Many were old friends from across the county.

The first briefing was to be at 11 a.m. in the incident room.

Henry decided, if he had time, he would go in and listen. He had not yet heard who the dead body dressed in police kit was, and curiosity nagged away at him.

Conroy's big fat Mercedes was the only car in the zoo car park.

Rider drove his Jag past, made a big loop and pulled alongside with a scrunch of tyres on gravel. By this time Conroy was out and standing there, awaiting Rider who climbed creakily out of his car.

Conroy was a vision in cream, with a woven silk three-piece suit by Hermés, off-white T-shirt, and a pair of white canvas trainers by Converse. He'd seen the outfit in *Esquire* and decided he liked the look. It was him. It had set him back over a thousand pounds.

The two men shook hands. Conroy gave an almost imperceptible nod to his driver and the Mercedes moved away.

'I've told him to come back in an hour. That OK?'

'Fine by me,' Rider said indifferently, 'but what'll we talk about for that length of time? Your fashion sense?'

Conroy laughed guardedly and patted Rider on the shoulder. 'We'll think of something . . . but John, how are you? Nice to see you. You look bloody rough actually and you smell like a fuckin' brewery. Did you drown in a bottle of gin last night? Christ, it's a good job the cops didn't pull ya – you'd still be over the limit.'

Rider glared at him through narrowed eyes, already wound up by a man he hadn't seen for five years, although he'd tried to keep abreast of his nefarious activities.

'And you look like some pathetic ageing rock star in that suit and with that pony tail,' he retorted.

'Whoa, come on, John,' the other said placatingly. 'Let's have a walk and a talk, take a look at some animals, maybe do some business . . . yeah?'

Rider didn't really want to be here with someone who represented much of what was bad about his past, yet his innate curiosity had been aroused. What did this bastard want? He nodded reluctantly.

'Good man.'

They walked towards the zoo entrance.

A lone car pulled onto the far side of the car park, catching Rider's eye. A white Jap thing. Two people on board – men, staring in their direction. They looked as out of place as Conroy and Rider. But although he noticed the car and experienced a vague disquiet, Rider didn't pay it much heed. He wasn't a gangster any more, so why should he?

Henry found himself in exalted company, sharing a lift with a dying breed of officer. Two Chief Superintendents, the rank being one of those abolished in police shake-ups of recent years. There were a few left, but not many.

One was Fanshaw-Bayley, Henry's ultimate boss. The other was the Head of the North-West Organised Crime Squad generally referred to as the NWOCS, Detective Chief Superintendent Tony Morton.

The NWOCS were an elite team of detectives whose sole brief was to investigate organised criminal activity in the north-west of England, from Cumbria to Cheshire. They were based in Blackburn, Lancashire. The squad had been in existence for just over ten years and under Morton's direction had been responsible for some of the biggest, most spectacular busts and arrests ever seen in the north-west.

Morton – his home force was Greater Manchester – was a very sharp detective indeed. Henry knew he had begun his career on the hard, mean streets of Salford and Moss Side, and worked his way up the ladder of promotion through sheer hard work and uncompromising thief-taking. Henry had a great deal of respect for the man, who was in many ways a role model for him.

When Henry stepped into the lift, the two Chief Supers glanced quickly at him and resumed their conversation. They talked in hushed tones but were not trying to hide what they were saying.

Morton was speaking. He was clearly upset.

'I am totally fucking devastated, Bob . . . so all I'm saying is that you can have every single member of my squad for this job for as long as it takes. Me too. We'll drop everything and give this priority. Catch the bastards – catch 'em and crucify 'em! It's a real blow to us, I can tell you. Christ, I can hardly think straight.'

FB placed a reassuring hand on Morton's shoulder.

'I understand, Tony. If it'd been one of mine, I would've felt the same – gutted.'

'Yeah, thanks, Bob.'

The lift came to a halt on the floor where the incident room was located. FB gestured for Morton to step out ahead of him. Henry stayed in, finger on the doors-open button. When they were clear he took his finger off.

The last thing he caught was Morton saying, 'What I don't understand is what the hell he was doing there by himself, all tooled up. It doesn't make sense, though he was a bit of a loner.'

By which time the doors had closed and the lift was ascending towards the canteen.

With interest, Henry mulled over what he'd just heard.

At least it confirmed one thing: it *was* a cop who'd been gunned down – a member of the NWOCS.

Next question for Henry: Who?

'I think sometimes you should revisit your past, don't you? Does you good. We get so caught up with ourselves as grown-ups we forget simple pleasures like zoos.'

Conroy was doing the talking as they walked around, pausing briefly at each cage or enclosure to examine the exhibits. Other than themselves, the zoo was empty, and it seemed a cheerless place on that fine, but cold morning.

Rider was actually mildly impressed with the place. Though small and unspectacular, it was well tended and the animals seemed in good health. He wasn't really taking in what Conroy was saying because most of it was drivel. But then he moved up a gear and got Rider's attention.

'I hear you bought a club recently.'

'You heard right. Doesn't news travel fast?' It was only last week he'd completed the full transfer, though he'd actually been operating the place for about a month.

'It's a small world we inhabit,' Conroy commented.

They leaned on the outer rail of the lion enclosure and looked through the wire mesh at the sleepy inhabitants. One of the big cats rolled onto its back. A lioness glared at the two humans and licked her lips.

'*You* inhabit,' Rider corrected him. 'A small world YOU inhabit. So, yeah, I've bought a club.'

'What sort of place is it, exactly?'

Rider started walking again. Out of the corner of his eye he saw the lioness stand up, stretch and pad towards them.

'Exactly? A grotty rundown disco with a bar and a late-night food licence . . . and if I put some money in it I might make some back. Eventually. What's your interest?'

They were now strolling side by side along the enclosure.

Walking next to them, staring at them and grunting frighteningly was the lioness, her muscles tensing with each step under the tawny coat. Rider couldn't tell if she was feeling playful or hungry, but the size of her massive jaws and paws made him relieved there was a strong fence between them.

17

'Partnership,' stated Conroy.

Rider stopped in his tracks. Conroy carried on a few steps before realising he was alone.

The lioness stopped too, lifted her black nose and looked down its length through haughty black eyes.

'Fuck off!' blurted Rider. 'Why should I want to go into partnership with you?' He pointed at the lioness who had settled back on her haunches to watch the discussion like a tennis umpire. 'I'd rather climb in with her.'

'Oh, come on,' began Conroy.

'I'll head back to the car, if that's all you came to say.'

Rider walked away, leaving Conroy open-mouthed and on the edge of anger. The lioness growled at him, emitting a sound which seemed to emanate from her belly, gathering momentum as it passed through her throat into her mouth. Conroy jumped. He stuck two fingers up at her and said, 'You can fuck off too.'

He stormed after the disappearing Rider. No one had walked away from him whilst he was talking in the last ten years. People listened to him. If they didn't, they got something broken.

By the time he caught up with Rider, he'd adopted a pleading tone of voice which held just the merest hint of threat in it. Rider knew his way of speaking well.

'Look, John, I expect you're wondering why I want a piece of action up here, by the sea.'

'To peddle drugs, I imagine, which is your main source of income,' Rider said through the side of his mouth, still walking.

'John, stop and fucking listen to me!' Conroy took hold of Rider's arm and yanked him to a standstill. Rider halted abruptly, faced Conroy and looked dangerously down at the hand which was wrapped around his upper arm. Then he stared into Conroy's eyes.

The hand dropped away.

'Sorry,' mumbled Conroy. Good, Rider thought. He's still afraid of me. 'I want to explain something.'

'You gotta minute.'

'I need to expand. I own the east of this fucking county, all the way up from Blackburn to Colne. Clubs, pubs, council estates. All mine, but I need to move on. They're poor people across there, only so much money. I'm stagnating and Blackpool has got to be the place for my next move. So what better, eh, John? You've got a club, and those doss-houses you run . . . let's get back together again and make some fucking bread.'

Rider folded his arms defensively and looked into the enclosure at which they were now standing. There was a high wall surrounding a dry moat and a circle of grass with a few trees in the middle of it. On one of the trees sat a huge, Silverback gorilla, arms folded like Rider's.

Rider couldn't help but smile.

'This place has great potential. Eighteen million visitors every year.

Pubs, clubs . . . that gay scene – those twats love the speed – no real organised stuff here, just two-bit villains with no strategic mind like me. We'll make a fucking killing. Me and thee . . . like the old days.'

They were standing more or less shoulder to shoulder, looking at the gorilla as they talked, and he at them, as though listening.

'He could be a doorman,' Conroy laughed.

Rider gave Conroy a sidelong squint. There was something not quite right about this but he couldn't pin it down. 'Ron, you're lying about something here. I can tell when you ain't telling the truth. Your nostrils flare when you talk.'

'Eh? I am not lying, John,' Conroy said earnestly, his nostrils flaring. Instinctively he put his hand over his nose, realised what he'd done, then self-consciously pulled it away. 'So what about it? Me and you again?'

Rider sighed, leaned on the outer wall of the enclosure, resting his weight on his hands.

'There's a few things,' he said easily. 'First I don't like you. I don't like your cop connections or your political ones . . . they give me the creeps. I wouldn't go into any deal with you because I don't think I could ever trust you after the way you shafted Munrow.'

'Hey, business is business, John. Not that I'm saying I did shaft him. What is important is that I never shafted *you*.'

'Hm, maybe not – but whatever, I don't like drugs and I won't entertain them. It took me five years to get off the sods – and I still want to mainline, even now, stood here, and if I go in with you, I'll slide back. I want to stay clean. And, as I said, I don't fuckin' believe you for some reason. You're a sneaky bastard and you're up to something. I can feel it in my piss. So the answer's no. And you know me. I say something – I mean it.'

Conroy hardened. His jawline tensed and relaxed a few times. 'I want in to that gaff of yours, John. Now I've asked you nicely. Don't make me tell you. Nobody says no to me these days.'

Rider stood slowly upright at this. He considered the words uttered by Conroy and their implication.

He spoke, but did not look at Conroy because he felt that if he did, he wouldn't be able to resist tipping the bastard over the wall in with the gorilla.

'You've obviously forgotten who you are talking to. Don't ever threaten me and don't try something you'll regret.'

Conroy made no response.

Rider, becoming angry, raised his eyes to the sky and said, 'Do you understand?'

Again nothing.

Rider's head swivelled. He looked at Conroy who was standing there as rigid as stone.

Then Rider saw the reason for Conroy's lack of acknowledgement.

The muzzle of a gun was being pushed hard into the back of Conroy's head, just under the point where the hairband held his pony tail. Rider, though rusty in such matters, recognised the type of gun immediately – a K frame .357 revolver, six shot, constructed of stainless steel. He was close enough to read the words *Smith & Wesson* stamped on the barrel. It was a type of gun he had once owned illegally, once used and once dealt in. He knew what kind of damage it was capable of inflicting on a human being.

Rider's eyes followed the barrel to the hand, to the arm, to the person who was holding the gun.

He was a tall guy, youngish, dressed sportingly in a black Reebok tracksuit. He had dark, unkempt curly hair and a three-day growth on his face. Thin, gaunt, he looked as though a good meal would have killed him. His eyes were wide and watery, almost no colour in them, and he sniffed continually. He looked high and excited.

A couple of metres behind him stood a similarly dressed male who was no more than a teenager, dancing on the balls of his feet, agitated. He waved a semi-automatic pistol loosely in front of him, pointing in the general direction of Rider.

Rider's eyes locked briefly with Curly.

'You finished your little speech, hard man?' he demanded wildly of Rider. 'Eh? Eh?' With each 'Eh' he jammed the gun harder into Conroy's skin.

'Yeah, finished,' said Rider. His eyes took in both men as he half-turned to see better.

'Good, fuckin' good,' snorted Curly, really hyper.

The only thing in Conroy's favour was that these men were at the peak of a score. People like that made mistakes. They also tended to kill other people, too.

'What's happening?' Rider said, hoping to establish a dialogue to give him time to think.

'Can't you fucking see? We've come to kill this cunt.' He rammed the gun into Conroy's head again.

Conroy let out a little squeak.

'Oh, right. I see,' said Rider, nodding his head. He lifted both hands in an open-palmed gesture. 'You do what you gotta do,' he said to Curly, who he had now sussed as a rank amateur, as was his pal behind him. Professionals don't talk, they act. If they had been pros Conroy would be splattered by now. Rider guessed this was their first direct hit and it wasn't easy. He knew. 'I won't interfere. Not my business.' To Conroy he said, 'Sorry, pal. Nothing personal.'

Conroy's mouth sagged open in fear. His eyes were bursting out of their sockets. 'You twat,' he managed to breath.

Rider shrugged.

Curly's thumb went to the spur of the hammer and pulled it slowly back.

Rider watched it, fascinated. He saw the firing pin come into view, the cylinder rotate the next bullet into position.

This was the only chance. He took it.

At the exact moment the hammer locked into place he lunged at Curly. With his right hand he palmed the gun away from the back of Conroy's head as though he was slamming a door shut.

What he couldn't prevent was Curly's forefinger from pulling the trigger, but this happened as the muzzle of the gun cleared the danger area of Conroy's skull. The bullet discharged just inches away from Conroy's ear.

Rider continued with his self-propelled momentum, pushing the gun further away, his fingers closing over the top strap and cylinder of the gun, gripping tightly and twisting it easily out of Curly's hand. At the same time he stepped into a position which put Curly between him and the other gunman.

Suddenly disarmed and disorientated, Curly staggered back a couple of steps. This should have been a simple hit, no complications. Now things had changed.

For a start, there was no gun in his hand any more.

Behind Rider, Conroy sank to his knees, holding both his hands over his left ear. From such close range the shot had almost burst his eardrum.

Rider eased the gun into the palm of his hand and looked down his nose at Curly, in the way the lioness had earlier surveyed him.

Before he could say anything, Curly made a bad decision.

He threw himself to the ground and yelled, 'Shoot 'em, Jonno. Shoot the cunts!'

Jonno, his almost-adolescent companion, was as bewildered as Curly. He dodged and weaved on the spot, trying to get a shot in without hitting Curly – but was slightly off-balance and wide open.

To be on the safe side, Rider shot Jonno once.

He didn't want to kill the poor kid – even though he knew that if the gun was loaded with magnum shells it wouldn't matter where the hell he hit him, he'd probably die from shock if nothing else – so he aimed in the general area of the youngster's legs.

It wasn't a magnum. He could tell from the recoil.

The .357 slug slammed into the outer part of Jonno's right thigh with an audible 'slap' as the flesh burst, ripping through the muscle and lodging by his thigh bone.

Jonno screamed and dropped his gun. His hands went to the leg and clamped round the wound as he lowered himself to the ground. Blood spurted out between his fingers. He was shivering already as the shock waves pounded up through his abdomen.

Curly looked up at Rider, who pointed the gun at him.

'No, don't, please,' he gasped desperately.

Rider was about to enjoy some sport with Curly, but this was quickly curtailed when someone shouted, 'Oi!' from a distance. Two people who looked like zoo officials approached cautiously.

Deciding enough was enough, Rider ignominiously heaved the half-deaf Conroy to his feet and dragged him out of the zoo whilst waving the revolver about so people would keep their distance.

There were one or two questions Rider wanted to put to him.

Henry leaned back in his chair, laid down his pen and picked up the statement he had written about his little altercation with Shane. He re-read it thoroughly once more. If it came to the crunch, he hoped it would answer all the questions.

He was satisfied with the content, but winced when he came to the feeble excuse for not putting an entry onto the custody record. It wouldn't hold water if the Police Complaints Authority ever got involved.

'Morning, Sarge – sorry, Inspector.'

Henry glanced up. Derek Luton was standing there, smiling and very smartly dressed.

'You coming to the briefing, Henry?'

'Yep, certainly am.' Henry laid the statement carefully in his desk drawer and stood up. 'All psyched up for this, Degsy?'

'Can't effing wait,' he said, rubbing his hands together enthusiastically.

Henry slid his jacket on. They walked towards the door. 'I hear it was a detective from NWOCS that got blasted,' Henry said.

'Yeah, believe so.'

'Name been released yet?'

'At the briefing, I think,' said Luton.

'I heard Tony Morton telling FB he would deploy his whole team for this. You could end up working with one of the elite.'

'I'll try not to wet my keks,' laughed Luton.

Just before they reached the door the phone rang on Henry's desk.

'Shit. I'll see you up there.' He aboutfaced and walked slowly back, hoping it would stop ringing before he got to it. It didn't.

Rider was in the bar of his newly acquired club. It was dark and cool but smelled of old tobacco and spilled beer, beer which had permeated into the carpet, making each tread a sticky one. The whole place was suffering from neglect and bad management, needing gutting and refurbishing.

Rider sighed and let his eyes skim over the place. It was huge – a former casino, though the last time a roulette wheel had spun was in the early 1960s. Beyond the bar, dance floor and eating areas was a warren of corridors and rooms going up three floors. Rider wondered if he'd bitten off more than he could chew. It was going to cost a lot to get it up and running properly, but the joint had real potential.

All it needed was cash and dedication.

Jacko the head barman was polishing glasses. He had come with the place – as had a few other staff – was a good worker and very proud of his territory behind the bar. It was the only area in the whole club that was spotless.

Rider had only known Jacko about six weeks but had been impressed by him from the start. He appeared honest, loyal and committed to the place. He and Jacko had taken to each other and Rider had no hesitation in keeping him on. A good bar manager could be the lynchpin to the whole operation, and Rider knew a good one when he saw one.

The rest of the staff he sacked. They were lazy, idle, incompetent and dishonest.

He drank the last of his third gin and put the glass on the bar. Jacko came, picked it up and wiped underneath it.

'Another, boss?' he enquired.

Rider shook his head. He was relaxed now. He'd gone through that light-headed, nervy phase that always seemed to affect him after a confrontation. Jacko took the glass away.

Conroy returned from the pay-phone in the entrance foyer, made his way to the bar and told Jacko to get him a Bell's. He scowled into his drink as he tipped it back down his throat then proffered his glass for another, this time a treble. His head was throbbing.

'Left me fuckin' mobile in the car,' he said. 'Just phoned the driver to tell him to pick me up.'

'How's the ear?'

It was clanging like Big Ben.

'I'll survive.'

He took a mouthful of the whisky, ran it round his mouth, swallowed and gasped. He stared at the smooth liquid for a moment and at length said, 'Haven't seen that move for a while, John.'

'Mm?'

'Disarming – yanking a gun outta someone's hand. Used to be your party trick, that, dinnit?'

'Not especially,' said Rider. He had done it twice before, though the gun hadn't gone off on those occasions. He was getting slow. 'One day I'll miss and some fucker'll get blown away.'

Conroy appraised Rider critically.

'You never lost your bottle, did you? All you did was become a drunk.'

'I got out of it, that's all. I'd had enough.'

'Everyone said you'd lost your bottle.'

Rider squirmed uncomfortably. Conroy was getting under his skin and he didn't like it. 'A few things happened. I got a conscience, I got pissed off looking over my shoulder for cops all the time, wondering when you were going to grass me up. I saw how bad the whole scene was and I realised I needed to get out of it before it killed me, or I ended up as a lifer. I was thirty-five, a junkie and a piss-head. I suddenly thought, "Let's get outta here and try to get to forty-five, preferably not in a prison or a coffin". Now I'm just a piss-head, got a life of sorts, some brass and no ties to bastards like you. I don't deal drugs. I don't loan people money at extortionate rates. I don't beat people up any more just because they've looked at me funny, and I don't get other people to maim or murder for me.'

'Very bloody deep,' said Conroy sarcastically. 'You sound like a complete angel.'

Rider bristled. His lips puckered angrily.

Conroy emptied his glass. He shook his head sadly as he spoke. 'Sorry, mate, but you've been involved in it for too long. You owe too many people and too many still owe you, good and bad. And you wanna run from it? No chance, because it's all just caught up with you today.'

'How?'

'Talk about ironic. Here's you, eh? Quits the big time, wants to be left alone, get respectable – if you can call being a DSS landlord respectable. To me it stinks. Selling dope to ten-year-olds is more fucking respectable than what you do. But then today I come along – someone you haven't seen for years – and bang!' He pointed his right forefinger at Rider's temple and clicked his thumb like a hammer. 'Some bastards with a gun turn up, try to slot me and you save my life and half kill one of 'em. Talk about ironic.'

'Why?'

'You want to know what this is all about? It's about me and Munrow—'

Rider raised his eyebrows. 'I thought he was still inside.'

'You thought wrong. The bastard's out and he's after my territory. They were his boys today, no doubt about that, so word'll get back to him and you'll be linked to me. And you know what he's like – bull in a friggin' china shop.'

'You mean you're in dispute with him?'

'Dispute? That's a pretty little word. Nah, we're at war, John.' He spoke through gritted teeth. 'It's just starting, but it'll be big, bad and ugly – just the kinda rumpus you used to enjoy.'

24

Chapter Four

There is one thing about Blackpool, Henry Christie thought whilst driving south down the sea-front. It is never a dull place.

Completely unique. The world's busiest, brashest, trashiest resort, attracting floods of tourists every year. It is a finely tuned machine, expertly geared to separating them from their hard-earned dough.

Even in the low season when all the residents – police included – can take midweek breathers, the weekends draw in thousands of day-trippers, eager to enjoy themselves and throw their money away.

The public face of Blackpool is that of a happy-go-lucky place where everything is perfect: funfairs, candyfloss, the Tower, the Illuminations and children's laughter.

Henry Christie rarely saw this side of Blackpool.

He dealt with the flipside which most people never experience but which, as a cop, he could not avoid. There was the massive and continually expanding drug culture and the criminal manifestations behind it – burglary, theft, violent robberies and overdoses; each weekend the influx of visitors who attended the nightclubs left a legacy of serious assaults by itinerant, untraceable offenders; there was the growing problem of child sex and pornography; and the explosion of a huge gay culture had brought its own problems to Blackpool, related more to the prejudice of others, resulting in many gays being the subject of beatings or even rape by heterosexual males.

Then, of course, there was murder.

Murder was a frequent visitor to Blackpool.

Mostly the deaths were down to drunkenness and street brawls between youths, unlike yesterday's carnage in the newsagents. And unlike the one Henry was en route to now, that Sunday morning just before noon.

He slowed and drove off the road, across the tram-tracks and onto the wide stretch of Inner Promenade opposite the Pleasure Beach – a huge funfair – in South Shore. Parking in the shadow of one of the world's hairiest roller-coaster rides – the Pepsi Max Big One – he looked up at it and shivered. He'd once been bullied into riding it by his wife and daughters, and was convinced he was going to die when the trucks plunged vertically and corkscrewed impossibly on the tracks at speeds of up to 80 m.p.h.

25

The souvenir photograph of them all holding on for dear life revealed the terror in his face.

Never again.

Several police cars and an ambulance were parked on the Promenade, all unattended. A long black hearse was in amongst them, with two pasty-looking body-removers on board, eating burgers. A small crowd had gathered and were peering with interest over the sea wall, near to the pier.

He pushed his way rudely through them, ducked under a cordon tape, nodded to the policewoman standing by it and made his way down the slipway onto the beach.

The sand was firm and dry, fortunately. Henry did not want to spoil his suit nor take the chance of getting his shoes messed up. Just like a detective.

The tide had gone out about two hours before and the edge of the sea seemed a mile away. The beach gave the appearance of being clean and golden, very much like the town it fronted. The reality was that it was one of the dirtiest beaches in Europe.

However, it was a peaceful and pretty winter's day with a low sun rising in the sky. One of those days when it felt good to be inhaling breath.

Not a day to die.

A small group of police officers and a couple of paramedics were gathered around what, at first sight, looked like a bundle of rags at the foot of one of the pier struts. There was an obvious pathway in the sand leading to and from the scene.

Henry tried to psych himself into the right frame of mind to be the senior detective at a scene. The one who would have to make the decisions. The one everybody else would look to for a lead.

Oh joy, he thought.

She couldn't have been more than twenty years old. It was difficult to tell for sure. She was five foot five inches tall, very thin with spidery arms and legs, all bones, no muscles.

Henry watched as the deathly-faced undertakers lifted her body easily from the trolley and onto the mortuary slab, dumping her there unceremoniously.

Her drenched outer coat had been removed and searched, revealing nothing. Now she was lying there in what she had been wearing underneath: a T-shirt top, a short one which was nothing more than a piece of cloth covering her breasts, and a micro-skirt in what had once been stretchy black Lycra and would have only just covered her lower belly and the top of her thighs. There was no underwear.

Henry closed his eyes briefly. Stay detached, he ordered himself. She's a piece of meat, nothing else. Then he opened his eyes and allowed himself to look again.

But no matter how he tried he could not view her as a carcase. That was probably the reason why she was here, dead, because some bastard had thought she was nothing more than meat – something to be used, abused and discarded.

A scenes of crime officer videoed the body from all angles, focusing in on several areas. Then he took a few stills, the flash giving her pale damp body a sickly glow.

'Shall I cut her clothes off?' a female voice said into Henry's ear. It was Jan, a mortuary technician. She smiled brightly and held up a large pair of scissors, opening and closing them like a seamstress, indicating her eagerness.

She was nothing like the stereotypical mortuary attendant. In her mid-twenties she had ashen, pretty features, jet-black hair rolled into a bun, and large, black-rimmed spectacles. She wore a green smock which hung from her neck almost to the floor, and though deeply unsexy as a piece of clothing, it could not disguise her large, round bosom. She was a constant source of puzzlement to the majority of male police officers, most of whom fancied the pants off her but never dared ask her out.

Henry had heard them make many jokes about necrophilia and sex on mortuary slabs, but he knew no one had ever made any progress with her. He also knew she was happily engaged to a local jeweller and was working towards a career as an undertaker. She was odd – definitely – off the wall and a little bit whacky, but she was also pleasant and good-natured.

'No,' said Henry. 'Let's take 'em off and bag 'em.'

'OK,' she shrugged brightly.

In the past Henry had experienced some real struggles removing clothing from dead bodies: those stiff with rigor mortis being the classic ones. This girl was easy, pliant, almost cooperative.

He and Jan hoisted her into a sitting position. Jan held her there whilst Henry shuffled the T-shirt over her head and eased her arms out one at a time.

It was like undressing a drunk, though this one would never sober up.

Next he eased her skirt down over the hips, down her legs and off.

Jan placed a wooden block under her neck, like a pillow.

Henry's eyes surveyed the naked body . . . and the injuries.

The sea had washed the blood away, but even so, it was apparent she had been subjected to a violent, sustained attack. Henry tried to imagine her last moments and felt vaguely sick.

Before he could inspect the body more closely, the Home Office pathologist, Dr Baines, came into the mortuary dressed in a smock, pulling on a pair of plastic gloves.

He looked dreadfully worn out. Henry knew he'd been up most of the night carrying out post mortems from the shooting. There was still two more to do, and dealing with the body of this female was something he could well do without. Had it been any other detective than Henry, Baines would have said, 'No, get somebody else in.' But he and Henry were old friends, sometime drinking partners, and they owed each other favours.

'Bad business last night,' Baines commented.

Henry nodded.

'So, big H, what've you got for me here?'

Baines walked to the slab and cast a critical, professional eye over the body.

'Found on the beach this morning by a jogger, near to South Pier. No identification yet, but we're working on it. She had an overcoat on, a skirt and T-shirt. No knickers.'

'Nothing else?'

'Nope. Got a search team scouring the beach now before the tide comes back in. If they don't find anything we could be struggling.'

Baines sighed. 'Nasty. Very nasty.'

'How long would you say she's been in the sea?'

Baines eyes looked up and down the body. He touched her skin, parted her legs and inserted a thermometer inside her rectum. He checked the reading. 'Hardly been in, if you ask me. Doesn't show any of the usual signs of long-term immersion. Possibly been tossed about by the tide, but nothing more.'

He picked up the girl's left arm and twisted it gently outwards so he could see the soft skin on the inner elbow. He tucked the arm back and moved his attention to her legs, looking behind each knee.

'Junkie?' Henry asked.

'Junkie,' confirmed Baines. He began to count, 'One, two, three . . .' pointing as he did.

'. . . Twenty-two, twenty-three, twenty-four,' he concluded a few minutes later. 'So that's twenty-four stab wounds in the chest, stomach, upper arms, upper legs,' he said, very matter-of-fact. 'Probably had a knife up her vagina by the looks. Her face is a real mess too.' He counted the number of punctures around her head and neck. 'Twelve facial and neck stab-wounds at least. See?' he said to Henry. 'It looks as if the left eye-socket has been repeatedly pierced. Impossible to say how many times the attacker plunged the knife in there.'

He turned his attention to her arms again. 'Numerous incised wounds – slash-wounds, if you like – on her arms and the palms of her hands where she tried to protect herself from the onslaught. She went down fighting for her life, if nothing else. The attack continued long after she died.'

'Can you tell me anything about the knife at all?'

The doctor pondered thoughtfully. 'Probably not.' He bent forwards and peered at one of the stab-wounds in her stomach. 'My guess'll be very imprecise,' he warned. He put a thumb and forefinger to either side of the wound and parted it gently. Henry felt slightly sick when it popped open.

'Problem is,' Baines continued, 'skin stretches before a knife actually pierces and when the knife is pulled out it springs back into place. Sometimes the hole can look smaller than the knife which caused it.'

28

He stood slightly back and looked at the open wound which reminded Henry of a tiny, thin-lipped doll's mouth. 'This wound is one of the neatest on the body: the knife was plunged straight in and pulled straight out. Looks like a knife with two sharp edges – here, you can see the wound has two acute angles at each end.'

He allowed the hole to close. 'Probably a slim instrument, but it'll be difficult to tell how long the blade is. Might get some indication when I open her up, but don't hold your breath. It'll be guesstimates. The knife has obviously been twisted about and rocked backwards and forwards in many of the other wounds. Basically, a fuckin' mess – sorry, Jan,' Baines acknowledged the quiet attendant, 'but this girl died a brutal and horrific death and though it's a cliché, it was a frenzied attack. Nobody deserves to die like this.'

'Thanks,' said Henry. He'd been jotting down a few notes in his unofficial pocketbook. He closed it and slid it into his pocket which began to chirp like a bird, making him jump. He extracted the pager with an apologetic look on his face and walked to a corner of the room where he picked up the phone on the wall and dialled Blackpool Communications.

'I know you're busy with that suspicious death,' the woman said, 'but do you recall that other job I mentioned to you?' Henry said he did, but thought it had been a joke of some sort. 'No, no joke,' the comms operator said. 'Can you possibly attend? There's a uniformed patrol there and a Detective Sergeant who'd like you to go. Apparently there's more to it.'

Henry hesitated. For evidential reasons he felt he should stay for the post mortem, but it wasn't strictly necessary. 'OK, I'll go,' he said and ended the call.

Baines and Jan were standing on either side of the corpse, whispering to each other about the plan of action for the PM. They looked at Henry as he finished the call.

'I'll have to leave you with this for the moment,' he apologised. 'Got to have a quick look at another job, then I'll be back.'

'Anything interesting?' asked Baines.

'Someone's shot a gorilla up at the zoo.'

'Really? Never done a PM on a gorilla.'

'Sorry to disappoint, but I think it's still alive – just severely pissed off.'

Chapter Five

Once Conroy had gone, Rider sat and ate a late breakfast at the bar. Croissants and tea.

For the first time in his life, Rider was content with his lot. He liked the club and the 'guest-houses', as he preferred to call them, rather than DSS doss-houses. His basement flat underneath the first property he'd bought was an oasis of sheer luxury in a desert of basic living. It was his permanent home, the first he'd ever owned. He had the financial means to buy a luxurious detached house, but he'd grown accustomed to the flat which was perfectly large enough for him and his occasional guests. He had never put roots down anywhere before and he was loath to upstakes just for the hell of it. There was no need to.

He thought bleakly about his criminal past.

Back then his life had been a continual series of moves from one house to the next; to some dive of an hotel room to some flea-pit flat, then maybe a night in the back room of a pub. All in the mean streets of Manchester or some depressing East-Lancashire mill town.

Even when he'd started making real money from drugs, guns and lending money, the lifestyle didn't change, just the quality of places he could afford. One thing he vividly remembered about it all was the constant indigestion, probably brought about by stress, though he didn't realise it at the time.

He could never recall spending a full year in any one place because the whole nature of the existence made continuous movement a necessity. Standing still in those days meant you became an easy target, maybe of the law, or some toe-rag with a score to settle – and there was always plenty of them about.

He sipped his tea. Christ, he thought with disgust, twenty years of living like that.

In the end it got to him. Never knowing where he would be sleeping, or with whom; but always sure that once he was settled in and feeling comfortable, he'd have to get up and leave.

It was no good.

As a young man, fresh out of borstal it had been exciting. A life of hands-on crime, living solely off wits, strength, intimidation and violence. Building up a criminal empire which stretched throughout the whole of

East Lancashire and parts of Manchester, based on gambling, prostitution, loan sharking, gun dealing and the biggie – drugs.

In the end it wore him down, and his outlook on life slowly changed. Gradually he found he wanted 'normal' things, such as somewhere static to live, a woman, kids maybe. Time to sit and read a book once in a while.

It hit him one day as he was edging his car through a McDonald's Drive-Thru after a morning collecting debts during which he'd smashed the kneecap of one guy who'd missed a couple of repayments. He found himself staring at a family of four and he discovered he was jealous.

That was one of the reasons for pulling out.

There were plenty of others.

He'd become an alcoholic and such a big drug-abuser that he made some of his clients look clean. The habits were costing him a grand a week – big money – and whittling away mercilessly at his profits.

He also found that he came to hate people being afraid of him all the time. Always, at the back of their eyes, he could see uncertainty and fear. He had traded on the ability to instil terror when he was younger, but he found his reputation to be an impediment as he got older and his values changed. Most people he came into contact with were shit-scared of him and he didn't like having that effect.

The formation of the NWOCS also played a part in his departure. The fact that the cops had set up such a squad sent out its own message: Gangsters were not going to be tolerated. Rider knew of Conroy's cop connections, but was not naive enough to think the protection Conroy enjoyed extended to him and Munrow. He knew Conroy wanted things his own way, to be in control, but by that time, with a drug and booze-sodden brain, Rider was past caring. As far as he was concerned, Conroy could have it all.

The final and biggest reason was that he, Conroy and Munrow were not operating as a team any more.

Conroy had big, strategic ideas.

Munrow was a thug with little or no finesse.

And he was a complete shambles who could only see as far as the next fix.

They were in constant conflict with each other and Rider knew that if he didn't get out, sooner rather than later, he would have killed both the bastards.

So he made the decision, pooled all his cash and left.

Somewhat smugly, and from a safe distance, he found himself proved right on one thing. Soon after he quit, the cops arrested Munrow and several other bit players following an armed robbery. Conroy remained free as a bird (and Rider had his own ideas as to why) and flourished. Munrow, meanwhile, didn't manage to wriggle at all.

It could so easily have been Rider. He had been expected to take part in the robbery.

31

Now he was as happy as he'd ever been. He enjoyed Blackpool, running legitimate businesses, employing a few people and keeping his nose clean. He hadn't found a woman – not a regular one – but he was prepared to tread water.

Fuck, he thought bitterly. I hope to hell-shit Munrow doesn't rope me into this nonsense.

Conroy had not been very precise when he'd talked about the 'war', but it sounded bad. Munrow was out of prison, wanted what he believed to be rightfully his and Conroy was reluctant to give it to him. Naturally. So things had started bubbling . . . and Conroy was worried.

'I've moved on in a lot of ways,' he'd said to Rider. 'Like you,' he added, making Rider wince. 'I'm a corporate player now. I run a tight business – none of that hands-on shite like we used to. Too fucking dangerous by half. Keep everything at arms' length now, just rake in the profits. Not like Munrow. He's still in a time warp. I've expanded into new fields, built up new contacts and I'm on a very big deal. Munrow's on the verge of ruining it.'

He refused to divulge anything more to Rider, including the reason for his interest in the club.

He'd left shortly afterwards, leaving Rider brooding over breakfast.

A thought struck him. 'The bastard,' he said out loud. 'He didn't even thank me for saving his life!'

Smeared blood covered the inside of the strengthened glass, making it difficult for Henry to see through to the sole occupant of the enclosure.

'I couldn't believe what I was seeing,' a zoo official called Draycott was telling him. 'There were only four customers in the zoo at the time . . . it's very quiet just now, and all they wanted to do was shoot each other. A bloody shoot-out, right here, in Blackpool Zoo. It was like a scene from a film or something.'

He had already described what he'd witnessed to Henry and now he was in the process of coming to terms with it. Henry let him speak, asking occasional questions to clarify things.

'So one knocked the gun away from the other's head and it went off?'

'Yeah, that's right. Moved really quick. Really impressive. Next thing it was in his hand and he was in charge.'

'And what happened at the point when the gun first went off?'

'Boris here,' he thumbed at the gorilla, 'was sitting in his tree watching these guys, and when the gun went off he just tumbled out of the branches, right spectacular-like, and thudded to the ground. Shot by mistake, obviously. I thought he was dead at first.'

'And the men?'

'Bit confused there.' Draycott screwed up his nose. 'The one who originally had the gun jumped to one side and shouted something, don't

32

know what, and the one who grabbed the gun – if you see what I mean – shot his mate in the leg.'

'Very confusing,' Henry agreed.

'Oh yeah, very. Anyway, I shouted to them and they scarpered, basically, flashing guns at us.'

'All together?'

'Separate. First two legged it pretty quick; second two were a bit slower because one'd been shot. The girl in the entrance booth saw their cars and wrote the numbers down.'

'That should be helpful,' Henry said. He knew the girl was presently giving a statement. 'And the poor gorilla?'

'Yeah,' said Draycott. 'He's my main concern now. He dragged himself in here, sat down in one corner and bled like a stuck pig. His keeper went in but got attacked. Then he did this with the blood, wiping it all over the glass as you can see.'

'So it looks like he got shot in the shoulder?'

'Definitely. Looks a bad wound.'

Henry bent low to where there was an area of glass free from blood. He peered through.

The gorilla was sitting in one corner of the enclosure, nursing his left shoulder with his right hand, rocking backwards and forwards, chuntering to himself. He was a magnificent animal. Heavy and thickset with a short, broad torso. His head was large and wide, forehead massive and low, overhanging his eyes which were close together, small, deepset and black. His arms looked very muscular. Henry had to admire anyone who had the courage to step in with him, even when he was uninjured and in a playful mood. He suspected the keeper had been lucky to escape with his life today.

The gorilla's coat was matted with blood in a swathe which ran from his left shoulder, right the way across his chest to his stomach. He had lost a good deal of blood.

The wound was still bleeding profusely. Henry could see a sliver of jagged white bone sticking out between the gorilla's fingers. It was an injury which needed treatment quickly.

Suddenly the gorilla stopped rocking and became still and silent. His eyes flickered up and saw Henry looking through the glass. For a second their eyes locked in a kind of primaeval gaze. Then the gorilla's lips drew back into a fearsome snarl, revealing a powerful set of teeth which were capable of ripping a man to shreds. A deep bark of annoyance, followed by an angry roar, boomed from the gorilla's throat, making Henry's stomach somersault. The animal then flung himself across the enclosure towards Henry, battering the glass with his raging fists.

Henry drew back instinctively. He knew he was safe with that thick glass between him and the beast, but he could have sworn the glass bowed when the animal pounded almost 340 kgs of sheer muscle against it.

The air rushed out of Henry's lungs in a gasp. He was speechless for a moment. Eventually and rather inadequately, he said 'Wow.' He could feel his heart pounding, could taste the quick rush of adrenalin which had gushed into his body. He closed his mouth, pulled himself together and smiled shamefacedly at Draycott. 'Some beast.'

The attack on the glass had been brief. Boris had now slunk back to the comfort of his corner. He sat down and began to shiver uncontrollably, shock setting in.

'Where the hell's that vet?' Draycott begged to know.

The statement taken from the girl at the turnstile was not really worth the paper it was written on. She had not noted any numbers, and all the statement contained was a vague description of two cars which the men had boarded, their colour and a very partial registered number which she'd dredged from memory. Evidentially pretty crap.

Henry handed it back to the PC who had taken it.

There was little else for him to do at the zoo. The only real way forward would be if the wounded man turned up in a casualty department, or dead somewhere.

But, bearing in mind the nature of the incident – a hit that went awry, or so it seemed – even if he did turn up at a hospital there would be little hope of him talking. Henry favoured the latter possibility anyway: he'd more than likely turn up in a ditch somewhere having bled to death. That way there would definitely be no chance of him speaking to the cops.

Henry's stomach panged with hunger.

It was 2.30 p.m. and apart from some toast that morning, he'd eaten nothing all day. He walked to the zoo cafeteria, ordered a sandwich and a coffee and sat down to eat before returning to the mortuary to catch the tail-end of the post mortem.

As he sipped the brew he had difficulty in focusing his mind on anything other than the look which had passed between himself and the gorilla before it charged him. He knew he was probably overplaying the significance, but hell, it had been just like looking into the eyes of another human being. There had been intelligence and knowledge. Henry shook his head and felt very sorry for such a creature having to live in captivity.

He hoped Boris would pull through.

The last thing he wanted was to be investigating the murder of a gorilla.

'You look serious.'

Standing next to Rider at the bar was Isa. He hadn't heard her arrive. She was staying in a guest-house opposite the club. He had been deep into the club's books, trying to make some elusive figures balance. A struggle. He pushed the calculator to one side.

'Life is serious,' he said, forcing a false smile which then metamorphosised into a real one. Isa always had the capacity to cheer him up.

34

'I could make it more fun for you, John,' she said and kissed him lightly on the cheek.

'No doubt you could, hon,' he conceded, 'but afterwards it'd still all be there.'

'Must be bad.' She laid a hand on the back of his head. He could smell her lady-scent through her clothes. It made him slightly woozy for a moment. He pulled her towards him and hugged her gently, then released her. She stepped away.

Rider missed the look of longing in her eyes. They had always been good friends, other than for one night when a little flirtation went too far and they ended up making love. But it had proved to be a one-off, much to Isa's frustration, because she had been hopelessly in love with Rider for longer than she cared to mention. He seemed to continually miss the signs and she didn't have the guts to tell him. Because above everything else – at least from his perspective – they had been and were once again, business partners. 'I think I saw Ron Conroy being driven in his Merc. Am I right?'

Rider nodded.

'He's the reason you look like you've seen your arse, isn't he?'

'Yeah, but let me worry about him. My problem. No need for you to get involved.' He slid off the bar stool before she could say anything and stood up. 'So, what do you think about this place now you've had a good look around, got the feel of it?'

'When you look beyond the shit and the sticky carpet and try to imagine it how you describe, not bad, not bad at all.' She nodded appraisingly. Her mouth turned down at the corners as she considered. 'Loads of potential, but it needs so much money spending on it, John. Even if you were going to run it as a straight disco it would need gutting. Those ceilings look like they're about to come down. And I don't have too much money to invest, not at the moment.'

'I do. Don't worry about that aspect of it. I'm not asking you for anything other than your expertise and I'll pay you well for that. But what d'you think about the plan – the north's first lap-dance joint? Right here in Blackpool, the tackiest place in the world?'

'Seems a good idea and in the right town.'

'Good. Your job will be to provide the dancers and manage them.'

'Not a problem,' she said. Isa Hart ran a respectable escort agency in Manchester, specialising in escorts for the 'Busy, discerning professional', whatever the sex. A profitable business in itself, it also provided a sound front for many other less respectable activities including the provision of exotic dancers for the Middle East, strippers for high-class men's clubs and one-off functions, gay dancers and, of course, where Isa had started all those years ago – running call girls.

She had known Rider for many years. They had jointly run several ventures in the strip-joint and call-girl territory, but these businesses had crumbled when Rider hit the bottle and the coke.

35

They both gazed down the bar, across the vast dance floor and beyond to the raised seating area which was the restaurant. Rider's plan was to get rid of the dance floor, and build a huge circular bar on which the girls would dance to pounding rock music and relieve the customers of their money.

He could see it all. Brash. Glitzy. Rude – very rude. Yet well run, tightly policed by his staff, fun and completely in keeping with Blackpool's image. The clientèle would not be able to touch the girls and there would be no hint of prostitution. They would simply dance provocatively, virtually naked, in front of and almost in the laps of customers. Money would be handed to them and they could be 'bought' for individual dancing.

To Rider it was a beautiful image, which was one of the reasons he didn't want to sell the place to Conroy.

He had a goal now, an aim in life, and he wanted to achieve it.

And he had plans for the rest of the building too. There were another two storeys above which used to be offices for the casino and although the floors were generally rotten and dangerous, he planned to bring them up to scratch and open a restaurant and pub on the first floor and convert the second into new offices.

'The planning application goes in next week. We'll see what reaction it gets. Should be favourable.'

'You mean you've greased some palms?'

Rider merely smiled at her and raised his eyebrows.

The doorbell rang.

Jacko, who'd been restocking the bar, sauntered away to answer it while Rider pointed out a few more things to Isa.

A few moments later, Jacko was back, flustered.

'Cops,' he said.

Rider closed his eyes despairingly as he remembered something. The bell rang again.

He dashed behind the bar, reached under the counter, rummaged for a second and pulled out the gun he'd commandeered from Curly. He shoved it into Jacko's hands who held it like he'd been given a dog turd.

'Take that upstairs and hide it – hide it somewhere they won't find it, just in case they want to search the place. Well, go on, go on!' He shooed Jacko away. 'Make yourself scarce, Isa.'

'What do they want?' she asked wide-eyed, the sight of the gun having thrown her.

Rider did not reply. He turned and walked to the front door, grating his teeth angrily, swearing at the thought of Conroy. Today was becoming like one of the good old days, and the sad thing was, annoyed though he was by the whole débâcle, he was quite enjoying it, in a sick, perverted sort of way.

* * *

After Henry had finished at the zoo, he made his way back to the mortuary. Dr Baines, the pathologist, didn't tell him anything he hadn't already guessed. The girl had died from multiple stab-wounds. Any one from a total of forty could have been the fatal blow.

Baines promised a written report as soon as possible. That meant anything up to a week because of workload.

Henry thanked him, waved goodbye to Jan and gloomily returned to the office, where he immediately sought out FB. His boss was in the murder room set up for the newsagents job, in deep conversation with Tony Morton. Henry had to wait to step in.

FB looked blandly unconvinced when Henry said he wanted a full team on the beach corpse.

'Sorry Henry, this takes priority in terms of manpower and resources.' He flicked his hands at the incident room. 'The sordid little murder of a junkie who was probably on the game and deserved what she got doesn't even rank.'

Anger bubbled up inside him at these crass remarks, but he managed not to punch the living daylights out of FB.

'She actually deserves as much as anyone,' he replied calmly.

FB gave one of his famous sneers and said, 'That's as maybe, but the reality is you're gonna have to manage this one as best you can with the resources available – i.e. whoever's left in the office.'

'They're all on this sodding job. Can I have Derek Luton back?'

'Nope – you'll have to make do.'

'Jesus,' Henry uttered under his breath.

FB relented slightly. 'Tell you what. I'll give you one HOLMES terminal and an operator to go with it.'

'Big fuckin' deal,' Henry snapped.

'Don't push it, Henry,' FB warned him.

'Overtime budget?'

FB laughed.

And that was that.

In the CID office, the Support Unit Sergeant who had been leading the team searching the beach for evidence was waiting. He handed a small black leather clutch bag with a gold clasp and shoulder strap triumphantly to Henry.

The find cheered Henry.

Eagerly he cleared his desk top, spread out a sheet of polythene and opened the water-sodden bag, emptying out the contents. He had been hoping that there would be something in here to give him a quick lead, even though there was nothing to suggest the bag even belonged to the dead girl.

And the contents of the bag were, at first glance, going to be of no use whatsoever in solving the murder.

A crumpled packet of Benson & Hedges cigarettes, three left in, a plastic throwaway lighter and a syringe with a rusty needle. Everything soaked in sea-water, the cigarettes being not much more than tobacco mush.

'Fuck,' said Henry, disappointed, but not completely surprised.

It would have been nice to have tipped out a driving licence and passport with her name on and a diary detailing her most recent acrimonious split with her latest lover who had threatened to kill her . . . but it was not to be.

He tipped the cigarettes out of the packet then carefully ripped out the gold paper innards. Nothing.

He looked closely at the lighter, flicked the mechanism and found it worked. It gave him nothing else.

Neither did the syringe. Inside it, though, looked to be the crystallised remains of some controlled substance.

He turned the bag inside out, finding the black nylon lining to be ripped, he probed with his fingers into the space between the lining and the bag. Nichts.

'Don't suppose you found anything else?' he asked the Support Unit Sergeant hopefully.

Negative.

Shit.

Despondently Henry picked up the bag again and twirled it around between his hands. He looked through it once more . . . and saw something. Tucked into the bottom corner of the mirror pocket, folded several times, was a small piece of paper.

Very easy to miss, he reassured himself.

He pulled it out, holding it tentatively between finger and thumb, laid it out on the desk. It was sodden, almost to the point of disintegration.

Using the tip of a ball-point pen he unfolded it, trying not to tear it. He ended up with a triangular piece of paper which could have been the corner of a page, possibly a telephone directory. Some words – thankfully in pencil – were written on the paper and quite legible. An address – a house number and a street name, but no town specified.

Henry made the assumption it was Blackpool.

Ten minutes later, together with another detective, he was pushing his way through the main door of a block of flats in South Shore, about to do one of the things he most enjoyed doing: knocking on doors.

It looked a likely place, and although he tried not to stereotype people, he could well imagine the dead girl to have lived in such surroundings.

He rapped his knuckles sharply on the first door he came to and looked around whilst waiting for a reply.

The hallway, which reeked of cat piss, was littered with uncollected post, milk bottles – empty, unwashed – and a baby buggy. Oddly enough, no cats were to be seen. Henry glanced over his shoulder at the tubby Detective Constable who was accompanying him. 'See, told you. They all smell the same, these places.'

The detective, Dave Seymour, nodded. 'I know, boss.' He was an experienced officer with more years on the CID than Henry and only a couple to go before retirement.

Henry raised his hand to knock again just as the door opened reluctantly – but only as far as the flimsy security chain allowed. Henry could easily have put his shoulder to the door and burst through.

Behind the door stood a thin, pale-faced female holding a screaming baby to her flat chest. Her eyes were red raw, sunken. One of them bore the remnants of a nasty-looking green bruise. From inside the flat came the sound of a TV turned up to a high volume.

She clocked the two men as detectives straight away.

'What do you want?' she asked cautiously, appraising them.

'We're investigating a death,' Henry told her, having to raise his voice to compete with the baby-TV combination. 'Could we have a word, please? Inside.' He showed his warrant card.

'I don't know nothin' an' I haven't done nothin',' she said nervously, juggling the baby up and down. The child picked up her tension and the volume from its lungs increased by several decibels.

'We're just after some information, that's all,' Henry informed her. 'We won't keep you long – honest.' He smiled.

She tutted, put the door to, unhooked the chain and let the two detectives come into her living accommodation. It consisted of three tiny rooms: a bed/living room with a mattress covered with grimy sheets in one corner, a couple of big, second-hand armchairs and a good quality TV set on top of a small cupboard; a minuscule bathroom, and a kitchen with a three-ringed cooker, sink and no fridge. In overall area, the flat was no bigger than a small towing caravan but was much less luxurious.

A large amount of baby clothing littered the place; in one corner of the room was a high pile of unused disposable nappies. The room smelled of sick and pooh with just a hint of cannabis.

What a fucking life, Henry thought. She must be all of seventeen.

'And you are?' he asked.

'Jodie Flew.'

'You alone here?'

'At the moment, yes,' she answered tartly. 'What d'you want?' She brushed back a strand of greasy hair from her face. The baby's volume decreased. Seymour crossed to the TV and switched it off.

Henry told her, gave a description of the dead girl and asked Jodie if it were possible she knew her, or if she lived in one of the flats.

'Well, maybe. Dead, eh?' Jodie was not too concerned by the news. 'A new tenant moved into one of the flats upstairs, day before yesterday, don't know which one, but I only seen her a coupla times in passing. Could've been her, from the description. Hard to say. You spoken to the landlord?'

Henry shook his head.

'He lives downstairs.' She pointed to the floor. 'If he isn't in, he'll be at his club, that one on Withnell Road.'

Henry thanked her and made to leave.

'Any idea where that bastard of a boyfriend of mine is?' she asked as they stepped out.

'Should we?'

'Well, he's always in trouble for something or other. He went to the match yesterday and he hasn't come back yet. I know he gets pissed up an' all, but unless he got himself nicked, it's a long time to be away, even for him.'

'What's he called?'

'Shane Mulcahy.'

Henry blanched at the mention of the name. He knew Shane hadn't given this as his address, otherwise he wouldn't have knocked on the door in the first place. 'Does he live here?'

'Most of the time. Sometimes crashes out at his mum's.'

'Did he give you that?' Henry nodded at her.

'What? The kid or the black eye?'

'Whichever.'

'Both.'

Henry regained his composure and said, 'No, don't know. Why don't you give the nick a ring and ask the Custody Sergeant?'

'What with? I don't have a phone and I don't have any spare money until the Giro comes. That bastard took it all with him yesterday. I'll ring his soddin' neck when he comes back.'

She slammed the door behind them. Henry heard the chain slot back, then the TV get turned up.

Seymour said, 'Isn't that the one you kneed in the knackers?'

'You make it sound like an unprovoked assault, Dave. It was self-defence.'

They went outside and trotted down the steps to the basement flat. Henry rapped on the door.

'There's one thing about it,' Seymour said dryly. 'There's a one hundred per cent chance of him giving her a black eye again, but only a fifty per cent chance of him fathering another little Shane Mulcahy.'

The front entrance to the club was a pair of large wooden doors, gloss painted a deep shiny maroon.

Henry looked at Seymour with a surprised expression when the doors had been virtually closed in their faces by Jacko with a curt, 'You'll have to wait here while I get the boss.'

'Interesting reaction,' said Seymour. He leaned on the doorbell as though pushing it hard would make it ring out in a more official tone.

'Something to hide?' mused Henry.

They both waited for the 'boss' to arrive.

En route to the club, Henry had asked comms, via his PR, to see what could quickly be unearthed about a John Rider on the PNC and Indepol, Lancashire's own crime intelligence computer.

There was no response for a few minutes. He and Seymour had by then arrived at the club and were obliged to park outside whilst waiting for the reply. Parked up in front of them was Rider's Jaguar.

Checking up on people was pretty standard for Henry, no matter who he was dealing with. If they had ever been of interest to the police, he wanted to know.

After a tedious five minutes, the radio operator got back to him. 'From the PNC – two previous, both over ten years old. Want details?'

'Affirmative.'

'Nineteen seventy-nine, armed robbery in Blackburn. Two years. Hijacked a security van. Nineteen eighty-two, again in Blackburn, living off immoral earnings. Two thousand pound fine, eighteen months suspended. Received?'

'Yep.'

'Not a lot on Indepol. There's an old "target" file for him in existence somewhere, probably Manchester. There's an RCS and NWOCS reference. That's it . . . and PNC is flashing a warning signal. Apparently, if it's the same guy, he uses firearms and is violent.'

'Thanks,' Henry acknowledged, as usual not using radio terminology such as 'Roger and out,' because it made him feel slightly foolish.

'Pimp and blagger,' said Seymour.

'Firearms and violent,' added Henry. 'All very well to know.'

The door opened.

'Mr Rider?' Henry asked.

A nod.

'Your employee is very rude.'

'Not half as rude as I can be. What can I do for you?'

'Can we come in?'

'Do you have a warrant?'

Henry looked pityingly at Rider. 'We have a statutory right to enter licensed premises at any time.' Or so he thought. He wasn't completely certain, but he sounded it. 'We need to ask some questions about one of your tenants who was found dead on the beach earlier today.' He wasn't completely sure about that, either.

Rider sighed. 'Come in then.'

Conroy's whole afternoon had backfired very badly indeed. He slouched angrily down in the back seat of his Mercedes which sped smoothly eastwards along the M55. What an almighty fucking cock-up!

Firstly there was the matter of John 'holier-than-thou' Rider, who like some sort of demented religious convert had forsaken all things criminal. Conroy had expected a soft touch – a serious misjudgement.

He'd been a hundred per cent certain he would be able to walk all over Rider and make a very one-sided deal which would give him access to the club. It had been apparent though from the first moments of their encounter that Rider wasn't the slobbering drugged-up drunk he'd been expecting to meet. He was very much the Rider of old who was not to be messed with.

It didn't alter the plan, though.

Conroy still wanted into the club – and very soon.

All it meant was that the next approach to Rider would be more formal and if necessary backed up with force. How much force was a matter for Rider, but there would be no room for negotiation. Conroy would get what he wanted.

Then there was the other matter . . . Munrow.

Conroy shifted uneasily. He could still feel the muzzle of the gun pressed into the back of his head. His ear throbbed like hell. That was the last thing he needed at the moment – a fucking gaolbird starting a war just because he felt he'd had his nose put out of joint. It'd be more than his nose when Conroy finished with him. It'd be his brain.

'You callin' Dunny, boss?' Conroy's driver asked over his shoulder, interrupting the thought process.

'Shit – yes.' Conroy sprang forwards. 'Gimme the phone.'

The driver handed the mobile over to him. Conroy punched a number in.

'It's off,' he said. 'Yeah, you heard right. Bring the stuff back.'

The next ten minutes were very uncomfortable for all parties. Not because of the nature of the enquiry, simply because Rider hated to be in the presence of police officers, particularly detectives, and resented answering questions, incriminating or otherwise, merely on a point of principle. And he particularly resented Henry Christie, whom he disliked on sight.

To Rider, Christie had an aura about him that the rather plodding Seymour didn't possess. It was nothing to do with the way he dressed – because for a detective, Christie dressed quite conservatively. Nor was it the way he spoke, as Christie's voice was quite monotone.

It was that he oozed inner savvy. It was the look in his eyes, the way they constantly took measure, occasionally narrowing to a slit as they ran over Rider. The way he listened to answers, but at the same time his mind seemed to be considering something of greater importance. It was the way he assessed Rider, chewed over what information there was to be had, what information was hidden, and weighed him up. Probably coming to the right conclusion.

Basically, he unnerved Rider.

From the other side, Henry did not like Rider either. There was an immediate animosity between them. Not that Henry cared. There was friction between himself and a lot of crims. It was a good thing, he thought. Kept them on their toes.

But this man Rider . . .

As he answered the questions, Henry tried to analyse him. Something about the guy made Henry do a double-take. What the hell was it? Henry could feel there was something more to this man, who on the face of it came across as a middle-aged, overweight, seedy club and doss-house owner.

Henry took a few minutes to discover what it was.

Then he knew.

He'd only ever met a few other such people in his life and he shifted slightly on the bar stool, his arse literally twitching.

Rider was no common criminal. This man was, or had been, big time. Top notch. There weren't too many about. Some liked to think they were, but mostly they were nothing. This man tried to cover it in bluster and bad temper, but just below the surface Henry could see exactly what he was.

And it was in the eyes, too. They always gave the game away. There was that violence lurking there which said, 'I could kill you, cop, and not give a toss.'

But it was rusty. Henry could see that, too. This man had been out of the game for a while, but it was still in his blood. He could be very dangerous again.

Yes, thought Henry, Rider was something special. His mouth went dry at the thought.

Now he wanted to know everything about this man, the sooner the better. He cursed his lack of professionalism for not knowing already.

Rider responded begrudgingly to the detectives' questions.

Yes, the dead girl's description sounded like one of his new tenants. Couldn't remember her name at the moment; it would be on the rent book. From Blackburn, he thought. No, didn't know very much about her. No, that wasn't unusual. He was a landlord, not a fucking snoop. So long as the rent came, he didn't give a toss. Yes, top flat, number twelve. Came in two days ago. Yes, they could go in and have a look round the flat. Probably wouldn't be locked. She didn't bring much stuff with her. She was alone. Was that all? Bye bye.

Henry thanked him. As he did he recalled the statement taken from the girl at the zoo. It mentioned a big red car taking off after the shooting. There was a big red Jaguar parked outside the club.

Henry could picture Rider involved in something like that.

'Oh, by the way,' he said, sliding off his bar stool onto his feet. 'Have you visited the zoo today?'

'No.' Too quick, very tense all of a sudden.

'Let's hope you haven't,' said Henry, 'because if you have and I find out I'll be back here faster than shit off a shovel.' He spoke very matter-of-factly and in a way that Rider found intimidating.

'Don't know what the hell you're on about.'

'See you now,' Henry said affably.

He and Seymour walked out.

Rider remained at the bar. Jacko and Isa materialised out of the woodwork. Jacko stayed behind the bar. Isa asked him what it was all about.

He gave a sneer. 'Nothing – just one of my tenants. Nothing to worry about.' But he *was* worried, and frightened. 'Fuck that bastard Conroy!' he said between gritted teeth and slammed the bar top with his fist. 'Fuck him for getting me involved again.'

Out on the street Henry took the number of the Jag and radioed it through for a PNC check.

The two detectives got into their car, an unmarked Rover Two series. 'He didn't even ask "Why?" when I mentioned the zoo,' Henry said. 'I find that intriguing. I mean, if a cop asked you if you'd been somewhere, surely you'd—'

Henry's audible musing was interrupted by a very garbled message on the personal radio. A patrol was shouting, but most of the words were impossible to make out – with the exception of, 'Assistance! Assistance! Officer down!'

Chapter Six

'We've to take the stuff back to the warehouse – the deal's off for some friggin' reason,' Dundaven said to his passenger, whose name was McCrory.

He ended the call on the mobile and tossed it onto the dashboard of the Range Rover. They had been mooching around Blackpool, killing time in amongst all the tourists, pretending to be trippers themselves, whilst waiting for the call from Conroy. The theory was that they would look less suspicious on the move rather than parked up in some back alley somewhere. Two guys sitting in a motor always attracts attention.

The mobile had chirped whilst they were driving south down the Promenade from Gynn Square, stuck in the flow of traffic.

However, McCrory breathed a sigh of relief at the news. 'Thank fuck for that, Dunny.' He was getting decidedly jumpy, trolling around the place with enough firepower in the back to arm a unit of the SAS. 'Let's get the crap outta here.'

Stopping and searching persons and vehicles is one of the most fundamental functions of a police officer. Its effectiveness in preventing and detecting crime cannot be over-stressed. Stop-searches result in thousands of arrests each year, mostly for minor criminal and drug-possession offences, as well as more spectacular ones. The Yorkshire Ripper, the Black Panther and members of the IRA responsible for planting bombs in the north of England were all arrested by officers exercising their basic powers.

Many officers stop-search using the numbers game: if enough people and vehicles are stopped, the theory goes, sooner or later there will be a result.

Some officers simply have a nose, an eye, an ear – an instinct – for pulling the right person or vehicle at the right time.

Or in some cases, the wrong time.

PC Rik Dean was one such officer. He had three and a half years' service, but at the age of thirty-two, had another eight years' experience behind him as a Customs and Excise officer.

Blackpool Central had been his first posting as a cop and he loved the place. The work was hectic – Blackpool never stood still – and the social life was even better now that he was divorced.

He was one of those policemen who just seem to fall over villains. He didn't know why – it just happened. When he stopped a car, odds could be laid he'd find a hoard of stolen goods; if he pulled a person, he'd find heroin. And he didn't know why. He'd look at someone, or a car, his brow would furrow, his head would tilt to one side and he'd say, 'Let's have a look at that.'

Which is what he did that Sunday afternoon.

He was working the 2–10 p.m. shift. When he paraded on duty he was given a thick wodge of arrest warrants, mainly for people who had failed to appear at court, and was told to go and execute a few of them. The warrants, that is.

He was partnered with a policewoman called Nina. She was nineteen years old, had only recently finished her initial training and joined the shift, and was still wet behind the ears, slightly hesitant and shy in everything she did. Rik had decided she could execute the warrants to build up her confidence in dealing with people. At ten o'clock when the tour of duty finished, he might suggest a drink in the bar. And who knew where that could lead . . .

Apart from being a cracking thief-taker, Rik was also a serial police-woman seducer, with five so far to his credit. He couldn't resist a woman in uniform, and they seemed unable to resist him with his trousers down.

Again, he did not know how he did it. Just happened. If he could have distilled, bottled and sold his policing and womanising skills he would have made a fortune. Or so he thought and often joked.

The afternoon had been fruitless and frustrating, made more so by the way the station was buzzing frenetically with chatter about last night's massacre at the newsagents and this morning's murder on the beach. Detectives were everywhere, suffused with their own importance, carrying bits of paper, looking serious, talking in whispers, attending briefings.

And Rik was envious. He wanted to become a detective and get involved in jobs like those.

'No reply,' Nina said wearily. She climbed back into the passenger seat of the Maestro and dropped the warrant onto the pile in the footwell. 'That's eight we've tried with no luck,' she complained. 'I'm getting bored with this.'

'Me too.' He started up the engine and the less then elegant police car moved off. It was 4.30 p.m. and they'd been pounding on doors solidly since the start of the tour. 'Let's kick it in the head for a while and cruise.'

'Yeah, good idea.'

'If you see anything you fancy stopping, just give me a nudge, will you?'

'Yeah, will do.'

Rik was not really in the mood to do much. His thoughts were on enquiries, arresting murderers and big-time crims.

Nina sat back, removed her hat and ran her hand through her cropped, spiky blonde hair. She heaved a deep sigh which pushed her bust tightly up against her tunic. Rik saw the rise of the material out of the corner of his eye and gulped. Nina smiled. She had ideas for ten o'clock too.

Unfortunately for both, their thoughts of a future liaison would soon get put on indefinite hold.

Rik drove down the Promenade, coming onto it from the north at Gynn Square, travelling slowly south. There was a huge amount of traffic about, as well as pedestrians. From a sluggish beginning, the brightness of this January day had attracted many day-trippers into town.

The evening was drawing in now and many were planning to leave.

He drove little faster than walking pace, content to watch.

'We'll mosey down south, come up by Squires Gate and work back round to Marton. There's a couple of warrants for up there,' he said.

'Suits me fine.'

Rik's mind was coasting in neutral. He was not interested in working hard that afternoon. His thoughts were a mixture of how best to word his application for CID, what might happen between him and Nina, and how great it would feel to be a detective.

He saw the vehicle for the first time as he reached the junction with Talbot Square and stopped at the traffic lights at the head of the queue. From this point southwards, Blackpool's Promenade is basically a dual carriageway, two lanes in either direction.

Rik had pulled up on the inside lane.

He was looking around aimlessly, eyes flitting about between the task of driving, glancing at female pedestrians and gazing out to sea.

Policework was way down the list.

The fact that the vehicle which pulled alongside him at the lights was a Range Rover 4.6 HSE, green with a grey flash down the side and bull-bars wrapped around the grill, did little to arouse his curiosity. He cast his eyes over it but thought nothing.

Nor did he pay much attention to the passenger, a male, early twenties, who happened to look down at him and catch his eye ever so briefly. The man turned quickly away and said something to the driver whom Rik could not see from his lowdown position in the Maestro.

The lights went to green.

The Range Rover surged ahead of the police car. Rik was not concerned about that. He was happy enough to let other cars overtake and speed along as they wished. Catching speeders was the job of the traffic department, not his.

He did notice that the vehicle had been registered in Liverpool, the last two letters of the index number being KB.

That was enough for him to ask Nina to radio in and ask for a PNC check. With the high volume of cars stolen from that area he had no qualms in checking any vehicle registered there.

The reply was that it was not stolen, but the current owner was not listed on the computer. The previous owner had notified DVLA of the sale of the vehicle two months before. Even that did not have much effect on Rik – not consciously. Thousands of vehicles were without current owners. It usually meant they had recently changed hands and the paperwork was still going through.

He drew in behind the Range Rover which had stopped at the next but one set of traffic lights on the Promenade at the junction with Chapel Street. Tussaud's Waxworks were on their left.

Now Rik could see the driver's face reflected in the door mirror. The man continually checked the mirror, looking back at Rik whilst speaking animatedly to the passenger.

That was probably what swung it for Rik. He hardly knew any drivers who checked their side mirrors as often as this one.

The lights went to green.

Once again the Range Rover accelerated away.

The Maestro, not built for speed or agility (what exactly was it built for, some officers had been known to ask) had a problem keeping up, but the volume of traffic held the bigger car back. By the time they reached the next set of lights, Rik was behind it again.

Now Nina was sitting up, taking notice. 'Something wrong?'

Somehow the atmosphere had changed. She could sense Rik's new alertness, like a charge of static.

He played it down, shrugged. 'Just gonna pull this guy. D'you fancy issuing him with a producer?' He was referring to the form HORT1 issued by police to drivers for them to take their documents into a police station to be checked within seven days.

'Sure.' She peered at the Range Rover but failed to see anything wrong with it. She believed the PNC check she'd done had been simply routine, nothing else. 'But why, what's he done?'

'Nothing . . . probably nothing,' said Rik. 'We'll stop them after they've gone through the lights.' His head was at a slight tilt, his brow furrowed.

The Range Rover was indicating a left turn at the lights which would take it onto Lytham Road.

When the lights changed, the big vehicle moved off as though turning left, but halfway into the junction the indicator went off and the vehicle veered right and kept going straight down the Prom.

Rik thought he was in for a chase. He absently fingered the transmit button on his personal radio.

He flashed his headlights a few times and turned on the blue flashing roof-light and pipped his rather pathetic horn. He wished they'd fit proper two-tone horns.

Initially the Range Rover did not respond.

Rik was about to call for back-up when, drawing level with the Pleasure Beach, the Range Rover pulled into the side of the road and stopped.

48

Rik pulled in behind, leaving a gap of ten metres.

Neither occupant of the Range Rover got out.

'Go and give him a chit,' he said to Nina. She had already prepared her clipboard and put her hat on. 'And smell his breath. He could've had some bevvy. I'll hang on here.'

He had a premonition that the driver might just try and speed away.

He was right.

When the Range Rover had pulled up initially alongside the police car at Talbot Square traffic lights, McCrory looked down to his left and nearly had heart failure. 'Shit, Dunny,' he said through clenched teeth. 'Cops. Fuck, fuck, fuck.'

McCrory was a small-time thief and drug addict in his early twenties who was known to his acquaintances as 'Bits 'n' Bats', often shortened to 'Bits', due to his habit of helping himself to other people's property, their bits 'n' bats. He had ingratiated himself onto the lower rungs of Conroy's organisation without ever knowing who his ultimate employer was, and had proved himself to be a trustworthy deliverer of packages, unusually for a druggie. Never completely aware of what he was carrying, these packages ranged from drugs, the occasional handgun and cash.

Today he had been hired to assist in the delivery of what was in the back of the Range Rover to Rider's club. As he had lumped the firearms into the vehicle he had palpitations. He had no illusions about what he'd been required to deliver in the past. He could guess at drugs, and maybe money sometimes, but he had never even considered that he might have carried guns before. Just the action of putting his hand on them made him break out into an ice-cold sweat. He felt completely out of his depth, but he was unable to back out. He'd already been hired, received half his fee, and did not have the guts to say no thanks. That would have made him appear unreliable. Maybe expendable.

The man in control – who McCrory believed to be the controller of the purse strings – was called Hughie Dundaven. He was a gruff Scot in his early thirties who had been involved with Conroy for several years. He had risen quite high in the hierarchy and ran a couple of council estates in the Burnley area for Conroy and oversaw some clubs. He had been responsible for hiring McCrory, but he was having his regrets.

'Just fekin calm down. Relax. Be cool, we'll be reet,' he said.

'Be fuckin' cool?' McCrory blurted. 'Jeez, an' how am I expected to be fuckin' cool?' All he wanted to do was jam a needle up his arm and escape this madness. Buckets of perspiration rolled off him. He shivered and squirmed as though he was sitting on a hedgehog.

He was beginning to grate on Dundaven's nerves.

'Just shut the feck up. It's only a cop car. They're not goin' ter stop us.'

'He looks suspicious to me.' McCrory panicked as he caught the eye of the policeman and twisted away.

49

'Dinna fekin look at him then, you knobhead. Act natural. If he sees you jumpin' about like a prick he will stop us, wonnee? Otherwise there's no reason tae.'

The lights changed. Dundaven shot away.

And there was no earthly reason why they should have been stopped. The car was clean, decent, and he was driving fine.

When stopped at the lights near to Tussaud's, the police car was behind them. Dundaven had paid no heed to it until McCrory, looking through the back window of the Range Rover, had panicked, 'He's still there. I don't like this, Dunny. It's doin' me head in. I need a fix.'

That was the point where Dundaven looked into the door mirror and ranted to McCrory, 'Will you fekin calm doon, you twat! You's gettin' tae me now. It's nothin'. He's drivin' doon the Prom, lookin' at the totty, just like you'd do if you were a cop in Blackpool . . .' And all the while he could not stop himself from looking in the mirror, in which he could see Rik's face, looking back at him.

At the next set of lights Dundaven was undecided which way to go, even though he was signalling left. He wanted to get to the motorway but wasn't sure of the quickest route. The last moment saw him cancelling the signal, going straight ahead down the Promenade. He swore at McCrory for getting him riled up, the useless cunt.

McCrory peered backwards over his shoulder almost constantly.

'He's still with us,' he observed unnecessarily for Dundaven, who could quite clearly see through his mirrors. 'Still with us . . . oh fuck, oh fuck, Dunny, he's flashing us to stop, he's flashing us to stop! Oh my fuckin' God!'

McCrory flipped round in his seat to face the front. He shrunk low as if he hoped a hole would appear in the floorpan into which he could be sucked. In a grand gesture of despair he dropped his shaking head into his hands. 'We are fucked. They are gonna find all that lot in the back. We . . . are . . . completely goosed, Dunny. On my daughter's life, we are going to prison.'

'No, we're not,' Dundaven's harsh voice grated.

He pulled into the side of the road, stopping like a good motorist should, and keeping the engine ticking over. He quickly reached between the seats and rummaged underneath a car blanket. He extracted two weapons – sawn-off shotguns with the stocks removed.

McCrory's eyes widened. 'Oh God, I need to OD on heroin like now. A fuckin' shooter!' he whined. Now he *knew* he was out of his depth.

Dundaven forced one of the guns into McCrory's unwilling hands. Then he wound his window down and waited patiently for the arrival of a rather pretty policewoman.

Nina adjusted her cap again. She walked past the front of the police car, aware that her male colleague was eyeing her up appreciatively; aware, also, she was responding to the admiration by swaying her behind ever so slightly provocatively. Nothing anyone else would have noticed, but enough for Rik, whose intestines did a little skip of pleasure.

She went to the driver's window of the Range Rover, standing in the roadway, but feeling safe as Rik had put the blue lights and hazard warning lights on. She held her clip-board in two hands, resting the bottom edge of it on her tunic, against her belly.

'Hello, is this your car?' she asked Dundaven. She smiled genuinely.

He returned a wide smile, which was also genuine.

Glancing down she caught sight of the shotgun in his lap.

And the one in the hands of the passenger.

'Yes – and this is mine too,' Dundaven said.

The gun swung up.

Nina did the thing which probably saved her life.

Automatically she brought up the clipboard and shielded her face. Dundavan pulled the triggers, firing both barrels at her. The poorly balanced gun kicked back in his grip and he almost dropped it.

The lead shot from the two cartridges ripped the plastic coated clipboard to shreds in Nina's hands. This obstruction, though slight, managed to dissipate some of the force of the blast.

Even so, she took it full in the face. The knuckles of both her hands where she had been holding the board were pulped by the shot.

She staggered back into the road, her hat flying off.

A passing car swerved, but caught her almost full on. She cartwheeled onto the bonnet and crashed into the windscreen. The motorist braked sharply and her limp body was thrown back onto the road.

'Get the other one, the driver,' Dundaven screamed at McCrory.

'What the fuck . . . ?' quibbled the hired hand.

'Get the other one – shoot him.'

McCrory knew better than to argue. In a trance of acquiescence he got out of the Range Rover, ran down the side in a low crouch and when he got to the rear nearside corner he pointed the weapon at the police car. Not really aiming, hoping he hit nothing, McCrory pulled the triggers. Without waiting to see what, if any, damage or injury he'd caused, he scurried back to his seat. Tears were streaming down his face. 'Oh man, oh man,' he kept saying to himself.

Rik could not believe his eyes for a moment.

The figure of Nina stepping backwards like a boxer who'd been k.o.'d had made him angry for a second. One of the rules was you always spoke to drivers on the pavement, but if you speak to them in the road, don't forget where you are. Be careful.

Then the car struck her and a man appeared at the back of the Range Rover brandishing a shotgun.

Rik was half out of the car at that moment.

He saw McCrory, whom he recognised instantly as the passenger, saw the gun, and launched himself back into the police car across the two front seats. The hand brake slammed into his chest. He realised he'd made a bad choice. If the man wanted to kill him he was trapped. The windscreen shattered, peppered with shot, spidering out like cracked ice. It did not give.

Rik winced and fumbled for his radio. He blabbered his first, virtually incoherent message into the mouthpiece, expecting the man to appear at the side of the car and blast him to Kingdom Come.

Nothing happened.

Rik took a chance. He raised his head. Through the cracked screen he saw the Range Rover accelerating away.

He pushed himself out of the car and ran towards Nina's prostrate form in the road. Her face was a gory mess. Rik recognised the wound as consistent with a shotgun blast and now everything made sense. She had walked backwards into the car because she'd been fucking shot.

A bone in her left thigh was sticking raggedly out through the skin. Her left arm was twisted and looked to be badly broken. She wasn't moving. Rik thought she was dead.

'Repeat your message, caller,' he heard his radio say.

He looked at the Range Rover getting further and further away, then to Nina. He knew where his priorities lay.

The first police car to respond squealed around the corner of the nearest side road. Henry Christie was at the wheel.

Chapter Seven

Normally Henry was a poor listener where the personal radio was concerned. Most of the time he had it turned right down or off. Generally he used it solely for his own convenience, but that afternoon he was glad he'd just checked Rider's car and the volume was up.

He and Seymour were probably less than two hundred metres away from the incident. They were on the scene within seconds.

Henry's experienced eyes took it all in. The policewoman lying on the road. The shattered windscreen of the police car. The shocked, ashen face of Rik Dean, a bobby Henry would have been very happy to have on the department. The public beginning to gather and gawp.

He pulled up alongside. Rik ran to him.

'Down there, down there,' he pointed wildly. 'Green Range Rover. Two on board, white males. Shotgun. Shot her. Shot at me! Christ!'

'OK pal, you stay here and look after her. Assistance'll be along in a few seconds,' Henry told him.

He rammed the gear lever into first and put his foot hard down on the accelerator.

Henry's CID Rover was not equipped with blue lights or sirens. Nor was it 'souped-up' as so many misinformed members of the public would like to believe of police cars. It was a bog-standard saloon with no extras, bought at a massive discount with another forty-nine of the same model, all in a puke-green colour which tended to sell poorly to private customers. Hence the discount. Although quite new in terms of date of manufacture, it had been mistreated, badly driven and sneered at over the last eighty thousand miles of its police service. A typical cop car, in fact.

Despite all that, the engine was still pretty lively.

Henry had to rely on the rather pathetic-sounding horn, flashing his headlights and massively exaggerated hand signals – some rude – to make progress down the Promenade. He drove dangerously, taking risks which would make him sweat on reflection. In and out of the traffic. Fitting the car into gaps that, by rights, were not wide enough for a motorcyclist, but which miraculously opened up as he hit them. He prayed his luck would hold out.

Next to him, Seymour held loosely onto his seat belt, swaying and rocking with the momentum, coolly relaying their position to comms in a flat unemotional voice. He might as well have been sitting in a pram.

'Tell them to get the helicopter up,' Henry said. He braked sharply, making the car stand on its nose, veered acutely to the left and narrowly missed an on-coming Bentley.

He shook his head at his driving skills. It was just like being on his mobile surveillance course again.

But there was nothing to say that the Range Rover was even on the coast road now. Could easily have turned off, doubled back, anything.

Henry carried on. Wherever he went it was a gamble.

It was surprising how far a vehicle can travel in a short time.

Although Henry had been on the scene very quickly, he was probably about ninety seconds behind the Range Rover even then. By the time he'd spoken to Rik, he was probably about two minutes behind.

And, of course, the Range Rover wanted to get away.

The occupants weren't going to dawdle along and take in the sights any more. They wanted freedom.

And though Henry was driving like a maniac down the Promenade towards St Annes, he was constantly having to brake, slow down, swerve. If the Range Rover was having just a fraction of an easier time of it, the distance between them would be constantly increasing.

The comms operator, having got the full story from Rik and other officers now at the scene of the shooting, circulated the registered number of the Range Rover to all patrols. Within a minute or so the whole of Lancashire Constabulary were on the lookout for it. She also confirmed that Oscar November 21 – the force helicopter – would be in the air within minutes.

Four minutes after leaving the scene, Henry was driving through St Annes, a less brash, slightly posh resort to the south of Blackpool.

If he's anything like smart, Henry thought to himself, he'll dump the Range Rover pretty fucking soon, if he hasn't already done so. It was an observation voiced a moment later by Seymour. Great detectives think alike!

'He could be anywhere now,' Henry said with frustration. He eased his foot off the gas. 'Shall we continue to gamble?'

'I don't think we have a choice, boss.'

Henry visualised the pathetic bloodied figure of the policewoman lying on the road and agreed. They had to give it a shot for her.

His right foot pressed down again. They sped out of St Annes, through the next town, Lytham, emerging onto the A584, heading towards Preston. His hopes of coming up behind the Range Rover diminished with each passing second. He decided to drive to where the A584 joined the A583, at Three Nooks Junction. If he'd had no luck by then, he'd call it a draw and drive back to Blackpool.

He knew that another major enquiry would need kick-starting. And if the policewoman died – was she dead already? he asked himself – it would take precedent over the murdered girl on the beach.

The idea of two police officers being killed in two consecutive days in the same town appalled him. Some coincidence.

Beyond the built-up area, the A584 becomes a good, fast dual carriageway for about three miles before it links up with the 583. Henry gunned the Rover as fast as it would go. In the circumstances, that meant the needle hovered around 105 m.p.h. Rather generous, Henry felt, but it didn't stop the steering wheel rattling like mad in his hands.

They reached the traffic lights at the 583 within minutes.

No sign of the Range Rover. The trail was growing cooler by the second.

For no reason other than they didn't want to give in so easily, Henry slowed down, turned right at the lights and drove towards Preston.

Neither was expecting anything now.

'I'll go as far as the Lea Gate,' Henry said, naming a pub some way up the road, 'and spin it round in the car park.'

Seymour nodded.

The radio had gone quiet. No other patrols had spotted the vehicle. Very depressing, particularly for Henry. It would be a hundred times more difficult to make arrests from enquiries. Much easier to catch the bastards red-handed.

Seymour saw the vehicle first.

On the forecourt of a petrol filling station on the opposite side of the road. By the time he'd blurted it out, Henry had cruised past. He craned his neck round. Yeah. Could be the one. Too far away to see the registered number. Two men with it. One by a pump, filling it up. The other in the driver's seat.

'It must be,' said Seymour.

'Let's check it out.'

The road at that point was not a true dual carriageway. Two lanes did run in either direction, but they were separated by white lines, not a central reservation.

Henry was travelling slowly in the inside lane. With a rush of adrenalin, and little thought for a tactical approach or safety, he wrenched the wheel down and performed a U-turn across four lanes of traffic.

Cars skidded and braked everywhere. Horns blared angrily. V-signs and dick-head gestures were flashed. People swore.

Henry ignored them.

He'd seen his target and was homing in.

And likewise, Dundaven had seen the approaching danger. He knew it could not be anything other than the law.

'Leave that. Get back in,' he screamed through the open window at McCrory who was in the process of filling the thirsty machine with endless gallons of juice. He flung the nozzle to one side, spraying excess petrol across the forecourt, and ran to his seat, slamming his door behind him.

Henry veered onto the forecourt off the road.

Dundaven put all his weight on the accelerator and aimed the huge Range Rover purposely towards the oncoming police car. Intention: to ram and disable.

'Hold on,' Henry cried out and wondered fleetingly whether his right, left, or both legs would be broken.

The two vehicles met virtually head-on. The bull-bars wrapped around the front of the Range Rover crunched into the front lights and radiator grill of Henry's motor, bringing both to a skeleton-rattling halt.

Dundaven kept his foot rammed to the floor and pushed Henry's car across the forecourt, causing it more and more damage. Then he slammed his brakes on, went into reverse and put his foot down again. With a screech of tearing metal the Range Rover extricated itself, tyres squealing and smoking on the concrete surface.

When he had enough space to manoeuvre, Dundaven was back into forward gear and was pulling away.

Dundaven's right hand appeared out of his window, waving the shotgun in the general direction of the police car. He loosed off both barrels at the two officers who cowered down like frightened rabbits. It was a badly aimed shot, taken as the Range Rover was speeding past, and the discharge missed them completely. Once again the recoil was very great and he was unable to keep hold of the gun which jerked out of his hand onto the forecourt. Then he was gone, slewing across all four lanes of the dual carriageway and accelerating away towards Preston. The massive engine responded superbly to the throttle.

In contrast, the rather smaller engine of Henry's car had conked out.

He twisted the key in the ignition and prayed there was not too much damage. The starter motor coughed pathetically. Henry almost threw up his hands in despair, got out and kicked the car in anger.

But before he did, he tried it once again.

Roughly it fired up. He dabbed the gas pedal a couple of times and the unwilling engine came back to life like it had been in shock.

The process of restarting seemed to take for ever. Time which was allowing those two bastards to escape. In actual fact he was only a matter of seconds behind his target when he recrossed the road, which by now was becoming accustomed to dangerous driving.

The view down the front of Henry's car was no longer smooth and sleek. Instead it looked as though a heap of tangled metal had been clamped to the radiator, the bonnet having creased up like a blanket after a bad night.

He pushed the car to the limits of its performance in each gear and all the while he expected it to die on him. Surely, he thought, the collision must have damaged some of the workings.

'Keep going, y'bastard,' he intoned under his breath.

Because now he was mad. The driver of the Range Rover – apart from shooting a police officer – had rammed him and tried to kill him. He did not take kindly to that.

Seymour, cool as ever, was talking slowly into his radio.

Henry threw a quick glance at him. Blood was pouring out of a cut just below the left side of his scalp where he'd cracked it on the door. When he'd finished passing his message, Henry asked him if he was all right to continue.

Seymour scowled at Henry as though he was a complete prick.

'Let's catch these cunts,' he said grimly.

If Dundaven had been given the chance, he would have dumped the Range Rover at the first opportunity and stolen another car. That would have been the sensible thing to do.

He did not have that option.

The cargo in the back made it impossible. So he was stuck with what he'd got and had to make the effort to get it back to safety.

He was pleased by the way things had gone at first. He'd got out of Blackpool easily. The problem he next faced was that he needed to refuel the vehicle. The big engine was guzzling petrol faster than a tramp guzzled cider, and he didn't have enough left to get back to Manchester. Not at the speeds he'd be travelling at.

The refuelling had been going well.

McCrory, still stunned, was responding with blind obedience to everything. He made an excellent petrol pump attendant.

Then the detectives spotted them.

Dunny had hoped to ram the cop car into oblivion, but the manoeuvre had been nowhere near as effective as intended. This was confirmed by McCrory, who was keeping tabs out the back window.

'They're there, they're behind us,' he shrieked.

'I should've wasted 'em,' growled Dundaven with regret.

'There's another cop car with 'em now,' McCrory said.

Dundaven checked the mirror and glimpsed the blue light. He overtook a slow-moving bus, causing oncoming traffic to avoid him, then cut back in and shot through the next set of traffic lights which were on red. In the middle of the junction he had to slam on, twist and turn, accelerate away, keeping going all the time.

McCrory leaned forwards and peered up through the windscreen.

'Now the fuckin' helicopter's there,' he howled in anguish. 'We haven't got a hope in hell, Dunny. We are fucking doomed. On my daughter's life, we are doomed.'

'Shut yer pathetic hole,' Dundaven warned him. 'We are not doomed.' Well, I'm not, he added silently.

He mounted the pavement with the two nearside wheels and overtook a series of cars on the inside, pulling back onto the road inches before he hit a lamp post.

He was thinking quickly, weighing up the odds which were shortening against them. McCrory was a liability. If they did get caught, he would definitely talk till the cows came home. Though he didn't know much, he knew a little and the cops could follow up on it. Dundaven made a decision.

The shotgun McCrory had used on the police car was at McCrory's feet where he'd dropped it in disgust. Dundaven pointed at it. 'Put two more shells in that and hand it to me.'

Without enthusiasm, the other man picked the weapon up. His fingers were shaking as he did what he was told.

'What you gonna do with it?' he asked and placed it into Dundaven's beckoning left hand.

'Open yer door just a crack an' I'll show ya.'

'Eh?'

'Just fekin do it!'

McCrory pulled back the handle. The door was unlocked and slightly open.

'This is what I'm gonna do.'

He put the weapon to McCrory's head and pulled both triggers. This time when the gun recoiled he made sure he kept tight hold of it.

McCrory was catapulted out the side door.

By the time the chase hit the outskirts of Preston, Henry had been joined by a traffic car and the force helicopter. Other police vehicles in the area were converging.

The Control Room at force headquarters had taken over all communications. Their first instructions to Henry were that he should withdraw from the pursuit immediately and let the traffic car take up the following position.

It was one of those radio transmissions that, for some reason, Henry did not quite receive. This was one he was not going to give up. He'd face the consequences later.

He managed to stay in sight of the Range Rover as it bobbed and weaved through traffic. His own driving was more restrained and careful . . . but not by much.

They were about fifty metres behind, with nothing between them, when the passenger door opened and the body of a man seemed to leap out of the vehicle.

It corkscrewed out, appeared to stick gruesomely to the side of the Range Rover for an instant before suddenly losing grip, flopping onto the ground and bouncing into the road in front of Henry.

'Jesus, look out!' bellowed Seymour, losing his composure for the first time.

Henry's reactions had now become fine-tuned. He had a micro-second to react and steered brilliantly around the body, his car lurching madly on two wheels, close to overturning. The body continued to roll and bounce along behind them. The driver of the traffic car didn't have a chance in hell of missing it. He did well, but ran over it with all four wheels.

Henry saw it happen in his rearview mirror. He cringed as he experienced the impact by proxy and watched as the front wheels of the traffic car, then the rear, went over the legs and lower abdomen of the poor unfortunate man.

The traffic car braked and stopped.

'One down, one to go,' muttered Seymour. He shifted in his seat and made himself comfortable whilst holding a bloodsodden handkerchief to the cut on his head.

It looked like being a long one.

Dundaven's dilemma was now which route to take. He needed to get back to Manchester if at all possible. If he could get onto the estates in Salford he knew he could shake the cops, helicopter included.

But Salford was thirty miles away.

The most direct route was to head to the M6 at Junction 31, then onto the M61. Once on the motorway his options became limited. The police, if they could get enough vehicles together, could box him in, slow him down, make things very difficult. Not that he intended to stop. Ever. Whatever the situation he would keep on going . . . but on the motorway, the cops would have the upper hand.

The other choice was to head into East Lancashire, which he also knew well, being the area where he operated. Blackburn, maybe. It was a big-enough town where he could probably abandon the Range Rover and go to ground. Then he'd have to face the consequences from Conroy. Definitely not appealing. He'd rather be arrested.

He was quickly running out of options.

Whichever he chose, he knew that if he continued to drive like an idiot, refuse to stop, maybe ram a few more cop cars, and wave the shotgun about, all they would do was follow him at a safe distance. That was their policy. They didn't like getting people hurt. It tarnished their image.

He needed to make a decision quickly.

He was travelling down the steep hill, Brockholes Brow, away from Preston towards motorway Junction 31.

In his rearview he saw the crunched-up front end of the police car he had rammed on the forecourt, right up there, giving him nothing, pushing him hard.

Seymour had staunched the bloodflow from the cut on his head. He dropped his red-drenched hankie on the car floor where it landed with a squelch. He delicately touched the wound again and winced. Blood dribbled out again. He swore and held the sleeve of his jacket over it and pressed.

Henry had drawn up right behind the Range Rover on the steep Brockholes Brow. Only a matter of feet separated them.

Injured though he was, Seymour was full of bright ideas.

'If I had a pound of sugar,' he said laconically, 'I could lean out of the window and put it into his petrol tank. That'd stop him.' He had noticed the filler cap had not been secured. Petrol had splashed out on a couple of bends.

'Just check the glove box,' Henry said urgently. 'I think there's a bag of sugar in there.'

They both cracked up laughing.

'I just love chases,' Seymour said. 'Such fun.'

Brockholes Brow is a very steep hill about a mile long with a speed restriction of 30 m.p.h. They were touching eighty in their descent, whilst dangerously overtaking, cutting in, braking, accelerating. Only just missing other cars, leaving a trail of chaos behind.

Henry stuck with it all the way, as if he was being towed.

He didn't hold out much hope of this bastard being stopped by fair means. The man was obviously – and quite rightly – desperate to get away. He'd shot a cop and God knows what'd happened to the passenger. Henry couldn't begin to comprehend that. It was like a nightmare.

No, he thought. There were only two ways to stop this guy: if he ran out of petrol, or if the police employed foul means.

Another traffic car joined in behind Henry. There was one positioned at the foot of the hill, ready to pull out in front of the speeding Range Rover.

As the tons of hurtling machinery hit the flat, the driver of that waiting police car saw what was coming. He decided that discretion was the better part of valour. He wanted to get home for tea, so he sat there and let them all fly past. He tagged on behind.

The pursuit was taking on the appearance of *Death Race 2000*.

For a January Sunday in the north-west of England it had been an excellent day. Warm, sunny, still. One of those special winter's days – but a winter's day nonetheless.

And daylight does not last long in winter, however good the day has been.

By 4.50 p.m. as the chase approached the motorway, the night was drawing in. Quickly.

Street-lights were flickering on. Car headlights had been on for a while.

The darkening day was the reason why, at the last moment, Dundaven chose to take the motorway as a route to freedom. Maybe the cops wouldn't have it all their own way, he thought. Once he got on the motorway he would keep his lights off and drive blind. He knew that a good long stretch of the M61 was unlit and this would be to his advantage. Even with the helicopter and its searchlight up above.

He hardly reduced his speed on the approach to the first roundabout which forms Junction 31, keeping in as straight a line as possible on the wide, newly constructed road. He raced underneath the M6 bridge, with the River Ribble to his left, negotiated the second roundabout and picked up the M6 south.

He was feeling pretty confident when he came off the slip road and entered the motorway proper, easily overtaking the police Range Rover which was lying in wait for him.

Henry switched on his headlights, hardly expecting them to work. He was mildly surprised when both lit up, even the offside one which had been damaged in the collision. It shone at a very acute upwards angle, lighting up the spare wheel on the back door of the Range Rover.

'Handy if the Luftwaffe appears,' Seymour said.

They both started giggling again.

Each had settled into the pursuit now and were enjoying it, in spite of its dangers and the obvious lunatic they were after.

The traffic car behind Henry now flexed its muscles, pulled out, easily overtook him and cruised alongside Dundaven.

Silly manoeuvre.

Or as Seymour put it, 'The stupid prat.'

He was not wrong.

Dundaven looked sharply to his right, mouthed something down at the officers, yanked his steering wheel and barged into the side of the traffic car. The driver fought for control but spun spectacularly away, bounced off the central reservation barrier and the car flipped onto its roof. It continued to spin like a top until a car speeding down the outside lane, driven by an unsuspecting member of the public, smashed into it. Then another.

Dundaven in the Range Rover, Henry in the CID car, left this twisted chaos behind.

Seymour peered back but had difficulty making out exactly what had happened in the deepening gloom. He swore grimly and faced front again.

Henry grabbed the PR and shouted, 'No one is to try and pull this vehicle again. *No one!* Relay that to all patrols.'

From up in the sky the searchlight which hung on to the underside of the helicopter came on. For good reason the light was known as the 'Nightsun'. It emitted a light equivalent to 30 million candle-power. The whole light was fully remote, controlled from within the cockpit of the helicopter, and the beam width could be focused tightly onto a target. Which it was on the vehicle below.

The pursuit came off the M6 at the next exit, straight onto the M61, no slowing down necessary.

Dundaven increased his speed. Within moments the big vehicle was touching 115 m.p.h., courtesy of its 4.6-litre engine.

By contrast, Henry's car started to flag. The engine, less than half the size and ten times as worn, tried valiantly, but had extreme difficulty keeping around the 100 m.p.h. mark.

Dundaven hared easily away. The gap increased with each second.

There was no escaping the helicopter, however, which had a cruise speed of 125 m.p.h.

Seymour confirmed their position to Control Room, and that he believed their ultimate destination could well be Greater Manchester.

He asked for their patrols to be alerted.

'Unless we get him stopped on the motorway, we'll lose him,' Henry concluded. 'Here, give me the radio again. Perhaps there is something we can do.'

A traffic patrol officer called Sharp sat behind the steering wheel of his pride and joy: a brand new Volvo estate car, kitted out in the new orange, blue and white livery of the Lancashire Police.

He was parked on Anderton Services on the M61, literally only metres from the boundary with Manchester and about six miles south from the current position of the chase which was less than five minutes away from him.

His call sign came up and the Control Room operator asked him a question to which he replied, 'Yes, one on board.'

He was given authority to use it.

It was his lucky night.

He drove quickly down to the bottom of the services exit road and stopped on the hard shoulder. He turned on every light his car possessed so no one would fail to see him. He scurried around to the tailgate of the Volvo, opened it and pulled out his new piece of kit.

He was shaking with nervous anticipation.

History in the making.

The first officer in Lancashire to use 'The Stinger'.

Dundaven drove hard down the motorway, leapfrogging as necessary. Overtaking on the inside or hard shoulder. Followed all the while by that fucking helicopter.

Resting on his knee was the shotgun.

Holding the steering wheel with his right hand and left knee, he deftly broke the weapon with his free hand. The remnants of the two cartridges which had killed McCrory were expelled. Without letting the speed drop, he reached back between the seats and felt under the blanket where the shotguns had been secreted originally. He found a box of cartridges and dumped them out onto the bloodstained passenger seat. He skilfully slotted two into the empty barrels and closed the weapon.

Once loaded, he transferred the steering to his left hand, the shotgun to his right. Then he attempted to do what he always did to people or things which annoyed him.

He leaned out of the window, braced himself against the doorframe, aimed as best he could and wrapped his forefinger around the double triggers.

This was happening as he sped past Anderton Services.

He hardly noticed the place really; vaguely saw the police car with its lights ablaze and thought he might have seen the figure of a cop standing by the car. But that was all. What he was bothered about was getting a good shot at the helicopter.

The Hollow Spike Tyre Deflation System is its technical name. Better known as 'The Stinger', it consists of a lightweight plastic frame with metal spikes protruding from it and is designed, in manufacturer's parlance, 'to safely resolve pursuit situations'. By rolling out the frame like a red carpet across the path of a vehicle, the hollow spikes imbed themselves in one or more of the tyres. Gradual deflation and subsequent loss of speed follow. That's the theory.

The Stinger had been used in several police forces with a good deal of success, though vehicles had been known not to pick up spikes in their tyres. Lancashire had eventually bought a large number of the systems. This was the first time one had been deployed.

Sharp was ecstatic as he watched the fleeing Range Rover bump over it. He yanked it back in and bundled it into the back of the Volvo.

Had it done the trick, was the next question.

Dundaven fired both barrels upwards, remembering to keep hold of the weapon. At the same time he felt a dull 'thu-dud' when the wheels went over something in the carriageway. A hump or something. Maybe raised tarmac over a repair. Nothing really.

The observer in the helicopter saw Dundaven's head and right shoulder leaning out of the window and the shotgun aimed at them. He informed the pilot and both of them said, 'What a wanker he must be if he thinks he's going to even come close.' They stayed exactly where they were on station above him.

He missed completely, all of the shot eventually falling harmlessly away.

'That'll show the fuckers,' Dundaven said with satisfaction.

He dropped the shotgun onto the passenger seat and returned his concentration to driving. Not that far to go now.

The Range Rover slewed to the right.

He corrected the steering, thinking nothing of it. A gust of wind.

It happened again.

'Wooaw,' he gasped. The wheel almost ripped itself out of his grip. This time it was a little harder to control at 117 m.p.h. 'What the fuck is happening?' he demanded out loud. Puncture, maybe?

It veered to the right again. Dundaven held tightly to the wheel, trying to keep the speed up but finding it increasingly difficult. With each second the vehicle became more and more unstable. Next it went left. Something was very definitely wrong.

With a flash he remembered the cop on the motorway.

And the bump on the road.

He groaned angrily and reached for the shotgun.

'The Stinger!' he hissed.

Sharp, the traffic officer, had caught up with Dundaven in less than two minutes. The speed was now lower than fifty and dropping.

The helicopter radioed the apparent success to all patrols.

Within another minute Henry was back in the chase.

Seconds behind him was another traffic car and an Armed Response Vehicle (ARV) – which was double-manned – each officer armed to the back teeth with a variety of weapons.

Another helicopter appeared in the sky, the one belonging to Greater Manchester Police.

Dundaven saw everything converging on him. He fought to keep the speed up, but could not halt the decline. Having picked up spikes in both front tyres, the Range Rover was proving impossible to control. It seemed to have had enough of him and wanted to stop the whole crazy business. He was powerless, like the rider of a horse which had a mind of its own.

He slowed and stopped in the centre lane.

The helicopters hovered above, lights blazing down on him.

There were no other cars about other than cop cars, because three miles back Control Room had activated the overhead matrix signs and brought the motorway to a standstill.

Dundaven fondled the shotgun for a few moments. Deep in thought he tossed it out of the window, sat there and bowed his head.

It was over.

Henry talked Dundaven out, giving him precise instructions through a loud-hailer.

Slowly. No sudden movements.

There are armed officers. Their guns are pointing at you. If you make any sudden movement, or do anything other than what I say, you will be shot. Be in no doubt about that.

Open the door with your right hand. Push it fully open.

Put your hands on your head. Interlock your fingers.

Get out very, very slowly.

Right leg, left leg. Slowly. Get out. Stand up. Face me.

Walk very slowly towards me.

Keep looking at me.

Slowly or you will be shot . . . that's it . . . another two steps.

Stop there.

Keep facing me . . . keep looking at me . . . do as I say.

Keeping your hands on your head, go down onto your right knee.

Now stretch out your arms at shoulder height. Pretend to be Jesus.

Keep your left arm stretched out. Lean forwards and place your right hand on the road. Now your left. Lower yourself to the ground, keep your nose flat to the road, lie face down on the road.

Put your arms out again.

Stay exactly where you are.

An officer will now approach you. He is armed and if you move, he will shoot you in the back.

You must do what this officer tells you . . . otherwise you'll be shot.

He was expertly searched. His wrists were secured up his back in rigid handcuffs. He was placed in the rear of a police van which had been called to the scene. Two burly cops climbed inside with him. The back door was locked. Henry instructed them to take him directly to Blackpool.

Henry picked up the shotgun and placed it carefully on the back seat of his car.

He and Seymour looked into the Range Rover, baulking at the sight of the blood and bits of skull and brain splattered all over the passenger side.

Henry opened the back door.

When he lifted the blanket he realised why Dundaven had been so anxious not to get caught.

'Looks like we've bagged a gun-seller,' said Seymour.

Chapter Eight

It is claimed that the best job in the FBI is to be stationed at the London office, situated on the fourth floor of the American Embassy in Grosvenor Square.

Karl Donaldson agreed wholeheartedly with the proposition.

He had been appointed as an assistant to the legal attaché some twelve months previously, having fought off fierce competition for the post. Since then he had never been happier in his professional as well as his personal life.

In the last year he had acted as FBI liaison with many British police forces, MI5 and MI6. Thanks to cooperation between himself at the FBI, Scotland Yard and the Spanish police in Madrid, a Colombian-backed money-laundering scam handling billions of dollars of drug-trafficking money between the US, Channel Islands and Isle of Man and a crooked Egyptian finance house, had been smashed and literally dismantled.

Donaldson had recovered and seized over two billion dollars and destroyed a service to the cartels which had probably seen twenty times that amount pass through it in four years. He had also been involved in the investigation of many other international conspiracies, several of which were ongoing, some of which had come to nothing.

The work, he found, was demanding, exciting and fulfilling.

Just as his personal life had proved to be.

Previously having been a resident in Miami, he had moved to England and married Karen Wilde, cop, formerly a Chief Inspector in Lancashire. They had met and fallen in love whilst Donaldson – then a special agent – had been investigating mafia connections in the north of England. Karen had transferred to the Metropolitan Police and was presently seconded to Bramshill Police College, where she held the rank of Temporary Superintendent.

Without having tried particularly hard, they were expecting their first child.

Life was being very good to them both.

But occasionally there was a downside – which Donaldson was experiencing now.

He was sitting at a window seat on the direct GB Airways flight from London to Madeira. In spite of his destination, that lush green Portuguese island in the Atlantic, Donaldson's face was set hard, as it had been for the whole of the three-and-a-half-hour journey.

The plane was on its final descent into Santa Catarina Airport on the east coast of the island.

He gazed out across the wing. He could not be said to be taking in the steep banking of the plane, nor the expert manoeuvring, the twisting and dipping, in order to line up with the runway; his aesthetic sense did not appreciate the clear blue sea below, shimmering in the sunshine, nor the tantalising glimpses of the island itself.

Neither did it particularly concern him that the runway is one of the shortest in Europe, the end of which drops literally into the sea.

Normally he would have revelled in everything.

He readjusted his seat belt and braced himself for the landing which he knew would be characterised by extra reverse thrust and sharp braking. It was surprisingly smooth and lurch-free.

Within minutes the plane had taxied to the small terminal building.

Donaldson reached up and opened the overhead locker, lifting out his only piece of luggage, a small overnight bag. His stay was to be short, but not sweet.

The heat of the day hit him whilst walking from the plane to the terminal.

Even though it was January, Madeira was much warmer than London. He experienced a very brief reminder that, since being posted to London from Florida, he had seen little sun.

He went straight to Customs, showed his American passport and sailed through.

A dark-faced man with a black moustache and brown, intelligent eyes, approached him.

'You are Mr Donaldson, I believe, from the FBI in London,' the man said. '*Muito prazer.*'

Donaldson nodded. '*Muito bem, obrigado,*' he replied. It was one of the few Portuguese phrases he knew. He was not familiar with the language, but spoke Spanish well and German fluently. With his knowledge of the former he expected to be able to read menus and road signs, but nothing more complicated.

The two men shook hands formally, no smiles.

'I am Detective George Santana. May I welcome you to Madeira on behalf of the police service. Please accept my deep regret that the circumstance of your visit is not more pleasurable.'

Donaldson nodded. They had walked out of the airport. A car drew up to the kerb, driven by a policeman in uniform.

'I'd like to see the body as soon as possible.'

Donaldson touched down at one o'clock on Monday afternoon. By that time, Acting Detective Inspector Henry Christie had been at work for seven hours and was beginning to flag. He had only finished Sunday's tour of duty at 2 a.m. and with less than four hours' sleep under his belt, his eyes felt like a bucket of grit had been thrown into them.

He rubbed them once more with his knuckles, blinked a few times and ran a hand around his tired face. He stifled a big yawn, but only just.

The evening before, Hughie Dundaven had been booked into the custody system at Blackpool by about eight. He remained compliant in terms of his behaviour but said little and refused to divulge his name and address. He demanded to see a solicitor, which was one of his legal rights.

He had been strip-searched and all his clothing was seized for forensic. He was given a white paper suit – a 'zoot suit' as they are fondly called – and a pair of slippers to protect his modesty. Nothing in his property gave any indication as to his identity. All he had in his wallet was cash. Six hundred pounds of it.

Non-intimate swabs were taken from his hands. Hair was plucked from his head for DNA sampling – the norm for all prisoners arrested for serious offences.

He refused to sign a consent form to allow his fingerprints to be taken.

By the time this had all been done it was ten o'clock. Dundaven had not yet been interviewed about anything.

The duty solicitor rolled in shortly after this and had a confidential chat.

Henry had appointed a DS and a DC to carry out the initial interview, but the solicitor said his client was not prepared to be interviewed at that time of day. He should be allowed to rest – all prisoners were entitled to a period of uninterrupted rest for eight hours in any twenty-four.

Henry hit the roof. He demanded an interview and got it.

It turned out to be a short one, just to establish why Dundaven had been locked up and to give him an opportunity to give his side of the story.

He refused to say a word.

By the time that farce had ended it was midnight.

Dundaven got his wish then. He was led to a cell, where under a rough blanket he slept like a baby.

Henry and his detectives convened in the CID office where, over coffee, they planned next morning's strategy.

Then he went to the property store where Dave Seymour and the ARV crew had unloaded and listed all the property from the Range Rover.

Henry raised his eyebrows. 'That's an awful lot of firepower,' he said appreciatively, looking at the guns and ammunition which had been laid out and labelled.

'Enough for an army,' agreed Seymour.

Henry helped to list the last few weapons, noting their make and serial numbers, careful to handle them so as not to leave or disturb any fingerprints. The guns all looked new and unused.

The logging of the weapons was completed at 2 a.m.

Just before going home Henry phoned the hospital and asked about the condition of the policewoman, Nina. He was told, 'Critical.'

He hung up with a tear in his eye. He did not know the girl, but it was the principle of the matter. He'd been involved in other investigations where police officers had been killed. These days the mere thought of it happening could move him to tears. He realised that as he grew older – he would be forty later in the year – he was getting less and less detached. In days gone by, nothing seemed to affect him. For some reason, everything did now.

'Turning soft,' he said, wiping the back of a hand across his nose. He got up and went home.

When his head hit the pillow he could not sleep. He tossed and turned uncomfortably, drifting off occasionally, sweated, and disturbed Kate who, in her sleep, told him to 'Pack it in.' Whatever that meant.

Frustrated and knackered he gave up trying to sleep and was back in the office by six, getting his head around how he could cover everything that was happening with the few staff he had.

Two dead bodies: one in the mortuary in Blackpool, one in Preston. Both unidentified.

A cop in ICU, probably going to join them.

And a gorilla with a bullet in his shoulder.

A weekend in the north's premier holiday resort. Come to Blackpool and get your head blown off or a knife in your guts . . . or, he went on to think shamefacedly, get kneed in the groin and lose a testicle.

He tried to delete the last one from his list and crossed his fingers mentally. Perhaps it would go away.

The identification of two bodies would only be a matter of being patient and waiting. He would be surprised if they didn't come back on finger-prints.

He looked at the paltry list of detectives available to him. Not many. Most snaffled for the newsagents job. He shook his head, his brain like cotton wool. The management of resources really does your head in.

'Right, get on with it,' he ordered himself. He picked up his pen and began to decide who would do what.

The same DS and DC who had initially interviewed the prisoner could carry on with that investigation, together with Dave Seymour. It was well within the scope of any competent detective: interviews, exhibits, paper-work. All Henry needed to do was guide them, and keep an eye on the wider picture. At least there was a body in the cells, which made it a whole lot easier, even if Chummy was being uncooperative.

Whereas it was less straightforward with the dead girl. They still had to find out who'd done that one.

Henry's remaining staff consisted of two DCs. Simply not enough to deal with the job. The thought of prostrating himself in front of FB was not appealing – but he was sure that if he pushed, FB would wilt.

He had to.

Blackpool police station was going to be extremely crowded.

The gorilla, Henry decided sadly, would have to wait.

And so would every other minor crime for the foreseeable future. The uniform branch would have to investigate everything that came in.

And that was how he spent his morning.

Administration. Deploying personnel. Wheeling and dealing for extra staff. Ensuring paperwork was done and the necessary circulations made. Pacifying the media, which had descended on Blackpool *en masse*. What really bugged him was that they were more interested in a wounded gorilla than a policewoman on her deathbed, or a young female on a mortuary slab. He didn't allow his annoyance to show.

Basically he did all the things that went along with being a police manager – a million miles away from a car chase with crashes, flying bodies, helicopters, Stingers and shotguns.

He would rather have had his head down, getting into the ribs of that bastard down in the cells, making him talk by using his interview skills. But that was not his job any more. His was to manage, to delegate, to empower. Perhaps he was safer sitting behind a desk. At least it stopped him from getting into trouble.

The ride into Funchal, Madeira's capital, took thirty minutes. At his request, Donaldson was driven directly to the morgue so he could get the worst part over with soonest: identifying the body of a friend and colleague.

The morgue was bare and functional, but clean. Donaldson was glad about that. It could have been much worse.

The body was on a drawer in the huge fridge.

Santana pulled it out and drew back the harsh white sheet.

Donaldson suppressed a gasp. Not because of any marks of violence or because it had been mashed to a pulp. Neither of those things applied to this body. Rather because he was looking at the face of someone who had been young, vibrant, very much alive not many days before. Someone he and his wife had grown very close to over the last few months.

He sighed, nodded, looked up at Santana. 'Yes. That's her.'

It was like a violation of sorts but it had to be done.

Donaldson took hold of the sheet, drew it back and exposed the naked corpse, closing his eyes for a moment to halt the sensation of dizziness.

He had never seen her without clothes before. He never thought he would. He could not deny that, even though she had been a good friend and work colleague, he had occasionally allowed his eyes to drift across her breasts, or down her long slim legs – and speculate. Special Agent Sam Dawber had been beautiful; she also had the personality and brains to go with it. But Donaldson's admiring looks were only sporadic. He was deeply in love with his wife and other women did not enter the equation.

'Sorry, Sam,' he said softly to her now. 'Please forgive me.'

He folded the sheet at her ankles.

She looked peaceful in death. Serene. Her skin was more tanned than when alive, but she'd been on Madeira for almost a week and the weather had been exceptionally good. Her back, bottom and backs of her legs were red and mottled where the blood had settled. There was a tinge of blue around her mouth, which was slightly parted.

'You say she was found dead in her bath in the hotel room?' he said to Santana. For some reason the act of speaking made him feel better able to examine her, detaching him from the task. He peered closely at both sides of her neck.

'Yes, apparently drowned. She may have been drinking heavily and fallen asleep in a stupor. There were many bottles of spirits in the room. Much of it drunk. Maybe she took her own life?'

Donaldson stopped himself from giving Santana a withering look. At the same time alarm bells sounded in his head.

He nodded and continued the minute examination. He picked up her left hand, opened it out and looked at her nails.

'Who found her?'

'A chambermaid.'

'I want to speak to her.'

He was now peering at a cut and bruise on the hairline on Sam's left temple, which was only visible when her hair was pulled back.

Santana said, 'Sure, can be arranged today. Why?'

'Routine,' Donaldson answered with a shrug. 'All sudden deaths of FBI agents are fully investigated.'

'But there are no suspicious circumstances,' Santana said defensively.

'To you, maybe not.'

'To any detective.'

'Look, George, I don't mean this as a slur to your professionalism, but I know – knew – this woman.' Donaldson bent down and inspected her inner thighs. 'For a start, she didn't drink,' he said, standing up again. 'When will the autopsy be carried out?'

'This afternoon, four o'clock.'

Initially Donaldson had had no intention of staying for it. He changed his mind. 'I want to be here.'

'Why, do you not trust our doctors now?'

'She was a friend and colleague, George. I owe her that much, don't you think?' He was extremely puzzled and worried by Santana's frosty reaction.

Santana nodded formally. 'I apologise.'

'Forget it. When did you say she was found?'

'Ten, yesterday morning.'

'So there's a good chance her hotel room will still be vacant,' Donaldson

71

said. 'Can we go and have a look round it? And could you give me her belongings? I need to take them back.'

Santana nodded. 'No problem.' But behind those two words Donaldson detected there was – and that he, Donaldson, was becoming a pain in the ass all of a sudden.

Well, so be it.

The hotel room had been cleaned from top to bottom. New guests were arriving in the morning. From the crime-scene point of view, therefore, it had nothing to offer.

Donaldson was very annoyed. 'This should have been left untouched until I had the chance to go through it,' he said.

'It was checked by my people and there was nothing of interest, and certainly nothing to support your obvious belief that a crime has been committed here.' Santana was abrupt. Then his voice softened. 'She died by accident and there's nothing more to it. No one to blame, no one to arrest. You should accept that, my friend. Maybe you didn't know her as well as you thought.'

Donaldson gave that short shrift.

'Can I see your scenes-of-crime photographs?'

Santana's mouth drew to a tight line.

'You haven't taken any, have you?' Donaldson said with disbelief.

A short shake of Santana's head confirmed this.

Donaldson's eyes closed despairingly. He demanded to speak to the chambermaid.

She understood English well. And had little to offer. Yes, she had found the body in the bath. It had frightened her. She had called the manager who had taken over and informed the police. The brooding presence of Santana hovering over her shoulder did little to help matters. He seemed to intimidate her. Donaldson would have preferred to talk to her alone, but there was little chance of that happening.

The autopsy did not help much either.

Donaldson prepared himself for this stage by buying a compact 35mm camera and two colour films from a shop in Funchal. Hardly ideal, but the best he could do under the circumstances.

While the pathologist waited impatiently, he took photographs of Sam's body before the knife went in. Once again he felt like an intruder and whilst he did it, his mouth twisted into a grimace of distaste. Had there been another way, or another person to do it, he would happily have handed the task over.

He took several shots of her head, trying to get a good close one of the cuts on the hairline. And shots of her shoulders and thighs, just above the knees where he had seen some slight bruising.

When he was satisfied, the pathologist moved in.

The procedure was carried out competently enough by the doctor who

72

was from the new hospital, Cruz de Carvalho, in Funchal. He was accompanied by an assistant who recorded his observations in writing. The doctor spoke in Portuguese and then translated for Donaldson's benefit.

Sam's head injury and the bruising on her body was duly noted and recorded.

At the FBI agent's insistence the doctor took scrapings from under Sam's fingernails and bagged them.

Then he placed the dissecting knife in the soft flesh at her throat and sliced easily into the skin. Donaldson turned away. Within moments there was a perfectly straight incision right the way down the middle of her slim body to the pubis.

Donaldson forced himself to watch. He was aware that, if not careful, the last memory he would have of her would be as a hollow cadaver, all organs removed, skull hacked off, brain sliced up on a table.

Eventually the chest cavity was opened, the ribcage removed, the heart and lungs cut out. The lungs were heavy and needed two hands to lift them across to the dissecting table. Here they were sliced open, revealing the foam consistent with drowning. Typical post mortem appearance.

Water was also found in the stomach and trachea.

After two and a half hours' work the doctor had finished.

He washed off after he'd sewn her roughly back up. Donaldson pestered him with questions.

'She drowned,' the doctor insisted. 'The head injury you talk about is consistent with banging her head on the edge of a door. It did not kill her, but may possibly have stunned her for a few moments.'

'But what about those bruises on her shoulder and legs? Are they consistent with someone grabbing her and holding her down?'

The doctor, 'Ummed . . .' and considered it. He dried his hands. 'There is that argument, I suppose,' he concluded, 'but without supporting evidence . . .' He shrugged. 'She was here on a walking holiday, I believe,' he continued. 'These are bruises she could easily have got doing that.'

'So what's your theory?' Donaldson pumped him.

'If she had been drinking' – here he held up a blood sample taken from her – 'and this will tell us for sure, then I think she got drunk, staggered into a door, banged her head. This may have sent her dizzy. She had filled a hot bath and when she climbed in, the combination of alcohol, the blow to the head and the hot water made her pass out. She drowned. Misadventure. Accident. Whatever you want to call it.'

'But not murder?'

The doctor shook his head.

Santana, who had watched the autopsy and listened to the conversation, cut in at that point. 'An unfortunate set of circumstances. No mystery as you imply, Karl. No one to blame. Very sad.'

Henry had eaten a rather large meal and was glaring accusingly at his empty plate when a file of papers dropped onto the canteen table in front of him.

The harassed, overweight form of Dave Seymour stood there. Tie askew, top shirt button open, jacket flapping untidily. His eyes were red raw. He had spent the day interviewing Dundaven. It was 6.30 p.m.

'He's now got some smart-assed solicitor from Manchester acting for him,' were the first words he said to Henry. 'Some guy named Pratt of all things. But he isn't.'

'What d'you know about him?'

'I phoned the RCS in Bolton and asked them. Just a sec . . .' Seymour left Henry and went to the serving hatch where he selected a meal and returned to the table. He sat down opposite. 'Seems him and his firm are known for representing shite, from criminal dealings to property stuff. Very fuckin' seedy by all accounts.' He shovelled a large load of potato pie into his mouth. This didn't prevent him from continuing to talk. 'At least he got his client to tell us his name and date of birth.' Seymour pointed with his knife to the name written on the file.

'And what do we know about him?'

'Not much yet. We think he's involved in the drugs scene over in East Lancs, but not much more than that.' A forkload of mushy peas disappeared down his throat. 'Think he's a pretty big player.'

'Any pre-cons?' Henry asked.

'Yep, but they don't tell us much. Petty stuff.'

'Terrorist connections? Organised crime?'

'Organised maybe. Nothing terrorist.'

'And the passenger in the Range Rover – the flying man?'

'A lowlife shitbag called McCrory. Junkie. Petty thief. Good shoplifter, as most druggies tend to be. On the periphery of Dundaven's scene. Bit of a gofer, I'd say.'

'And what's Dundaven's story?'

Seymour closed his eyes in despair. 'You wouldn't fucking believe it. The shitehawk's trying to wrangle out of it and dump everything on his dead buddy. He says McCrory asked him to drive to Blackpool yesterday 'cos he wanted to pick something up. Turns out to be guns – from a man in a pub, would ya credit?'

Henry sniggered. 'Oh, the ubiquitous man in a pub; we'll catch the bastard one day.'

'Yeah, well, they pick up the guns, so the fairy tale goes . . . don't know which pub it was, by the way . . . and Dundaven is horrified, bless his soul. He says he's too frightened of McCrory to say anything – him being a real hard case, as he put it. Says McCrory produced two shotguns and blasted Nina and dinged one off at Rik Dean's car.'

'McCrory did the shooting?'

'That's what Dundaven says. Next thing, McCrory's holding a gun to Dundaven's belly saying, "Let's go". Poor ole Dundaven has to do whatever he's told, but being a law-abiding citizen, what he really wanted to do is hand himself over to us.'

'So why did he ram us and shoot at us?'

'Duress. Fear.' Seymour shrugged. He swallowed more pie with a forkful of peas.

'Bullshit,' said Henry. 'And the next bit? This should be worth hearing.'

'It is,' laughed Seymour, and recited: 'So overcome with emotion and grief is McCrory that he puts a gun to his own head, opens the door and tops himself.'

Henry laughed out loud. 'He expects us to believe that?'

'Deadly serious about it.'

Henry stopped laughing. 'And then?'

'Fear makes him continue the chase, ram the traffic car and take a potshot at the helicopter.'

'So where do we stand with all this? What can we prove?'

Seymour had devoured his meal. He went and bought a pot of tea and two cups. He poured one for Henry.

'There are no direct witnesses to refute what he says, unless Nina pulls through. Rik Dean was sat in his car and couldn't truthfully say who shot her, because the car is much lower than the Range Rover, and his view was obstructed by the spare tyre on the back. Same for us. We couldn't actually *see* him waste McCrory, could we?'

Henry considered it for a few seconds. It wouldn't be long before the first twenty-four-hours' detention would be up. Then for an extra twelve he'd need the authority of a Superintendent to carry on questioning Dundaven without charge. He decided he would seek that authorisation and keep the pressure on Dundaven.

He told this to Seymour and added, 'Even if you haven't got any admissions from him, keep pushing him and then, as late as possible, charge him. Throw the book at him. Charge him with everything you can possibly think of, including the driving offences. If there's enough shit, some of it'll stick.'

Donaldson was booked into the Quinta da Penha de Franca. He had been allocated one of the seaview rooms in the new annexe. Very nice and comfortable, with a balcony overlooking the pool and the ocean beyond.

The night was dark, tranquil and quite chilly.

He shivered, walked back into the room from the balcony, closed the door and drew the curtains. He stretched out on the bed, clasping his hands behind his head and mulled over his thoughts on Samantha Jane Dawber, whose devastated body was lying in a fridge with all its vital organs – including the brain – thrown loosely into the torso and sewn up. Her cranium had been packed with newspaper and her facial skin stretched back into place and stitched so tightly that her features were stretched and distorted.

There was no respect in a morgue. Death was simply a business. A sausage factory.

Samantha Jane Dawber.

Sammy Jane.

Sam.

She had been posted to London six months earlier and easily fitted into the small team. She was recently divorced, but the break-up – without kids to worry about – did not seem to have affected her too deeply. She kept in regular touch with her ex, a Special Agent from the New York office.

Donaldson fell into an easy working relationship with her. When she subsequently met Karen, his wife, they too became friends.

It had been a good six months.

With her assistance (she had done most of the legwork) he had helped the police in Cornwall to crack a long-running fraud case. She was a good worker who took the job seriously, constantly updating herself on criminals who drifted around the international scene. One of her favourite games was to get the mugshot books out – which contained hundreds of photos – remove about fifty, cover their names, shuffle them and challenge Donaldson to name them. Usually he might recognise five or six. Without fail she could name every one, every time.

Sammy Jane. All-American girl. Whatever that meant.

Now dead in a way Donaldson didn't like.

She 'got into' walking in a big way since coming to England. She often dragged the Donaldsons out all over mainland Britain to hike over hills. One memorable walk had taken place in the Lake District over a weekend when Henry and Kate Christie had been invited along. Donaldson and Henry had met and become friends on the same enquiry when he'd met Karen. It proved to be a tough walking weekend, both nights of which ended up in exhausted revelry in way-out pubs in the middle of nowhere. He and Henry had got extremely drunk and were watched with severe pity by the womenfolk.

Donaldson remembered the laughter of those two days. Sam's giggles and wry outlook on life had been infectious.

Her visit to Madeira had been prompted by an urge to explore the *levadas* – footpaths running alongside irrigation channels – that crisscross the island. That was the plan.

Donaldson sat up and made himself not cry. He shook his head, breathed heavily and attempted to combat the sobs building up inside him.

He won. It was a close-run thing.

'Phew.' He blew out his cheeks. He rubbed his eyes and looked across at Sam's luggage which he'd deposited on the spare bed. Maybe the reason for her death was amongst that lot. He hadn't sorted through it yet.

In his heart he was convinced she hadn't died a pathetic drunk in a bath. That was not Sam.

Reaching across to her suitcase, he flicked up the catches.

John Rider coughed long and hard. He managed to clear his chest and throat, picked up the King Edward cigar from the ashtray, put it between his lips and re-lit it with a 'pa-pa-pa' until the flame had taken properly.

He blew out a ring of smoke.

'You OK, John?' Isa enquired, gently resting a hand in the centre of his back.

He squinted sideways at her and nodded. 'Never better.'

'You should give up.'

'One of life's last few pleasures,' he said to justify the habit.

Isa tried to hold his gaze a little longer, but he looked away and reached for his drink. She emitted a short, dissatisfied sigh and her mouth warped in frustration for an instant before returning to its normal self.

She took a step to the bar and leaned on it.

Jacko gave her a mineral water and she took her first sip of it, wishing she had the guts to tell Rider how she felt about him. It's ridiculous! she told herself. A woman of your age and experience being unable to tell some two-bit ex-gangster that you love him. Her overriding fear was that it could spoil both their friendship and business partnership if he didn't reciprocate.

The club was extremely quiet. Monday. January. Blackpool. Hardly worth opening. But Rider believed it might as well be open as shut right up to the refurbishments starting.

Rider, perched on a bar stool, hoped he had come back to emotional equilibrium. Yesterday had been a nightmare. That Henry Christie. Looked quietly ruthless. Looked like he knew about the zoo. Looked like he wouldn't let it rest.

Then the news about the gorilla splashed all over the telly and the papers. That had really gutted Rider, the suffering of an animal.

Today, thankfully, had been peaceful. A couple of detectives, not including Christie, had visited and searched the flat which might have been the dead girl's. They had found nothing but might possibly have got an ID from her property and fingerprints on a glass. Rider gave them a short statement.

And that was that. Back to square one. Normality. Or so he hoped.

There were very few customers in the club. A few lonely souls. A few canoodling couples ensconced in the alcoves. Later, when the pubs closed and the disco cranked up, it would get busier. Not much. It would close at 12.30 a.m.

Rider couldn't wait to get stuck into the place. Get the builders in, ripping the guts out of it, giving it a full body transplant. Transforming it into a ritzy, glitzy entertainment spot. If the planning application was successful, the builders would be in within six weeks. Four months after that, barring accidents, the doors would re-open just in time for the summer trade.

He shivered in anticipation. His eyes drifted around the floors, walls and unsafe ceiling, seeing it all. His baby.

Two young men at the far end of the bar caught his attention. Initially they had been sitting in one of the booths and Rider thought they might be gay. They had sauntered up to the bar, leaned on it and rudely rapped bottles on it to attract Jacko's attention.

Rider's bowels gave a sudden flutter.

He knew the sort. Not too far removed from the two who had appeared in the zoo, but maybe not as far down the road as them, being slightly younger.

Jacko served them each with a bottle of Foster's Ice. Both drank from the bottle, their teeth showing as they swallowed each mouthful, almost as if it was painful. The 'in' way to drink.

Rider beckoned Jacko over.

'Know 'em?'

Jacko knew most locals.

'No. Blackburn lads,' he said. Over the years of working behind bars in Blackpool, Jacko had learned to identify regional accents, quite specifically in many cases. He could tell easily whereabouts in Lancashire a person came from and his other regional specialities were the West Midlands, Scotland and London. He was rarely wrong. The Blackburn accent was a common one in Blackpool.

'You happy with them?'

'They've done nothing wrong.'

'Yet.'

'Yet,' agreed Jacko.

Rider glanced down at them. One eyed the other and nodded. He held out his bottle at arms' length and smashed it onto the floor. It shattered spectacularly.

'Yet,' said Rider again under his breath. He lowered himself from the stool. Before he could get to them, the other one swept his left arm across the bar top, catching half a dozen newly-washed pint glasses, sending them crashing to the floor. As though he was throwing a knife at a target, he lobbed his bottle of Foster's into the optics behind the bar. A large bottle of Bell's and a few glasses exploded.

'This is a shit-awful place,' the young man roared.

'Oi oi oi,' shouted Jacko, running down the bar.

'Hold it, Jacko!' Rider screamed.

The two youths turned to face Jacko and Rider, adopting the threatening pose so beloved of the British hooligan/hard case: legs apart, fingers gesturing to come forwards, eyes bulging in their sockets, rocking on the balls of their feet.

'C'mon then, y'cunts,' one sneered.

Normally Rider would have been happy to wade into troublemakers, but something held him back here; that nod given by one to the other which meant premeditation, not simply drink. He was wary.

'Hang back, Jacko,' Rider hissed through the side of his mouth. He was aware of Isa hovering by his shoulder and the eyes of every other punter focused on the scene, something witnessed all the time in bars throughout the world. 'OK lads, we don't want any trouble here. I'm sorry you don't like the place, but you've had some fun. So now get out.'

'Or what, pal?'

'Look, if you want me to call the cops, I will. But we can call it a draw now, you can leave, nobody's suffered and we'll all put it down to experience.'

'Boss,' Jacko began. 'The damage . . .'

Rider held his hand up to silence him.

'What if we don't wanna leave?'

'Yeah, pal, what you gonna do?' they taunted.

Rider became controllably angry. Not afraid. Still cautious.

He pointed a finger at them. 'If you don't get out of here, boys, you'll face the consequences, one way or another. If you think me and Jacko here can't handle you, then you're very much mistaken. We'll lay you both out until we're satisfied – then we'll call the cops. It's that simple. If you want hassle and aggro, fair enough, the choice is yours. You can call it quits or end up in a police cell with matching injuries.'

Rider held his breath. The two youths looked at each other and nodded reluctantly after weighing up the odds.

It was all too easy, but Rider's relief clouded his judgement. Perhaps after all they were not the sort of people he believed them to be. Maybe they were just kids flexing their muscles.

Angrily they shouldered their way to the exit, accompanied by Rider and Jacko. They left peaceably.

'What about the damage?' Jacko said into Rider's ear again.

'Chalk it up to experience.' Rider held up a finger when Jacko began to say more. Jacko shook his head disgustedly and made some under-the-breath remark about 'every Tom Dick and Harry thinking they can get away with it from now on.'

Rider ignored him.

When he was sure they'd gone, Jacko returned to the bar. Rider stood alone at the club doors. He lit a cigarette, noticing his hands were shaking. Whether it was drink or nerves he wasn't sure.

Puzzled, he tried to figure out what that had all been about. At least they'd gone without a fight. He blew out a lungful of smoke and turned back into the club.

Karl Donaldson walked slowly along the sea-front in Funchal, the port on

79

his right, towards the marina and restaurants. The night was cool and fresh, pleasant for walking.

He was dissatisfied by the way things had gone. Sam had died tragically – *accidentally* – and he could not prove otherwise.

Hard to accept.

What he really wanted to do was bring in a team and get a real investigation going with real detectives. He knew it was an irrational desire and that he'd never get the go-ahead for it. What he was trying to do, as Santana had rightly hinted, was blame someone for her death, just like a grieving relative.

But there was no one to blame. Sam had died accidentally and that was an end to it. It hurt him to think he hadn't known her as well as he thought. She could well have been a secret drinker, an alcoholic . . . and yet somehow that wasn't Sam.

All that remained for him to do was arrange for the body to be flown back to the States, tidy up the loose ends here paperwork-wise, and fly home to London and his wife. He missed her like mad.

'You speak English?' a female voice said to him.

'Yes, I do,' he replied without thinking.

'You're American,' she said, picking up on the accent immediately.

Donaldson held back a swearword. He'd been so wrapped up in his melancholic thoughts, he'd walked straight into it without realising. The timeshare tout. That dreaded disease, now a worldwide plague which had even reached the tiny island of Madeira.

'Yes – and I'm not interested, thanks.'

'I'm not selling anything,' she persisted pleasantly, smiling.

'Of course not.'

'Please,' she said as he began to outpace her. 'Give me a minute of your time.'

Fuck, what did it matter. He was going home tomorrow. And ever the sucker for the pretty face – which the girl did have, along with other attributes – he gave in. Within five minutes he had promised to visit a timeshare development (although the words 'time' and 'share' never reared their ugly heads), had been given some literature, and was on his way.

He turned down onto the marina and wandered past the series of restaurants there, finally plumping for one where he received least hassle from the salesmen-cum-waiters. He ate a good meal. Tomato soup and onions with a poached egg floating in it, followed by *espada*, the island's very own fish which looked like a creature from a horror movie, and a bottle of Viñho Verde.

Ninety minutes later he emerged full, light-headed and completely resigned to Sam's fate to be branded a closet drinker.

He was back in his room fifteen minutes later, emptying his pockets and undressing with not much coordination. The wine had had more effect on him than he'd imagined. His eyes managed to focus very briefly on the leaflet the timeshare tout had foisted on him. He was about to screw it up and bin it when he stopped, laid the paper out on the bedside cabinet and thought for a moment, difficult though this was.

Out of curiosity, he went over to where Sam's belongings had been piled up and dug out a flight bag; he unzipped it and pulled out a money pouch, the type worn around the waist. He remembered Sam wearing it on the Lake District trip. Inside was all the money she had left in her possession – about five hundred pounds in sterling travellers' cheques and six thousand *escudos*. There were other bits of paper folded up: restaurant and bank receipts, a receipt for a coach tour of the island – for tomorrow – and the thing Donaldson had been looking for . . . the same timeshare information leaflet he had been given.

He unfolded it carefully and laid it next to his on the bedside cabinet.

Yes. Exactly the same. Other than the time and date of the visit, written in by the tout. He sighed heavily. So what?

Then he turned the sheet over and saw that Sam had written two extra words on hers – two words which he had missed when he'd originally gone through her belongings. Donaldson recognised her writing – big, loopy, almost child-like.

Scott Hamilton!!!! The exclamation marks were Sam's.

Donaldson, after removing his socks, visited the bathroom. Whilst he sat there he thought, Maybe timeshare *is* for me, after all.

11 p.m. Monday. A continuous tour of duty of seventeen hours. At last, Henry Christie wrapped up his day. He was fast approaching a state of zombie-dom.

He rechecked his 'to do' list in front of him, hoping that everything which needed to be done, had been.

Dundaven had been charged with some firearms offences, bail refused. He would be up before the Magistrates tomorrow, when the police would apply for a remand in custody for seventy-two hours, otherwise known as a 'three day lie-down'. This would enable Henry's team to question him at a more leisurely pace and complete further enquiries. Several addresses had come to light in the east of the county and they were all going to be hit at six the next morning. Everything was arranged for that: firearms teams, Support Unit officers and detectives. All coordinated by Henry, who sensed something big and nasty lurking behind Dundaven.

The three days would give a clearer indication of Nina's condition. Whether she lived or died would affect further charges. Murder or Attempted Murder? In any case, Dundaven was going to be charged with McCrory's murder.

The other enquiry on his plate – the dead girl on the beach – seemed to be pretty slow. She had been identified from fingerprints and some documentation found in her bedsit.

Marie Cullen had been a prostitute, working on the streets and in the clubs of Blackburn. Other than that, the police had very little to go on. Two detectives were going east in the morning to do some spadework. Henry thought this one would be a toughie. Prostitute murders usually were.

He had a stinking headache, his sinuses acting up as though they had been clamped with alligator clips.

He opened his desk drawer and sifted through the contents to find some paracetamols. He was sure he had some. Whilst doing so he noticed the statement he'd drafted about the incident with Shane Mulcahy. He pushed it to the back of his drawer and hoped it would go away. He found no tablets.

Derek Luton, looking tired and haggard, wandered into the office, stretching and rolling his neck.

'Degsy – you got any headache pills on you?'

'No. That's why I came in here myself. Got a real splitter.'

'Ah well,' said Henry resignedly, 'we'll just have to suffer. How's it going?'

'Good. Yeah. Excellent, in fact. Really interesting. I've been out taking witness statements with a Detective Sergeant from the Organised Crime Squad, guy called Tattersall.'

'And are you getting anywhere?'

'I think they have some sort of line on the gang, but they're keeping it close to their chests at the moment. They seem to have really got in the driving seat now, because it was one of their lot who got it. FB is letting Tony Morton run with it.'

'What's the name of the cop who got killed?'

'A DS – Geoff Driffield. From Manchester, on secondment to the squad.'

'Can't say I know him. What the hell was he doing in that shop all kitted out and tooled up and all alone?'

'That remains a mystery,' said Luton. 'Apparently he was a bit of a loner. His days on the squad were numbered because he wasn't a team-player – more of a glory-seeker. Theory is, he got some gen about the gang, discovered where they were due to hit and wanted to make a name for himself. Backfired.'

'That's a fucking understatement.' Henry glanced at his watch. 'Gotta go, bud, early start tomorrow.'

The club never cranked up that night. Hardly anyone ventured in after pub closing time. Rider shut up shop shortly after midnight. No point flogging a dead horse. By 12.30 he and Jacko were the only ones left inside. The customers had drifted away without complaint, as had the remainder of the staff. Isa had kissed Rider on the cheek and gone to bed in the guest-house opposite the club where she was staying.

After washing and drying the glasses, Jacko locked up the bar. He hated leaving a mess because it was always depressing to return to. He set the alarm for that area, gave Rider a quick wave and sauntered out into the night.

Rider was alone.

He savoured the peace for a few moments whilst drawing the last few puffs out of his cigar. He stubbed it out and after checking all the likely places a burglar might hide, he too left.

They hit him as he walked to the car.

Two of them. Balaclavas. Baseball bats, or maybe pick-axe handles.

They came from the shadows, giving him no time to react.

The first blow landed on his back, right on the kidneys. A surge of pain, like a bolt of lightning, scorched up through him. But he didn't have too much time to savour this because the second blow, from the weapon wielded by the second man, connected with his lower stomach.

The blows were only milli-seconds apart.

They had the effect of putting severe pain into him, winding him and disorientating him. His body didn't know what to do. Part of it screamed to him to stand upright and respond to the pain in the back; another part wanted him to bend over double. The compromise meant that his body contorted to pay homage to both blows.

By which time more violence was being used.

The sticks flashed, raining blow after blow on Rider: shoulders, arms, ribs, stomach, arse, upper and lower legs.

Rider was driven callously to the ground in such a manner he was unable to scream or respond in any way which might have brought him some assistance. All screams became gurgles, all shouts whimpers. All he could do was take it, roll up in a ball, cover his head and hope that oblivion was not far away.

In a beating, thirty seconds is a long time, especially for the party receiving it. During that time, Rider's body probably took in excess of forty well-delivered hard blows.

Then they stopped.

Rider groaned pathetically. His whole body felt like it was on fire. A raging, searing, Great Fire of London type of fire – one which destroyed everything in its path.

His cheek was pressed against the cold pavement. His mouth sagged open. A horrible gungy liquid dribbled out: a combined brew of snot, blood and whisky.

In agony he pushed himself up onto all fours. His breathing was shallow, laboured, painful.

Then it all began again.

The first blow of this renewed attack smashed into the base of his spine. This time he did emit the beginnings of a scream – but the sound was cut short when the next blow connected with the side of his head. This sent him spinning across the pavement towards the front wheels of his car and mentally into a void.

They stopped before he lost consciousness.

He was face down, half in, half out of the gutter, his nose pressed into a grid. The sound of the drains below belched into his subconscious. The smell of shit invaded his nostrils. In a flash of clarity he wondered if he had soiled his own pants.

One of his attackers grabbed a handful of his hair and yanked his face upwards, almost tearing the hair out by the roots. He shook Rider's head until his eyes half-opened.

'Just a message, this,' hissed the man from the cover of his balaclava. 'You choose very carefully who you side with, OK? It's in your interests not to get involved. D'you understand me, Mr fucking-tough-nut Rider? Next time you're dead.'

He let Rider's head drop with a dull thud into the edge of the pavement.

A second later he passed out.

Chapter Nine

After four fitful hours' sleep, Henry found himself standing in front of a large squad of police officers, cups of tea in their hands. It was 5.45 a.m. and they were in the canteen at Accrington police station. The reason for meeting here was that five out of the six addresses they had uncovered in relation to Dundaven were in East Lancashire, and Accrington was central for them all. The sixth address was in Bury, just over the Greater Manchester border.

There were forty-eight officers, eight for each address. Four Support Unit, two CID and two firearms. The Support Unit were specialists in entering premises quickly and also in search techniques for buildings and persons. The plan that morning was to get in quick on the warrants Henry had sworn out the day before, take no crap, search thoroughly and if necessary, make arrests.

Henry cleared his throat and called for attention. The room fell immediately silent as all eyes turned to him.

He briefed the officers about what they should search for, reminded them of their powers and the law, begged them to cause as little damage as possible, try not to shoot anyone unless absolutely necessary, and wished them luck.

They separated into their various teams whilst Henry marvelled at the sheer size of some of the Support Unit officers. He was no pygmy himself, but some of them towered over him. Even the women. They all checked their equipment – door openers, dragon lights, extending mirrors, various tools, guns and CS sprays.

Within ten minutes they had all dispersed, leaving Henry and a Detective Sergeant sat in the canteen.

By 6.30 the teams were all in place. Five minutes later the first door went through.

It was a good feeling.

The Jacaranda da Funchal was one of the most pleasant complexes he had ever seen; if he hadn't been there for some other reason, Karl Donaldson could easily have succumbed to the hard sell which was actually disguised as a soft message.

He had walked the two miles to it from his hotel: west out of Funchal, beyond the rather staid but magnificent Reid's Hotel, and to an area known rather unoriginally as the Tourist Zone. It was a fairly unprepossessing part of town, much of which reminded Donaldson of a bomb site with many open tracts of wasteland, some with half-demolished buildings, others nothing but rubble and dust. Oh, and tourist hotels.

When he found the Jacaranda it was pure oasis. Set in about ten acres of gently shelving land, it had everything someone who wished to buy a timeshare could dream of: health club, tennis courts, two pools (one indoor, both heated), and the apartments themselves were luxuriously equipped to a very high standard.

Donaldson was very impressed. He stood there and surveyed the place, dressed in his best tourist shorts and shirt.

The sales patter made him want to sign up there and then – but he had been trained to resist brainwashing, tough though it was.

He could imagine Karen's face to be told they now owned a timeshare in Madeira.

Eventually, begrudgingly, the salesman gave up on him and handed over his free gift – a flight bag – and turned his attention to other, more responsive clients.

Which gave Donaldson a chance to break off and wander round the complex alone.

He was armed with the compact camera which he'd bought to photograph Sam's body. He made his way to the posh reception area where a pretty Madeiran lady was busy behind a large desk, inputting on a PC.

'*Ajude-me, por favor*,' he said with a broad smile. '*Fala ingles?*'

'*Sim*,' she nodded. 'I do.'

'*Bom*,' he replied, relieved. 'My name is Donaldson. I'm from the United States and I believe Scott Hamilton works here?'

'Yes, Mr Hamilton owns the Jacaranda.'

'Oh, great. We're pals from way back when. I'm here on a kinda short visit and thought I'd drop by and say howdy.'

The direct approach. He was under no illusions this would work. He expected nothing, so was pleasantly surprised when the opposite happened.

The receptionist, Francesca, whose name was on a badge pinned to her blouse, immediately picked up the phone, punched in a short number and spoke very quickly. The name Hamilton came up several times, but Donaldson did not manage to catch much of the conversation. She put the phone down and smiled. She had pitch-black hair and her beautiful white teeth contrasted spectacularly to produce a very alluring effect which was not lost on Donaldson.

'He will come and see you,' she said.

'*Obrigado, Francesca*.' Donaldson noticed her eyes were a wonderful shade of brown which was in keeping with her lovely olive complexion.

'Please sit down.' She pointed to a comfortable-looking sofa on the other side of reception. He obeyed, completely dominated by her – in his dreams. She returned to her console and began tapping away, occasionally glancing across at him.

A few minutes later a man in his late twenties appeared from a door behind Francesca's desk. He was dressed in a silk, cream-coloured, short-sleeved shirt with an open neck, blue chinos and black open-toed sandals, no socks. He wore plenty of jewellery, mainly gold. His hair was black, combed away from his face and his sideboards sloped and tapered past his ears. A minor goatee was stuck onto his chin like a slug. He looked very slick.

And to Donaldson, very much like a player.

He approached Donaldson, a quizzical look on his face.

Donaldson stood up, not wishing to be disadvantaged. He held out his hand, which the man ignored.

'I don't normally see salesmen,' he said, 'but you asked for me personally. I gotta say, you don't look much like one.'

'I, er . . .' Donaldson began. He glanced quickly at Francesca, who studiously avoided eye contact. He recovered quickly. 'It's always possible you wouldn't have seen me if I'd been completely honest. You are Scott Hamilton, I take it?'

He nodded and rolled his tongue around his mouth with a slurping noise.

'I'm Karl Donaldson. I'm an FBI agent. You knew a colleague of mine, Samantha Dawber, now dead.'

Hamilton was totally unfazed. His bottom lip pouted while he considered the name. He shook his head. 'Nope, I think not.' Super fucking cool.

'She wrote your name down on a piece of paper before she died, and as she passed on in mysterious circumstances, I'm obviously investigating. I think she may well have visited the Jacaranda. She had some of your literature in her possession.'

Hamilton shrugged. 'Maybe she did, maybe she didn't. Lotsa people visit the place. But I don't know her anyway.'

'She obviously knew you. Otherwise why would she have written your name down?'

'I'm the manager of the place. My name's on all the literature we produce. Not unusual. People write my name down.'

He hadn't spoken too many words but Donaldson gave him a Brooklyn origin, tainted and watered down by some time in LA. He also gave him credit for being a hard-nosed son of a bitch. He had a desperate urge to grab the man's goatee and rip it out of his chin and make him squeal like a kicked puppy. In fact, he promised it to himself.

'She put four exclamation marks after it. Why in hell would she do that, pal?' Donaldson was on the edge of losing his own cool. 'It seems damn odd she's gotten your name down on a piece of paper and she's ended up dead soon after.'

'What the fuck you implying?'

'Nuthin,' said Donaldson innocently.

'I don't much like your tone, mister . . .?'

'Donaldson. Karl Donaldson. FBI. London office.'

'And what exactly is your jurisdiction in Madeira?'

'I'm empowered worldwide to investigate offences committed against American citizens on foreign soil.'

'Well, here's one you'd better start investigating then,' said Hamilton, leaning towards him. 'I'm an American citizen and I'm being harassed unlawfully by the FBI. Fucking investigate that!'

He got closer and closer to Donaldson as the words tumbled out of his mouth. The FBI agent remained impassive and said with a click, 'Pal, you've just cooked your goose.'

'Get off this property.' Hamilton turned to Francesca. 'Call Security. I want this man removing.'

She scrabbled for the phone.

'I'm going,' said Donaldson.

Hamilton turned away and stalked towards the door.

Donaldson called out, 'Just one more thing.'

Hamilton spun back, an angry look on his face – which Donaldson captured for posterity with a flash of the camera.

Henry sat hunched at his desk at Blackpool Central police station. In true detective fashion he was easing the last crusts of a meat pie into his mouth with one hand, the other cupped underneath to catch anything that didn't make it. Hot gravy dribbled painfully down his chin. He had nothing to wipe his mouth with, other than his hands. Then he had nothing to wipe his hands with, other than his desktop blotter.

'Acting Detective Inspector Christie, isn't it?'

With a mouthful he turned and looked up, and tried to stand up when he saw who it was. 'Yeah, it is . . . sorry.' He swallowed.

'No, don't get up.' The man perched on the corner of Henry's desk. 'I'm Detective Chief Superintendent Tony Morton from the North-West Organised Crime Squad and this is WDC Robson, Siobhan Robson.' He cocked a thumb at the officer, then held out his right hand.

'Yes, I know. Look, sir, I'm sorry but my hands're a bit greasy at the moment. I'm not sure you'd appreciate me shaking yours – unless you wanted to lick it after.'

Morton gave a short laugh and the female detective giggled brightly. The DCS withdrew his hand with a shrug and a smile.

Henry leaned back to get a better view of his visitors.

'It's Henry . . . am I right?'

'Yes, sir.'

'I believe you're up to your eyeballs in major enquiries.'

'Pretty much. Can I help you in some way?'

'I was just curious about the Dundaven enquiry, how it's progressing. We've been monitoring that man's activities for a while and in one fell swoop you've got him slap bang to rights.'

'Mmm, at a cost, though.'

Morton did not understand for a moment. Then it clicked. 'Ah yes, the policewoman. Very unfortunate.'

'Not to mention the guy whose brains he blew out,' said Henry. 'And the multi-vehicle pile-up on the motorway he caused by deliberately ramming a traffic car. I'm amazed no one died in that.'

'So, how goes the investigation then?'

'Very well,' said Henry. He had no reason to be anything other than open with Morton, a man he greatly admired and whose squad he would gladly have worked on. 'We hit a few addresses this morning, all connected with Dundaven, but found very little – which surprised me. But we're not going to let it rest. I get the feeling he's well connected and I'm going to keep chipping away at him. We haven't found the origins of the guns yet and that needs to be bottomed. They're all new and I'll bet they're from a warehouse somewhere. When we pinpoint that, it'll give us another angle to dig at – and dig we will.'

'You seem very determined.'

'I am,' said Henry thoughtfully. 'I don't like people who shoot at coppers, nor do I like people who sell guns.'

'Very laudable,' commented Morton. 'But sometimes it's difficult to be so thorough – the practicalities of the job, time constraints, pressures, especially working in local CID. I know the caseload is enormous.'

'Yeah, I agree . . . but I'll do my best. I won't let it rest until I'm completely satisfied I can't go any further with it.'

'How will you know when you can't go any further?'

'Intuition . . . brick walls . . . some dickie-bird'll tell me.'

'Well, good luck, Henry. Stick at it.' Morton turned to the female detective. 'Ready?' She nodded assent. 'Seeya, Henry.'

'Bye,' Siobhan said, giving him a little wave and a smile.

He watched them leave and wondered what the hell that was all about.

Five hundred kilometres off the west coast of Africa, on the tiny island of Madeira, Karl Donaldson was back in his hotel room.

It was 6 p.m. Night had fallen quickly. With it came rain which lashed against the balcony doors of his room.

He had recently returned from making the final arrangements for Sam's body to be on the same flight as himself to London next day. From Heathrow he would connect it with New York.

He was not looking forward to the journey, knowing she would be lying stiff, cold and desecrated in the hold below. He shivered at the thought.

Pangs of hunger growled in his stomach.

He had a quick shower, changed and walked from the seaview annexe where his room was situated through the rain across the metal footbridge which spanned high above the main road into Funchal, and up to the main part of the hotel, the Quinta. He went into Joe's bar, had the dish of the day – which happened to be *espada* – and half a bottle of Atlantis Rose.

An hour later, after the meal, he moved the few metres across to the bar and settled down for a couple of beers whilst reflecting on the events of the day.

Just what the fuck was Scott Hamilton up to? And more to the point, who was he? Why did Sam write his name down? Did he have something to do with her death? Or was he, Donaldson, just clutching at straws?

It frustrated him that he might well be able to find out about Hamilton, but might not ever be in a position to answer any of the other questions. Even so, there was no way he would ever – EVER – accept that her death was misadventure or accident. He was convinced she had been murdered, but how the hell could he prove it?

Lost in thought, he did not notice the approach of the woman. She appeared from nowhere, and touched his shoulder gently. Donaldson twisted his head upwards.

It was the receptionist from the Jacaranda.

She was wearing a trenchcoat, but no headgear, and was soaking wet, her black hair plastered to her head and face. Her mascara had run from her eyes, making her look like she'd been crying. Maybe she had.

'Francesca,' Donaldson said in surprise, remembering her name. He got to his feet.

'Mr Donaldson,' she said with a quaver in her voice.

'You're soaked to the skin.'

'It's OK, doesn't matter.' She unfastened her belt, the buttons of her coat and flapped it a couple of times to shake the excess rain off the gaberdine material. Underneath she was wearing jeans and a T-shirt. 'May I sit down?'

'Sure, sure, help yourself.'

She sat.

'Drink? Coffee – wine – whatever?'

She shook her head. Donaldson eased himself back into his chair, eyeing her uncertainly, trying to judge what was about to happen.

She was obviously on edge; her body language screamed it. Her hands twitched nervously, could not keep still. She brushed wet strands of hair back away from her face with shaking fingers. She seemed hardly able to bring her eyes up to meet Donaldson's.

'So, Francesca, what brings you here?'

'I want you to understand I enjoy my work,' she said quickly after a few moments' consideration. 'I'm quite well paid and I'm lucky because I have no real qualifications. If I did not work at the Jacaranda, I would probably be a waitress.'

Donaldson nodded. He decided not to say anything, let her fill in all the blanks, though he wasn't sure what this all meant.

'I don't want to lose my job. I support my mother. My father died two years ago . . .' She shrugged, suddenly unable to continue. She glanced quickly towards the door and her mouth opened slightly as she appeared to see something. Donaldson peered round to look. No one was there. She was seeing ghosts.

'You are from the FBI?' she asked meekly.

'Yep.'

'That lady – Samantha – she too?'

'Yep.'

Her eyes looked deeply into his for a couple of seconds, then tore away. She appeared to stifle a sob.

'Look, Francesca,' Donaldson said, hoping he was going to hit the right note. 'I think you've come to see me for a reason. Does it concern Samantha?'

'Yes.' It was a hoarse whisper.

'So, what is it?' he probed softly. His eyes found hers once more. 'You can trust me,' he added, thinking, Famous last words.

'Can I?' Her eyes dropped again and stared at her hands which she was wringing tightly together, like drying them underneath a warm-air machine.

Donaldson reached across. He laid one of his hands over hers. They felt clammy and wet. 'Yeah, you can.'

Slowly Francesca took control of herself and raised her face. Quietly she gasped, 'I think she was murdered.'

Donaldson's insides did a double-back somersault, but his exterior, he hoped, remained a vision of placidity.

'We can't talk here,' he said. 'Let's go to my room. You can dry yourself off and we can talk privately. I'll get some coffee sent up. Come on.'

He stood up and offered a hand, wiggling his fingers in a gesture of encouragement. She hesitated a moment before taking it and rising slowly from her seat.

The rain had not abated. If anything it was heavier than before, backed by an ever-increasing wind which had started to howl. Donaldson turned up his collar and hunched into his jacket. Francesca buttoned up her long coat and tied the belt into a loose knot.

With a hand laid on her back, Donaldson guided her through the gardens of the Quinta, out of the walled grounds and onto the steep cobbled road which led down to the gate which opened onto the footbridge.

When they actually stepped onto the bridge, Donaldson was slightly ahead of her, now leading the way. The rain and wind were particularly bad here, exposed to the elements. Below, the main road was busy with traffic. The combination of wind, rain and traffic noise deadened all senses, making hearing and seeing difficult.

Which was Donaldson's single pathetic excuse for not being switched on properly at a time when he should have been turned on and tuned in. Her nervousness should have rubbed off onto him. The furtive glances towards the door. The NVCs. They should have given the game away.

Instead, his chin was tucked down into his chest, his mind tumbling with the possibilities of what she was about to reveal to him. And he almost ran headlong into the man who was standing at the opposite end of the bridge, next to the elevator which descended into the hotel annexe.

At the last moment Donaldson saw him and pulled up sharp.

'*Desculpe*,' Donaldson said, pronouncing it 'dishkoolper', meaning excuse me.

The man stood his ground, barring the way to the elevator doors. He was a big bloke, unshaven, tough-looking, wearing heavy jeans and a reefer jacket, both hands in the pockets, thumbs snagged on the edges.

'Excuse me,' Donaldson said again, hoping he had read the situation wrong, because the man and his code of dress did not really shout hotel guest.

The man shook his head.

Fuck, a set-up, were the next words which leapt through the American's mind. *She's led me out here and I came like a fool and now I'm gonna get what Sam got. Goddam dickbrain!*

Then he heard her say, 'Behind.'

He looked, expecting her to be holding a gun or something, but no. Even in the rain, he could see her face was a mask of complete terror, as beyond her, walking slowly towards them across the narrow bridge, was another guy. Of similar proportion to the other – big and brutal-looking. Donaldson's legs gave him a twinge of fear.

He had not been set up.

One of the drawbacks of working on foreign soil was that his authority to carry a firearm was withdrawn. He understood why, but it was one of those little things he had been unable to grow accustomed to. The instinct to reach for a gun was still there and his fingers literally twitched. In the past this lack of a weapon had been a problem of life and death magnitude. He was pretty sure he was about to discover that once again.

He and Francesca, who was now visibly cowering, were trapped. Hemmed in, one man either side of them. There was no escape across a bridge not wide enough for three people to stand abreast and a forty-foot drop either side, splat onto the road.

Because it was expected of him as an FBI employee, Donaldson kept himself fit and agile by means of regular workouts and daily runs. Before moving to the London office that had been a necessity; working in the field always carried the possibility of ending up in conflict situations where fitness could be a life-saver.

Since taking up the less strenuous appointment at the Legat, fitness had become more of a habit of pride than a operational necessity. He never truly believed he would find himself in such a position again – facing potential attackers. Nowadays he dealt with liaison, processing information, intelligence gathering, speaking to people on the phone – basically sitting on his ass in a smart office, pushing a pen and letting other people get into hairy situations.

But now he was glad that fitness was a part of his day-to-day life. He knew he was going to need the reserves it had given him.

FBI recruits are taught, wherever possible in conflict situations, to use their brains and mouths first; if that fails, switch to defensive tactics.

The last resort was deadly force.

Donaldson guessed he was about to skip the first two and go straight to the third option.

He squared up to the man by the elevator, who must have known exactly what he was thinking.

The man moved fast. He pulled his hands out of his pockets and, with his right, swung something in a wide arc towards Donaldson's head.

He saw it coming, ducked low, put his left arm up to protect himself and took the full force on the forearm of what turned out to be a double motorcycle chain, welded together for extra weight and power. It wrapped itself around his arm like a python, cutting into the skin despite the protection of his jacket sleeve. He screamed in pain and staggered into the railings. The man drew back the chain with a flourish, as if he was demonstrating a bull-whip, and moved in. His big left fist rocketed into Donaldson's throat, driving him back harder against the railings, from where he slumped to the hard metal surface.

Donaldson was vaguely aware of a scream from Francesca and the sound of a scuffle behind him and a rasping male voice, shouting.

Donaldson's attacker launched a big kick towards his exposed groin. He grabbed the foot just centimetres before it connected with his balls and clung desperately onto it whilst the man tried to shake him free, and pounded him repeatedly in the side with the chain. Fleetingly, Donaldson saw the traffic passing below, under the bridge. It was a long way down.

Donaldson bit into the big man's leg, right on the calf muscle at the back of the shin. He sunk his teeth in as hard and nastily as he could, trying to bite through the oil-tasting denim, knowing he couldn't, but trying anyway.

Bites work well in fights.

The man let out an agonised roar. With a superhuman effort he yanked his leg out of Donaldson's grip and teetered backwards, holding the bitten area.

Donaldson was up onto all fours, shaking his head. His toes sought grip on the slippery wet metal surface and he tried to launch himself at the man. He didn't connect as hard and accurately as he would have liked, but when his left shoulder rammed into the man's lower belly, it forced all the wind out of him with a rushing groan. He pushed him off-balance. The man toppled over and landed on his back with Donaldson about to dive onto him.

Still with the chain in his hand, he swung it wildly at Donaldson, who ducked properly this time, feeling the whoosh of air as it sailed past his head. The man whipped it back in the opposite direction so quickly that this time he caught the side of Donaldson's face, knocking him from his position of advantage, sending him sprawling against the railings again.

Donaldson was on his feet first, recovering well, despite feeling that his jaw had been broken by the impact of the chain across it. He hit the man hard, determined to finish it. Twice in the face, Donaldson's fists bunched hard like iron blocks, right-handed, two blows to the side of the jaw. The impact of each jarred his knuckles, but it did the job. The big man, who was only halfway up to his feet, dissolved like a jelly.

Donaldson spun round, concerned for Francesca.

He was too late. The second man had her pinned up against the railings, a hand clamped around her throat, trying to push her over. She struggled, twisting, fighting and clawing like a cat, but the man was too strong. With one last great shove, she went over the railings; her legs came up, she screamed, then was gone into the void.

'*Nooo!*' howled Donaldson, racing towards the second assailant, who simply turned and ran across the bridge into the rain and the darkness of night.

There was a screech of brakes below, a dull thudding noise, then the metallic crunch as cars collided. Donaldson stopped and looked over the railings. It was hard to make anything out properly. There was confusion on the road. He could just about see the figure of Francesca underneath the wheels of a car. A hand stuck out, seeming to be reaching for something. Then it stopped moving.

Donaldson's jaw was not broken, although it had swollen to twice its normal size and was as hard as iron. A nasty-looking, raised red-raw wheal ran from his right eye down across his chin with indentations in it, into which the chain could have been fitted perfectly. It looked as if someone had driven some sort of wheeled kitchen implement across his face. His eye was swollen and black too.

The painkillers prescribed by the doctor at the hospital were not working. He didn't want them to work. He wanted to feel pain . . . because he was that way inclined at the moment.

He was listening to Detective George Santana who was talking about the attacker in custody. Donaldson was not liking what he was hearing.

'Romero is a well known tough-nut. Convictions for robbery and violence. He works as a team with another no-good local criminal. We are looking for that man now. It looks like robbery was the motive, and it went wrong. They have robbed tourists before.'

'So what you're goddam trying to tell me is this incident has no connection with Sam Dawber's death. It was purely coincidental, am I right?'

Santana shrugged. 'What is the connection?' he said evenly. 'You tell me what it is and I'll believe you and investigate it.'

'Francesca was going to give me information about Sam's death. She'd already told me Sam had been murdered. We were going to my room so she could tell me everything she knew. There's just too much of a co-incidence, George.' Donaldson counted on his fingers. 'Sam writing Hamilton's name down; my visit to the timeshare, his reaction to me; Francesca turning up to see me and then those bastards waiting for us on the bridge. It don't take a genius to see it all, so go on, George, you tell me there's no connection,' he concluded, challenging Santana.

Santana nodded and conceded. 'You are probably correct. But it is very circumstantial, even with the best intention in the world.'

Donaldson breathed a sigh of relief. Ally-fuckin'-looya, he thought.

'However,' cautioned Santana, 'unless Romero tells us something, there will be a problem making a connection.'

'What has he said so far?'

'Absolutely nothing. He's an old hand. We may never crack him.'

'Fuck,' uttered Donaldson. He was completely deflated, frustrated and pissed off. It was the powerlessness, the lack of control that was really irritating him. Being in a foreign country made it all a million times worse. Everyone else spoke a language he could just about say 'Hello' in, and their police force seemed either unable or unwilling to run with the ball. God, he wanted to scream. Unfortunately he could not open his mouth wide enough to do so. He would probably be on liquids for a week until the swelling went down.

'OK George, I know you ain't impressed by my gut feelings about this, but I ask you, *implore you*, to keep an open mind about it. Keep your ear to the ground – don't just forget it once me and Sam get on board that silver bird tomorrow. I'm sure Sam was onto something and it obviously involved Hamilton. And if you do find anything out, let me know soonest . . . and really give that Romero some pain.'

Santana nodded. He laid a hand on Donaldson's shoulder. 'I will, my friend. Trust me.'

Yeah, thought the American. What you're really sayin' is, 'Get off my island and leave me in peace, you Yankee busybody.' Once I've gone, you won't give me a second thought, will you – and whoever killed Sam'll get away with it.

A jolt of pain leapt through his jaw. He cupped his face gently in his hands and his thoughts turned to Francesca. The words he'd said to her stuck in his craw and tried to choke him.

You can trust me.

Liar.

* * *

95

'Right, people,' said Henry, addressing the small team of officers who were dealing with the Dundaven enquiry. It was 10.30 p.m. They were all raring to race off for a drink; Henry was ready to go home and sink into bed, but not before he'd said one or two things.

'First of all, well done re today's work. We've started making some inroads into this man Dundaven and I'm sure that if we stick at it, we'll turn up some real dirt and it'll snowball . . . if you see what I mean. But there's still a lot of questions need answering. What was he really doing in Blackpool? What were his intentions if he hadn't got pulled? What was he going to do with the guns? Where have they come from, where are they going to? Who is the bastard answerable to? In other words, who is his boss?

'From tomorrow I think the important thing is to get the prosecution papers sorted out, get the file right, ensure there's no loopholes anywhere. In that respect each of you review the file critically and then get me, then CPS to do the same. Let's make it watertight.'

There was a general nod and murmur of consensus.

Henry saw the female detective, Siobhan Robson from NWOCS at the back of the room listening. She had a smile playing nicely on her lips. Henry acknowledged her with a quick nod.

'At the moment, Nina is alive and making some progress, but still critical. They've operated on her again today and she was in surgery for four hours. The doctors say it was a success, but there's more to come. She's young, strong and brave and there's every chance she'll pull through.' One or two of the detectives showed by their faces they were relieved to hear the news. 'So, tomorrow, first thing, we'll charge him with Attempted Murder on her . . . but if she doesn't pull through, we'll simply amend it to Murder. He's been charged with McCrory's murder already.

'We need to start rooting around into McCrory's background too, which might be easier than Dundaven's. So far we've only found his mum, bless her soul. She thought he was an angel.'

'He is now,' chirped one voice. There was a titter of laughter.

Henry smiled too. 'Let's find out about his connection with Dundaven. That could maybe open some chinks . . . So what I'm saying is there's a bloody long way to go with this yet. This is just the start, OK? Right, thanks again, everybody. See you all in the morning . . . unless there's any questions?'

'How's Guy the gorilla?'

'Doc says he's doin' just fine.'

They had all been standing around the office. They shuffled slowly out past the figure of Siobhan Robson, who looked at Henry, gave him another smile, then left herself.

Henry watched her go with interest. She was very, very nice indeed . . . but he was above those sorts of thoughts. He sat down heavily.

Whatever happens, mass murder, terrorist attack, suicide bombing, I will not be coming into work one single minute before nine tomorrow, he thought. Wild horses won't even be able to drag me out of my pit before 8.15.

He'd thrown his pager into a drawer and was thinking of the delights of his duvet when one of the DCs who had been working on the murder of Marie Cullen came into the office.

Her name was Lucy Crane.

'Hi, Luce.'

'Boss,' she said, chewing gum. She was a no-nonsense detective with an air of toughness about her which belied her five-and-a-half foot frame. She was also a lesbian. 'Summat pretty interestin',' she said in her broad Lancs accent. 'Could be summat, could be nowt.'

She threw a piece of paper down in front of him with a name scrawled across it.

'Locked up one year ago for kerb crawlin' in Blackburn. The prostitute who was showing her fanny for him was Marie Cullen, arrested at the same time.'

'Very interesting,' said Henry. He reread the name just to make sure he hadn't misread it. As if he didn't have enough on his plate. 'Any up-to-date connection between the two?'

'Haven't got that far yet.'

'Who else knows about this?'

'Just me.'

'Keep it that way for the time being.'

'Reet, boss.' She was unfazed but she'd had longer to get used to the idea than Henry, who now found he wanted a drink.

'C'mon, let me buy you a pint,' he said. Kate and his bed would have to wait just a little while longer.

Chapter Ten

Doctors are supposed to have a sensitive touch, but the consultant who, at ten o'clock the next morning, was probing along John Rider's ribcage with fingertips like pieces of dowling must have been the exception that proved the rule. Rider flinched each time he was touched.

After the ribs the doctor moved to the skull, handling it like a rugby ball. Equally roughly he pulled up Rider's eyelids one at a time with his thumb and shone a penlight torch into his pupils. Then he listened to Rider's heart and lungs by planting a stethoscope on his chest which felt like it had been left in a freezer. The doctor made a few muttered comments about giving up smoking and drinking or death would not be far away. After this he tested Rider's blood pressure – which was extremely high – with a tourniquet so tight Rider thought his arm might drop off.

The consultant stood up and sniffed haughtily. A nurse handed him a set of X-rays which he held up to the light and inspected. He hummed, muttered to himself and handed them back to her.

Then he regarded Rider over the frame of his pince-nez which were balanced precariously on the tip of his bulbous, pitted nose.

'How do you feel?'

'Like shit,' said Rider honestly.

'Only to be expected. You had a rather severe beating, but although you're black and blue, it doesn't seem to have done any permanent damage. Two of your ribs are broken, but they'll heal in their own good time. Your spine is bruised, but will improve once you get mobile. And, of course, the cheekbone under your left eye is fractured. The rest is superficial bruising. Your skull is OK. The reason you were kept in was because you passed out. Basically, you're fine. The most dangerous thing for you at the moment is your blood pressure and the state of your lungs. Give up smoking, Mr Rider. It kills, especially at the rate you smoke.'

'I know, I know.' Rider sulked like a schoolboy.

'You don't wish to make a complaint to the police, I hear.'

'No. Wouldn't be any use. They had balaclavas on.'

'Your decision,' said the consultant. 'But you really must cut back on the fags – that's my medical advice to you.'

Rider nodded.

'You are now discharged from hospital.'

Isa and Jacko collected the invalid twenty minutes later and helped him down the corridor to the car park where the Jag was waiting. Rider rolled painfully into the back seat and Jacko drove him back to the basement flat. Throughout the journey Isa leaned back over the front seat and looked with concern at Rider who winced with every bump they hit.

Between winces, he glared back at her accusingly.

'You're going to do something stupid, aren't you,' she said bluntly. 'I can see it in your face.'

'Depends on your definition of stupid.'

'My definition? OK – my definition of stupid is someone who can't control his emotions, someone who has done well for himself and dragged himself out of the gutter of violence, but then steps back into it at the first opportunity because he wants revenge. That's my definition of stupid – an idiot who wants revenge because that's all he understands. That's what you're going to do, isn't it? Get revenge.'

He said nothing with his voice, but his expression said yes.

She closed her eyes in despair and held back the tears because she didn't want him to see her cry.

'Please don't do it, John,' she appealed quietly. 'There won't be any winners from it.'

'Isa,' he began with a dangerous tone, 'those two guys nearly fucking killed me. All they needed to do was say to me, "Don't get involved", that's all. I didn't actually need telling, truth be known. I wasn't going to get into some fucking gang war that has nothing whatsoever to do with me. But they went well OTT. They were fucking out of order. There's no way I'm gonna let this pass. No way. Jacko – turn in here.'

'Eh? The zoo, you mean?'

'Yes, the fucking zoo I mean, you moron,' he growled.

'But why?'

'Will you just do what you're fucking told to do! I want to see if that gorilla's OK – all right?'

'Anything you say.' Jacko slowed the car and headed up the driveway to the zoo. 'Barmy if you ask me,' he mumbled.

Despite the agony attached with movement, Rider leaned forwards between the seats. His mouth was only inches away from Jacko's ear. 'If you ever call me barmy again, Jacko, I'll fucking kill you. D'you understand?' he rasped hoarsely.

Isa stared at him, completely dumbstruck.

Jacko's mouth dropped open. He didn't dare look at Rider. As a barman, the same threat had often been uttered to him by drunken, violent customers, but it had meant nothing. Rider's words, however, shook him to the core. He was very frightened of the man who was now his boss.

Rider gave Isa a warning glance and leaned back in the leather seats. His face bore the beginning of a sneer. His top lip quivered. His eyes seemed to change to deadly, emotionless orbs. There was a cruel, determined look on his battered features. A look that Isa hadn't seen for ten years, one she had never wanted to see again, one which meant deadly trouble.

He had metamorphosised before her eyes. He had reverted to type.

Rider looked out of the car window, his nostrils flaring angrily. He was aware of the change, too. Like a monster had been reawakened inside him; or some dreadful death-bearing virus, perhaps. Part of him wanted to fight and neutralise it, to destroy it for ever, but it was growing with every second, becoming an unbeatable force, taking over his whole being and personality; driving him on.

A force that meant he would extract revenge.

The worst thing about it was that he was quite enjoying the sensation. Rather like injecting a controlled drug. Something he knew he shouldn't do, but once it was done and the euphoric sensation was creeping through his veins, it was great. Like he'd been asleep for ten years and had now risen from the ashes.

Those bastards didn't know what they'd unleashed.

He saw the tears forming in Isa's eyes. Ignored them.

But before he went over the edge, there was one last good thing he wanted to do.

About twenty minutes after seeing John Rider, the consultant visited another of his patients on the morning round. The name of the patient was Shane Mulcahy and two days before, the consultant had been forced to remove a severely damaged left testicle.

Throughout Shane's short stay in hospital, the only period he had been quiet and pleasant was when he'd been under general anaesthetic. Otherwise he had proved himself to be the stereotypical lout, minus the lager. Nothing was good enough for him. The food was 'shite'. He would have preferred beefburgers and chips all the time. He was rude to the nurses, whom he called 'tarts', to the doctors, of whom he was slightly afraid, and his fellow patients, who he thought were all silly old bastards.

In short, he had been a complete arsehole.

'Well now, how are you feeling, young man?' the consultant asked, checking the notes.

'How would you fucking well feel if you'd had one of your bollocks kicked off?'

'Not terribly well, I imagine. Having said that, I'd probably be much less of a pain in the arse to everyone.'

Shane sneered up at him, folded his arms and looked away, his lips muttering silently, his face in a sulk.

'Let's have a look then.'

A nurse drew the curtains around the bed, pulled back the bedclothes and removed the dressing.

'Like what you see?' Shane sniggered, trying to cover his embarrassment in a show of bravado.

The nurse took a deep breath, looked coldly at him and said, 'I don't like anything about you.'

'Twat,' he hissed.

The consultant bent over and inspected the shaved and swollen genital area. He probed around more harshly than necessary. Shane let out a yelp of pain and a tear formed in his eye.

'Sorry,' said the consultant.

'Like fuck you are.'

'You're fit to go. Make an appointment at Out Patients for Friday. A couple of weeks and you'll be as right as rain. It won't affect your manly functions in any way.'

'Good. An' I want you to be a witness against the cops for me. I'll be seein' me solicitor as soon as I get out of here and I'm gonna sue those bastards for every penny they've got.'

'I shall do what I have to,' the consultant said. He wrote something on the notes and hung them back over the end of the bed. 'Though I deplore what happened to you, I would make the observation that you probably deserved what you got.'

At 10.30 a.m. they were in an unmarked CID car heading east out of Blackpool along the M55. Henry was driving; Lucy Crane was passenger.

'What do we know about this guy?' Henry asked.

He actually knew as much as Lucy, having discussed the man at length in the bar the night before, but wanted to hear it all again.

Lucy riffled through the papers on her knees and extracted a photocopied entry from *Who's Who*. She read out a few salient points, ad-libbing occasionally, about Sir Harry McNamara, multi-millionaire businessman.

'Educated Lancaster Grammar,' she was saying, 'then Oxford . . . blah blah . . . owns a big transport company, worldwide business . . . went into politics mid-80s . . . became an MP in '83, but retired in '87 to pursue his business interests. Supposedly donated lots of money to the Tories and is a good friend of the former Prime Minister, who visits him privately from time to time. Lives in Lancashire. Has homes in London and the Channel Islands.'

'Rich bastard in other words,' commented Henry. 'Not that I'm envious, you understand.'

'Nor me.' She turned up some newspaper cuttings and skimmed through them. 'Second wife an ex-model . . . been linked with a couple of glamour pusses – and prostitutes. Weathered a storm a couple of years back linking him with a hooker. Wife stood by him and they declared their undying love for each other . . . how touching . . . arrested in Blackburn last year for kerb crawling and drink driving.' The last piece of information came from police reports.

'The Marie Cullen connection . . . makes you wonder,' sighed Henry.

'Doesn't make him a killer,' Lucy warned him.

'Makes him a good starting point.'

They came off the M6 and headed towards Blackburn.

After having kicked it around the office for a while, Henry and Lucy had decided on the direct approach, to treat McNamara as if he was nobody special, just another member of the public who knew the murdered girl.

Henry had considered making an appointment to see him, but chose not to. Like all witnesses, he wanted to catch him unprepared. Judging by what little he knew of the man, the element of surprise would probably be short-lived anyway. McNamara was no one's fool and he would recover quickly – in seconds, probably. Henry wanted to savour that tiny stretch of time before McNamara became the overbearing, obnoxious sod he apparently was when dealing with 'lesser' people.

Prior to setting off Henry had phoned Blackburn police and by pure luck managed to speak to the officer in the plain-clothes department who had arrested McNamara.

The officer recalled the incident vividly.

McNamara had been one of the most difficult prisoners he had ever dealt with. He had demanded to speak to the Chief Constable, belittled the officer, threatened legal action and refused to be searched. He stalled, demanded every right – which he got – spoke to some high-flying Manchester solicitor who gave him 'certain advice'. Then he played the system. He claimed himself to be unable to give a specimen of breath because of a lung infection, unable to give blood because of a medically-documented fear of needles and unable to give a specimen of urine because of a bladder infection. He vehemently denied the kerb crawling, stating he was having car trouble.

Eventually he was charged and bailed with both offences.

In court he was represented by a barrister who specialised in drink-driving legislation; he produced two doctors who testified as to his medical conditions and a motor mechanic who swore blind that McNamara's Bentley was having mechanical problems that night – something to do with a fuel-line blockage.

Rent-a-witness.

The charges were dismissed by Magistrates who did not believe a word but had no choice other than to accept the expert opinions.

McNamara then instituted civil proceedings against the police for a variety of matters, ranging from malicious prosecution to assault and a myriad of other things. As civil claims tend to, it was still going on.

'All in all,' the officer admitted to Henry, 'it amounts to the fact he's got money, power and influence. If you're dealing with him for anything, watch out. He's a slippery sod and he bears grudges.'

Henry thanked the officer. He and Lucy then began their trek across the county, intending to combine an on-spec visit to McNamara with a few enquiries around Blackburn about the dead girl.

They skirted Blackburn on the arterial road. Henry picked up the B6232 Grane Road, which would take them up onto the moors.

Five minutes later they pulled into the long driveway which led up to McNamara's farmhouse. Henry said to Lucy, 'Just so you know, I'm dropping the word "Acting" when I introduce myself. Plain "Detective Inspector" rolls off the tongue better and he has no reason to know I'm really just a Sergeant.'

'OK,' she smiled. 'Delusions of grandeur, maybe, but OK.'

The bulky figure of Sir Harry McNamara, former MP for the South Blackburn and Darwen constituency, stood thoughtfully at the conservatory doors of his restored farmhouse on the moors overlooking Blackburn. It was another clear winter's day, no cloud or mist, and he could see the Lancashire coastline some forty miles to the west and the little blip that was Blackpool Tower.

Usually days like these made him appreciate what a wonderful part of the country he lived in, with scenery to rival anywhere else in Britain – indeed the world. And he had seen much of both.

He placed the expensive, bulbous cigar between his fat lips and took a long draw, blowing the resultant smoke out into the atmosphere where it wisped away.

Today, however, he was not considering the countryside. He was thinking deeply about the conversation he'd had with a police Chief Inspector from Blackburn who had earwigged a phone conversation between the cop who arrested him last year and some detective from Blackpool. The police in Blackpool, it would appear, were investigating the murder of a prostitute and McNamara's name had cropped up.

He stepped out of the conservatory and walked across the patio to the edge of the lawn. Even though the grass had not been mown since the onset of cold weather, it looked well. He dropped the cigar butt onto it and crushed it to death with the sole of his shoe.

Philippa, his second wife, who was twenty-two years younger than him at thirty-five, appeared in the conservatory. She had picked up his mood following the phone call and – as other minions did (and she was under no illusion that she was anything more than just another minion) – had withdrawn to a safe distance. She was wary of her husband's temper, which could be violent at times. This time, however, there was something different in the air. He was angry, that much was obvious, but there was fear there too.

'Harry,' she called sweetly, 'can I get you anything?'

He had his back to her and did not do her the courtesy of turning. Just shook his head, made no verbal response.

'Tea? Coffee? Something stronger?' she persisted gently.

He closed his eyes momentarily in a gesture of impatience. Still not turning he said, 'No,' firmly.

103

She left.

When he was sure she was out of earshot, he pulled a mobile phone out of his pocket and dialled a local number.

'We need to have chats, soon,' he said.

'When?'

McNamara gave a time and date. No location because the venue was always the same. He ended the call abruptly.

He spent as little time as possible on mobiles. Handy though they were, they were also dangerous. He knew he could very easily be a target for journalists with scanners, particularly with his reputation. He preferred the old-fashioned landline where possible.

'Harry,' McNamara's wife called from the conservatory door.

'I said I don't want anything!' he barked.

'I know,' she said, 'but the police are here – two detectives. They want to see you about something. Harry, what is it?'

'How the hell should I know?'

Brushing roughly past her, he mooched over to the house and went to the entrance hall where, indeed, two detectives were waiting to see him.

'Sir Harry McNamara?' the male detective said politely, a smile on his face. He held out a hand. McNamara shook it. 'I'm sorry to bother you at home, but we need to have a chat with you. Hope you don't mind, hope it's not inconvenient. Oh, by the way, this is DC Crane and I'm Detective Inspector Christie. We're from Blackpool CID.'

'Come into the study,' McNamara said. 'I hope this won't take long. I'm rather busy and need to go out shortly to a business meeting.' A lie, but these two cops wouldn't know.

'I can't make any promises about how long it'll take. Depends on what you tell us,' Henry informed him.

McNamara nodded and led the detectives to the study which was off the hall. Henry caught sight of McNamara's wife standing in the kitchen. It was only a brief glimpse of a tall, sad-looking woman, lonely and quite beautiful.

The officers were not asked to sit, nor were they offered refreshment. McNamara made it clear he was doing them a favour. It was an imposition for him.

'What do you want?'

Lucy did the talking, Henry the watching.

'We appreciate this might be quite delicate,' she began. 'We're investigating the murder of a young woman in Blackpool. We think you knew her and we're obviously speaking to everyone we can find with connections to her. As a matter of routine.'

'No, I don't know her,' McNamara said immediately. 'I don't know anyone in Blackpool.'

'She's not from Blackpool, she's from Blackburn and her name is Marie Cullen.'

Henry watched McNamara's face, which flushed like a toilet.

'No. The name means nothing to me.'

'She was a prostitute and was arrested for soliciting about a year ago in the King Street area of Blackburn. You were arrested at the same time for kerb crawling and drink driving. She was seen to get in your car.'

'And as you two probably know, I was acquitted of the charges at court. The poor woman who was embroiled in the same incident was not known to me then, nor now. I did not, nor do not, know her. It was just an unfortunate set of circumstances for which the police will be paying dearly when it reaches civil court.'

'You're saying you don't know Marie Cullen?' Lucy asked.

'Yes. That is what I'm saying, so I suggest we stop at this point. I have never seen the woman since that night and if you even begin to make out that I have done, I'll sue you. Now I'm asking you to leave.'

They were ushered out and moments later were climbing silently into the CID car. Henry started the engine.

Then they looked at each other. Simultaneously they both said the same word and burst out laughing.

The word was 'Guilty'.

Once on the road, Henry said, 'I think he knew we were coming, Luce, which I find pretty worrying. Let's bob into Blackburn police station and have a nose around, maybe speak to the officer who dealt with him again.'

'Good idea.'

The top ten worst moments of my life, thought Karl Donaldson. I'm not exactly sure which one this has replaced, but I think it's definitely sneaked into the top five.

He was certain the number one spot would never be breached – the time when he'd held the dying body of a friend and colleague who'd been cruelly gunned down by a mafia hit man. That had been a hell of a bad moment, which still hurt two years later.

But this was pretty damned bad too.

The casket containing the post mortem mutilated body of FBI operative Samantha Jane Dawber was taken from the hold of the GB Airlines plane which had just touched down at Heathrow from Madeira. It was transferred under Donaldson's watchful eye onto the back of a small flatback truck with big tyres, an amber flashing light and a curious-sounding horn, across the apron on what seemed like an interminable journey to the British Airways New York flight.

He watched it while it was loaded into the belly of the huge jet, amongst all the other luggage.

Donaldson desperately wanted to be on that flight too, in order to accompany her all the way home and hand her over to her Mom and Pop.

To be able to tell them everything he knew about her life and death; tell them what a fantastic person she was, a wonderful caring friend, a dedicated professional. And tell them he'd arranged for another autopsy to take place because he wasn't remotely satisfied with the one already done.

The hold was locked.

Donaldson said, 'Bye, Sam, look after yourself.'

It was hard to hold back a tear and a sob, but he did. He was sad that he would miss the subsequent funeral, but he knew Sam would understand because something told him he would be busy at this end, unearthing stuff about Scott Hamilton and maybe getting to grips with the real reason for Sam's death. And, of course, the other death he felt totally responsible for – Francesca's.

Karen met him at the other end of Customs.

When he melted into her arms he allowed himself that tear. Karen too had obviously been in a state of denial. They cried silently for a few moments, holding each other tight, oblivious of the gawping stares of everyone else.

Eventually they let go. Time to look at each other properly.

'Your face is a terrible mess,' she said, looking at the dirty chain-mark and black eye.

'It'll heal.'

'And you look completely whacked.'

'And you look completely gorgeous.' He glanced down at her stomach, which was just beginning to show signs of expansion. He touched it and said, 'How's your belly?'

'Full of arms and legs,' she smiled, 'but fine.'

'Long hot bath and a good night's sleep is what I need,' he said, taking her hand and walking towards the exit.

She looked at him critically. 'Hope that's not all you want. I mean, there is absolutely no way I can get pregnant now. We should take advantage of that sort of situation, don't you think?'

'Then I suggest we get home as soon as possible.'

Detective Constable Derek Luton was extremely proud of himself.

He had been a police officer for only six years, spending five on uniformed patrol duties at Blackpool. During those years he had dedicated himself to becoming a detective and he had achieved his aim far sooner than he had anticipated.

From his appointment onto the branch, he had been working on Henry Christie's team and had set himself to learn everything he could from Henry who, it was quietly considered, was a cracking detective.

Not because he broke the rules (though it was rumoured he had once given a prisoner cocaine in return for information); nor was he oppressive to prisoners, nor was he a maverick, but because he was thorough, occasionally a genius, occasionally very brave . . . and he had a bit of a reputation too, which added to his general aura.

Henry himself would have cringed at this last bit. Eighteen months earlier, he had stupidly become involved with a young policewoman. His marriage to Kate had only just survived it and Henry had learned a salutary lesson: keep your dick in your pants. He didn't like to be reminded what an ass he'd been.

But Luton worshipped Henry, who had taken him willingly under his wing. He knew he had a lot to learn from Henry's vast wealth of experience. And now Henry had let him get involved in Blackpool's biggest-ever murder case. Five civilians, one dead cop.

Brilliant.

'The Lottery Killings', as the media had dubbed it.

Not only that, by pure chance Luton had been paired up with a seasoned detective from the North-West Organised Crime Squad.

Bliss!

Luton had aspirations of being much more than a local CID officer. In the fullness of time he wanted to move to the Drugs Squad, then Regional Crime Squad and ultimately, la crème de la crème, the NWOCS, the gangbusters. Fuckin' magic, they were, he thought enthusiastically.

The murder investigation – which NWOCS had bulldozed their way into and taken over – would, Luton hoped, provide some sort of insight as to how they operated. Maybe even get him noticed as a potential future recruit.

Initially he was very impressed.

Taking witness statements was a skill most police officers, whatever the department, get good at. Luton considered himself to be above average, as was expected of a CID officer – but the statements taken by the guy Tattersall from the NWOCS he was working with were superb – packed full of detail, and reading like a story.

Tattersall even got the witnesses to sign some blank statement forms so that there would be no need to revisit when they were eventually typed up. Not usual practice, but a time-saver.

The statements had been taken from four witnesses who had seen the first robbery at the newsagents in Fleetwood, the one the gang had done before heading south to massacre the people in Blackpool. They were all very similar.

In fact, the statements were so good that when he got the chance, Luton took a quick photocopy of the originals for future reference. Copying material he judged to be good quality was a habit he had acquired early in his service. He kept everything in a binder and often referred back for guidance, though as his experience grew he went back less and less and the binder was relegated to his locker.

A couple of days into the investigation, Luton began to have vague, nagging doubts about the NWOCS.

He raised some of the questions which Henry had posed on the night of

107

the shooting, that fatal Saturday, because he felt they weren't being addressed. Or he wasn't aware of them being addressed.

Questions such as: How did the robbers get from one shop to the other so quickly?

It was possible they could have done it – but only if traffic was virtually non-existent on the roads.

When he put it to them, he was fobbed off with, 'In their fucking car, how d'you think?'

Questions like: Why should the gang suddenly revert to murder? They were violent, yes, probably capable of murder. But killing six people?

Luton was patronised.

'Drugs,' he was told. 'We believe they were on speed.'

Then he asked if the possibility of two separate gangs operating had been considered.

That really got their backs up. Luton found himself shut out completely, ending up with a lame duck job doing house-to-house enquiries along the supposed route of the gang from one shop to the other. A job for uniforms.

And he couldn't understand why.

He didn't specifically link it to the nooky questions he'd been asking.

No one said anything to him, so when he asked he was told it was to give him experience of all aspects of a murder enquiry, which he had to accept. At the back of his mind he had a nasty feeling he'd upset somebody, but didn't know who, how or why.

Late that Tuesday evening, three days after the shootings, Luton was alone in the murder incident room at Blackpool police station. The usual 9 p.m. debrief of the day's activities had been done and everyone involved in the job had either gone for a drink or gone home. Moodily, Luton had stayed behind, kicking his heels, drifting aimlessly around the silent room, pissed off with proceedings.

He was pretty sure the NWOCS had a lead on the gang and that only their officers were following it up, keeping it very much to themselves. He was annoyed that he wasn't being allowed to do anything in that direction.

In one of the baskets next to a HOLMES terminal, having already been inputted, was a thick stack of witness statements. They were all now neatly typed.

Absently, he picked up the top one and glanced at it. He recognised the name of the witness as one of the people he and Tattersall had interviewed about the Fleetwood robbery. Luton's eyes zigzagged down the page, not specifically reading it closely, until something jarred him into concentration.

He had been present when the statement had been taken and he remembered it quite clearly. This particular witness had been very precise in his recollection of events and had given a quality statement.

Holding the statement in two hands, Luton sat down on a typist's chair

108

and with a very puzzled brow, began to read it through again – very carefully this time. He hadn't realised that he had been holding his breath until at the end he exhaled long and unsteadily.

Then he read it again. Just to make sure.

After that he flicked through the statement tray to see if he could find the original. It wasn't there.

He knew where he could find a copy.

Leaving the typed statement on the desk next to the computer terminal, he got up and walked out of the room. He ignored the lift – too slow – and shot down the stairs three at a time until he reached the CID floor where his locker was situated.

With a cold expression, Jim Tattersall had been watching Luton's activities from the door of the incident room. As the young detective stood up, he twisted quickly out of sight into a darkened office, from where he saw Luton almost run to the stairs.

When the stairs door closed, Tattersall walked swiftly into the incident room and went to the seat Luton had been using.

He saw the typed statement on the desk.

Tattersall's face hardened as he realised that Derek Luton had discovered something he should not have done.

The photocopy Luton had made of the original statement was in a binder at the bottom of his locker. He unhooked the binder and pulled it out, together with the three other statements he had witnessed being given. He hurried straight back upstairs, arriving there breathless.

The incident room was still empty. Good.

He crossed quickly to the desk where he'd left the statement, sat down and compared it with his photocopy of the original.

He nearly choked. It was different! Somewhere in the translation from longhand to type it had been changed, only slight changes, but crucial ones.

Suddenly the room seemed airless and hot. He could not believe what his eyes were telling him.

Statements had been doctored.

He ran a hand over his face. Once again he compared them. In the original, the time of the robbery in Fleetwood had been written as 7.10 p.m. The typed copy stated 7.01 p.m. Luton could easily have forgiven this as a typing error and maybe it was. Pretty bloody elementary, though.

No way could the next change have been down to a mistake of fingers. It was much more fundamental, but still quite subtle.

The original statement had been quite specific about the descriptions of the men responsible. The witness had a very clear memory of events. He had described all the men as being quite small, about five foot six to five foot eight. And though they had all worn masks, he described their hair colours and even guessed at possible ages – seventeen to twenty-three. All young men.

The typed statement changed this to: 'They were all of medium height' – and the individual descriptions of the men had been amended too, making them much more general than specific. The age range had also been changed: 'anything from seventeen to thirty-seven'.

One of the men had spoken during the raid and the witness had described his voice as 'gruff, with a local accent, and I would probably recognise it again'. The typed statement read, 'He had a Lancashire accent and I probably wouldn't recognise it again.'

The changes meant that the men could have been any one of a quarter of a million males in the north-west of England and were evidentially worthless.

Another slight but significant change was the time that it took to rob the place – reduced from four minutes to two. This meant that the men had left the premises at the new time of 7.03 p.m., giving them ample time to make it to the newsagents in Blackpool . . . if, in fact, the men who had robbed the shop in Fleetwood were the same ones responsible for that subsequent, appalling crime.

Luton sat back and allowed his head to flop backwards so he was staring at the ceiling.

What was going on here? he asked himself. What did all this mean?

Had other statements been changed too?

'DC Luton, isn't it?'

Luton sat bolt upright and spun round on the chair.

'Oh, hello, sir.'

It was Tony Morton, Head of the NWOCS, and Jim Tattersall.

'Working late? I won't be approving the overtime,' Morton said with a short laugh. There was no humour behind it. He and Tattersall were standing at the door. Luton panicked inside as he wondered how long they'd been there watching him.

They walked towards Luton who, easy as he could, rotated back to face the desk. He picked up the typed statement and dropped it casually back into the basket, then rolled up his photocopies with shaking hands.

'So . . . what're you up to?'

Luton faced them again. A wave of intimidation gushed through him. Like nausea.

'Uh – nothing,' he stammered. 'Just having a read of a few statements. Seeing where we're up to . . .' His throat was arid, constricted, but he could not understand why. He felt as if he'd been caught doing something naughty, yet here was the perfect opportunity to tell Morton – in the presence of Tattersall – exactly what he'd found: someone had been tampering with witness statements. It was his duty to do so.

Fuck that, he thought. These two looked like they were in this together.

'We have statement readers for that sort of thing,' announced Morton.

Tattersall loomed silently and menacingly behind him.

'Yes, I know, sir. Just interested, that's all.' He tried to slip the rolled-up photocopies smoothly into the inside pocket of his jacket. Actually there was nothing smooth about the way he did it because his nerves got the better of him. For a start, there were about a dozen sheets of A4-size paper, not specifically designed to fit into inner jacket pockets, especially when there is a wallet, diary and two pens in there already. Basically the statements did not fit, but he made them go in by crushing them up and forcing them. The result was a huge bulge like a rugby ball in his pocket.

'What've you got there?' Morton asked.

Luton stood up. 'Nothing, sir. Just some of my notes. If you'll excuse me.'

He made to walk past Morton who held out a hand, placed it across Luton's chest and prevented him walking away. Luton thought for one horrible moment he was going to reach into the pocket and grab the statements.

'Is everything OK?' he asked, eyebrows raised. Luton nodded dumbly. 'Any problems, you can come to me with them.' He looked Luton squarely in the eyes and Luton was certain Morton must be able to feel the beating of his heart; the organ was thrashing around in his chest like a crazy man locked in a cell.

'No, no problems,' croaked Luton.

Morton removed his hand. Luton said good night, sidestepped Morton and Tattersall and walked coolly to the door, where he then bolted.

He hit the stairs, he calculated, at somewhere approaching 100 m.p.h. and threw himself down them like a pin-ball. Within moments he had descended to the level of the CID office – which was as deserted as the incident room had been.

He needed to see his role model. But his role model wasn't there.

'Henry, where the shite are you when I need you?' he chunnered under his breath. He went to Henry's desk, picked up the phone and dialled Comms. No, they had no idea where the Acting DI was. He dialled Henry's home number. Kate answered.

'Kate, sorry to bother you. Is Henry there, it's Derek Luton here.'

'No, he's not back yet,' said Kate. 'Are you all right, Derek? You sound a bit strained.'

'Absolutely fine. Just breathless from the stairs,' he said oddly.

'You want to leave a message or anything?'

'No, it's all right. I'll catch up with him later,' he said in what he vainly hoped was a more controlled voice. 'Bye.' He hung up.

'What to do, what to do,' he said to himself whilst he danced on the spot like someone on hot coals, opening and closing his fists. Then: 'Get a grip, you knob,' he remonstrated. He quickly scribbled a note for Henry on a yellow post-it and stuck it prominently in the middle of the desk blotter, as opposed to around the edge where the rest of them were stuck like flags. He hoped Henry would see it straight away.

In the back yard of the police station it was brass monkeys. After these past few pleasant days, the January nights had turned harsh and bitter. Luton strode out of the ground-floor rear entrance and headed towards his car at something approaching a jog, all the while looking over his shoulder, but feeling completely stupid for doing so.

He got to his car in one piece. Stop overreacting, dickhead, he told himself. Why should anyone want to do anything to you? Complete crap.

However, when he was in the driver's seat, he made damn sure all the doors were locked before starting the engine.

Instinct was telling him two things.

One – you've just uncovered something very smelly indeed.

And two – watch your back, pal.

When Luton had gone from the room, Morton walked over to where he'd been sitting and picked up the top statement from the file.

'Fuck,' he said. 'What the hell is this doing here, for everyone to see?' He looked hard at Tattersall.

'I came back to put them away,' he replied. 'That's when I found him.'

Morton's nostrils flared angrily. 'We cannot afford to take chances,' he said. He shook his head. 'D'you think he's sussed it?'

'He's sharp. Think about all those questions he's been asking. I'd say yes, he's sussed it.'

After a thoughtful pause, Morton spoke. 'As I said, we can't take any chances.'

There was a knock on the door.

Luton did not have to wake up to check the clock. He was already awake and knew it was 2 a.m.

Annie, his wife of six months, had been asleep; not as deeply as usual. His tossing and turning and sweating meant she could not get comfortable. It was like sleeping with a restless dog.

'What time is it?' she groaned groggily.

Luton told her.

There was another knock on the door.

'Who is it?' she asked.

'Dunno.' He slid out of bed, covering his nakedness with a dressing gown. He went to the bedroom window and peered out, shading his eyes with his hands like goggles. The weather had really turned and sleet was blasting down the avenue on an icy wind. Luton could make out the dark shape of a man at the front door, huddled up against the elements. He couldn't see who it was. 'Might be Henry,' he said. 'I left him a note to contact me.'

Annie turned over and disappeared underneath the quilt. 'Well, tell him to get stuffed,' she murmured. Seconds later she was back in the land of snooze.

Luton let the curtain fall back into place. He slid his feet into his moccasin slippers and went downstairs. The front door was solid with just one pane of mottled glass in it. He pushed his face up to it, peering out, flattening his nose. 'Henry?' he called.

Luton could not identify the person properly but when there came a muffled, 'Yeah,' in reply he breathed out in relief. Despite the time, Luton was pleased Henry had turned up. There were some burning issues to discuss.

He slid the chain off, pulled back the two bolts, unlocked the mortise and opened the door. A strong gust of Arctic cold wind whipped in around his bare legs and gripped his testicles.

The figure outside had his back to Luton, standing in shadow.

'Henry?'

The figure turned. Luton recognised the face immediately and registered the gun in the man's right hand. It had a bulbous silencer on it.

A hushed *Thk!* hardly made an inroad into the sounds of the night. The bullet drove into Luton's forehead, spun like a missile through his brain and exited out of the back of his skull.

He was dead. Standing, but dead.

His legs buckled like a sucker-punched boxer. They collapsed under him and he toppled over, blood gushing in a torrent all over the hallway.

Just to make sure, the man leaned forwards, placed the gun at Luton's temple and put two more in because it was surprising how some people lived if you didn't make certain.

Annie woke for some reason, not quite sure why. She shivered. It was ever so cold in the bedroom. Her arm, which had been out of the quilt, was like a block of ice.

She rolled over, pulling the cover over her head, and reached out for her husband – who was not there.

Startled by this, she came fully awake and opened her eyes. It was still dark. She focused on the digital clock-face on the bedside cabinet. 6.20. God, it was so cold. And where was he? What was Derek doing up at this time of day?

Somewhere in the recess of her mind she recalled the two o'clock knock on the door.

Four hours ago. Surely Henry had gone home!

She climbed out of bed and hastily grabbed her fluffy dressing gown and bunny-rabbit slippers.

It was bloody freezing on the landing. Real penguin temperatures. A gale was blowing, as if the front door was open. She switched the landing and hall lights on.

She'd almost reached the foot of the stairs before she realised what she was looking at, lying in a lake of congealed blood and half-covered in wet slush.

She sank to her knees, her hands covering the silent scream.

She was unable to do anything, but stare.

Then she found her voice and started an unwordly, inhuman wail of horror.

Chapter Eleven

The three men met at an exclusive golf and country club set in the high, lovely countryside between Blackburn and Bolton. This was where all their meetings took place. The club was owned by one of the men and the other two held small, but profitable stakes.

The owner made the arrangements for the meetings with the management of the club (which was scrupulously operated) to ensure they would not be disturbed for at least two hours while they used the pool and the sauna. It was a good atmosphere in which the men could relax and unwind and discuss business matters.

The meetings usually concluded in the same way: girls were brought in for two of them, and a young man for the third.

They always arrived and departed separately, at least twenty minutes apart.

That Wednesday morning was an emergency meeting.

It had snowed overnight and the hills were covered with a white blanket. It was not pleasant flakey snow, but wet and slushy and grimy.

The first of the men to arrive was the owner of the club, Ronnie Conroy.

He had learned his lesson from Blackpool and now, as well as his driver, he was accompanied by two armed goons. No one was going to sneak up on him again.

The big Mercedes purred up the long driveway, past a couple of snow-covered trees and greens, stopping outside the grand entrance to the club.

Conroy walked straight into the club, striding quickly through the reception foyer and into the manager's office. After checking the arrangements had been made, he went to the changing rooms and got into his swimming gear. He dived into the heated pool and swam a few slow lengths whilst he considered matters.

Ronnie Conroy was a worried man.

There are perhaps a hundred and fifty to two hundred people, all men, who are the top operators and control eighty per cent of the UK drugs trade and they lead lives of lavish wealth, often in communities far away from their trading heartlands. They are far removed from street dealers and the day-to-day violence of bars, housing estates and night clubs upon which they shower their product.

With a few exceptions, these men all reside in houses with swimming pools, stable blocks and acres of grounds. They own race horses, private planes or helicopters and homes abroad; the ones with children send them to private schools. Many are active within their adopted communities, living apparently blameless lives, supporting churches, charities and often find themselves on school boards.

They all own legitimate businesses which act as a front for their more nefarious activities; they are usually cash based businesses, more often than not in retailing.

Ronnie Conroy, one-time partner of John Rider, had grown into one of these top operators.

What Conroy really imagined himself to be was a businessman, not a gangster. The words *Company Director* were proudly displayed on his passport. The fact that the bulk of his company's profits came from supplying drugs, prostitution and selling guns was something he never mentioned in polite company. In fact, his neighbours in Osbaldeston, a leafy village on the outskirts of Blackburn, believed he was a car dealer.

Conroy had been connected to Rider for many years, and another man called Munrow. The three of them had bonded professionally, though their personalities often clashed, and had built up an empire of criminal activity in the east of Lancashire and Manchester which had operated for well over ten years from the mid-seventies. Hard, violent years. Much of their time had been spent kicking the shit out of other would-be's to keep their own heads out of the sewage.

The profits had been good, but not as substantial as they could have been in a more peaceful, cooperative regime.

Conroy had realised this, but his pleas to Rider and Munrow to make peace with other gangs fell on deaf ears. They were both highly feared individuals who got pleasure from inflicting pain, intimidating others and ruling – literally – with iron rods, unless they were using pick-axe handles instead.

Their heavy tactics simply fuelled fires. Then halfway through the 1980s, there was an explosion of blood as gang fought gang for supremacy.

When the North-West police forces formed a dedicated squad to combat this menace, Conroy had been one of the first to see the light . . . and things fell very neatly into place for him just at the right time.

Rider seemed to lose his nerve. He ran and never returned.

Munrow was an awkward bastard. He wouldn't run from anyone. For safety's sake, he had to be sacrificed one way or another – and Conroy was just the man to do it.

Without ever knowing the real truth – that Conroy had informed the cops – Munrow was arrested halfway through a robbery in Accrington. He and a gang of three armed men were surrounded by a heavily armed police contingent who had been briefed that the gang were ruthless and dangerous and should not be given any quarter. One of the four tried running. He was gunned down with a complete lack of mercy.

Munrow surrendered quickly, suspecting, but never being able to prove, that Rider – who should have been the fifth member of the gang – had grassed on him. Subsequently he was jailed for nineteen years. This was the longest sentence even a judge who had been bribed could realistically run to. Even that had been a push to justify, but in his summing up he damned Munrow as a 'menace to society', 'evil', and other epithets. The promise of a villa on the Costa del Sol can work wonders, even to the judiciary.

From that point on, with Rider and Munrow out of the picture, Conroy flourished.

And so did his colleagues within the police force and local politics.

He pushed a new culture of cooperation, which was fairly easy to achieve because, using information provided by him, the police in the form of the newly established North-West Organised Crime Squad were able to round up, prosecute and jail most of his rivals. The ones who escaped the legal net were killed in a series of shootings for which no one was ever captured.

Within eighteen months of Munrow's convictions, Conroy controlled a string of council estates throughout East Lancashire, over a dozen clubs, fifty pubs and a few schools.

But, after eleven years of peace and prosperity, Conroy found himself facing the biggest threat to his empire ever.

Munrow was back on the streets after serving a little more than half his sentence. He had come out of Strangeways like a bad-tempered bear who wanted his porridge back.

He and Conroy had met to discuss things in an acrimonious encounter which achieved zilch. Conroy was not about to give him anything. Furiously Munrow had left, stating, 'Well, if that's your attitude, I'll take everything.'

He began to keep that promise.

That was problem one.

Then Dundaven had been arrested and there was the distant, but real possibility that police enquiries could end up on his doorstep. Problem two.

'Fucking aggravation,' he said out loud as he dived under the water. It was getting like old times.

Action needed to be taken.

He surfaced with a gasp, did the crawl to the edge of the pool and dragged himself out, showered, stripped and stepped into the sauna where things were very, very hot.

Twenty-two minutes after Conroy had arrived, the second member of the

117

trio drove up to the country club in a less conspicuous motor. Had the registered number been checked on the Police National Computer it would have revealed that the registered keeper was of 'blocked' status. This meant that information about the owner could only be passed over landline, not by radio, and only to police officers. This was often the case with vehicles used by the police for undercover work, particularly on specialist units. The computer screen would have also told the operator that this particular car belonged to the North-West Organised Crime Squad, based in Blackburn. It did not go on to say that the car was allocated to Detective Chief Superintendent Tony Morton for his exclusive use.

Morton parked up and went into the club by a side entrance, ensuring he didn't have to pass through Reception.

He went towards the pool where at the door he was faced by Conroy's two guards. He submitted bad-naturedly to their body search with a sneer on his face. Then he changed, showered and went directly to the sauna.

Conroy sat there naked and unashamed, sweat streaking down his body, his limp penis resting on his thigh like a pet.

Morton nodded to him, threw a ladle of water on the coals and hopped onto the top bench and laid out full-length.

Although Karl Donaldson had been offered FBI-owned accommodation in London, he had declined, choosing instead to live in the small town of Hartley Witney, about half an hour's train journey from the capital. It was also within minutes of Karen's workplace – the Police College at Bramshill – where she was seconded to the teaching staff.

Living in Hartley Witney meant early starts and late finishes for Donaldson, but the unhurried lifestyle and surrounding countryside made it worth the effort. One of the great pleasures in his life had come to be getting off the train at Winchfield, the nearest station to home, at the end of a long day to be greeted by Karen and driven home to their little rented cottage. It was like living in some sort of Noël Coward time warp. He loved it to bits. A stereotypical American's view of the English way of life, spoiled perhaps by the Jeep Cherokee he had bought so he could keep just a faint grip on America.

He allowed himself a late start that Wednesday morning, sleeping for almost twelve hours. It was after ten when he arrived at the FBI office in the American Embassy.

His chain-beaten appearance and black eye caused much interest, as did his story about Sam and her death. After a short conference with his colleagues he went to his desk with the intention of writing up a very detailed report and a strong recommendation that the matter should not rest there: a full investigation should be set up with the cooperation of the Portuguese authorities.

After that he intended to contact New York and set about finding out everything he could about Scott Hamilton.

Those were his good intentions.

What he hadn't bargained for was the multi-storey building of paper-work which had accumulated on his desk during his absence. It looked like he'd been away for six months, not a few days. He experienced a vague tinge of annoyance that someone else hadn't taken it on.

He shrugged. That was life in any office, he guessed.

His first instinct was to sweep all the papers off into a bin. Very, very tempting. He sighed and screwed his professional head on. He eased himself stiffly into his chair. His bones and body were still feeling bruised and battered. He took the top item from the pile and perused it.

Within minutes he felt as if he'd never been away from the place.

Half an hour later, the final member of the trio arrived. His car was the biggest, flashiest of all three – a Bentley Brooklands which had set one of his companies back just short of a hundred grand.

He wasn't too concerned about walking in through Reception and who might possibly spot him. He was a regular there, well-known to be a part-owner and believed he could be seen with whom he damn well liked.

The other two were sitting in opposite corners of the sauna.

Conroy was still naked, but Morton had a towel neatly folded across his lap, covering his dignity.

The third man burst in. He was completely naked, his large loose stomach hanging down over his pubes. He sat somewhere midway between the others.

'I think we've got problems,' Sir Harry McNamara said.

They adjourned to one of the plush conference rooms. A large picture window overlooked the golf course and beyond to the moors which swept away towards Bolton. On a clear day the view was magnificent. Today the weather had worsened and slanting snow reduced visibility to a matter of metres.

Coffee, sandwiches, biscuits and brandy had been brought in. A *Do Not Disturb* sign hung on the outside of the door – rather pathetically as no one would have countenanced disturbing them. The two apes with big bulges under their arms and sloping foreheads saw to that.

McNamara was doing the talking.

'I don't need to tell you both that things are reaching a critical stage here, and the last thing we need is to have our equilibrium rocked in any way.' He dunked a ginger biscuit deeply into his coffee, immersed it for a good few seconds to allow it to soak, then placed the whole soggy mess into his mouth. 'My part of the negotiations have gone extremely well and my contact – my very nervous contact – will be here soon to view the samples.' He sighed grimly and looked with undisguised scorn at Conroy. 'Only we don't have anything for him to look at, do we?'

119

'It was just fucking unfortunate that Dundaven got picked up,' Conroy snapped defensively.

'What were you thinking of, taking them to Blackpool in the first place?'

Conroy stiffened. 'You're the one who wanted them stashed well away from your warehouse, just in case. Rider's club seemed as good a place as any. I shouldn't have given the bastard any choice. I should've just told him I was going to use it . . . and, of course, those two guys turning up with shooters complicated matters, threw me off-course a bit, y'know?' He touched the side of his face. 'Having a gun stuck into the back of your head, then going off next to your ear ain't pleasant. My ear still rings like fucking chapel bells . . . It was a bad fucking day all round.'

'And that's another thing,' McNamara latched onto. 'What's the position with you and Munrow? We won't be doing business with anyone unless we can show we're in control. What's the current state of play?'

'I have no fucking idea at all. It's a waiting game. I don't know what his plans are. He's an unpredictable, dangerous twat.'

'Take him out,' said McNamara.

'Oh – like, yeah. Easier said than done. There's not many willing to go up against him.' Conroy turned his attention to Morton. 'Has that bastard Rider shot in the leg turned up yet?'

Morton shook his head.

'One big fucking cock-up, all this,' Conroy said in dismay. 'All at once.'

Quietly, Morton said to McNamara, 'Ron's not the only one who's got a problem, is he Harry?'

McNamara clammed up tight. He reached for the brandy bottle and tipped more than a generous measure into his coffee.

Conroy laughed. 'You haven't been picked up for kerb crawling again, have you, you daft cunt?'

Nothing came from the millionaire.

'Shall I tell him?' Morton said, who, when nothing came, went on, 'The police in Blackpool are investigating the murder of a prostitute. One by the name of Marie Cullen. Ring a bell, Ron?'

Conroy nodded and glowered sourly at McNamara. 'You haven't, have you?'

'She threatened to go to the press about our relationship,' McNamara blurted under pressure. 'She wanted money to keep quiet. She could have ruined me.'

'You mean she'd had enough of you beating the living crap out of her every time you fucked her. Is that what you mean, you sadistic bastard?'

McNamara placed his cup down. He rose from his chair and without warning plunged himself across the room at Conroy who was standing at the window with a drink in his hands.

They fell into a heap, McNamara's fists flying, rolling across the carpeted room, crashing into chairs. But, though McNamara was bigger

120

than Conroy, his technique was lacking badly and within moments he found himself face down on the floor, nose pressed into the shagpile, with Conroy's left hand pushing the back of his neck down. In his right was a switchblade which he pressed dangerously into the side of McNamara's neck.

'Don't ever try a fucking stunt like that again, or I'll skewer you like a pig,' Conroy panted heavily.

Morton pulled him away. 'Gents, gents,' he cooed.

Conroy released his grip and stood up.

Spitting phlegm, McNamara drew himself onto all fours and gasped, 'At least I'm not a little-boy shagger.' He wiped his face.

'I don't hurt them,' said Conroy.

'Gents, please! Come on, we've got problems to solve here, solutions to find,' Morton said with patronising smoothness. 'Let's not make things any worse than they are.' He helped McNamara to his feet. 'We've *all* got problems and we need to air them reasonably, otherwise we might as well go our separate ways . . . and in the long term that could do us all damage, knowing what we know about each other. We need a corporate approach here. Heads together.'

Conroy brushed himself off. The blade had disappeared.

McNamara returned to his seat, wheezing slightly, and lit a cigar.

'Point taken,' said Conroy.

'Harry?' Morton probed the tycoon.

Reluctantly the man nodded.

'Good, let's get on with it then.'

Conroy stalked moodily over to the window where he stood, arms folded, staring out at the snow.

To McNamara, Morton said, 'I'll do what I can to help you, Harry, but I've got to know one thing. Did you kill her?'

'Bitch deserved it,' McNamara spat.

Morton sighed. 'In that case, you do have a problem. A monumental one.'

'Why? Can't you do anything to get them off my back? That's what you're paid for, isn't it?'

'It's not so simple in this case. I don't hold any influence over the cops in Blackpool. I managed to get my team onto the newsagents killings because it's one of my men who ended up dead there and we need to control the investigation. But there's no way I can get anyone onto Cullen's murder . . . I couldn't justify it.'

'Shit,' said McNamara.

'And you're in a similar position too, Ron, but I might be able to get a couple of my people onto the Dundaven enquiry on the pretext that we've got an interest in him, just to keep a watching brief on it. That way at least I could pre-warn you of any developments in your direction.'

'I don't see it as that much of a problem. Dundaven won't talk. If he

121

does, I'll ensure he commits suicide on remand. My difficulty is getting a shitload of guns up here in time for the viewing.'

'No – you're wrong there,' Morton warned him. 'If finding guns was your only problem, you'd be laughing. Both your problems are much, much bigger than that.'

He had the rapt attention of both men.

'Your – *our* – problem is a very nosy, tenacious detective who doesn't quite know anything at all just yet, but given time, knowing him and his reputation, he's very much on the verge of discovery. And that problem,' said Morton, 'is called Henry Christie.'

Long hours hunched over a desk did nothing for the small of Karl Donaldson's back. Reading and writing in a completely ridiculous posture gave him severe pain in the lumbar region. Around lunchtime, having spent two hours sifting meticulously through the accumulated paperwork, he knew he should get up, stretch, have a walk round. Otherwise he'd be set like a statue in that position.

He leaned back creakily and rubbed his neck.

'I'm not cut out for this crap,' he said to no one in particular. 'Desk jockey.'

All this close-up work was playing havoc with his eyes too. He had a horrible feeling he might need spectacles soon. In his book that was the ultimate concession to the onset of middle age. That and a beer gut.

He ran a hand carefully over his face, touching the chain-mark, black eye and swollen jaw. The combination pulsated continually, even though he'd now succumbed to Nurofen. Suffering pain wouldn't bring Sam nor Francesca back to life.

He had almost reached the foothills of the mountain of paperwork. He quickly signed off an Intelligence bulletin from Madrid without reading it too carefully, then a name in one of the paragraphs caught his eye.

It was a surname: *Mayfair*.

The item referred to the fact that a sharp-eyed FBI operative who happened to be on a surveillance job at Madrid Airport had spotted two people whom he believed were the Mayfair brothers, Tiger and Wayne. They had arrived on a flight from Lisbon, both using assumed names and not travelling together. It was an unconfirmed sighting but the agent was reasonably sure it was them . . . the two men believed to be responsible for a number of contract killings throughout the US and Europe. Wherever they went, death seemed to follow, but as yet no law-enforcement agency had tied them evidentially to actual murders.

The item went on to state that a photograph of the two was to follow, taken by airport security cameras. Donaldson skimmed through the most recent Interpol bulletins from Portugal and saw nothing which would indicate that the Mayfair brothers had been active professionally.

He took a photocopy of the bulletin and updated the office file on the

Mayfair brothers as this was his responsibility.

Next on the pile was a teleprinter message. Donaldson read it and his eyebrows rose with pleasure on reading the name of the originator . . . *Acting DI Henry Christie* . . . which was why he read the whole thing a second time. He was glad he did. He picked up the message, cleared a space on his desk, pulled his portable PC towards him and logged into the FBI system.

'The way I see it,' Morton said pensively, 'this is a three-sided thing. Firstly, Harry, there's your angle: Christie's a digger, a stubborn guy who doesn't mind who he upsets. This means he'll be on your case until he cracks it, or it defeats him. My guess is that he'll crack it because it's nothing more than a run-of-the-mill murder case. He will get you, given time.'

McNamara winced and drew on his cigar.

Conroy cackled with laughter, which ceased as soon as Morton turned to him and said, 'And in your case, as Christie himself stated to me, he doesn't like people taking pot-shots at cops. If only for that reason he'll net you along the way.'

'Not a fuckin' chance.'

'He will,' Morton assured him. 'He's already searched all those premises and—'

'And found nothing. He's way off the mark.'

'Just practising his aiming.'

The three men were all now seated, in positions where they could easily see and hear one another. There was invisible tension in the room, caused mainly by Morton's assessment of Henry Christie and his abilities.

'And how does he affect you?' McNamara pointed at Morton.

Morton sat back and thought for a moment. 'Firstly, I'm pretty sure it was Christie who put the seeds into the mind of the unfortunate DC Luton about there being two gangs operating. Luton brought it up, but we laughed him out of the office. But it worried us. Then, last night, we found Luton reading through the witness statements we'd amended. I'm sure he was dealt with before he spoke to anyone else. Having said that, he seemed to be expecting Henry Christie at his front door, but that says to me they haven't yet talked.

'Which means that Christie doesn't actually know shit about anything yet, but him being the person he is, it won't take him too long to make connections . . . and then he becomes a problem for me, Harry, in answer to your question.'

'Then top him,' said Conroy. 'If he poses a threat, do him.'

'Yes,' McNamara agreed. 'We've done it before.'

'No,' said Morton firmly. He stood up and paced the room. 'We only take out police officers in exceptional circumstances. That's always been agreed. It causes too much interest. Too many people want those sort of murders solved. We only get rid of the people who know too much and who are likely to cause us immediate damage. People like Geoff Driffield and Derek Luton. They were both too near.'

'But you said he'd find out,' complained McNamara.

'Look, at this stage he knows fuck all,' the detective said. 'And if we kill him now there'll be so much heat that some bugger might crack. Two cops are already dead in Blackpool; one is still in ICU. If another one gets it . . .' He left the implication floating in the air like a bad smell and shook his head.

'Accident?' suggested Conroy.

'They need to be arranged,' Morton pointed out. 'Not easy to do without arousing suspicion.'

'Pay him off then,' said McNamara. 'Pay him to look the other way.'

'Mmm, I thought about that . . . but I know a little about Henry Christie because of that big mafia case he was involved in a while back, and I don't think money would work. He once turned down an offer of several million dollars to look the other way. He arrested the man who made that offer, saying he liked to be offered bribes because he enjoyed locking up the people who made them. So, no. That won't work.'

'Put the fear of God into his family.'

Morton looked sharply at Conroy. 'We don't intimidate wives and kids,' he said.

'So what then?' asked an increasingly irritable McNamara. 'I want the cunt off my back – now.'

'Well,' said Morton, 'he's a very talented detective.'

'Yeah, Detective Sergeant Perfect by all accounts,' said Conroy snidely.

Morton went on, 'A good investigator, bit of a ruthless touch, but straight as a dye . . . Think about it.'

Conroy was first to catch on. 'Just the sort of honest detective you'd want on your elite squad.'

'Exactly – and funnily enough, we have a vacancy for a Detective Sergeant right now. The last one died on the job.'

Chapter Twelve

Henry Christie's ears were not burning. He was far too busy to even contemplate that others could be talking about him, as once again his sleep pattern had been very much interrupted. It was past midnight when he finally got into bed, having spent much of the evening cruising the streets, seedier pubs and guest-houses in Blackburn with Lucy Crane to try and find some of Marie Cullen's colleagues who might be able to add a bit of background to the dead girl. It was a fruitless and frustrating night.

A uniformed cop knocking on his front door at 6.30 a.m. had been the precursor to another horrendous day in Blackpool.

Henry, in a deep, dreamless sleep, had been the only member of his family to hear the knocking, or at least the only one to respond to it. He dragged himself downstairs, feeling like the man in the toothpaste advert with halitosic-laden germs dancing a jig on his furred tongue.

When he opened the door his heart dropped. He thought he was about to be given bad news concerning Nina. He had phoned the hospital from home before going to bed and was told she had taken a turn for the worse: critical – likely to prove. Henry assumed the Police Constable was here to tell him the news personally. He steeled himself for the punch.

He expected an upper cut from the right.

The head-butt to the bridge of his nose caught him completely by surprise and toppled him over, figuratively speaking.

He had to make the PC repeat it three times because his brain refused to take it in.

Derek Luton dead? Found shot to death on his front doorstep? Looks like his brains have been blown out? Wife almost catatonic? Derek Luton? *Dead?*

Henry couldn't get his head round the enormity of it. Not enough sleep. Head's a shed. Too much going on in too short a space of time.

Degsy Luton dead?

Henry finally raced upstairs, threw on yesterday's gear, underwear included, then got into his car and drove directly to the scene, Luton's house in Blackpool north shore, which had not yet been touched by scenes of crime.

Yep, Henry could confirm it. He had had his brains blown out. What a fucking mess. Henry had to steady himself as a flash of memory snapped into his mind's eye – another world away, but still vivid and recurring – of a man who had had his brains shot out right in front of him.

He took a deep breath, pulled himself together and got to work – directing, delegating, informing those who had to be told, going into automatic crime-scene management. He was aware, again, that his acting rank meant that everyone was waiting for him and that as senior detective on the scene, he was in charge. It gave him a slight feeling of excitement and, if he'd been questioned about it, he would have admitted enjoying it. The role, that is. Not this particular situation.

Once everything was underway, he went next door to where Annie was being comforted by a policewoman and a neighbour. A GP had administered some calming drugs to her, with a prescription for more. The doctor was just leaving when Henry arrived.

He sat down next to Annie on the edge of the settee. Luton's widow stared blankly ahead, her fingers twisted into tight fists. A mug of tea, untouched, was on the coffee table.

'Annie,' he said softly. He placed an arm around her shoulder. She jumped as if she'd been pinched, looked at Henry and realised who he was. She turned into him, gripping him, burying her head into his chest. She released a wail-cum-scream which shook her whole being from head to toe and held on tighter to Henry as the tears began to pour out. Henry held on, too, making reassuring noises, stroking her hair and trying not to cry himself.

He spent much of the morning with her, not wishing to delegate this particular unenviable task to anyone else. Not that he was a great one for dealing with grief. Actually he was very poor at it.

In over six hours' gentle coaxing, Annie did not say anything which was of any use to Henry. She was a bubbling wreck, unable to string two words together without bursting into tears. Henry did not push. That would have been counter-productive. By the same token it meant the police were getting nowhere at a fast rate of knots. And Annie was the only witness they had at that moment in time.

Whilst Henry was grappling with the problem of having to draw information out from a distressed witness, another problem which he had wrongly assumed might have gone away reared its head in the form of an ugly skinhead called Shane Mulcahy.

Since his discharge from hospital, Shane had spent the last remnants of his and his girlfriend's dole money on a concoction of drink, drugs and a Chinese takeaway – this despite her protestations that they needed the money to buy food for them and the baby. He'd simply smacked her open-handed across the face, then given her a kick up the arse when she hit the floor. 'Don't fuckin' tell me how to spend our money.'

For fourteen hours he had been in a state of inebriation coupled with the combined whizz-bang effect of amphets and the monosodium gluta-

126

mate in the sweet-and-sour chicken. 'Near total bliss' would have been Shane's poetic attempt to describe his condition; however, there was little that was poetic about Shane and he chose to describe it as, 'Great, been outta my fuckin' 'ead.'

He awoke face down on the bare floorboards of the bedsit he shared with Jodie Flew and their offspring. His nose was pressed against the hard wood with dribble having collected in a pool around his cheeks. He wiped his face as he pushed himself into a sitting position. He felt rougher than a bear's arse – a comparison he often used because it suited his sense of humour – and in his mouth there was a taste he could not quite place: somewhere between vomit and sugar. A pain bolted across his head behind his eyes, like a surge of electricity between two electrodes. He swore.

It did not occur to him to wonder why he was on the floor. It was a position he often awoke to.

Jodie was asleep on the mattress.

The baby gurgled happily in a cot in the corner of the room. Shane heard it fart.

He tried to stand up. When he moved he winced. His lower abdomen felt as though a scalpel had been left in by the surgeon. But in comparison to the previous day, the pain was ebbing.

He dressed himself in the jeans he'd worn for the last two months – he was proud of their unwashed state – found a crumpled T-shirt underneath the TV set and put his denim jacket and stolen Doc Marten boots on. Ready for the day ahead. He left the meagre living accommodation without bothering to disturb Jodie or the baby. He didn't really want to have anything to do with either of them.

Next stop was his solicitor.

The stop after that was Blackpool Central police station.

It was busy at the enquiry desk. Lots of press and TV people seemed to have camped out there, covering the spectacular crime wave which was coursing through Blackpool that week.

Shane and his legal representative were kept waiting for twenty minutes. The skinhead became increasingly agitated. When at last the Civilian Public Enquiry assistant beckoned to him, he stalked across, leaned on the counter and put his aggressive face right up to hers. His red-raw eyes were wide and menacing, his features distorted into a snarl, examples of which had been captured by media photographs of skinheads many, many times over the years. 'I want to make a complaint of assault against the police, luv,' he said.

She recoiled in disgust from his pungent breath and body odour and the threat of violence. 'I'll get the Duty Inspector,' she said. Her nose was screwed up because there was a bad smell under it.

'So that leaves Munrow,' Conroy said. 'I mean, what's the fucking judicial system coming to these days? That bastard got nineteen years, f'fuck's

sake. Shouldn't nineteen *mean* nineteen? The guy is a menace to society –
and that's a quote direct from the judge himself.'

'That's what you paid him to say,' interjected McNamara with a laugh.
He was feeling better now that some action was going to be taken on his
problem.

'Yeah, he did a good job, God rest his soul. Pity we didn't have any
influence on the prison board,' whined Conroy. 'So,' he said, turning to
Morton, 'come on, Mister Problem-solver Extraordinaire – put your mind
to this one.'

'He either needs to be brought into the fold, rather like Henry Christie,
or possibly paid off – or eliminated,' Morton responded, counting his
fingers as he ticked off the choices.

'Well, I can't talk to the man. He makes me wanna stick an iron bar
around his head as soon as I see him, so the first one's out of the question,'
Conroy replied, using his own fingers. 'Secondly I don't want to pay him
one single chuffin' cent, so you can forget that one.' He held up three
fingers. 'I like the sound of the third option – kill the cunt.'

'But you've already said you haven't got anyone capable of going up
against him,' McNamara pointed out.

'Doesn't mean I don't want the bastard rotting in hell,' Conroy said
sullenly.

Silence descended on the room and the three men watched each other
thinking.

'He does need to be sorted,' Morton said. 'One way or the other, for the
sake of credibility. No one's going to do business with us if we can't keep
our house in order.'

They fell silent again.

McNamara lit another cigar. Morton poured a coffee. Conroy bit his
nails and played with his pony tail.

'How about a professional?' suggested McNamara.

'Be just my luck to hire an undercover cop. To be honest with you,
boys, I don't actually know any professionals, believe it or not. I know
people you can pay as little as five hundred dabs to. They're ten a penny
in Salford, and any nigger in Moss Side'll have a crack – but they're
all so fuckin' unreliable. Munrow would probably drop them first.
The only person I know who could do it properly, if he was wound up
enough, would be John Rider. But he doesn't want to get involved. He's
gone completely cuckoo. In his day I would've put him on a par with
Munrow, maybe above for being a violent sod. Now he's a bit of a wreck,
really.'

'He saved your life,' McNamara said.

'True, true.'

'If he had a reason to kill Munrow, do you think he would?' Morton
asked.

'What d'you mean?' Conroy looked puzzled.

128

'What I'm saying is – give him a reason and he might just do the job for you. But give him a reason. Quick.'

'This is getting to be Nightmare City,' said Detective Chief Superintendent Fanshaw-Bayley. He and Henry were walking down the rear yard at Blackpool police station. 'I appreciate you've got a lot on your plate at the moment, Henry, but you need to pull out the stops and solve this one PDQ. The Chief Constable is going berserk. Seems to be an open season on cops in this town this week and she wants results, like yesterday. And she's ordered two more ARVs into town to go high profile. I'm gonna bring Ronnie Veevers in to head this one.'

'You'd better throw resources at it,' Henry said. He'd once been the victim of FB's penny-pinching ways (or so he thought) and this time he didn't want to start out at a disadvantage. 'That's the only way you'll make progress on this one.'

'Is there any reason to think all these shootings are connected?' asked FB. They entered the ground floor of the station and walked towards the lift.

'It shouldn't be ruled out,' Henry ruminated, 'but so far I can't see a link.' The lift arrived eventually and they stepped into the small space. 'The DS in the newsagents; I don't know a great deal about it, but I'm pretty uncomfortable with what I know, but it's not my pigeon, thank God. Then Nina getting shot by Dundaven . . . now Derek. What could be the link? The only one I can think of is the North-West Organised Crime Squad. The DS was on it, Nina was shot by someone who was one of their targets and Derek was working along with them. And let's not forget the gorilla in the zoo which has generated more media interest than all three of those put together. Poor old Boris. Shot out of his tree.'

'Is the NWOCS linked to that one in some way?' asked a mystified FB.

Henry gave a short laugh. 'Not unless Boris was working undercover for them, too.'

'But other than Tony Morton's crew, there's really no connection – so far.'

'So far, no. Even the NWOCS's connection is clutching at straws. There's nothing to say that all three got shot because of their dealings with it. It just happens to be there, that's all.'

The lift rose to a creaky halt. They got out and walked into the CID office which was abuzz with activity, subdued chatter and some tears. Luton would be sorely missed. His enthusiasm had been infectious.

They walked to Henry's desk. He perched on the corner of it whilst he continued his conversation with FB.

'If we could make some connection it would be great, because then it would give us something to chip away at. But at the moment, they are three completely separate jobs. The DS in the newsagents, whatever the reason for him being there – and I'm sure it'll come out in the wash – was in the wrong place at the wrong time; Nina got shot because she was being a good cop and shit like that happens occasionally, comes with the territory... but as for Derek, I am completely stumped, boss. Maybe it was a burglary gone wrong, or one of his previous prisoners bearing a grudge against him. Maybe mistaken identity. Dunno. We'll have to look at all angles.'

He shook his head sadly. A wall of tears was building up inside behind his eyes when he thought of the wretched figure of Degsy Luton sprawled out in his hallway, head blown apart, brains, blood and bones on the carpet and up the wallpaper, all the way down into the kitchen. Grotesque and so very, very wrong.

'Basically no leads,' said FB.

'No.' Henry's mouth twisted bitterly. 'And as for Boris, I haven't even started on that one. That's gone well-cold. Fuck!' he said angrily. 'Anyway, perhaps when Annie comes down from her trauma she might be able to help – with Degsy, that is, not Boris.'

'Right,' said FB. He drummed his fingers on his thighs. He tapped his feet, bit his bottom lip and made a clicking sound in the back of his throat. FB's decision-making process was in action. 'Couple of things. Firstly, how far are you with Dundaven?'

'He should have been in Magistrates by now and remanded in custody. Nothing came of the raids, really. I personally think there's a long way to go with it yet – but as far as Dundaven himself is concerned, it's boxed off. He won't see daylight except through bars for a long time now.'

'Do you want to continue with it? Will it be worth it?'

Henry nodded. Actually he didn't have a clue if anything more would come of it, but he wasn't about to admit that to FB. 'I'd like to keep four detectives on it for a month and then reappraise it.'

FB considered this. Then, 'You can use two.'

Thanks a bunch, Henry wanted to say. 'And Derek?'

'Full team from this afternoon, unlimited overtime – within reason – for up to two months. Authorised by the Chief.'

Wow! Henry almost choked, so impressed was he. Then he remembered the implications so far as he was concerned. Because Inspectors did not receive overtime payments, he would earn nothing extra financially, but experience all the other drawbacks. Long hours. No sleep. So what else was new?

However, he held back the urge to grovel in front of FB and plead to be dropped down a rank. He had to look on the positive side of things. It was all good promotion-board material. Juggling three plates at once, having the responsibility to keep them spinning. He hoped he had the ability to stop them from crashing around his ears. 'Oh, jolly good,' he said.

FB lowered his voice and moved slightly closer to Henry. 'There is something else we need to discuss, and that's the other murder – the prostitute on the beach.'

'Oh?' said Henry guardedly. He had been expecting some repercussions, but even so he could not resist making one of those remarks which so often put him firmly in the bad books of his bosses. Mischievously he threw FB's quote back in his face. 'You mean the one who deserved what she got?'

The look on FB's face told Henry he'd hit a bum note. FB's eyes narrowed and he said, equally mischievously, 'Just remember one thing, Henry, if you go for promotion this year, I'll be on the other side of the desk, so don't be so fucking cheeky.'

'Fair enough.' Henry knew what side his bread was buttered on. 'So, what about her?'

'Two things. Firstly, because of Derek's murder I'm going to scale her enquiry down.'

There's nothing to scale down, Henry thought. He made no reply but his body language told FB exactly what he thought of that one.

'Henry, you and I both know we haven't got a million detectives to play with. It's a question of priorities and she's way down on the list.'

She'll be glad to hear that, Henry thought, but kept his mouth closed again. He stopped his foot tapping which betrayed his annoyance.

'Secondly, we've had a very irate ex-MP on the blower to Headquarters, shouting and bawling, demanding to speak to the Chief . . . no, she didn't . . . threatening to sue the living shit out of us. He actually got to speak to the ACC, Brian Warner, and told him you'd been harassing him, making false claims, suggesting he was the one who murdered the girl.'

'Never actually got to that stage.'

'Even so, that ex-MP, and you know who I mean, is one very powerful and influential person with friends in very high places. He needs careful handling.'

Henry cut in angrily. 'I won't compromise the search for a killer just so I don't upset some rich bastard who chums around with the great and the good.' He folded his arms haughtily.

'Henry,' said FB patiently, 'I'm not saying you should. Just watch him, that's all. Do everything by the book. Record everything. Justify every-thing. Watch your back, in other words – that is, if you're going to have any further dealings with him.'

'I will have,' said Henry. He had made that decision because of what FB had just told him. It particularly annoyed him when people like McNamara started throwing their weight around after being justifiably and reasonably dealt with by the police. 'In fact, I'm going to arrest him on suspicion of murder now because he's really got my "mad" up.'

FB groaned inwardly. 'C'mon, let's grab a brew.'

Henry stood up, brushed his rumpled clothing down. He needed a shower and a change. His underpants were notably uncomfortable.

Without bothering to check his desk he followed FB towards the lift. A typist walking the other way then dumped a bundle of newly typed reports and files onto his blotter; on top of that the Admin. Officer placed the remainder of the day's other correspondence.

The meeting concluded at 1.15 p.m., no Minutes having been taken, but certain agreements having been made. All three men were ready for their treats which were waiting in the reception foyer of the club. A fifteen-year-old boy – thin, wan and pathetic-looking – for Conroy; women for the other two. High-class hookers who were going to cost a lot of money.

Shadowed by the gunmen, the three wandered into Reception, their conversation much lighter and more relaxed than it had been. They talked about football and cars.

A man approached them.

Conroy's guards stepped in between. Their hands slipped inside their jackets, a simple gesture which carried a menacing message. They didn't seem to realise that had the man been a professional, they would all have been well dead by then.

But he wasn't.

His name was Saltash and he was a pimp. He preferred to be referred to as a 'procurer'. His business card stated *I Procure the Needs of People* on one side and *Procurer to the Professionals* on the other.

'It's OK,' Conroy said quickly, calming his jumpy bodyguards. His men became easy and drew aside. 'What've you got for us today, Saltash, you slime-ball?'

Like an over-attentive, smarmy waiter, Saltash bowed courteously and led them to his 'products' – another misnomer he liked to use.

'For you,' he said to Conroy. He indicated the young lad with the flourish of a magician. 'This is Gary . . . Gary, stand up.' Gary stood. He had a very spotty complexion and wore a sneer of contempt for Conroy. 'Meet Mr Conroy.'

Conroy smiled. He liked them to have a bit of spunk about them (his little joke).

Saltash continued, 'For you, Mr Morton, I've brought along Angela again – I know you like her and she adores you. Angela!' Saltash motioned with his thumb.

Angela rose. Tall, leggy, dark, mysterious. Aged somewhere between twenty-four and thirty-six. She was virtually lovely, but slightly raggy around the edges. She had a deep, grainy voice with a southern accent which made Morton's hair tingle. And she spoke dirty, especially when drawing breath during oral sex. Morton adored her. She thought he was a fool.

She slid her arms around his neck and kissed him. 'Baby . . . we need to fuck,' she whispered.

'And for you, Mr McNamara . . . Gillian.' Gillian was already on her feet. She was as tall as Angela but had much more of everything and she was black. She shook hands with McNamara whose face had already hardened into a cruel mask of lust.

Saltash's experienced eyes saw that all was OK.

'Usual prices?' Conroy asked. This was always his treat.

The procurer nodded.

'Usual services?'

Another nod of consent.

Conroy handed him an envelope. It was always a cash transaction. He looked at Gary who stood there looking bolshie. 'Get up those fucking stairs,' he hissed.

The defiant front wilted to one of passivity and acquiescence. Like a frightened dog, the boy did as he was told.

The other two men led their ladies upstairs.

As ever, three rooms had been put aside for their pleasure.

Saltash went into the restaurant and ordered a three-course meal with wine.

He thought he had a wonderful job.

The Duty Inspector hated what he was doing, taking a statement of complaint from a youth he knew to be a troublemaker, drug user and thief, with a string of convictions as long as a wet day in Fleetwood. It as a good test of the Inspector's interpersonal skills that he didn't get up, go round the table and complete the job Henry Christie had started a few days before, and rip Shane's one remaining testicle from its moorings.

'I shall pass these details onto the relevant people,' he explained to Shane at the conclusion. 'I shall tell our Scenes of Crime Department to come and visit you later today to get a photograph of your . . . um . . . operation scar and you will hear very shortly from the Discipline and Complaints Department, I expect.'

The Inspector then bit his lip as he handed Shane a leaflet about how to complain against the police and how complaints are subsequently investigated. He showed him out of the police station – together with his legal adviser – as though he was a valued customer who would receive the most favourable attention. *Please do call again.*

What riled the Inspector was that was exactly how the D & C Department would perceive Shane: a client.

It made him sick to his stomach.

But, that said, Henry had obviously gone too far.

All the enthusiasm had drained out of Henry when, twenty minutes after having been told – informally – of Shane's complaint against him, he sat down heavily at his desk. On top of everything else he was dealing with, the news had rocked him like a body blow.

He felt deflated and threatened.

The horrible spectre of a Crown Court appearance loomed ahead, with all its attendant publicity. As he sat there, head in hands, he decided that if he did end up facing a judge and jury, there were only two words he would say: 'Not Guilty.'

All he wanted to do was sit and cry, he was so depressed. The workload, long hours and lack of sleep over the last few days had taken their toll; today's additional weights – the violent death of Derek Luton, news that McNamara was making noises in high places, and the complaint from Mulcahy – were not far off being the last straw. The one that broke the detective's back.

'Right,' he said to himself. 'Let's get this into perspective.'

Firstly, a court appearance was the worst thing that could possibly happen. Most complaints filed against the police fizzled out and came to nothing. This one could be the same. Henry believed he had used 'reasonable force' in order to subdue Shane who had, after all, attacked him with a knife. It was more than likely that when the file of evidence was submitted it would come back with *No Further Action Recommended*. It was his word against Shane's. The only thing going against Henry was his stupidity in not filling in the custody record.

Secondly, McNamara did not intimidate him. In fact, Henry relished the prospect of taking on people in high places.

Thirdly, Degsy's killer had to be found and a Detective Inspector with his mind on other matters would not achieve this.

And fourthly, long hours and hard work killed no one. Or so it was said.

'Right,' he said again. 'Get a grip and deal with everything as it happens.'

However, it was with slothful reluctance that he took the top piece of paper from the pile on his desk and read it. Correspondence waits for no man. Failure to deal with it simply means more. It doesn't stop coming just because there are other things to do.

He began to deal.

The procurer drove his three products back to Blackburn later that afternoon. He delivered them to various locations. Gary asked to be dropped off near to the railway station. Angel was left outside a motel on the edge of town where Saltash had another client waiting for her. Gillian wanted to be taken home.

The whole journey had been unusually quiet. Normally the two girls were full of laughter and mischief whilst Gary, for his age, had a very inventive sense of humour. Today was different. They were all withdrawn, sullen and somewhat tense. Saltash was quite happy that there was no chatter. He was over two thousand pounds to the good – tax-free, of course – and each of his products had pocketed two-fifty plus whatever tips they had been given. That was their business.

Gillian was the last of the three to be dropped off. She had seemed unusually distracted; it was her mood that had rubbed off on the others.

Saltash stopped near to her council flat in Shadsworth on the outskirts of town.

'Here we go,' he said brightly. 'I'll pick you up here at ten tomorrow. Busy day, lots of dosh to earn.'

She was sitting in one corner of the back seat, her long legs drawn up underneath her, coat tucked in, staring blankly out of the window. The snow in Blackburn had turned into wet, sleety rain. Very unpleasant.

'Come on, Gillian, I want to get home,' he snapped when she did not get out straight away. He twisted round and cast his eyes back at her. Slowly her head turned away from the window and she looked into her pimp's eyes.

'He was Marie's main customer, wasn't he?' She wrung her hands.

Saltash's eyes dropped momentarily. 'That's none of your business.'

'He killed her, didn't he?'

'I don't know. Anyone could've killed the silly bitch. She was wild and stupid and probably got her come-uppence. But I'll tell you one thing, Gillian; if you go mouthing off what you've just said to me, I'll kill *you*. Understand?' He licked his lips.

A tear rolled down her cheeks. 'He degraded me today,' she said with a choked sob. 'And he talked about Marie when he did.'

'Listen, you brainless tart, you degrade yourself every fucking day by what you do. Hasn't that sunk in yet? You make good money pandering to the whims of pathetic, rich men, so don't knock it, babe. In five years you'll have enough to pack it in – but if you want to go now and work for tuppence ha'penny at a supermarket check out, then fine, fuck off and do it. But don't moan to me because a customer's a bit kinky. Goes with the show, girl.' He pointed animatedly at her as he spoke.

'And Marie? Does that go with the show? Ending up dead on a beach?'

'Maybe,' he said cruelly.

'I thought you were supposed to protect us?' she cried.

He had no answer.

'Oh fuck you!' she yelled into his face, opened the car door and emerged into the sleet.

Walking across the pavement she could still feel the sore places on her ankles and wrists where he'd tied the ropes to pin her to the bed. That she could handle. Many did that. It gave them a sense of dominance. What she found impossible to deal with was the cold knife-blade which McNamara had touched against the lips of her vagina and threatened to ram in.

Just like he'd done with that other poor bitch.

The phone rang. Henry grabbed it, delighted by the distraction.

'Henry, you old son of a b,' came the ebullient American accent down the line.

He brightened up immediately. 'Karl, how ya doin'?'

'Nice-ish,' said the FBI agent. 'I guess you heard about Sam.'

'Karen phoned Kate the other night and mentioned it. Sorry to hear about it. She was a nice person.' Henry had met her the once on that weekend trip to the Lake District.

'Murdered.'

'Really?'

'Yep. Can't prove it, but I'll try. You know me.'

'Certainly do. Anyway, pal, business or pleasure?'

'Well, it's always a pleasure to do business with you, Henry,' the American said genuinely.

'Karl . . . you're making me blush. Now cut the crap.'

'OK. Been reading a routine circulation of yours re the seizure of some firearms after a shooting up on your manor . . . manor – is that the right phrase, bud?'

'More a Metropolitan term, but it'll do. So, what about these firearms?'

'They're part of a haul from a break and enter at a warehouse in Florida, just outside Miami. Two months ago. One heck of a haul too: machine guns, rifles, pistols, bazookas, SAM's . . . you name it, plus the ammo to go. Several million dollars' worth. Enough to equip a small army.'

'From Florida?' Henry said, astounded. 'What the hell are they doing in Lancashire then?'

'Who knows?'

'You coming up here then, Karl?'

'Naw, not for a while anyways, but I'll do my best from down here to help you with information, as and when – or if – I get it. For the time being I'll fax you all the details of the haul. Maybe you should have another word with your suspect? Then I'll speak to the Miami Field Office to see what else they can tell me about it.'

They chatted on for a few more minutes before concluding the call. Henry, cheered by the news and the conversation, picked up the last piece of correspondence and found himself humming *Starfucker*. The tune stopped abruptly when he saw the post-it sticker slap bang in the middle of his blotter. He ripped it off and read it.

In the precise way Derek always operated, the note was timed – 10.15 p.m. – and dated.

It read, *H. Need to speak to you urgently. Found something well odd.* It was signed *Degsy.* Then a P.S. *I'll be at home. Whatever time you get back, call me or come round, WHATEVER TIME!! It's urgent. D.*

Within seconds, Henry was hurtling down the stairs.

The line was very bad. Donaldson had to listen very intently through the static to hear the voice at the other end. It didn't help that the person was speaking in a Portuguese accent and was calling from Madeira.

'Special Agent Donaldson?'

'Yeah. Sorry, you'll have to speak up. I can hardly hear you.'

'It is me, George Santana, speaking from Funchal.'

'Oh, hello,' said Donaldson slightly more formally. He rated the

Maderain detective very low on the Richter Scale following his experiences in that country, but was obviously very interested in why he should be ringing. He was the last person Donaldson expected to hear from, and quite honestly had grave doubts about the man's professional ability. He'd concluded, from very little evidence, that either the guy was not a 'real' detective, with no feel for a case, or he was on the take. Or both.

With a startlingly loud crackle which nearly burst his eardrum, the line cleared. Then they could have been conversing in adjacent rooms.

'Ahh, that's better.'

'Yes, I can hear you well, also,' said Santana. 'I have some news for you about the person who was arrested for the assault upon you.'

'Uh-hu, Romero,' nodded Donaldson. His fingers automatically touched the chain-track across his cheek. He expected the worst: he'd escaped, or been released without charge, been given a pardon. Something along those lines.

The news stunned him.

'He's dead. He was found hanging in his cell in the prison where he was being held pending court. It was very suspicious.'

That's handy, Donaldson thought cynically. Another possible witness found dead, unable to testify.

'That is not all,' Santana continued. He sounded out of breath. 'The one we believed to be Romero's partner in crime is dead also. He was found floating in the harbour near to the ferry. Throat cut from ear to ear. Of course we do not actually know if he worked with Romero when you were attacked—'

'Yes we do, George,' the American snarled.

'OK, OK, we do,' Santana submitted.

'Why tell me all this, George?'

'Because I have been obliged to think long and hard about this. I admit I was very unconvinced about Agent Dawber's death being of a suspicious nature. However, following the other girl's death, then the man in the harbour, then Romero – who we are not convinced hanged himself, I believe there is more to this than meets the eye.'

'Hooray,' Donaldson could not resist saying. He held back from blasting out that it had taken two more deaths for it all to be taken seriously.

'There is also more,' Santana said. From the tone of voice, Donaldson could visualise the sheepish look on his face. He waited for it.

'The samples taken from under Agent Dawber's fingernails?'

Donaldson's gut wrenched. 'Yes?'

'Human tissue. It looks like she scratched somebody's face.'

Donaldson closed his eyes and fist in celebration. Thank God he made the pathologist take the samples!

'We are unable to match with DNA from here, regrettably.'

'Send me the sample. I'll get it done.'

'We've yet to find any hard evidence against anyone at this stage. The

137

result of the analysis of Agent Dawber's blood shows a high alcohol content – which doesn't help you, I'm afraid.'

'Take a good long look at Scott Hamilton at the Jacaranda. He's the connection.'

'Exactly what we are doing. He is now under twenty-four-hour surveillance.'

Annie was deeply distressed. It manifested itself in different ways. She moved from almost violent hysteria to a silent, trance-like state in a flash. Tears flowed, dried up, burst again. One moment she was on her feet, the next sat down, head buried in a cushion, trying to deal with the enormity of the situation.

She had returned to the house, in spite of others urging her to stay out. She wanted to remain *in situ*, in the home she and Derek had created in the six months of their wonderful marriage. To stay with memories which, with the exception of the final one, were good ones. She wanted to touch the things they had owned, bought and paid for together with their hard-earned cash.

The hallway was being inspected by a forensic team. Two scientists clad in white plastic suits were crawling about, lifting fibres, scraping up blood; a scenes of crime officer was daubing excessive amounts of grey fingerprint powder all over shiny surfaces, leaving dirty marks that would be hell to clean later. They were finding little. It had been a very clean kill.

The house would never be the same again, physically or spiritually.

Annie was in the lounge with her mother and a male police officer who had replaced the policewoman. Both seemed to have no clue what to say or how to deal with her.

She was in the middle of one of her trance-like states. Her eyes stared unseeingly at the gas-fire from her position on the settee. Heavy rain lashed against the window. Snow doesn't last long in Blackpool.

Henry sat next to her.

'Annie? I need to ask you some questions. Important questions. Things we need to know quickly. Annie?' He found it hard to tell if he was getting through to her. 'Annie, do you hear what I'm saying?'

No response.

He laid a hand softly on her shoulder. She shivered and came back from wherever she'd been, blinked at him for the first time in the half-hour he'd been there. He kept her gaze locked into his. 'Annie, we need to talk.'

She swallowed, nodded and ran the back of her hand across her nostrils and sniffed up.

'What did Derek say when he got home from work last night?'

She screwed up her pretty face and tried to concentrate. Her brain was making this difficult. She put a hand on his and squeezed it, then collapsed against him. Deep sobs shook her whole being, like a monster struggling

138

to free itself from inside her. Henry put his arms around her. She crushed her face into his chest and cried.

In twenty minutes she'd cried herself out.

For the moment.

Henry's shirt and tie were soaking wet, a mix of tears, snot and saliva.

Annie sat upright. Henry handed her a paper handkerchief. She wiped her face with it and blew her nose.

'Questions,' she stated. In answer to his look, she said, 'Ask them now, Henry, while you've got the chance. I'm in control of myself at the moment. Not sure how long it'll last.'

'What did he say when he got home last night?'

'Very little.'

'Did he seem his normal self?'

'No . . . odd, distracted.'

'He must have said something, Annie.'

'Kept muttering about a statement, how he couldn't believe it. He'd been there, yet it was different, changed . . . something like that, anyway. He was waiting for you to call. He was sure you would. I didn't know what he was on about.'

'He'd left a note on my desk, but I went straight home last night. I didn't go into the office.' Like maybe I should have done, Henry thought agonisedly. Then: Fuck that for a thought. What's done is done. 'And what happened after that?'

'We went to bed round about midnight. He read for a while, then he was tossing and turning, going to the loo. I was aware of it, but I was asleep. D'you know what I mean, Henry?'

He nodded.

Annie stopped talking. He hoped she wasn't about to weep again.

'I don't remember anything else,' she said faintly.

'Think, Annie,' he encouraged her softly. 'It could be important.'

She stood up and crossed to the window, staring at the rain. There were two police cars and a van outside. The whole of the garden had been taped off. Officers from the Support Unit were on their hands and knees, searching for evidence in what was quickly becoming a quagmire.

'There is something,' she said eventually. 'He got up. I mean, obviously he got up or he wouldn't be dead now. Hang on, hang on, let me get a grip.' She put her head into her hands and pummelled her forehead with the base of her hands, wracking her brain, shimmering with frustration. She turned to Henry again. 'Yes, that's it. He got up. Someone was knocking on the door. He went to the window. He said it was two o'clock. Then he went downstairs. I turned over and went back to sleep.' Her eyes rested accusingly on Henry. 'He thought it was you at the door. He thought you'd come to see him . . . only it wasn't.'

Her face creased like a screwed-up ball of paper.

'Did he bring anything home with him?' Henry asked quickly.

'I don't know.' Her bottom lip, her whole chin quivered. She was trying vainly to keep control, but was slowly losing the struggle.

'Annie, we need to have a look through his things. There could be something to help us. May we?'

'Yes, sure, but someone's already done that.'

'What?' said Henry, perplexed. 'Who?'

Annie didn't know.

Henry turned to the policeman. 'Who?' he demanded.

'Two detectives from that lot in Blackburn.'

'The Organised Crime Squad?'

'Yeah, them.'

'We couldn't find anything, boss,' Siobhan Robson said to her Detective Chief Superintendent.

'What sort of a search did you do?'

She sighed with frustration verging on anger. 'Cursory – that's all we could do. We couldn't very well tear the place apart, could we? It would have looked a bit too suspicious.'

'Maybe he didn't have anything with him.' This was a suggestion made by a Detective Inspector called Gallagher, who had been with her during the search.

'Oh he did, I'm sure of it. Copies of the original statements at least. That's what the little bastard did – made copies, as we have seen from his locker. So where the hell are they? We need to find them – soon. And my bet is that they're in his house – somewhere.'

Henry stormed into the murder incident room. Two policewomen were inputting details into the HOLMES terminals. DC Robson and DI Gallagher were in deep, muted conversation with Tony Morton. As Henry closed in on them, they looked up and stopped talking. A smile appeared on Morton's face.

'Henry, good to see you. I've been looking for you.'

Henry liked and admired Morton. He thought he was a good cop who got results. But at that moment in time, Henry was enraged and when something annoyed him, his mouth had a nasty habit of speaking quicker than his instincts for self-preservation.

Without courtesy, he launched into a tirade of invective which stopped all activity at the HOLMES terminals. 'What the fuck right do you have to go rummaging about in Derek Luton's belongings for? Not only have you been heavy-handed about it and upset his widow, you could easily have tainted valuable evidence. You had no right, no fucking right.'

Morton's false smile fell from his face instantaneously. His expression hardened.

'And you, DS Christie, have no right, no *fucking* right whatsoever, to

140

talk to a senior officer like that. I've a good mind to slap you on paper, but from what I gather, discipline enquiries are not unknown to you.'

'I personally don't give a flying fuck what you do, Mr Morton. You and your élite squad of wankers are bang out of order. We'll probably never know what damage you've done. What the hell were you looking for that was so important anyway?'

Gallagher, the DI, who had silently witnessed the exchange, cut in. 'I can answer that, boss. After all, it was me who went to the house with DC Robson here. We thought he'd gone home with some important documents that we needed for this investigation. Some house-to-house logs he'd been doing.'

'House-to-house logs?' said Henry incredulously. 'What the hell was he doing on house-to-house? That's for numties!'

'He was assigned to my murder squad, and how I use my officers is my business, not yours,' Morton said stiffly. 'Now, Henry,' he went on placatingly, 'if we've trodden on your toes, we apologise, but we needed to find what he had. We did it carefully and with consideration and compassion for Mrs Luton's feelings. There's no chance we spoiled any evidence and if you feel Craig and Siobhan here were heavy-handed, I'll go round and see Mrs Luton and apologise. How's that?'

Shut up Henry, he told himself. Take a breath. Count to ten. This man's a Chief Super. He can knee-cap you if he wants.

'All right,' Henry accepted. 'Did you find the logs?'

'No,' said Gallagher. 'We'll simply have to revisit all those homes again.'

'Unlucky,' Henry could not resist saying.

There was a moment of strained silence. Gallagher's eyes narrowed slightly as he weighed Henry up.

The smile that was originally on Morton's face reappeared. To his two officers he said, 'Leave us,' and flicked them away with a wave of his hand. Gallagher nodded. He picked up a pile of papers, his eyes never leaving Henry's. Siobhan smiled nicely at him. Then they both went.

The two HOLMES operators resumed their tasks.

'Now then Henry,' said Morton. 'Come and sit over here.'

He guided Henry to two chairs next to a table on which was a coffee filtering machine. Henry smelled the rich aroma of a newly brewed pot and his body demanded a cup. Fortunately Morton poured one for him. He handed him the cup and both men sat down.

'I'll come straight to the point, lad. As you know, life goes on in this job of ours. When a vacancy arises, it gets filled, however it occurred. And sadly we now have a vacancy on this squad.'

'You mean Geoff Driffield – your guy in the newsagents?'

Morton nodded. 'We need people of a high calibre, as you well know. We have an enviable reputation of crime-busting to maintain and only the best will do for us.'

He regarded Henry with meaning.

'You mean me?'

Morton nodded. 'You fit the bill. I want you on the squad.'

Chapter Thirteen

A certain club in Manchester city centre on the periphery of China Town played host to John Rider that evening. He arrived shortly after eleven and established himself in a position at the bar which gave him an unobstructed view of everyone entering and leaving. He ordered a pint of Boddington's bitter as a gesture to Manchester, and after a long satisfying swig, began to sip it slowly.

The whole place was a dive. An unprepossessing doorway at street level, which could easily be missed, led down a tight set of steps into the foyer. The cashier was in a booth protected by armoured glass and two bouncers stood nearby – dinner-jacketed, bow-tied, black-shoed, fingers interlocked at groin level, thumbs circling.

The admission was five pounds – cheap for Manchester – the facilities limited and the drinks expensive. They were served from a three-sided bar. The dance floor was minute, or intimate depending on your point of view, and music pounded down from speakers suspended precariously from the ceiling. The disco lights ensured it was difficult to see the fixtures and fittings, which were in poor condition. Carpets were tatty, walls peeling.

Just like Rider's own club, money needed to be spent.

But unlike Rider's, the place was packed with punters.

Rider saw her arrive. Toni Thomas.

She was stunning. Long blonde hair, beautifully made-up face, off-the-shoulder strapless dress in glistening blue which stopped just below decency to reveal long shapely legs in silver stockings. The front of the dress plunged into a cleavage to be proud of.

She came in and drifted around the place like a goddess. All eyes followed her progress. She waved with soft gestures, acknowledged looks with pert smiles, some flirting, dainty laughter.

She was beautiful.

Rider almost fell for her there and then.

Toni Thomas, the person who in the last fifteen years had been Munrow's accountant and who Rider believed had kept some of his businesses going for him whilst he was inside. The legitimate ones, that is – the off-licence and the two launderettes. The person who might know where Munrow was to be found.

Because Rider wanted to pay him a visit.

He watched her smooch onto the dance floor with a man. The music had turned slow and sensuous. She unashamedly rubbed her genital area up and down the man's thigh, kissed him, touched his backside and squeezed his balls. His face was a picture of ecstasy.

When the music went up-tempo they came off the floor hand in hand, then parted company.

Toni went towards the toilets, straight past Rider without noticing him.

He put his glass down, slid off the bar stool and pushed his painful way through everyone to the Gents.

The toilets were apparently empty.

They were grim and unsanitary. The urinals were cracked and germ-laden. The cubicles looked ready to collapse like a house of cards. The stench hit Rider's nostrils. His face curled up in disgust.

Only one of the cubicles had the door closed.

Rider crept softly along the tiled floor, stopping outside the cubicle. He could hear rustling inside and some softly spoken whispers.

Two voices. Toni was not alone.

Rider laid a hand on the door and tested it gently. Locked.

For a moment he hesitated and thought about his actions. Something he would not have done ten years earlier.

He knew the soft approach would be useless. The only time for questions would be when Toni's head was being forced down the U-bend of the toilet and she was almost drowning in shit. Violence was the only method these people knew how to respond to. The quiet word, the exchange of pleasantries, was alien to them. Seen as spineless. But to have your head rammed down a bog, boy, they really understood and responded to that.

Rider nearly turned away and went home to his poxy little bedsits and his dreams of a big-time strip club. That's where he knew he should be, where he felt comfortable. This world wasn't his any more. He'd grown out of it.

Then he steeled himself and tried to forget the pain his body was still experiencing.

He was going to do it.

Shuffling back a few paces, he kicked the cubicle door open. It flew back with hardly any resistance and revealed the sordid tableau beyond.

Toni was kneeling in front of a man who was sitting on the toilet, his trousers down around his ankles. It was a different guy to the one on the dance floor. His hard cock was three-quarters out of sight in Toni's mouth. Very quick work. Must have been a pre-arranged tryst.

Toni kept the prick firmly where it was, as though interruptions like this were commonplace. With her mouthful she turned and looked side-ways up at Rider. She recognised him immediately. The organ popped out of her mouth and swayed unsteadily in her hand.

Rider waded in.

He reached across Toni, grabbed the shirt-front of the man on the toilet, and with no great effort – because the man was small and slightly built – lifted him bodily off the pan. He dragged him out of the cubicle and propelled him towards the Gents door, trousers around his ankles, penis having deflated instantly, now a shadow of its former self. He fell to his knees.

'Fuck off out of it,' Rider's voice said in a tone not much louder than a whisper. 'Now, if you know what's good for you.'

The man didn't argue. He jacked up his trousers and bolted.

Rider knew he had only a short time.

He stepped menacingly into the cubicle where Toni was hanging onto the toilet bowl as if she'd been violently sick in it. Her big blue eyes looked fearfully up at Rider; ten years ago she had lived in absolute terror of him and now he'd come back to haunt her. He had been very cruel to her in those days. Treated her badly, verbally, and once physically abused her. He had made it clear he despised people like her. And Munrow had laughed and failed to protect her. All he was interested in were her numeracy skills, otherwise she could be treated badly by anyone. He hadn't cared a fuck. She'd hated Munrow, but stuck it because the money and hours suited her lifestyle.

Quickly Rider snarled, 'You have a choice, Toni. Answer my question now, or I smash your beautiful face to fucking pieces . . . *then* you answer.' As he spoke, Rider knew he'd gone soft. In the few seconds since making the decision to act with violence and then going into action, he'd already backed off. Ten years ago her head would have been down the toilet already.

'Where is Munrow?' he asked, eyes blazing at her.

'John, I don't know. I haven't seen him since he came out,' she cried. Her voice was deep, gravelly and could arguably have been described as sexy. Tears appeared in her eyes. 'Please don't hurt me.'

'You had the choice.' Rider grabbed her hair with the intention of pulling her head back before driving it into the porcelain. He'd forgotten she wore a wig and all that happened was his hand came away with a finger-load of blonde silky hair. 'Fuck!' he hissed and threw it over the partition into the next cubicle where it landed with a splash in an unflushed toilet.

Toni cowered. She huddled in the corner with both hands covering the embarrassment of the short cropped hair underneath. She started to cry with short, jerky whimpers.

Rider stood back. 'Tell me where he is and I'll leave you alone. I don't want to hurt you, but I will, Toni.'

Through her tears, she informed him.

'Sensible fella,' Rider said. He couldn't resist patting her head patronisingly. 'By the way, get a better razor. I can still see your five o'clock shadow, even under all that make-up.'

145

Seconds later Rider was pushing his way towards the club exit. Racing in the opposite direction were the two bouncers, on their way to break up the reported fight in the toilets.

Once outside, Rider breathed deep. He was relieved to be out of that atmosphere and the clientèle in particular. Call it prejudice, he thought, but I hate transvestites.

The pub was situated in the Little Harwood area of Blackburn, about two miles from the centre of town. Twelve men had assembled in the back room. One of them stood at the door in order to prevent any unsuspecting member of the public from bursting in. The remainder sat facing the large TV screen, watching the live transmission of a Blackburn Rovers match on Sky. The Rovers were one down.

A serving hatch connected the room to the bar, but all the necessary drinks had been bought and the shutter had been drawn and bolted down. This business had to be conducted privately.

Charles Munrow pushed himself out of his seat and walked across to the TV. He switched it off. Silence descended on the room.

The other men watched him nervously. They were all tough, uncompromising individuals, but Munrow left them standing in terms of sheer brutality and animal violence.

He was nothing special to look at.

He wasn't six foot six with a scar across his cheeks, tattoos on his arms and built like a brick shit-house. He was very average-looking. Five-ten. Firmly, but slimly built, with a pinched, unfriendly face with very closely cropped grey hair. Nothing stood out, except that aura which warned without speaking.

In the days of the triumvirate of Munrow, Rider and Conroy, Munrow had been the most violent out of the three. Conroy would rather have had someone else to do his dirty work; Rider needed the right set of circumstances to light his blue touch paper, otherwise he was a pussy cat.

During armed robberies it was always Munrow who would shoot some poor bastard Group 4 guard's foot off. Just for the hell of it. Always him, when arguing, who would pull a triple-edged Stanley Knife blade and swish it across somebody's cheek. Cuts like those were impossible to stitch.

He had been brought up to be violent and loved it.

In the end he was the only one of the three who went to prison. It would have been him eventually anyway.

Eleven years in Strangeways had done nothing to soften his approach to life. He came out with a vengeance and the idea that he'd pick up the pieces where he'd left them. Assume his rightful position in gangland – at the top.

Things had changed dramatically.

The gangland he knew no longer existed. With the glaring exceptions

146

of Moss Side and Salford, it was all much more subtle and organised. Now the buzzwords were 'compromise' or 'negotiation' or 'strategies'. Words Munrow did not understand.

When he approached Conroy expecting to be let back in, he found the door wedged shut. He quickly saw the reality that he was not wanted any more.

All he had left was a rundown off-licence and two poxy launderettes which were throwbacks to the 1970s. Most people had their own washing machines now. Who on earth wanted to use a scruffy launderette?

He was virtually broke and needed to get back into the mainstream.

Which he decided to do by violence.

Munrow cast his eyes around the room. Some of the men were contacts from another era who had been left behind, like him; some were young bucks who wanted a chance to prove themselves. All were capable of murder. What's more, all were willing . . .

They were to be the nucleus of his new business team.

Munrow opened his mouth. Prison life had put an even harder edge on his tobacco-stained vocal cords. Behind every word he spoke there was the hint of a cough ready to break. He lit a cigarette, took a deep drag and spoke whilst the smoke was in his lungs.

'We control the doors,' he said gruffly. 'We control the drugs in and out. Simple, innit?' Smoke drifted lazily out through his nostrils and mouth. 'And tonight we're gonna make inroads into this problem of the doors. I don't want nothin' fancy. Just hard and fucking violent. We do three clubs tonight. Two at the same time – midnight – and the third, all of us together, at quarter to two. Dennis, are the cars ready?'

Dennis nodded. He was one of the balaclava twins who had dealt with Rider.

'Is everybody tooled up?'

Heads nodded. They were eager to go and get some action.

'Good. This should be fucking easy. They're all tarts on the doors these days. They won't be expecting us and we do 'em good and proper. In and out. Don't waste time. Make your point, then leave before the cops, or anyone else, has time to get there. And don't use shooters unless absolutely necessary . . . we'll leave that for later when we all get together.'

The bedroom upstairs at the back of the pub smelled of beer. From the plug-hole in the cracked sink emanated the unmistakable whiff of blocked drains. The walls were damp, paper peeled off, adding to the aroma.

There was another stronger smell in the room: that of decaying human flesh.

The room was an unhealthy environment for anyone to be in, let alone someone who'd been shot in the leg and had received no medical treatment for the wound.

Such as in the case of Jonno, the young man who had been shot by

147

John Rider a few days before at Blackpool Zoo.

He was lying in a flimsy metal-framed camp bed. He had drifted into unconsciousness again, a blissful state for his body which could no longer tolerate the excruciating pain from the badly infected wound.

Sat next to him on a stool, leafing through an old *Woman's Own* was the man Rider had quickly christened as 'Curly'.

Munrow came into the room.

The stench hit him, clawed its way up his nose. Gangrene. He gagged and covered his nostrils with his hand. 'How's he doin'?'

'Not good. Needs a doctor.'

Munrow eased the blood-stained sheet off Jonno's body and exposed the leg. The true aroma of the wound whooshed up towards him like an invisible swarm of flies.

The leg was in very bad condition.

The bullet had lodged in the outer part of Jonno's right thigh and the wound had quickly putrefied even though it had been repeatedly washed and cleaned. Now it was turning green and mouldy-looking, like Gorgonzola, and this was spreading rapidly through the muscles and into his groin. At the very least Jonno had lost his leg.

Munrow had been very reluctant to send Jonno to hospital or get a doctor to see him. That meant questions. Questions meant answers. Answers meant cops.

In the old days he would have brought in a friendly, paid-for GP. Now Munrow didn't have the contacts.

Jonno moaned and smacked his lips, which were dry and flaking. His almost-transparent eyelids flickered open a fraction. He mumbled something that made no sense. Sweat rolled off his forehead. He was burning up inside. His eyes closed wearily. He turned his head to the wall.

'What we gonna do?' Curly asked.

Munrow's cold eyes looked sideways at Curly. 'Dump him.'

Just after midnight Conroy was watching a pornographic video which had a weak and predictable storyline centring on the punishment of young schoolboys and occasionally their masters.

He was at his house in Osbaldeston.

Two bodyguards and their girlfriends were lounging about downstairs, probably snorting cocaine. Two more security guards and their Alsatians roamed the grounds outside.

Conroy was in the master bedroom, lying splayed out naked on the bed. His long hair had been freed from its pony tail. The huge TV monitor in the centre of the room was showing the video. He masturbated himself slowly throughout the feature presentation. Having watched the film a dozen times beforehand, it was his intention to hold himself back from shooting his load until the climax of the film, during a mass rape scene at the end.

148

It was one hell of a good film, calling for full audience participation. And it was nearing the end.

Six trouserless boys were led uncomplaining into the headmaster's study and told to bend over and touch their toes.

The headmaster picked up his cane and flexed it. The camera pulled back to reveal that he wore no trousers himself and was sporting a huge erection. Conroy quickened his pace. In a moment the police would swoop and the real fun would begin.

The phone next to his bed rang shrilly.

With a snarl of annoyance he picked it up, thankful he had not reached the point of no return.

'Yes? What the fuck do you want?' he barked.

'Boss . . .' It was one of his guards. 'We got trouble in town. Two of the clubs have been hit.'

'What?' he screamed. 'Who by?'

'The Thunderpoint and the Electric. All the doormen have been trounced.'

So it wasn't the cops.

Conroy abruptly lost his appetite for self-fulfilment and young boys on film. He picked up the remote and pointed it at the TV, blacking out the favourite part of his favourite movie.

'Get a car sorted. I'll be down in five. Get tooled up just in case.'

Conroy and his men were in Blackburn less than twenty minutes later. They went straight to the Electric which was within spitting distance of the railway station and was formerly a cinema.

He did not actually own the club outright, but held a fifty-one per cent stake in it, the remaining forty-nine per cent divided between Morton and McNamara through a complex series of financial manoeuvrings which kept their ownership as secret as possible. Conroy covered the door with his own men and this ensured that only his dealers had access to the clientèle and therefore he had a stranglehold on the drug trade inside. The Electric was not a big club, holding a capacity of two hundred. Nevertheless he cleared about £1500 per week through it in drugs money alone.

It was very rare for him to put in a personal appearance at such a low level. He tried to keep his distance from the streets these days.

Dundaven usually dealt with things here and Conroy was a tad uncomfortable as he sat in the manager's office and glowered at the head doorman who sat on the couch, a towel pressed into a nasty gash on his cranium. He had escaped lightly. The two other doormen had been whacked into oblivion and taken to hospital by ambulance.

The cops had been and gone, fobbed off by the manager, by the time Conroy arrived.

'What happened?'

'We didn't stand a chance,' the doorman whined. 'They pulled up

149

outside, two cars, three in each, balaclavas on. They were into us before we could do fuck-all.'

Conroy sighed. Men in balaclavas. Right up Munrow's street. 'And . . . ?' he urged the man on impatiently.

'And they beat the living crap out of us with baseball bats or pick-axe handles – I don't know which. You don't really care when you're being clonked. They both fucking well hurt.'

'Why weren't you ready? I thought protection was your job. It's what you're paid for, isn't it?'

The doorman looked sourly up at him. 'Ready? Give us a break,' he said. Although he knew he was talking to the boss, the pain in his head made him angry. 'Why should we be ready for that?'

'Because I fucking pay you to be ready, you fucking wanker! Where were your bats?'

'Behind the cash counter. If we had them on us all the time the cops'd pull us. We keep 'em out of sight and only grab 'em when we need 'em.'

'You mean you didn't need them tonight?'

'We was attacked – out of the blue. It weren't like trouble was brewing.'

'Did they say anything?'

'No.'

Conroy sat back and crossed his legs. He was annoyed and worried at the same time. Fucking Munrow! This had to be down to him. It was times like this that Conroy needed Dundaven. He would have arranged to sort Munrow out in the most appropriate way. But with Hughie locked away, a vital link in his set-up had been severed.

Shit. How to get Munrow out of his hair? Then he remembered Tony Morton's suggestion which, reading between the lines, went something like: Get John Rider to do your dirty work for you.

But how could he get Rider sufficiently riled with Munrow to take him out?

Conroy rolled his neck. It cracked obscenely.

'Let's have a look at the Thunderpoint. See if it's the same pathetic story,' he said to his bodyguards.

It was.

But at least he had had an idea about Rider and Munrow. A double whammy. One which would sort both of them out.

They were ready for the *pièce de résistance*.

Possibly the biggest club operating in Lancashire that midweek night was the Salsa, near Fulwood, just off the M55. Out of town, plush, up-to-date with state-of-the-art sound and lighting, it was frequented by footballers, Manchester pop stars and other minor celebs. The Salsa was a good, well-managed, profitable club with a capacity of almost fifteen hundred with it usually reached on Friday and Saturday nights.

The Salsa was the jewel in Conroy's crown. He owned one hundred per cent of it. A poor week netted him five grand in drug money alone. In entrance fees, which went through the books and were properly audited, the club grossed over £50,000 each week. Easily.

Conroy strove hard to keep it one of the best clubs in the north. It was the only one he ever visited. He often paid celebs to frequent it and give it the necessary credibility. You could almost guarantee to see somebody well-known, whatever night of the week. The off-chance of dancing on the same floor as a pop star or a five-million-pound footballer probably drew in an extra two hundred bodies a week.

It was a perfect target for Munrow to make his point.

From the car park they made their way in a businesslike manner to the front of the club. Staves and bats were secreted up sleeves or down trouser legs. Shotguns were held firmly under jackets.

The balaclavas went on at the last moment. Within seconds they had pole-axed the doormen and entered the club.

They rampaged through the place like a pack of wild dogs. Indiscriminately hitting innocent people, smashing tables and destroying the disco console.

Munrow made his final point by having two of the bouncers dragged onto the dance floor and laid face down.

In full view of all the customers, many of whom were drugged up to the eyeballs, he placed his shotgun in the soft flesh at the back of the left knee of one of the bouncers and pulled the trigger. He did the same to the other.

Munrow and his business associates then fled.

And not one witness, out of a total of four hundred and ten people, saw a thing.

Funny, that.

Chapter Fourteen

The avenue was wide, tree-lined and very pleasant. Extremely middle-class. On either side of the road was a grass verge which was covered with a coating of pure white fluffy snow. Behind the grass verges ran wide footpaths, behind which were the garden walls which fronted the houses. They were all detached, five- or six-bedroomed affairs with driveways which had an entrance and an exit. Set back at the rear of the houses were double garages the size of small bungalows. The gardens were all lawns and landscaping. Stockbrokers and solicitors abounded here, a good place for them to live, not far from Manchester and the towns of central Lancashire. They had their own little railway station nearby that made commuting a doddle.

Rider looked at his watch. 7 a.m. A couple of minutes before, a milkman had trundled down the avenue in one of those electrified carts, in and out of the driveways, and now the place was quiet again.

It was very dark. A real winter's morning. It would probably be ten before the night was completely shrugged off.

The dull ache in Rider's body became more than uncomfortable. He changed his position slightly for the hundredth time, yawned again, long and weary. It had been a long night.

He shivered and hoped it wasn't to be an unproductive one. Otherwise he'd have to revisit a certain transvestite and drown him/her in a toilet.

Rider was sitting in the front passenger seat of a tatty Ford Transit van parked up on the avenue, underneath the overhang of some roadside trees. The van was totally out of place, exposed. Rider knew it would only take one phone call from an early-rising public-spirited resident to bring the cops sniffing around. He was living on borrowed time and the later it got, the less he had.

With increasing restlessness he was observing the front of one of the houses about a hundred metres away.

It was fucking freezing and though the engine was ticking over like there were lumps of lead in the petrol, the pathetic heater was only gasping out lukewarm air. He wasn't dressed for the cold, only wearing his night-club gear of thin suit and tie.

Efficient as ever, Jacko, sitting in the driver's seat, was appropriately dressed for the winter weather in a duffel coat, thick socks, boots and cord pants. His gloved hands were resting on the steering wheel. He constantly had to wipe the screen with the back of his hand to see through the thin veil of frost which was forming relentlessly on the inside of the glass as their breath froze.

Jacko looked glum and unhappy. He did not want to be here. He desperately hoped nothing would happen.

'You should get a decent van,' Rider complained. 'I'm freezing my balls off sat here.'

'It is a decent van,' Jacko replied stonily. 'Is he gonna come or what?'

'Yes.' There was more certainty in Rider's voice than he felt.

'Then what?'

'Leave it to me. My problem.'

'I don't like this one little bit, John,' the other said nervously. 'Why get involved? I know you got battered, but this is a dangerous world – and I really don't want anything to do with it.'

'I know. You won't be involved. Trust me.'

Jacko gave him a contemptuous glare from the corner of his eyes.

Rider was experiencing some guilt in roping the barman in, but he had no one else to turn to other than Isa, and she wouldn't be much use in a situation like this. 'I appreciate what you're doing.'

The barman merely snorted, giving the impression he wasn't remotely taken in by Rider's words. He wiped the window again.

A vehicle turned into the other end of the avenue, lights blazing. It came towards the Transit. Rider got ready. But it was only the gritting lorry thundering past, showering the Transit with road salt.

'At least there's nothing left to rot,' Rider said dryly.

'One more remark about this van and we're going,' Jacko snapped. He meant it. 'You could've used your Jag.'

'And he might've recognised it . . . Hang on.'

Another vehicle turned into the avenue from the same direction, travelling slowly. A car. Instinctively Rider touched Jacko's arm. They both sank down.

This car turned into the driveway of the house they were watching and pulled up outside the front door. The security lights clicked on and bathed the whole front garden with white light. The car lights were switched off. A man got out, went up the steps to the door and pressed the bell.

Rider's throat constricted.

'Is it him?' Jacko hissed.

Rider couldn't say for sure. He was three hundred feet away and he could hardly see sod-all through the iced-up screen.

The upstairs house lights came on. Seconds later the front door opened. The man stepped inside, the door closed.

'Well?' Jacko demanded.

Rider shook his head. 'I'll take a chance.' He reached under the front seat and pulled out the revolver he had confiscated at the zoo. He held it up ominously, feeling a charge of adrenalin zip through him. His hand shook ever so slightly. Fear? Excitement? 'Give me fifteen minutes and if I haven't reappeared, call the cops, emergency or something. Use your imagination, 'cos it's likely one or both of us'll be dead.'

He jumped out of the van without looking at Jacko and trotted towards the house, making the first footprints of the day in the snow.

Henry Christie's two daughters – Jenny, fifteen and Leanne, nine – were both at an age when privacy meant a great deal to them. They had a room each and were very protective of their environments. They hated adults in their rooms, full stop.

Both were also acutely aware of their developing bodies, Jenny more so than Leanne, obviously. Should their dad, by accident, see anything more than he should, or even see their underwear in the washing basket, there would be screams of embarrassment. Usually from him.

His privacy and body, however, were fair game for them.

And at the same time as John Rider stepped out of the van that morning, Henry was thinking how unjust the world was when he couldn't even have a crap in peace.

He had settled himself, quite naked, on the toilet in the *en-suite* adjoining his and Kate's bedroom. He straightened out that morning's *Daily Mail* and looked forwards to ten minutes of bliss. He hadn't even had the time to digest the sports headlines when Leanne burst in without knocking, tearing into the littlest room like a chattering whirlwind in jim-jams, frightening the shit out of her father. He quickly covered his private parts with the newspaper. Leanne, seemingly oblivious to his predicament, commenced to show him some drawings she'd done at school the day before.

'Mmm, yeah, lovely. Nice – that's a good one,' Henry said, trying to appear enthusiastic. A trapped critic. At that point he was having a few problems holding back his natural bodily functions.

Then his eldest daughter, Jenny, appeared. 'Hi, Dad,' she said brightly. She came in and helped herself to a towel and a bottle of shampoo. On her way out she looked at him critically. He squirmed and coloured up. 'You've put some weight on,' she said and legged it with a giggle.

Leanne revealed another drawing which resembled . . . nothing. She explained it was someone riding the 'Big One'. With that Henry could appreciate where she was coming from.

'Ahh, yeah, great . . . Look, honey,' he said tenderly, 'your Daddy needs to have the loo to himself for a moment or two, so go and get ready for brekkie, will you?'

She sighed heavily and collected her masterpieces which she'd scattered all over the floor. She left, closing the door behind her.

'Mercy,' Henry said. He lifted the newspaper and Kate came in with one of her 'faces'.

Henry closed his eyes momentarily.

'Don't look at me like that,' she warned him. 'Are you seriously going to try and get on this squad?' It was the continuation of a discussion-cum-argument they'd begun when Henry came in from work the night before. Kate was obviously going to pursue this to the bitter end. 'Seems a bloody dangerous job to me. Everyone who has anything to do with it ends up dead.'

'Coincidence. No connection – and an exaggeration.'

'But why d'you want to go on it?' She crossed to the shower and turned it on. 'I thought you wanted to be a DI? Surely it'll put your promotion chances on the back burner?'

'Probably. But it's such a good opportunity, Kate. It's got a cracking reputation, the work's real interesting and very focused . . . and there's nothing set in stone that I'll get on anyway. They'll have to advertise the vacancy, so other people will be able to apply and everyone'll go through the rigmarole of interviews. You know I'm crap at being interviewed. My bottle goes.'

Kate unfastened her dressing gown and shrugged it off. Henry could not keep his eyes off her as she tested the shower temperature and adjusted the control minutely. Even after all these years – they'd known each other since they were sixteen – and two children, he loved the sight of her body minus clothing. Recently she'd been on a pretty ruthless exercise and diet regimen which had shed pounds and toned her muscles up just enough to – well, just enough. He glanced down at his own tummy and breathed in, slightly ashamed of himself. He was in good health, but didn't have the strength of character to stop eating things which were bad for him, and go to a gym. The result was showing around his midriff. Jenny had been right in her cheeky observation.

Kate stood and faced him with a sad look in her eyes. She was completely unaware of her nakedness and his position on the loo.

'I don't want you to go back on a specialised squad.'

'There's no guarantee I'll get promoted to Inspector. I think I should go for it. They approached me.'

'It's not the Inspector thing. It's the hours, days, weeks. You know what it was like when you were on Regional Crime Squad. I never knew when you were coming home next. I didn't like it and neither did the girls.'

'I work long hours now,' he protested.

'Yes, but at least you come home every day and you only work ten minutes away. It's different. You're not chasing all over the country, or Europe. It feels good having you close by, even if you work until midnight. And you virtually run that office, don't you?' she said, changing tack slightly. 'Surely that'll count towards promotion?'

'Don't bank on it. Once you get into that interview room, everyone's on a level playing-field.' He paused and gave her a pleading look. Big eyes.

155

Fluttering lids. 'Look, I really fancy this job, Kate. It's the chance of a lifetime. It's like dead men's Doc Martens.'

'Literally,' she commented gloomily.

'And as I said, I'm not guaranteed it.'

'Well, you know how I feel about it. We've only just got everything back to normal around here and now you want to rock the boat . . .' She shrugged. Her small breasts quivered with the gesture. She turned her back on him, stepped into the shower and slid back the curtain.

So that was really her hidden agenda. It wasn't so much the long hours away from home, it was the temptation that went with them.

She had a point, of course. Life at home had been incredibly good recently, following the 'blip' caused by Henry's stupidity and rampant sexual urges almost two years ago. Kate had truly forgiven him and for that he was extremely grateful to her. He loved Kate like mad and didn't want to lose her. But the guilt he carried about betraying her was always just under the surface and now, sitting on the bog, he realised for the first time that she too always had something at the back of her mind.

Something called mistrust.

She was obviously worried, but did not want to spell it out. Henry sensed that she equated specialist squad with adultery. All those hours and weeks she'd talked about meant temptation. Away from home. Strange places. Even stranger women, particularly the detectives.

He understood Kate's concerns, but was sure it would never happen again. His libido was in check.

And he seriously wanted to get on the Organised Crime Squad. It was right up his alley, the type of work he excelled in. Chasing and convicting good-class criminals.

Feeling unable now to concentrate either on the *Mail* or his bodily functions, he got off the loo and went into the bedroom to get dressed.

Rider edged around the perimeter of the garden, aware that his flimsy shoes were no barrier against the wet. He stayed far enough away from the house so as not to activate the security lighting which was fitted all the way around. He was trying to establish which of the bedrooms they were going into before he moved in and tried to gain entry.

The lights in a ground-floor room at the rear of the house came on. Rider assumed it was the kitchen, but the blinds were drawn. He could see the shadow of some movement but not enough to tell him anything. Then the lights came on in another room and through the patio doors Rider could clearly see into a lounge.

A man and a woman came into view.

The man was Munrow.

Rider did not know the woman, but from the brief conversation he had initiated with Toni Thomas, he had learned that she was a volunteer prison visitor and her husband was working in Saudi. Apparently she and

Munrow had struck up a relationship in prison and it had spilled into the outside world.

She obviously liked a bit of rough.

Rider settled onto his haunches in the shadow of the back fence. Munrow and the woman – Rider could see she was good-looking – stood side by side at the patio door and looked across the garden in his direction, or so it seemed to him. They each held a glass and were talking. She wore a dressing gown. Munrow was in a black windcheater and black jeans.

From his observation point, Rider appraised him.

He looked as fit and as hard as ever.

Once again, after having chosen a course of action, Rider wavered. In his condition, even if he hadn't been beaten up, he'd be no match for Munrow in a head to head. Rider had to physically stop himself from making his way back to Jacko and saying, 'Fuck it, we're going home.'

But he knew deep down in his soul that if he didn't take positive action now in a way which Munrow understood, he'd never be able to shake the bastard off his back. Ever. Munrow would walk all over him again and again. That was the sort of person he was.

If he dealt firmly with Munrow now, it would also send a strong message to Conroy to keep away.

The woman put her drink down and opened the patio door. She stepped outside with only slippers on her feet. The security light came on, illuminating the whole of the back garden. Rider hunched further down into the shadows.

In the snow she tiptoed to the bird-table and checked to see if there was any food on it. A moment later she was back in the house, patio door closed, and in Munrow's arms.

They attacked each other with a passion, kissing wildly, necking, tearing at clothing. She didn't have very much to remove and within a couple of seconds her dressing gown was on the floor and she was naked. Together they removed Munrow's clothes and she took obvious delight in peeling his boxer shorts off him, revealing what Rider had always suspected. A very big penis. Which she greedily took in her mouth as she knelt in front of him.

Munrow's head drooped back in ecstasy.

The woman clawed her way back to her feet, heaved herself onto Munrow by wrapping her legs around his waist and hands clasped around his neck.

Thus engaged, Munrow walked them both out of the room, easily holding her weight.

When they disappeared, Rider emerged from the shadows and sprinted low to the house. He flattened himself against the wall, gun in hand.

The security light went out. Rider moved and it came back on. He darted to the patio door and silently pushed the handle. Yes! It was open.

He was inside the house.

Munrow's discarded clothing was on the floor. Rider went through the pockets and found a single car key which he slid into his own. He trod carefully through the lounge and emerged in the hallway.

From upstairs the sounds of unbridled lust bounced down the walls. She was moaning to a rhythm, Munrow was gasping a beat behind. Oh, the din of sexual rapture, Rider thought.

He pulled a ski-mask over his head. Not because he wanted to hide his identity from Munrow, but from her. If things went pear-shaped in the next few minutes it would be better if she didn't see his face. He made his way cautiously up the steps to the landing, where the racket of intercourse became much louder from the bedroom second on the right.

After checking the first bedroom and finding it empty, Rider stepped lightly to the next door, which was open. He adjusted the ski-mask and tried to control his breathing – and the urge to scream and run away, forget it all, become a hermit. He counted to three and twisted into the bedroom, gun in right hand, supported by the left.

They did not notice him enter, being far too preoccupied in their own world of thrusting and grunting.

The couple were on the bed, facing away from Rider. The woman was on her hands and knees, face buried into a pillow, groaning wildly and Munrow plunged himself into her from behind with no subtlety whatsoever. It looked like he was meting out some form of medieval torture as he grabbed her thighs with white knuckled fingers and jab-jab-jabbed into her. She didn't seem to be complaining, meeting each of his rams with a powerful reverse thrust of her own. At the same time she was reaching backwards between Munrow's legs, cupping and squeezing his balls in the palm of her hand.

Not that he was a good judge of such things, but Rider made an educated guess that Munrow was not a zillion miles away from his climax. Rider wondered if it would give him an even greater thrill with a gun poked in his ear.

He decided to find out.

Two strides and he was standing right behind the heaving Munrow whose arse flexed, tightened and relaxed each time he drove his cock into her.

Without warning Munrow emitted a rhino-like squeal which made Rider jump.

The reason for it was that the woman had reached further back than Munrow's testicles and inserted the tip of her forefinger into his anus.

'Shove it in, baby,' he hissed. She obliged. He let out a long 'aaargh' – somewhere around middle C – and responded by slamming his full length into her. Rider wished he'd thought to shove the gun up there instead of in his ear. That would have been a real wheeze. Alas, the opportunity had passed.

Instead he sidled up to Munrow and stuck the muzzle under his left ear and cocked the weapon with an ominous click which always seems much louder than it really is.

In mid-forward thrust, Munrow stepped on the brakes, came to a dead halt. He contorted his head round, eyes wide, knowing exactly what he was feeling behind his ear.

Rider put more pressure on and said, 'Don't stop.'

'Honey, what's wrong?' the woman said. She looked round and saw the hooded figure of Rider pressing a gun into her lover's neck. She did what any normal person would have done: screamed and tried to wriggle free.

With his left hand, Rider grabbed the back of her neck and forced her face roughly down into the pillow, muffling the noise, suffocating her. He kept the gun pointed to Munrow's head and said, 'Shut it, you bitch, or I'll blow his head off and then rape you in the blood.'

He hoped it sounded convincing. Personally he was not remotely taken in by the threat.

Munrow hadn't moved.

Rider let go of the woman. She stayed where she was, ass in the air with Munrow stuck inside her. She started to shake and sob.

Suddenly Rider's resolve petered out. There was no way he could bring himself to force Munrow to finish the job.

'OK Charlie, we're gonna go for a ride. I suggest you come out of there, real slow-like – unless you want to take her along too.'

Munrow withdrew with a 'plop'. To his credit, despite everything, his manhood towered majestically, sparklingly damp, up to his belly button.

He opened his mouth.

This was no place for a debate. Not wanting to miss the chance, Rider inserted the gun into that orifice. 'Now then, Charlie,' he growled dangerously, 'this is a double-action revolver with the hammer cocked, so I don't even have to pull the trigger, just touch it, and I'll blow your fucking brains all over this pretty wallpaper. I want you to remember that because we're going downstairs now with this gun stuck in your mouth, so you need to be very cooperative, otherwise you'll be brain dead and she'll be dickless. Get my point?'

Jacko jumped. The security lights at the front of the house came on as Rider and the naked Munrow came out of the door, down the steps and walked towards the car – an old Ford Granada, like something out of *The Sweeney*.

Jacko could see the gun stuck in Munrow's gob.

Nausea ripped through the barman's insides. 'Oh shit,' he breathed. He coaxed the gear lever into first, released the handbrake, then the clutch – gently – but could not stop the van from kangarooing the first few metres as the engine and gearbox merged into one entity. One day he'd get the clutch fixed properly.

By the time he had pulled onto the driveway, Munrow had been forced

159

unwillingly into the boot of the Granada which was akin to a freezer. Rider had slammed the lid down over his shivering body.

Ski-masked, gun in hand, Rider walked casually up to Jacko who wound his window down. 'Follow me.'

'Where we going?'

'Fuck knows . . . just follow me.'

Rider got into the Granada and pulled the mask off. He slid that and the gun underneath the seat.

The car started first time.

From the boot he could hear Munrow's muffled banging and shouting.

There was no going back now.

The real bad weather had hit London. Public transport was at a virtual standstill. Traffic hardly moved in the heavy snow.

Even so, the conscientious Karl Donaldson crawled into his office at 7.30 a.m., having left home at 5.00 a.m. in the Jeep.

Some faxes and correspondence had appeared on his desk overnight.

One of the faxes gave the result of the second autopsy on Sam Dawber. It came to the same conclusion as the one performed on Madeira. Some more specks of human tissue had been found underneath her fingernails and was being DNA profiled. The bruising on her body was inconclusive.

'Goddam,' he sighed, resigning himself even more to the fact that he would probably never be able to prove Sam had been murdered. His only hope was a lead from the tissue, but being a pessimist at heart, Donaldson doubted anything would come of it.

A large fat envelope underneath this fax was from the New York Office and contained a photocopy of everything the FBI had ever filed on Scott Hamilton. Donaldson shuffled the papers out onto his desk. The file was almost half an inch thick. He scanned through it quickly.

Hamilton's main claim to fame was that he had trained as an accountant, had then been briefly jailed for skimming his employer's profits, and moved on to handle the financial matters of a well-known New York hood – i.e. laundering money for him. The Feds and the DEA had blown the racket sky high. The hood had been jailed (and since escaped), but Hamilton evaded incarceration by the skin of his teeth.

He branched out into some classy white-collar crime, defrauding people who should have known better. Currency and commodity frauds were his favourites.

He had been caught for a tobacco scam which backfired when the buyers turned out to be Fibbies. In particular, one Samantha Jane Dawber.

So that was how she knew him, Donaldson thought.

Hamilton got eight months for that.

He was not considered big time, as in mafia terms, but he was wealthy and worth watching as his activities sometimes straddled state and international boundaries.

He also had a violent streak and was suspected of dealing with a rival in a fatal manner. Nothing was ever proven. He was also believed to be a fixer, arranging things for third parties such as burglaries. Again, this was only intelligence, not hard evidence.

Since his prison release for the tobacco scam, he had dropped out of sight. There was nothing on file for almost two years.

Except the FBI now knew where he was – Madeira, running a time-share. Donaldson wondered what type of criminal activity the Jacaranda was fronting. He knew one thing for certain – it was going to be investigated ruthlessly.

He cast his eyes over the rap sheet for the cigarette fraud. Sam's name was down as Case Officer. It was a good bust. One to be proud of.

She probably couldn't believe her eyes when she spotted Hamilton on sleepy Madeira.

So why had she died?

Accident? Donaldson was convinced this was not right. More likely revenge for the jail sentence. Or had she stumbled across something more? And would he ever know? Probably fucking not.

The phone rang. He closed the file and answered it.

In days of yore, Rider would have known exactly where to take Munrow for a little chat.

Times change. He had no contacts to speak of any more, owned no suitable properties of his own, so was therefore forced to play it by ear.

After half an hour's driving he was heading up a steep winding road against merciless snow, out of the border town of Todmorden towards Bacup.

Halfway up the hill he turned off the road onto a farm track, where he pulled up out of sight of the main road. There was no sound coming from the boot. He prayed that Munrow hadn't died of hypothermia or inhaling exhaust fumes.

Jacko drew the Transit in behind.

Rider climbed out of the Granada and opened the boot. A shivering, numb Munrow lay curled up in the foetal position, arms folded tightly around his knees which were drawn up to his chest. He looked up at Rider, full of hate.

Rider produced the gun. He reached for Munrow's arm and heaved him out. He pushed the naked man roughly towards the back of the Transit, opened the doors and forced him in, climbing in behind, squatting on his haunches, gun held loosely. With immense satisfaction Rider saw that the huge throbbing erection had shrivelled to sub-acorn size. Now Rider didn't feel quite so threatened.

'Get out, pal,' Rider ordered Jacko. 'Go sit in the car.'

There was no need to tell him twice. He was gone in a flash, leaving Rider and Munrow alone.

Munrow's whole body was shaking with the cold. His skin had turned ice-blue. His teeth chattered audibly.

'I've brought you here for two reasons,' Rider said, giving the impression this was a pre-planned halt. In truth, he was winging it.

'Which are?' his captive managed to stutter.

'So you are obliged to listen to what I say and know I'm not bull-shitting.'

'Why the fuck should I listen to you?'

'Your own interests, Charlie boy. I mean to make a point and doing it this way is the only way you'll take it seriously.'

'Get fucking talking then.'

'OK. I don't give a monkey's ass about what's going on between you and Conroy. I'm not involved, never was, never will be. Your guys saw me with him because he wanted something from me, not because we're in business together. Understand?'

'You shot one of 'em.'

'Self-defence,' Rider said quietly.

'Don't believe you.'

'Your choice, Charlie. But think about this. If I was with Conroy, do you honestly think we'd be having this conversation right now, especially after your two goons beat the shite out of me the other night? Your head would be in pieces and they wouldn't find you until the snow melted . . . would they?'

Rider raised his eyebrows.

Rider wasn't sure whether he succeeded with Munrow. The other man could merely have been conning him just to get out of an awkward situation.

In the end, Rider had two choices – to kill him, or let him go and see what happened.

Rider always knew he would choose the latter. Just to make a point and ensure that Munrow realised Rider was no soft touch, he threw the Granada ignition key into a field adjacent to the lane where it disappeared in a snowdrift. He left Munrow standing there stark naked in the middle of nowhere, mouthing obscenities at him as Jacko reversed the van out of the lane, back onto the main road.

The man who only hours before had orchestrated vicious attacks on three nightclubs, now found himself helpless and freezing, scrambling over a drystone wall into the field to search for his key.

A humiliation he would never forget for as long as he lived.

Henry's heart went cold because he recognised the voice on the other end of the telephone line immediately.

Superintendent Guthrie. Discipline and Complaints.

Allegedly the most ruthless bastard they had in that department. A man, it was said, who dedicated his life to prosecuting police officers, who investigated each complaint with fervour. A cop who loved screwing other coppers.

'Henry. Need to come and see you. Have a bit of a chat. Think you know what it's about,' Guthrie said affably in the clipped way he spoke.

'Shane Mulcahy?'

'Spot on. You working Saturday – say three-thirty p.m.?'

No, I'll be in South America by then, Henry wanted to say. 'Yes,' he replied meekly.

'Good. See you in your office then. Bye.'

'Bye, sir,' croaked Henry. He replaced the receiver. A bead of sweat trickled irritatingly down his forehead. His hands trembled ever so slightly. The investigation process had begun.

He refocused his mind. There was a busy day ahead.

The team investigating Derek Luton's death were parading on at ten. Ronnie Veevers, the Detective Superintendent assigned to run the case, would not be arriving until noon. Henry was required to kick-start the job.

After this he wanted to see how the officers dealing with Marie Cullen's murder were progressing and to warn them about McNamara making smells at a higher level. Henry dearly wanted to arrest the man but knew that, at the moment, there was nothing to connect him to her murder, other than gut feeling. Which would not stand up in court.

Then he needed to know the current position of other enquiries.

Dundaven was in the cells on a three-day lie-down and needed to be interviewed with a purpose.

And maybe, if he could find time, he'd look into the shooting of Boris, the gorilla, and dig deeper into John Rider, see what he could unearth.

Lots to do. Not much time to do it in.

Firstly he called the hospital.

Nina had pulled through after a fraught night when they thought they were going to lose her. She had not regained consciousness, but showed slight improvement. She would undergo another operation today.

The news made Henry feel better and put his own problems into perspective.

The zoo told him Boris was much better too. But still in a real bad mood.

A cup of coffee was placed down on his desk. Henry spun round in his chair to see two smiling Chief Superintendents – FB and Tony Morton. They both looked smug, pleased with themselves – rather as if they were in co-hoots.

'Morning, Henry,' they said.

'Sirs.'

'Got some good news and some good news for you. Which do you want first?' Morton asked, beaming.

'I'll start with the good news.'

Chapter Fifteen

Detective Constable Dave Seymour was a raving homophobic. He could not countenance the thought of men 'doing it together'. Despite Equal Opportunity training, which sought to raise his awareness in such matters, gay men left him cold. 'Shit-shovellers' he called them.

The thought of lesbians was a completely different matter. When he visualised two women rolling around naked, frigging each other off, he was quite turned on. To him, a lesbian was just a woman who hadn't found the right man yet, whereas gays were dangerous, perverted individuals who should be put to death.

Which was why he wasn't too concerned to be taken off the Dundaven enquiry at short notice and drafted onto the Marie Cullen murder case, where he was teamed up with Lucy Crane. Lucy was a lesbian – a well-known fact because she had openly 'come out', and Seymour felt that, although married, he could be the right man for her.

'Once you've tasted the real stuff, you'll never go back,' he told her. 'A quality piece of meat is a million times better than any dildo.'

Lucy was driving; he was passenger. And ever since they had set off from Blackpool to go to Blackburn, he had never once let up with his sexual banter. By the time they hit the M6, she was heartily sick of it.

'Dave, shut up, will you?' she ordered him. 'You're getting on my tits.' As soon as she'd said it, she knew it was the wrong phrase to use.

'If only I was,' he cut in with a sly grin.

'And if you don't keep quiet I'll make a complaint against you for sexual harassment.'

'You'd never prove it,' he said smugly. 'My word against yours.'

She sighed deeply. 'Guess what, Dave? I've got a voice-activated tape recorder in my pocket and I've recorded your nonstop innuendo, requests for sexual favours and digs about my sexuality ever since we set off – and I'll use it if you don't shut your effing mouth. Yes, I'm a lesbian, I'm open about it and quite happy. No, I don't want to suck your cock. End of story. Let's get on with the job, shall we?'

Seymour had nothing to say. He glared nastily at her, grated his teeth for a moment and then mouthed the word, 'Bitch.'

He didn't know whether or not to believe her about the tape recorder. He wouldn't take any chances until he knew for sure.

The journey continued in silence, the atmosphere between them as thick as fog.

They were en-route to see if they could find some more of Marie Cullen's colleagues in the profession of prostitution.

Prostitutes! Seymour hated 'em.

The infrastructure of the British police service is riddled with bureaucracy. It has a slow, mechanistic structure within which it can take an eon for decisions to be made and then acted on. The militaristic lines on which the service is operated are being slowly whittled away as the police respond positively to the ever-changing society they serve; certain ranks have been abolished and the management structure has been flattened. But it is still slow, painfully so.

Except on the occasions when it wants to move quickly.

Particularly when high-ranking officers want to make things happen.

Which is why lowly Henry Christie felt he was in a world of unreality when Detective Chief Superintendent Tony Morton and his old bosom-buddy Bob Fanshaw-Bayley beckoned him into an empty office, sat him down and revealed the good news.

'Henry,' Morton began. 'As you already know I've earmarked you as a possible future member of the NWOCS. As such I've had a word with FB here to sound him out about it.'

Henry waited. Both senior officers were smiling.

'I know about your reputation and now I'm interested to see how you work first-hand,' Morton continued. 'So I went down on bended knee to Bob' – here the two high-rankers exchanged a glance – 'and begged him to let me borrow you for a few days to give us a chuck-up with this newsagents job.'

'And I agreed,' declared FB. 'Depending on your feelings, that is. We're not pushing you.'

Henry thought about it. He winced sadly. 'I've got too much on my plate at the moment. Otherwise I'd jump at the chance. It's happening a bit quick.'

'Henry, I like you. You know that. If you come and help us out now, then I can fix up a further six-month secondment, starting in April. That could possibly become permanent. Not possibly – definitely. I'll ensure it.'

'I'd like to, but there's Marie Cullen's murder, Dundaven . . . Derek Luton . . . I feel responsible. I couldn't really leave them in mid-air.'

'I understand that,' said Morton empathetically, 'but we're close to cracking the newsagents job. I'd like to see you working alongside my men just for the next few days, by which time we'll have a result. Then you can go back to your own stuff. Apart from anything else, this'll give you a chance to be in at the kill, as it were. And give me a chance to assess your suitability for the squad.'

'You'll only be absent for a few days,' FB pointed out. 'I'll keep an eye on your work, make sure it doesn't dry up.'

Henry leaned back. It sounded good.

'Think about it, Henry,' Morton said.

He didn't need to. A grin cracked across his face.

Morton held out his hand. 'Welcome to the squad, the cream of the crop.' His grip was firm and dry and he had the look of an angler who'd just netted a black marlin.

Completely bemused, Henry made his way back to his desk, chuffed to hell and back.

And yet . . . slightly disconcerted. *Steamrollered* was a word which sprang to mind.

Think this through, he told himself. What are the implications, professionally and personally?

Professionally, going on the squad would probably affect his chances of promotion. But he had always been in two minds about going for Inspector anyway as it would take him one rung further up the ladder away from 'real' policework. He'd have to talk management issues and strategies, all that crap. Stuff like that bored him shitless. He liked being operational, hands on, arresting people.

Going onto the squad would give him the opportunity to stay at this level and yet deal with high-class criminals. And maybe it would give him the time and space to delve into Dundaven and try to find the remainder of those firearms, the details of which Karl had sent him.

Personally . . . well, Kate should be told immediately, but he didn't dare pick up the phone. She would go ape. Henry decided to keep it until he went home that night so he could break it gently to her, face to face. That would be better than a phone call.

'DS Christie?'

Shaken out of his reverie, Henry jumped up at the mention of his name by DC Robson, the female detective on the squad whom he had briefly met before.

Henry had never been in a position to inspect her from close quarters. With her standing next to him, he had to admit that she was stunning. Black hair in a well-cut bob, shining brown eyes, small nose and a wide, soft mouth which needed to be kissed forcefully. He was aware that her complexion was porcelain perfect, dabbed with only the hint of make-up which made her high cheekbones stand out even more prominently. She was wearing a practical work suit – jacket, blouse and skirt – but it was nicely tailored and expensive.

The jacket swung open near to her shoulder and inadvertently his eyes crossed her lovely breasts and registered they were secured in a white, frilly bra which he could see through her blouse. She reminded him of a younger version of Kate. His heart gave a pathetic flutter.

Her intoxicating perfume almost overpowered him into a swoon.

'Hello. Siobhan, isn't it?'

'Yes. Well-remembered.' She smiled easily at him. Her tongue ran onto her top lip in a gesture that was thoughtful rather than erotic. Even so, it made Henry's guts jump.

He swallowed. 'What can I do for you?'

She held out her hand to be shaken and said those three memorable words.

'I'm your partner.'

'Is this it?' Seymour peered through the windscreen as the wipers, on double speed, worked overtime in an effort to clear the heavy rain which was bucketing down.

Lucy Crane pulled into the side of the road. She wound her window down and looked across at the high-rise development of council flats. She checked the note in her hand. 'Think so.' She rolled the window closed. 'You coming?' she asked Seymour.

'Suppose so,' he said with great reluctance. Their relationship had not improved and they spoke only when necessary.

They had got a list of all the women in Blackburn who had come to the attention of the cops in connection with prostitution in the last eighteen months. It was a fairly short list and quite repetitive. This was their third visit of the morning. It was a dull and tedious task trying to find someone who knew Marie Cullen and could maybe fill in some background for them. Two dead ends so far.

Also on the list were the names of two convicted pimps who operated in the area. Once they'd finished with the workers, they'd be moving onto the managers.

By the time they ran over the road and reached the entrance to the flats, they were both drenched.

'He had such an enjoyable time, he wants you again this afternoon,' Saltash said with a wicked smile on his face. 'So c'mon, get your well-fucked black arse into gear and let's get going. There's good money to be made in this for us both.'

'No, I'm not going. I don't like him, I don't like what he does and I can't stand the thought of going with someone who might have murdered Marie.'

Saltash didn't have the time or patience to argue. 'Get up, get your coat on and stop messin' around, Gillian, otherwise I'll have to slap you – and I don't wanna do that, honey.'

The black girl was sitting on the settee in her small lounge. She drew her knees up and presented a defiant face to her pimp. She shook her head. Her lips were taut and eyes blazing. Her body language screamed, 'Make me!'

Over the years Saltash had had many dealings with reluctant whores.

167

Sometimes they didn't know how lucky they were when he looked after them. They could have been on the streets, facing all sorts of threats, whereas he ensured that all the business he put their way was inside hotels or homes, places where they could give their full potential in a bit of comfort. Not down some dogshit-laden back alley or car.

When he had problems with them, he always resorted to the same well-tried and trusted remedy.

'You refuse to go, eh?'

He lurched across in an attempt to grab her black hair. Gillian ducked and he found his fingers groping for thin air. She squirmed off the settee with the intention of running into the bathroom and locking the door.

Saltash recovered quickly. He dived at her, rugby-style, wrapping his arms around her waist and bringing her down to her knees.

She struggled wildly. Her elbows jabbed backwards. One caught the side of his face, next to the eye-socket, with such force that he released his grip and his hands went up to protect his face. 'Fucking cow!' he screamed, reeling away.

Gillian dragged herself to her feet. She was angry. Instead of doing the sensible thing and bolting while she had the chance, she twisted round and launched a frenzied attack on Saltash, kicking and scratching him remorselessly, pummelling him with her fists.

He succumbed to the onslaught, trying to protect himself with his hands, parrying the blows which rained down on his head without a break.

'OK, OK, you win, you win,' he tried to tell her. She didn't listen, or if she did, she was past caring. As far as she was concerned, she was fighting for her life. She drove him back across the room. He turned to crawl away, all the fight having seeped out of him, giving her the chance to kick him properly. It hurt him. She was wearing Doc Marten boots.

'Jesus, Jesus, OK . . . Ahh . . . you've made your point!'

Gillian got her balance properly and aimed a perfect kick into his ribs. The force of it flicked him over and sent him rolling across the room, sprawling underneath the dining table where he lay on his back, panting, his arms clutched across his chest.

From this position he glowered at her. 'You'll pay for this, you stupid cow.'

She was unable to stop her head from shaking. 'No, I won't, no, I fucking won't, you bastard. I've had it with you and your snotty ways. You're supposed to look after us, but what happened to Marie, eh? You let her get killed, you bastard. I'm not going to finish up like her.'

Saltash attempted to ease himself into a sitting position. The pain which shot across his chest like a whiplash laid him back out again. 'C'mon honey, help me up.' He held out a hand and tried to look pleading. 'We'll work something out, I promise.'

Gillian ignored the outstretched fingers. She knew that if she yielded she would suffer. Firstly at Saltash's hands, then at McNamara's. That would not happen. She had to break free, one way or another. She had boiled over, put up with enough degradation. Her eyes searched the room and alighted on the portable TV set in one corner. She stepped across to it, unplugged it and lifted it as high as possible in her hands. She staggered across to Saltash who could not fathom out what was happening until it dawned on him in the split second before the TV crashed down onto his head. Everything went blank – with just a pinpoint of light at the middle of it. Then the light disappeared too. Saltash's TV set had been turned off.

She picked up his car keys and ran.

The two detectives consulted the address they had on their piece of paper and realised they had taken a wrong turning, were on the wrong floor, going in the wrong direction. Seymour tutted as though it was Lucy's fault. A great deal of self-control ensured she held back from punching him very hard.

They about-turned as a black woman appeared at the foot of a flight of stairs which led up to the next landing. The woman saw them, spun away and walked quickly down the concrete corridor. Neither of the detectives got a good look at her or thought anything of it, but made their way upstairs.

When they found the flat door open and the body of a man laid out on the carpet with a Sony portable smashed over his head and a pool of hot blood spreading slowly across the carpet, they were advanced enough in their deductive powers to put two and two together.

As fast as his bulky frame would allow, Seymour raced after the black woman whom they had good reason to believe was Gillian Sharrock, prostitute, with three convictions for soliciting and one for GBH, and also the person responsible for breaking a perfectly good TV set on some poor dead bastard's head.

She had disappeared into the rain.

The incident room was in darkness. The slide projector whirred, a slide clattered into place and the photograph of a man was thrown up onto the white screen at the far end. Slightly out of focus initially, the operator – DI Gallagher – brought the man up sharp and clear using the remote button.

The photo was obviously one taken covertly, probably from a pinhole camera in a button or maybe a briefcase. It showed a man sitting at a bar. It was good quality, demonstrating how much surveillance equipment had improved recently.

'Target One: Terry Anderson, also known as Terence Andrews, Tel Anderson,' said Gallagher, consulting his notes. 'Aged twenty-three, last known address believed to be a flat in Lancaster on St George's Quay. He is a fully paid-up member of the travelling fraternity – a gypo in other words, if you'll excuse me being non-PC.'

A titter went round the assembled group of detectives, which included Henry Christie.

'Works as a car-dealer and property-repairer, cash only, therefore no company records. Drives a Shogun and seems to have money to throw around. Has previous for armed robbery, bogus official jobs and a lot of violence. Tough individual. Known to carry firearms and is wanted for shooting at police officers in Lincolnshire a few months ago when he was disturbed on a burglary. Very nasty individual indeed. Lives off the proceeds of crime. All the details are in this folder.

'Henry – your team are responsible for him . . . we'll go into the details of the operation shortly. We believe he leads the gang who've been robbing the newsagents throughout the area and we have informant intelligence to that effect. He's the one who wields the shotgun, and he's the one, we believe, who blew our colleague away.'

Gallagher paused and allowed everyone to remember Anderson's face. 'Target Two . . .' Gallagher pressed another button. Another face appeared on the screen.

Henry smiled with undisguised satisfaction. Transferred, albeit temporarily, with the speed of light, and now given the responsibility of leading the team tasked to bring in the gang leader. He couldn't credit his good fortune! Back in a fully operational role, straight into the bosom of the NWOCS whose members greeted him like a long-lost brother. And straight away, without any animosity from anyone, in a position to make a name for himself. Absolutely wonderful!

He wondered how Morton had twisted FB's arm to allow this to happen so quickly.

He treated himself to a quick look at Siobhan Robson, sat next to him. She caught the look and her mouth fluttered a brief smile which Henry saw in the light of the projector. She looked forwards again. Henry's eyes closed tight and briefly in an expression of heavenly lust, then he tried to concentrate on Target Three, having completely missed Target Two. He was exquisitely aware that Siobhan's right thigh was touching, nay, actually resting against his left one. Totally innocent, he knew, but it still sent a tremor of excitement through him.

Pull yourself together, you idiot. You've got form for adultery and you weren't very good at it then, he remonstrated internally. And a girl like Siobhan is hardly likely to be interested in an old buffoon like you.

He cleared his throat, sat upright and put a gap between their thighs.

Until her leg, not his, closed the gap.

This time he ignored it – ish.

Target Four was being introduced by Gallagher.

The bloke on the screen now, in Henry's estimation, was a particularly sour-faced git. Another gypsy, as were all the men. Henry was sharply reminded of Shane Mulcahy. Both their features were quite similar. Shane

170

was made to look like a choirboy, however, when Gallagher read out Number Four's antecedents.

The four men – youths really – were a very bad bunch of people and Henry could readily believe they had turned from pure terrifying violence to killing in a moment. They all had the capability. It had only been a matter of time before the robberies became killing zones.

After the presentation the lights came back on.

Tony Morton took the floor. 'Now you know who we want to arrest. And please – don't let there be any cock-ups on this at all. No heroics, no gun battles, no shooting – just in and out and get 'em. Grab them before they have a chance to fart. We don't want any dead heroes like Geoff Driffield, who was trying to prove something to himself and the rest of the world.'

He took a breath. His eyes surveyed the faces of the detectives in front of him. 'And that's all I have to say. DI Gallagher will talk you through the operation itself. So . . . good luck.'

He stepped smartly off the platform and left the room, Gallagher taking his place. The latter checked his watch. 'In a few minutes, a firearms team will be coming to join us, together with some Support Unit personnel. There's no point in progressing this until they arrive, so I suggest you hang loose and be back here for three-fifteen prompt.'

'Tell me about Geoff Driffield.'

They were in the canteen which, apart from a couple of traffic wardens taking a mid-afternoon break from harrying motorists, was deserted. They were sat next to a window which gave a good view of Blackpool, the Tower in particular. They faced each other, hunched over cups of tea, in postures which were almost intimate. Anyone watching them would see they were easy in each other's company.

Siobhan sighed and collected her thoughts. At length she said, 'Driffield was always pushing for a result. He wanted glory all the time, and he wanted it all for himself. He must have cultivated some good snouts, and obviously he came up trumps with this gang – but then he didn't share it with anyone, poor stupid sod.'

'But going it alone? Crazy, even for a glory boy, isn't it?'

Siobhan turned the cup on the saucer and stared into it.

Henry looked at the top of her head. He could see the shiny hair right down to the roots. It was healthy and he wanted to touch it. Slowly, she shook her head. 'I think it's *exactly* what he wanted to do. In the past he'd had some good results going it alone, but he'd taken some stupid risks. I think that lying in wait for an armed gang was just a natural progression for him. He wasn't a team-player, and on a squad like this, you need team-players. You need to support each other, in more ways than one . . .' Her brown eyes rose to meet Henry's. They seemed to dance for him, a sort of seductive lambada.

171

'What happened on Saturday night, then?' he asked with difficulty.

'Geoff came on before anyone else and took off without leaving any details of where he would be. Next thing we knew, we were being contacted by your lot – we were on a surveillance job in Bury – and we got the news.'

Her eyes had not left Henry's face. She was taking in every detail, every contour and he likewise with her.

'H-how long have you been on the squad?' he asked her. He coloured up whilst he tried not to think about what it would be like to bury his face between her breasts and . . . well, he tried not to think about it.

'Six years. I'm from Greater Manchester originally.'

'Enjoy it?'

'Best job I've ever had.'

'Seems a long time to be in a specialist post.'

'Tony, the boss, likes to keep people who fit in well, support the aims of the squad, are prepared to work hard and who get results.'

'So you've got to toe the party line or else you're out, is that it?' Henry probed playfully.

For the briefest fraction of a moment a look of something like suspicion crossed Siobhan's face. So fleeting it was almost unnoticeable, but Henry caught it, and it disturbed him. What was it that the question stirred in her? Only later – much later – would he find out.

Her normal, natural look resumed. She tossed her head back with a laugh, shook her hair and ran her long fingers through its silky strands. Her lovely neck was exposed to Henry's eyes.

'No, nothing like that,' she said lightly. 'But Tony likes people who're with him rather than against him.'

'I'd better not rock the boat,' Henry said dubiously.

'No, better not.'

Tony Morton was seated in the Officers Mess at Blackpool police station, chatting to a uniformed Inspector. Gallagher came in and poured himself a coffee from the pot on the hot-plate.

Morton excused himself from the lower-ranking officer and went across to Gallagher. They moved to one corner of the room, out of earshot of anyone else.

'He's like a dog with two dicks,' Gallagher said triumphantly.

'Good. I thought he would be. The guy has difficulty keeping his keks up, apparently, where there's the slightest possibility of getting his end away. What about the other areas we discussed? We need to force those issues as soon as.'

Gallagher nodded. He floated a couple of ideas past his boss who immediately approved them.

The briefing which followed was very detailed, professional and thorough. Henry did not like Gallagher for some reason, but he was impressed by the way in which he had planned and delivered the meat and bones of 'Operation Cabal'.

No reason was given as to why the operation was so-called, and Henry did not ask. Nor did he actually know what the word 'cabal' meant. He made a mental note to look it up when he got home, whenever that would be.

An hour after starting Gallagher was winding up. 'OK, that's about it, men,' he announced, failing to include the four women present in the room, three being members of the firearms team. 'Because we've all been on duty for almost eight hours already, the Operation will commence proper at 6 a.m. tomorrow. This is to ensure you all get a good night's sleep, because it may go on for a very long time indeed. Don't be surprised if you're working fourteen-hour shifts – or more – once we're up and running. We'll do it until we catch them. So tell those loved ones at home. Right, any questions?'

There were none.

'Good. You must be in your ob points at 6 a.m. – so be there.' His face broke into a smile. 'Now go home, get some quality sleep and be ready to roll. That's it, folks! Henry, chats please.'

With Siobhan at his side, Henry made his way over to Gallagher, who handed him a small laminated business-size card. It was an authorisation to carry firearms.

Henry was stunned. He blinked. 'But I haven't carried a gun for nearly two years and I certainly haven't kept up my shooting skills.'

'Don't worry,' said Gallagher. 'Needs must. You'll be OK. I want you to go back with Siobhan to our offices in Blackburn where you can sign a weapon and a radio out and get some body armour from our store. You're almost one of us now, so you might as well use our equipment. You need to be armed for this thing, Henry. We're dealing with some real nutters here and I want everyone protected properly who's likely to come into first contact with them.'

One of those quivers of unease shimmered through Henry. The thought of a gun. Last time he'd held one in his hand he'd killed somebody. Deliberately. An act of self-defence.

He swallowed and stared at the firearms authorisation, dated that day and signed by the Chief Constable.

Boy, this squad really had some clout.

The offices of the North-West Organised Crime Squad were situated in what could loosely be described as the 'red light' district of Blackburn, just off the main town centre in the area bounded by King Street and appropriately enough, Mincing Lane. They were offices which had originally been used by the Lancashire Constabulary Traffic Department, before over the years becoming home to a series of specialised police units until eventually the NWOCS moved in.

Money had been spent on modernising and refurbishing the rundown array of buildings, which had proved an ideal location for the unit, providing office space, secure parking and a reasonably centralised location in the north-west.

Siobhan drove Henry from Blackpool in appallingly grim, wet weather, which as they went further east towards the Pennines, turned to sleet.

Despite the rain, several prostitutes were in evidence, walking the streets in totally inappropriate gear – high heels, short skirts, low-cut tops. Whatever the weather, business had to be done.

In the early part of his service Henry had spent a few years in Blackburn. He knew the area well and was surprised to see so little change. The district was still bleak, poorly lit and slightly seedy, just as it had been way back.

Blackburn was the only town in Lancashire that had a problem with streetwalkers and their customers. Fortunately, the red-light district was situated where there were few residents to annoy.

Siobhan pulled off King Street down an unlit, badly-surfaced side street and stopped at a reinforced gate with a barbed-wire top. She opened her window and ran a swipe card through a machine, tapped a three-digit number on a key pad and the gates swung open with a clatter. She drove in. Security lights came on and flooded the car park with bright white light.

On one side was a triple garage with a couple of offices above. On another side was the main building where the majority of offices were to be found. The other two sides of the car park were high walls.

Siobhan led Henry to the main building and after tapping in another number, this time of six digits, on a key pad, she pushed the door open. Once inside, the warning beeps of a burglar alarm pinged out. She went to the alarm control box in the hallway and tapped in yet another sequence of numbers. The pinging stopped.

'Goes straight to Blackburn police station, the alarm,' she explained. She ran the side of her hand down a pad of light switches. The interior of the building came alive and four strategically placed permanent outer lights came on too. 'Welcome to our humble little abode,' she said, opening her hands in a theatrical gesture. 'Come on through.'

She took him up a set of stairs and along a landing. 'Tony's office, that one,' she said, passing a closed door. She turned next left into a large, fairly open-plan office. It had been completely updated since Henry had last seen it nearly twenty years ago. The range of desks, PCs, filing cabinets and lumbar-friendly chairs was impressive. Police offices were usually kitted out with tatty furniture, broken chairs, telephone lines crossed dangerously all over the place . . . a Health and Safety nightmare. Not this place. There was even a coffee machine and a pure water dispenser.

'Nice,' remarked Henry, pouting with admiration.

174

One thing which resembled police offices everywhere was the phenomenal amount of paper stacked everywhere in baskets, and the walls which were plastered with notes, intelligence bulletins, photographs of crims and all sorts of other non-essential rubbish.

'This is where our team hang out,' Siobhan explained. 'The other team are downstairs.'

'You've got two teams?' Henry asked, surprised. She nodded. 'Why's that? I thought it was all one big happy family.'

'Oh, we're all happy enough, there's just two teams,' she shrugged.

Henry accepted the fact with a nod. He wasn't about to question it. At least he was on the same team as Siobhan Robson.

'This is where Geoff Driffield sat.' She pointed to the only desk devoid of paper. 'I . . . er, suppose it'll be yours when you get on the squad.'

Henry gave a short laugh at the assumption. The phrase 'Dead men's Doc Martens' sprang to mind. However, it looked a nice desk. *Dead man's desk*. And it hadn't taken them long to clear it. What a damned ruthless organisation the police is, he thought.

'That's the radio cupboard.' She waved in the direction of a large steel cabinet in one corner of the office. 'Here's the key. I'll just go and get you a bulletproof vest. They're kept in the store over the garage. Book yourself a radio and a couple of charged batteries out.'

She swished away. Henry heard her footsteps fading down the corridor, then the stairs, the front door slamming. He walked to the office window which overlooked the car park and watched her cross to the garage.

He unlocked the radio cupboard, assembled a PR and grabbed a couple of extra batteries. He knew what it was like to be unable to transmit because of dud batteries, and he had promised himself he would never be caught out again.

As with all police equipment, there was a book to record Issue and Return; he opened it and signed out the radio.

His eyes could not fail to notice the entries for the previous Saturday – and the fact that, according to the sheet, Geoff Driffield had signed a radio out at 1700 hours. As had four other officers – Tony Morton, DS Tattersall, DI Gallagher and DC Robson. All at 1700 hrs – 5.00 p.m.

Henry considered this.

Siobhan had said Driffield was a loner who had gone out alone, presumably armed with details of where and when a robbery was going to take place, with the intention of arresting the culprits himself and claiming the glory. Yet the sheet suggested a different story. Driffield appeared to have been on duty at 5.00 p.m. that afternoon – two and a half hours before the robbery – and he'd signed out a PR with four others. They surely would have noticed him sneaking off alone, wouldn't they? Maybe asked him where he was going? Shown a bit of interest?

Henry glanced out of the office window. The lights were on over the garage. He could see her moving about.

175

He looked down at the radio book again and frowned. Something very fucking strange was going on, Henry concluded. The entry in the radio book posed an awful lot of nooky questions for the squad. He ran a hand over his face, trying to rub some intelligence into his brain. The activity did not seem to work. Again he was tired beyond belief, definitely operating on one amp.

He closed the radio book and locked the cupboard.

On the table next to the door was an A3-sized book with the words *Duty States* imprinted on the brown cover. This was where officers booked on- and off-duty. Most officers in Lancashire now recorded their duties on a computer, but some specialist departments, not on the mainframe, were still obliged to use good old pen and paper. The fact that NWOCS used written Duty States did not surprise Henry. He opened the book and had a quick look at last Saturday's entry. Same story: Geoff Driffield and four others had booked on at 5.00 p.m.

With his tongue making a thoughtful clicking noise at the back of his throat, he closed the book, feeling uncomfortable.

A glance across the car park. Siobhan was still moving around over the garage.

Henry stepped out of the office, twisted into the corridor and tried Tony Morton's office door. It opened.

There is a term in policing circles for what he did next. It is called 'Dusting'. 'Dusting' is where, out of normal office hours, you sneak into a boss's office and search the place from top to bottom in the hope of finding anything of interest. 'Dusting' is a pastime in which many officers on night duty indulge, flitting through offices like burglars, hoping to uncover some dirt on anyone except themselves.

Henry was restricted by being unable to switch the lights on; however the car-park lighting cast sufficient for him to be able to conduct a cursory search.

He found nothing.

Then he looked at the walls. One was covered in an array of photographs and framed certificates, all relating to Tony Morton, his career and his qualifications; it was sometimes known as an ego-wall. Tony Morton had a big one.

Henry peered closely at the photographs, many of which were of Morton's classes in various police learning institutions throughout the years. One fairly recent one was of a Senior Command Course at Bramshill and Henry chuckled when he saw Karen Donaldson sat in the middle of the front row, named as Course Tutor.

One photograph showed Morton shaking hands with the Princess of Wales, another with Margaret Thatcher.

Two others particularly grabbed his attention. Actually grabbed it by the bollocks.

The first one was a large framed photograph of the front page of the

Lancashire Evening Telegraph, bearing the headline: POLICE SQUAD FOUND NOT GUILTY. A story followed, which Henry vaguely remembered, about an investigation into the activities of the NWOCS six years ago, following allegations of corruption.

A team headed by an ACC (one from Lancashire called Roger Willocks, now retired) had been tasked to investigate the squad, some members of which were supposedly feeding information to criminals about police operations. Nothing was ever proved and a six-month enquiry produced zilch by way of evidence. A photo of the ACC showed a very frustrated, pissed-off-looking man. Underneath the photo was a quote from him about what a superbly run unit the NWOCS was, and how it should be held up as a model for all such similar units. There was some incongruity between the picture and the words. They didn't seem to gel.

By counterbalance, there was another picture next to the ACC of a beaming Tony Morton; he was quoted as saying that the unit had been open, frank and helpful to the enquiry and was delighted to be completely exonerated of all allegations.

The next photograph, taken in 1993, Henry found both interesting and disquieting. It showed Morton shaking hands with the current Prime Minister and in the background lurked the bulky figure of Sir Harry McNamara. The caption underneath was about the PM visiting the NWOCS which had been established for some seven years and had produced some sterling results in terms of arrests and convictions.

Sir Harry McNamara. Suspect in a murder case which Henry was no longer investigating.

He heard the outer door slam, then the sound of Siobhan's footsteps running up the stairs. Shit!

Rider stretched out in the bath in his basement flat. The water was too hot, and could have been doing terrible things to his arteries. But it was bliss, laced as it was with Sainsbury's bubble bath. Things happen after a Sainsbury's bath, he thought languidly.

His body was a mass of bruises from the beating he had received. They were on the turn colour-wise, being a few days old, from livid purple to a manky sort of green which reminded him of cow-pats.

He had brought some reading material in with him. A novel he'd been intending to devour for some while and a couple of old evening news-papers. He went for a newspaper first, wanting to catch up on local news. The headline screamed about the shooting of a policewoman and the subsequent arrest and charge of a man called Dundaven, who was found to be in possession of a large number of firearms. An accompanying photograph showed the latter displayed on a table with the detective leading the hunt stood behind. Henry Christie.

Rider sneered at the face, but his mind was really on Dundaven, who he knew was one of Conroy's men, very high up in the scheme of things. He had been in Blackpool on the same day as Conroy, when the latter had been trying to get a piece of Rider's club – presumably as a means of selling drugs. Or did Conroy in fact want to stash *firearms* at the club?

There was a timid knock on the bathroom door. Rider knew it was Isa. Ever since returning from his jaunt with Jacko to sort out Munrow, she had been in a strange mood, like she wanted to say something but didn't know how. Rider hadn't given her the opportunity either because he suspected a potential earbashing.

'Yeah?' he said gruffly.

'I've got a couple of warm towels,' she called back from behind the door.

'Just leave 'em outside, thanks.'

'Can I come in, John? I want to talk.'

'I'm in the bath, Isa.'

'I bloody well know you are,' she replied sharply. 'I've seen you before, haven't I?'

That was true. A long time ago on a different planet, when he was a hardened criminal with a tough body and conscience to match. 'Come on then,' he relented and strategically moved a mass of bubbles so as to hide his pride and joy.

She came in and sat down on the toilet seat, dropping the towels on the floor. She was dressed in a bathrobe which was quite short and showed a good length of leg, reminding Rider how nice they were. Since Rider's beating, she had moved out of the hotel and into the spare room in his flat.

She looked at him, wondering how to start. 'I hope you realise you frightened the life out of Jacko,' she began. 'He's not used to that sort of thing, poor soul.'

'Nor am I,' Rider said defensively.

'You shouldn't have used him.'

'Point taken. Now, what else do you have to say?'

'I want to know if it's over, your revisit to gangsterland.'

'I hope so. As far as I'm concerned, it is. I made my point, which considering the hammering he gave me, was fairly muted. I think – hope – Munrow took it.'

Isa took a deep breath. It was as if a weight had been lifted, hearing those words.

Rider noticed that her eyes, which were a lovely shade of hazel, were moist and sparkling. His own eyes narrowed and his brow creased. He tried to guess what was going on in her mind.

'I'm glad, I'm really glad, John, because I've cleaned up my business too and everything I do now is above board. I was sick of expecting the next knock on the door to be the cops or the customs people.'

'What about the girls for the club?'

'Not a problem, but what I'm trying to say is that . . . I wanna sound you out about something, if I may?'

178

'Sure – fire away.' He was intrigued.

She cleared her throat. 'Don't know where to begin. I feel all weak and shaky when I think about it. You know all those years ago when we made love?'

Oh God, he thought desperately. His face dropped aghast. 'I didn't make you pregnant, did I?' At the same time he said it, the idea of being a father gave him a warm glow.

'No, no, nothing like that.' She waved her hands dismissively.

He was relieved, but yet . . .

'So, yeah, we made love and well, even before we did and certainly afterwards, I was – am – in love with you, John. I know it's all silly and stupid and juvenile – me, a woman who runs call girls – but it's true. I've always wanted to tell you, but never had the courage and it never seemed the right time. Until now.'

She stopped abruptly. Whilst speaking she hadn't had the bottle to look at him directly and when she did, the look of what appeared to be abject horror on his face stopped her dead in her tracks. She gasped, 'I'm sorry, John! I shouldn't have said anything. What an idiot I am! I've been holding a torch for you all these years . . . I'll go and head back home tonight. We'll still do the club, sure. I'm sorry – what a stupid fool I am.'

She stood to leave, tightening the belt on her robe.

Rider had been lounging back in the bath, laid out full-length in the deep enamelled tub. Now he rose into a sitting position, water surging off him like a wreck being recovered from the deep. He held out a wet hand. 'No, don't go,' he said with a weak smile.

'Don't laugh at me, John, or I'll punch your lights out,' she warned him.

'I'm not laughing,' he said sincerely. 'Come here.' He wiggled his fingers in an encouraging manner. 'C'mon.'

She took his hand with a degree of hesitation. He pulled her gently towards the bath so that she was standing right next to him. 'Come down here,' he murmured. Slowly she knelt next to the bath until their faces were on a level, eye to eye, nose to nose, mouth to mouth.

'This is my last try at getting a normal sort of life,' she said hoarsely. 'At least as normal as it can be for people like us.'

'And you love me?' he whispered.

She nodded. Her lips parted slightly. 'Desperately.'

He ran a hand around the back of her neck and eased her face towards his and kissed her on the mouth. Softly at first. Tentatively. Then, as their mouths moulded together and both realised they had found each other at last, the kiss became more urgent and wanting.

Henry was never completely sure how he achieved it, but by the time Siobhan hit the landing he was back in the main office, standing nonchalantly next to a notice board, pretending to read an intelligence bulletin.

179

He tried to look surprised when she bounded in through the door bearing a gift in the form of a covert VIP protection vest, designed for discreet use. In other words – underneath a shirt. Henry cringed when he thought how uncomfortable and hot it would be.

'It won't stop a sniper's bullet,' his partner declared, 'but according to the manufacturer it will prevent small-arms from inflicting wounds. It'll stop knife-slash attacks too.'

'Won't stop anyone blowing your head off either.'

'Don't be picky,' she said.

He took it from her and held it up between forefinger and thumb like it was a dirty nappy.

'We all wear them.'

'Even you?'

'Even me – but I wear a specially designed one.'

'Like a basque?' asked Henry, rather naughtily.

He regretted the comment briefly until she retorted, 'You'll have to wait and see, won't you?' and cocked an eyebrow in his direction. 'Right – a gun.'

She led him back into the corridor and to a door marked *Store*. She unlocked it and behind it was something the size of a broom cupboard with a squat, grey safe set securely into the back wall. Siobhan bent down to it and whizzed out a combination on the wheel which Henry could not follow. It opened easily.

She reached in and removed a revolver with the cylinder hinged open to show it was empty, and gave it to Henry.

'Not much choice, I'm afraid. This is the only one available. Most of us have Glocks.'

'Oh, I'm quite happy with this one,' he said generously, a statement which did not tie in with the tremble of his hand. Once again, he realised just how uncomfortable he was around guns. This was a Model No. 12 Smith & Wesson Military and Police with a two-inch barrel, weighing 18oz when empty. A good, reliable firearm. The .38 special ammunition with which it was loaded could travel over 1500 metres, and in Henry's hands was probably accurate up to about two metres. A trickle of sweat rolled down his spine and one or two demons stirred ominously in the pit of his bowels.

Siobhan gave him a box of ammunition and two speed loaders. She filled in an issue form, then asked Henry to sign it. Again, like the radio book, it recorded the issue and return of equipment – this time firearms. Henry scrawled his signature in the required space. There was another gap after his name for the authorising officer to countersign – in this case Tony Morton. Siobhan explained he would do that at a later date.

Henry looked quickly at Saturday's entries.

Geoff Driffield had signed a gun out. As had four others. 1700 hours. Everything was countersigned and approved by Tony Morton.

'Do you want to load up?'

He went back to the office. With nervous fingers he loaded the revolver and the speed loaders, fumbling the bullets and dropping one or two in the process. By the time he had completed the task, Siobhan had returned with a shoulder holster for him.

He slid his jacket off and eased his arms and shoulders through the webbing straps. Siobhan moved close to him and assisted him to adjust it so it fitted snugly. She was only inches away from him, fussing around like a loving wife might do for a husband who was getting ready for a special occasion. He could smell her warm breath.

'There you go,' she declared. 'How does that feel? Not too tight?'

'Fine.'

He could see the flawless complexion, the finer than fine silky hairs.

'I like webbing,' she said throatily, a smile playing on her lips. She eased her fingers around the straps of the holster, pulled herself onto tiptoe and kissed his mouth quickly, then drew away.

Henry was dazed into statuesque immobility.

She hoisted herself back up, kissed him again, and whilst doing so, sunk her teeth into his bottom lip, drawing a small squeak of pain/pleasure from him. His arms looped around her, crushing her body into his. Their groins ground together and her slinky wet tongue slid into his mouth.

It took a few seconds before reason triumphed over lust.

'Whoa . . . hold on.' He pushed her firmly away.

'What's the matter?'

'I'm sorry, that shouldn't have happened.'

'Why? Didn't you enjoy it?'

'On the contrary.' In fact the surge of pleasure he'd experienced was almost overwhelming.

'Because you're a married man?'

'That's one reason.'

'Any other?'

'We're work colleagues. I'm a supervisor. Recipe for disaster. I don't want to do anything foolish.' *Like I've done in the past*, he did not hasten to add.

She looked disappointed, but gave him a rueful smile and nodded. 'All right, I accept that.' Unoffended. But before she turned away she gave him an eye-to-eye which said, in no uncertain terms, there was unfinished business here.

Henry picked up the gun and slid it into the holster – only it didn't go in as he'd anticipated. He hadn't realised it was an upside-down holster – a type he had seen, but never used before.

He gave himself a mental warning to remember that, if he had to draw the weapon.

Otherwise he might shoot himself in the heart.

* * *

They made love twice in the following hour. The first time was fast, with little style, completely driven by desire. It lasted only minutes as they tore desperately at each other, biting, sucking, pushing, shoving, basically devouring each other in a frenzy. They came together in a tangled, panting, damp mess, then picked themselves up from the bathroom floor. Clinging tightly, not wanting to let go, they stumbled through to the main bedroom where they simply lay together, holding each other and realising their love in small murmurings.

When they were ready, the second time was much slower and considered. They explored each other, caressed, probed, rubbed and brought each other to the height of ecstasy.

They reached their second orgasm with Isa on top, riding slowly, her full breasts swinging gracefully above his face, until she felt him become harder and harder and his thrusts became more urgent. Then she ground herself onto his pelvic bone, taking him deep inside, and they both came with a long, deep climax which shook them to the core.

Exhausted, she collapsed on top of him, head buried in his chest; he stayed inside her, running his fingers up and down her spine, making her quiver delightfully.

'That was gorgeous,' she said languidly, breathing in long and pleasurably through her nose.

'Mmm,' he managed to reply.

They both drifted into a contented sleep until they were interrupted rudely by the shrill phone next to the bed. She rolled off him and he answered it.

It was the cops.

Bad news. Could he turn out? Now. The block of bedsits he owned near to the Pleasure Beach was burning down. People were trapped. Some could be dead. It looked like arson.

There were four fire-tenders, three police cars, a couple of ambulances and the road had been cordoned off. The noise of the engines of the tenders was deafening, a sort of roar and whine combined. The sound of radios transmitting and receiving, people shouting to each other and running all over the place simply added to the cacophony.

By the time Rider arrived the building was a shell. Massive amounts of fire and smoke damage had been caused to the ones on either side. The windows were all missing, blown out by heat and flames, and dense black smoke billowed out into the night, accompanied by the occasional flash of flame, though generally the fire was under control.

The fire brigade relentlessly pumped gallons of water into the building.

Two people had been unable to get out.

They had died.

One had burned to a crisp. The other had died through smoke inhalation. Rider pushed his way through the crowd of enraptured onlookers and ducked under the cordon tape. A uniformed cop approached him to block the way. Above the din of the incident, Rider introduced himself and asked to be directed to the Chief Fire Officer at the scene.

The cop pointed. Rider thanked him.

He trod carefully over several layers of hose pipes which lay across each other like a convention of boa constrictors.

The CFO was removing his breathing apparatus. Rider waited until he removed his face mask which left a clean area of skin around his nose, eyes and mouth. The rest of his face and neck was smoke-charred black.

'Deliberate,' the CFO told Rider confidently.

'Can you be sure at this stage?'

'Yes,' he said with authority. 'There are several seats of fire throughout the building. It looks like whoever started it worked his, or her, way down from the upper floors, lighting fires as they descended. That's not official yet, by the way, but I can tell. I've been to enough fires to know.' He wasn't bragging. 'Any clue who might have done this?'

Of course I fucking have, Rider wanted to scream. He tried not to let his face mirror his thoughts. He shook his head. 'No.'

'Well, this is a matter for the police now. Two people dead and deliberate seats of fire. It's a murder enquiry – as if they haven't got enough on this week.'

Chapter Sixteen

F riday. 6 a.m. They were all in position.

Henry, Siobhan and two members of the firearms team – Dave Bevan and Jack Philpot – were ensconced very uncomfortably in the back of a surveillance van parked on St George's Quay, Lancaster. The van was, purposely, a rather careworn Ford Transit, bearing the logo of a fictional electrical company.

All four officers were perched on narrow wooden seats in the rear of the van, squirming in an effort to keep the blood flowing to their extremities in the cramped conditions. It seemed the seats had been designed to make arses numb within minutes. They were certainly not made for comfort and relaxation.

Their combined breath condensed on the inside of the van and because it was so cold, froze in tiny globules on the metal surface. Henry guessed it was only a matter of time before stalactites formed. The heater had packed up and the extractor fan wasn't working. The joy and glamour of surveillance work, Henry thought gloomily. He hoped that the target, Terry Anderson, would do the honour of appearing soon.

Henry looked at the small chemical toilet and speculated as to who would be the first person brave enough to use it.

The van was parked about one hundred metres away from a converted warehouse in which Anderson was supposed to have a small flat. Through the one-way windows which allowed them to look out and no one else to peer in, they could see anyone entering or leaving the flats.

Four other officers were covering the rear. They were hidden behind a wall and Henry was extremely sorry for them. They must have been really suffering in the cold. The outside temperature was below freezing, but at least it wasn't snowing or raining. Hardly a comfort, though.

The remainder of the firearms team were parked in an unmarked van, tucked away in a mill yard about a quarter of a mile away down the quayside.

It was assumed with reasonable certitude that Anderson was not at home. The surrounding streets had been scoured for any signs of his Shogun.

Henry hoped that if he did turn up, he wouldn't drive in by the route which would take him past the mill yard. The firearms vehicle, albeit unmarked, had a definite aura of 'police' about it. Any self-respecting villain would clock it immediately.

There were two other routes to the flat. One from the main road which ran through Lancaster, the other around the perimeter of a nearby housing estate. Observers in unmarked cars were parked unobtrusively on these routes, watching for Anderson's arrival.

Henry was under no illusions about their prey.

Anderson was a very violent, professional criminal. He was very shrewd and ultra-suspicious. It wouldn't surprise Henry if he spent some time reconnoitring the area, checking for any signs of police activity, before he thought it safe enough to stop. If anything seemed out of place or spooked him, he would bolt and they would never catch him. Henry hoped the man wanted to get home desperately – for a shit, or something – anything which would make him less switched on.

The fact that the surveillance van was parked in such an exposed position, in eyeball contact with the front of the warehouse, didn't help matters. Because of the geography of the location – right on the riverside – there was nowhere more subtle to position it. Fortunately it looked a pretty genuine electrician's van and didn't stand out like too much of a sore thumb.

Henry glanced at his companions.

Dave and Jack, the two firearms officers, sat in thoughtful silence with bored expressions on their faces. They were dressed in dark blue overalls, body armour, ballistic caps and black lace-up boots. Each had an HK MP5 across his chest and a pistol in a holder around the waist.

'OK?' Henry enquired.

They both nodded, said nothing. Strong silent types.

Henry looked at the far more appealing Siobhan Robson, his partner. She was in tight jeans, a tracksuit top and a fleece-lined zip-up jacket. Her hair had been pulled into a pony tail and tucked under a dark green woollen cap. With her hair thus taken up, her ears were going blue with cold. It didn't stop them being nice ears, though. She stuck the tip of her tongue out at Henry and smiled with her eyes.

He responded with a quick grin, then raised his eyebrows and looked out through the window, mulling over the plan of action if Anderson turned up. It had been decided that he should be allowed to park his car, get out and walk to the front entrance of the warehouse. There he had to key a number into a pad to gain entry to the building. The teams should hit him just as he was doing this, grab him, flatten him, cuff him, search him, arrest him.

At least that was the plan. Everyone seemed to understand it and that in itself was a bonus.

He shivered and clamped his teeth together to stop them making a clattering noise like badly adjusted tappets.

Of course there was a good chance Anderson would never turn up. Ever.

It was five past six.

At which time John Rider was climbing into bed, having spent the night at the scene of the fire. He had made a comprehensive statement to the police, being as honest with them as he thought necessary. Yes, he had recently fallen out big-style with someone, but he wasn't about to tell them that. What had happened was beyond the ability of the law to deal with. It was for him to sort out now, once and for all. To put an end to this madness with perhaps one more act of madness.

Munrow would have to die.

There was no other option now, he believed.

Isa had been with him throughout the night, watching him closely, trying to judge his mood, guess his intentions. But Rider was good. He showed nothing, kept a straight face, kept his anger controlled. Turned inside himself.

They had returned to the basement flat a little before six, both gritty and grubby from the smoke. They shared a shower in which they soaped each other down and washed each other's hair. Shortly after six they climbed into bed and Rider made ferocious love to Isa in a way which brought her to a wonderful multi-orgasm, but which also left her feeling slightly afraid.

Afterwards, before they fell asleep, Isa asked him the big question.

'Are you going to kill him?'

A terrible, faraway look came into Rider's eyes which made Isa's skin crawl.

He nodded, rolled over and within minutes was asleep.

Isa buried her face in the pillow, unable to stop the tears.

Four hours later, Henry and his team in the van were beginning to warm up a little. A weak-willed winter sun poked its reluctant nose from behind the grey clouds and was making a little difference to the temperature inside the van. It had risen to freezing point, but it was better than nothing. Several cups of shared coffee from flasks were also having a positive effect on internal body temperatures. Unfortunately the liquid was having an adverse effect on the bladders of two of them, Henry being one. He was feeling an increasingly urgent need to pay a visit to a toilet, but not the chemical one fitted in the van, watched by the others.

It was becoming a predicament, one which would have to be addressed sooner rather than later.

Henry crossed his legs and gave Siobhan a lopsided grin which seemed to convey his inner torment.

To be honest, Karl Donaldson did not really expect to hear from George Santana again. So when he answered the phone he was amazed to hear the crackle of static that meant long distance, and the faint sound of Santana's voice at the far end.

'I have some news for you, Agent Donaldson,' Santana revealed after the opening exchange of pleasantries.

Donaldson waited to be told.

'We have been keeping your man under observation and there is nothing to report on that front,' the Madeiran detective said. 'However, we have learned that he has booked a seat on a charter-plane flight to the United Kingdom.'

'When and where does it land?' He expected to be told Heathrow, next Monday . . . something like that.

'Around four o'clock this afternoon. Manchester.'

Donaldson closed his eyes despairingly. He scribbled down the flight details as Santana said them, thanked him and hung up.

Fucking Manchester in six hours!

Not impossible – but pretty godammed difficult to arrange for someone to greet him and drop onto his tail.

He fleetingly considered ringing Henry Christie and telling him to haul ass to the airport – like they'd done once on a previous job. Then he remembered Henry was now on local CID in Blackpool and didn't have the roving commission that he'd had when on the Regional Crime Squad. He couldn't come and go as he pleased any more.

It left Donaldson with a dilemma. Should he go to Manchester himself and risk being spotted by Hamilton, or should he arrange for the cops in Manchester to put a surveillance team on him?

Six hours. Short notice to get someone to drop everything and follow a man whom they did not know, who was not really suspected of doing anything. It was pretty unlikely they would wear that.

So, by a process of deduction, there was only one solution.

He reached for the phone.

Twenty minutes later, Henry was almost weeping with the agony of trying to hold it all in. He had to pass water instantaneously, otherwise he'd burst in a spectacular fashion.

'I need to pee,' he declared, 'and I'm not using that!' He pointed accusingly to the chemical toilet.

'I could do with one too,' said Philpot, the firearms officer.

'Right,' said Henry. He looked out of the window. There was nothing moving on the Quay, vehicles, people, anything. He did a quick radio check using a prearranged code to find out if anyone had spotted the approach of Anderson and all came back negative. It seemed as good a time as any to break cover and dash across the road into the gap between two buildings and indulge in some blissful relief.

'We run across to that alley, go down to the far end of it and do it there. Then we wait for the all clear' – he nodded towards Siobhan – 'three clicks on the radio, and we'll pile back into the van.'

'Gotcha,' said Philpot, who for the last ten minutes had been fidgeting like he had a ferret down his trousers.

Henry opened the back door an inch. A blast of ice-cold air rushed in. He had another look to ensure it really was safe to go, dropped out of the van, sprinted across the road and disappeared down the alley, Philpot in hot pursuit.

They began to do what came naturally, their faces a picture of almost perfect pleasure.

Siobhan's voice came over the radio, the words in rapid fire. 'He's here. Target One's here. He's pulled up at the front of the warehouse!' There was a degree of panic in her speech.

'Fuck!' uttered Henry. He had to finish peeing because he didn't think he had a strong enough bladder to halt the process. Neither did Philpot. Both were in full flow, unstoppable. 'How the hell did he get here without us knowing first? C'mon, c'mon.' Henry urged himself. Down his radio he said, 'You'd better get the ball rolling, Siobhan. We'll be right behind you.'

If we can stop pissing.

Terry Anderson pulled up outside the converted warehouse in which he rented a one-bedroomed flat where he occasionally dossed down. He was driving his Shogun which bore Southern Irish numberplates. He applied the handbrake and switched off the engine only seconds after Henry and his urinating colleague had disappeared down the alley. Had Anderson been less than a minute earlier he would have seen them climbing out of the van. As it was, the quayside looked safe and sound. A few parked cars. A van. No pedestrians. Nothing out of the ordinary.

He had been scanning police airwaves and again, nothing was going on which indicated a surveillance operation was underway. He caught a few officers transmitting radio checks, but it meant nothing to him.

He felt pretty secure.

The scanner was lodged on the dash of the Shogun. He leaned forwards and switched it off at the exact moment Siobhan made her hurried transmission to Henry.

Anderson did not hear it.

He did not sit for long in the car. He had parked in the residents' bay on the opposite side of the road to the warehouse. He got out, locking the vehicle with the remote, and trotted towards the front entrance of the warehouse.

Out of the corner of his eye he saw the rear doors of the van opening. Instinctively he knew he was in trouble.

The sight of two armed cops, one in uniform, one in plain clothes, confirmed his intuition.

Anderson did not hesitate, caught as he was between his car and the protection of the building.

His three-quarter-length sheepskin coat was unbuttoned, as always. He flung it open, skewed round to face the two officers, and the mini-Uzi which was hanging on a strap around his neck fell naturally into his hands with the ease of much practice. He clicked off the safety with his thumb and immediately whacked a short burst at the officers, bending low as he fired.

The uniformed male officer took the brunt of the burst across his shoulders and chest. The bullets ripped into his unprotected right shoulder and the rest thudded into his body armour – which saved his life. The impact spun him round like a top and he staggered face-first back into the surveillance van, screaming as blood spurted out from the wounds.

The female officer hit the deck, diving out of sight behind a car.

Two more officers appeared from an alley, one in plain clothes, one in uniform. Anderson gritted his teeth and loosed off another short burst in their direction. They leapt back down the alley, into cover.

Anderson turned and sprinted along St George's Quay, disappearing out of sight underneath the railway bridge which spanned the end of the road.

Gun in hand, Henry ran up the alley towards the Quay. He could see Siobhan and the firearms officer jumping out of the back of the van and hear Siobhan's near-hysterical voice over the radio, urging the rest of the troops to get going. 'Move, come on, go!' or words to that effect. There was the dull 'du-du-du-du' – a sound Henry recognised immediately as that of an automatic weapon being fired. The firearms officer pirouetted, clutching at his shoulder which had exploded in bright red, and toppled back into the van, screaming. Siobhan dived for cover. One officer down.

By this time, Henry and Philpot had reached the end of the alley. They ran rather stupidly out onto the road and showed themselves.

Henry saw Anderson about seventy metres away. The smoking muzzle of the deadly black Uzi zeroed in on the detective. Henry jarred to a halt, threw himself at Philpot and they bundled back into the alley only a fraction of a second before Anderson pulled the trigger again and released a deadly burst of bullets.

Stone chips flew. One lodged in Henry's cheek. It was like being stung by a wasp.

They flattened themselves against the wall. Henry was breathing heavily already. Blood trickled warmly down his face. He wiped it away with the back of his hand.

He pivoted low out of the alley, gun in his right hand, supported by the left, bouncing on his knees. His elbows locked in an isosceles triangle ready to return fire, though painfully aware that the distance between himself and Anderson made the prospect of hitting him pretty remote . . . but all he saw was a glimpse of Anderson's back in the fleeting second before he went out of sight.

'Leader to Car One,' Henry bellowed down his radio. 'He's on foot,

189

coming towards you, wearing a light tan coat, sheepskin collar, carrying an automatic weapon which he has used.'

Car One was the unmarked car which was supposed to have been keeping observations at the entrance to the Quay to clock Anderson if he came in that way. If the occupants of that car had been doing their job right, they should have seen Anderson and warned the surveillance van. That was an issue Henry would be taking up with those officers later.

'You stay here,' he yelled across to Siobhan. 'Look after him – call an ambulance. C'mon, bud, let's move,' he said to Philpot.

He went after Anderson, mindful that things had gone horribly wrong in less than a minute. Doesn't take long for a job to get fucked up.

He and Philpot, who was much fitter and soon moved into the lead, ran to the end of the Quay where it becomes Damside Street, then onto the junction with Bridge Lane. Car One screamed down Bridge Lane from the direction of the city centre and squealed onto Damside Street, pulling up alongside Henry and Philpot.

The two officers aboard looked shamefaced. They had been away from their designated point and hadn't bothered telling anyone. There were two Kentucky Fried Chicken wrappers in the back seat.

Henry was fuming. He could not recall a time in his life when he had been quite so fucking enraged.

'You fucking wankers – where have you been?' he screamed through the driver's window. He couldn't be bothered to await a reply. 'You' – he pointed at the passenger – 'get out.' He turned to Philpot. 'You and this dipstick get going after him on foot. I'll get a lift to the southern end of town and work my way back down on foot. Right, get going, go on, fuck off!'

Henry leapt into the passenger seat and said, 'Drop me off at the Kentucky – you obviously know where that is.'

Dumbly the officer nodded.

Henry reholstered his gun.

He took a few seconds to marshal his thoughts before getting back on the radio. Then he directed two of the four officers who'd been at the back of the warehouse to make their way into the city centre and start searching. The other two were told to remain at the scene in case Anderson doubled back and also to assist Siobhan with the injured officer. He told the firearms team in the van to drive up to the police station, park their vehicles and begin searching from there. The two officers in the plain car tasked to watch the other route to Anderson's flat were given a free hand.

Flood the place, that's what he wanted to do. Flood the place and flush him out – if he was still there.

His mind was racing as he tried to consider all the angles.

The bus station, taxi rank and railway station all needed cover, as did every other way out of the city by foot and car.

He glared at the officer who was driving, but couldn't find the words to adequately express his emotions. He shook his head, exhaled an exaggerated sigh and kept his mouth shut. The officer concentrated on driving, totally aware he was being appraised by someone who probably wanted to throttle him.

Within two minutes they were at the southern tip of the city, at the top of Penny Street, one of the main shopping thoroughfares. Henry opened his door and as he got out said, 'You cruise the area and don't go to the Kentucky or I'll be sending your P45 to your home address.'

'Yes, Sarge,' said the chastened PC.

Henry stood upright. Blood dribbled down his face into the corner of his mouth. He wiped his sleeve across it. Then, with his hand on the butt of his revolver in the upside-down holster, he walked towards the centre of Lancaster. He moved slowly, pausing occasionally, looking, his eyes never resting.

The town was busy. It was difficult to spot anyone in particular amongst the throng of shoppers. He constantly relayed his position to the other members of the team and they to him.

Time was running out. Five minutes had passed since the incident and each passing second meant that Anderson was less likely to be caught. It was like looking for a needle . . . Henry tensed up, thinking he had spotted Anderson but no, it was a lookalike. Similar, but not him. Shit. There were so many places he could disappear to.

Henry had reached the junction with Common Garden Street. From this point northwards, Penny Street became a pedestrianised area. On the opposite corner was a branch of Marks & Spencer, Kate's favourite shop. Henry crossed the road, stood next to the shop window and stared down Penny Street into the impenetrable mass of people.

Damn, he cursed. He knew they had lost Anderson, just knew it. Henry's chance to make a good impression on the NWOCS – and he'd completely ballsed it up. Everything Morton had said he didn't want to happen, had happened. May not have been his fault personally, but he was the man in charge, the one who would have to answer all the awkward questions. The buck stopped firmly with him.

He glanced into Marks & Spencer.

And there he was, lurking behind a rack of sports gear.

They locked eyes.

Henry yanked his gun out of the holster.

Anderson stepped to one side, out of the cover provided by the sports-wear. The Uzi was in his hands. He fired at Henry, spraying bullets through the huge sheet of plate glass which separated the two men and made up the store frontage. Henry hurled himself to one side, dropping his weapon as he did so, and the whole window disintegrated spectacularly, like an avalanche, showering him with millions of shards of glass.

He was absolutely covered in the stuff – in his hair, down his shirt, in his pockets.

But he was unhurt.

The shopping had stopped in Penny Street. With screams and shrieks, everyone was running away or taking cover.

Anderson walked confidently towards Henry, Uzi in hand, a look of determination on his face and the intention of wiping out a detective. He lifted the small but deadly weapon and aimed at Henry's chest.

Henry saw Anderson's right forefinger curl around the trigger and pull it back. He saw the muzzle flash. Heard the crack and felt the impact on his sternum like a steam hammer. The force of the impact bowled him over and sent him sprawling in the broken glass.

But the bullet didn't penetrate, just seemed to knock the wind out of him as though he'd been rugby-tackled by six prop forwards.

For a moment he lay there dazed and slightly confused. Then what had happened sank in. He looked up and focused on Anderson.

It had been the last round in Anderson's magazine, and Henry was still alive because he'd worn the protective vest given to him by Siobhan the day before. In his dreams he gave her a big sloppy kiss.

Anderson had discarded the empty magazine, produced a full one from his coat pocket and was fumbling to slot it in, when he looked up and saw the six foot two, fourteen-stone frame of Henry Christie charging towards him through the space where there had once been a window.

Henry came in low. Anderson swung the empty gun at his head. Henry dodged it skilfully and his left shoulder powered into Anderson's solar plexus. He drove the wanted man hard backwards into a display of men's underwear which crashed around them.

The Uzi flew out of Anderson's grip and clattered away to one side.

The two men rolled and fought in a bed of boxer shorts and Y-fronts.

Anderson's fist connected with Henry's lower jaw, stunning him, sending shockwaves around his skull. Henry slumped off, shaking his head, allowing Anderson to get to his feet. He lashed out with his boot at Henry who immediately lunged at his legs to smother the kicks.

He overbalanced Anderson and this time the pair brought down a display of trousers and a mannequin.

They rolled through these, face to face, sometimes eyeball to eyeball, neither one able to get the upper hand. Anderson tried to head-butt Henry, who twisted his face out of the way only to expose his left ear to Anderson's mouth – who, never one to fight clean – bit into it hard and nasty, worrying it like a terrier, trying to rip it off the side of Henry's face.

The pain was phenomenal. Henry screamed. With a superhuman effort he wrenched his shredded ear out of Anderson's mouth and dug him hard in the ribs with a punch from his right fist. Anderson groaned.

The two men separated from each other, both scrambling madly in an effort to be the first one to get to his feet, to gain the advantage.

They made it simultaneously.

Six feet apart.

They stared at each other.

Anderson spat out a gobful of blood and ear onto the prostrate mannequin, which lay there dismembered. He wiped his mouth.

Henry could hardly draw breath. He was acutely aware at that precise moment how out of shape he was and that, maybe, he was getting too old for shit like this. His ear was giving him the most horrendous pain. He had never even contemplated how painful it could be to have someone bite your ear off. He put a hand up to it. Christ! It felt like it was hanging off. The hand came away covered in crimson.

Anderson smiled. He had blood on his teeth. He looked like something from a cheap horror movie, but the worst of it was that this was real life and the blood on the teeth was Henry's.

Anderson's right hand went to his left sleeve. Henry had a quick and awful premonition . . . he was right.

A huge knife slid out of the sleeve.

Henry's heart sank. The cunt was really well prepared for the worst. It was one of those quasi-military style knives where the handle was actually a knuckleduster and the blade was pretty damned near a scythe.

'Give up . . . Give up now,' Henry croaked hoarsely between rasping breaths. 'There'll be a dozen cops here soon and when they see that thing in your hand they'll blow you away. You'll be dead, I promise you, Terry.'

Anderson flexed his fingers in the knuckleduster and his grip tightened on the handle.

Henry prepared himself to be skewered.

From behind him came a sound he would never have believed he would be relieved to hear.

A weapon being cocked.

Anderson looked up past Henry's shoulder and the smile dropped off his face.

'Armed police! Drop your weapon!'

The cavalry had arrived.

Chapter Seventeen

Munrow remained in an exceptionally bad mood as he constantly reviewed yesterday's proceedings. He could not even begin to get over the way he'd been treated by Rider.

Left out on the moors in the middle of nowhere. Naked. Todmorden? Where the fuck was that? Freezing his bollocks off, having to undergo the torment and humiliation of trying to find an ignition key in a fucking snowdrift. Could have died of hypothermia. Then having to drive all the way back to his woman's house, covered in an oily car blanket, cowering down all the time, hoping no one would see him, or the cops pulled him. How in the name of shit would he have explained that to a Wooden Top?

So embarrassing.

He had been made to look a complete fool.

And nobody made Munrow look a fool. No one. No cunt got away with that – uninjured.

He sat brooding in a pub in the town centre of Preston, a pint of Thwaites Mild in his hand, waiting for the woman to turn up.

They had arranged to meet here so she could take him shopping for a new set of clothes befitting a free man. She had a rich husband in the oil business and a credit card with a ten thousand limit on it. The trap of an unhappy marriage made her want to spend to the hilt and, basically, stick two fingers up at Hubby who she knew was having it away in Saudi.

Munrow knew little about her, other than she was one of the prison visitors. Unpaid, doing it for a social service. She'd easily fallen under his powerful aura to the extent that they'd even contrived to screw in the prison classroom once, when he'd rear-ended her over a table.

He did not want to know very much about her. All he wanted from her was enough sex to see him through the post-prison rampant stage and then money.

One of his plans that afternoon was to induce her to make a substantial withdrawal and hand every penny over to him. Wham, bam, thank you, silly cow. He needed the money to pay off the men who had helped him cause mayhem in Conroy's clubs the other night. They were cheap to hire.

He took a big swig of his beer. His mind skipped to Conroy who, he imagined, would be shitting himself at that moment. Munrow's show of uncompromising strength would have worried him badly and he would no doubt want to talk pronto, although Munrow's plans did not include negotiations at that stage. More force needed to be shown, just to get the message across very clearly: Munrow was here to stay. He was back and wanted a chunk of the action.

Over the weekend he planned to hit some of Conroy's council-estate distribution houses in East Lancashire . . . then maybe there could be some talk. Or if the mood took him, he might just move his men into one of Conroy's Manchester clubs and take the place over. No talk. No fucking about. Yeah, he might do that.

It could be as simple as that.

As for Rider . . . that bastard would really suffer.

'Hello, sweetheart.' There was a tap on Munrow's shoulder. It was his woman. He had to admit she was – or had been – drop dead gorgeous. And she was cracking in bed. Amazing what a shit of a husband can do to a woman.

But deep down, Munrow sneered contemptuously at her. Naive, stupid cow. Didn't realise she was going to be screwed – in more ways than one.

For the time being he was going to play along. He hadn't satisfied himself sexually yet and those years behind bars had made him crave for it. He was going to have his fill before he robbed her blind, then dumped her broke.

He slid his arm round her slim waist and squeezed her breast. She bent down and kissed him hard on the mouth, breaking off eventually with a gasp.

'How are you feeling, darling?'

'Fine, got myself together now. Are you OK?'

'Yes, yes, thanks for asking.'

She had been on the verge of hysteria when he got back from his trip to Todmorden. At least she hadn't called the cops. He reassured her it was all one big mistake and things were fine. The less she knew the better. She had swallowed his cock and bull story and it was only when they both shared a hot shower and she knelt down in front of him and swallowed his cock and spunk did she really calm down.

After a few hours' sleep, Munrow had then scoured Manchester for the only person who knew exactly where he had been. The only person who could have given Rider the information about his whereabouts.

Toni Thomas, the bitch.

It was a waste of time. Toni was very noticeable by his/her absence.

'So, Debenhams? Burtons? Where do you fancy?'

Munrow came back to the present. He shrugged. 'Anywhere. You're buying, babe.'

The adrenalin ebbed out of Henry's body to be replaced by suffering.

He eased the protective vest carefully over his head – carefully because he did not want to knock his ear which was hanging off – laid it to one side and looked unwillingly down at his chest where the bullet from the mini-Uzi had struck his sternum.

There was a revolting, circular, deep purple mark with a single black spot at its centre which looked like he'd been struck by a hammer. When he breathed, he recoiled involuntarily. Jesus, he could not believe how painful it was. It gripped his sternum like a clawed fist. He was certain it must be cracked.

And his ear. His lovely ear. Bitten off by a madman. They estimated ten stitches to get it back on.

He was sitting on the edge of a bed in a cubicle in the casualty department of the Royal Lancaster Infirmary, a curtain drawn across. He removed the remaining items of his clothing, shoes, socks, jeans and underpants, shaking each item of clothing to try and dislodge the fragments of glass which had got into them and were slowly skinning him.

He was giving his underpants a very thorough shaking when the curtain was swished back. Siobhan appeared.

'Henry. Can't you wait?'

He couldn't help but smile. She withdrew tactfully and he called her in when he was half-decent, sat there in his Y-fronts.

'Sorry about that,' he said. 'The glass, you know?'

'How are you?'

'Shaken and stirred. How 'bout you?'

'I'll survive,' she said bravely. Henry could see that in spite of her smiles and the outwardly 'couldn't give a toss' attitude, she had actually been terrified when Anderson had opened up and the firearms officer had fallen next to her.

She took in a long deep breath. 'At least Dave's all right, though his shoulder is a real mess. He'll have pretty restricted movement in it.'

'I'll go and see him once I'm sorted out.'

They regarded each other for a moment. Siobhan's eyes took in Henry's bloodied, dangling ear, then lowered to inspect the other injury on his chest. 'That looks awful,' she grimaced.

'I know. Feels like I've been hit by a truck.'

'No, not that,' she said wickedly. ' Your beer belly.'

They caught each other's eye and burst into laughter – which Henry couldn't handle because it made him cringe in agony.

The amusement was curtailed when a fairly fearsome-looking nurse stepped into the cubicle, pushing a trolley bearing an assortment of trays, instruments, dressings and needles.

'I've come to clean your ear up. The doctor wants to sew it back on. He'll be here shortly.'

Henry was discharged two hours later, having had an X-ray which showed nothing broken, had his ear re-fitted and visited the firearms officer who had taken the bullet. The guy was in great pain, but stoical about the injury. He was about to go into surgery.

Henry also made a quick call home, told Kate briefly what had happened and that – God willing – he would be home as soon as possible. Bad as he felt, Henry wanted to get into Anderson's ribs.

Siobhan drove him down to Lancaster police station in the surveillance van. She found a space on the lower parking area. Anderson's Shogun had been seized and was parked in one corner of the yard.

'I drove it up,' Siobhan explained, 'but it hasn't been searched yet. I thought perhaps you'd want to do that.'

Henry frowned doubtfully, then dismissed the thought that it should have been searched already. He happily accepted that she believed he would want to supervise a thorough search of the vehicle. She handed him the keys to it, then they climbed out of the van and walked to the Shogun.

'Oooh, I could do with a wee,' she declared. 'You get on with it, Henry, if you like. I'll be back as soon as I've found a loo.'

She dashed off to the entrance to the Custody Office and was buzzed in through the security door, leaving Henry alone with the keys and the car. Thinking nothing of the situation, he inserted a key into the back door and turned it. As the door opened, Henry saw that a travel rug was laid out over something in the back.

He tugged it off and what was revealed made him puff his cheeks out in disbelief.

One sawn-off shotgun – an Italian SPAS 12.

And two mini-Uzis.

He did not touch them, merely stared at them in amazement. These were the last things he realistically expected to find in the back of Anderson's vehicle – the tools of his trade and quite possibly the guns responsible for killing Geoff Driffield and five other innocent people. How could the man be so stupid?

'What've you found?' Siobhan reappeared behind Henry's shoulder, peeked into the Shogun and was awestruck by the discovery. She hissed the words, 'Pure gold,' into Henry's good ear. 'If these guns tied up ballistically . . .' She did not need to say anything else.

Henry stayed silent, blinking at how easy it had been.

He called in a firearms officer to handle the weapons and disarm them as necessary, then after a full search of the Shogun which revealed nothing else, the guns were booked into the property store and locked in a safe.

DI Gallagher and DS Tattersall arrived at the station as Henry was about to have an initial interview with Anderson.

'Well done, you two,' Gallagher said to them. 'We need to thoroughly debrief what went on and, of course, go through the post-incident procedures for firearms incidents and consider counselling where necessary.'

He looked knowingly at Henry here, who, following a previous firearms incident had suffered a nervous breakdown caused by post-traumatic stress. Henry was fine at the moment but he knew these things had a habit of creeping up on people and addling their brains when they least expected it. He thought that Siobhan might benefit from counselling, although he didn't suggest it. The choice rested with the individual.

'What you need to do now is get your statement done,' Gallagher told him.

'We were going to chat to him now,' Henry said.

Gallagher shook his head. 'Bad practice. Me and Jim'll do that. We've been involved from day one. It's our pigeon.'

'It should be down to us,' Henry persisted.

'No – and that's final. You've done a good job, now leave it be and let someone else take it over.'

Henry's nostrils flared. He was getting angry. He put a lid on it and nodded. 'Did the other targets get arrested?'

'Two locked up, one still outstanding. They are in custody in Blackpool. We intend to interview Anderson up here though, then take him to Blackpool. They'll be in court on Monday morning. Look, you've both done a superb job today,' Gallagher concluded. 'Get the paperwork done, then go home, relax, do whatever you fancy. Enjoy yourselves.'

The men's clothing department in Debenhams, Preston, is in the basement. There was a vast array of clothes to choose from. Mind-boggling, really.

Munrow's mind was totally boggled. He had already been treated to about six hundred pounds' worth of gear from other shops in Preston and was therefore loaded with bags crammed to bursting with shirts, ties, trousers, jeans, shoes and chic sporting gear, and was frankly completely pissed-off. He stuck with it because he had not yet induced the woman to make that cash withdrawal he so desperately wanted. When she did and the money was in his fist, the shopping would come to an abrupt end.

He took a glance at his watch. Almost four. He groaned angrily. 'We've missed the banks.'

She gave him a patronising look. 'No, we haven't, sweetie.'

'But they close at half-past three!'

'You have been away a long time,' she chided him gently. 'Five o'clock now, mostly.' She took a breath and her eyes flickered a once-over. 'You really need a suit.'

They browsed through the tailoring department, Munrow glumly at her heels. His body language mirrored his state of mind. Fed up with shopping, impatient for her to get her money out. Shoulders slumped. Dragging his feet. Stifling yawns between scowling at her back. He was like a husband being hauled around. He also felt ludicrously out of place.

'I'd really like you to get some bespoke tailoring,' he heard her saying ahead of him. 'Fit you out in a really nice, made-to-measure suit. But that'll have to wait. For now, how about a couple off the peg?'

She stopped, turned unexpectedly, a broad smile of pleasure on her lovely lips. Her indulgence was making her extremely happy and at the moment she did not care who knew about it, or saw them. Even her husband.

Munrow thought he had changed his expression in time, but he was wrong.

'You're tired, aren't you, lovey?' she said sympathetically, misreading the signs. 'This is the last stop, promise. Then we'll book into the Post House and have a fashion show. And then we shall fuck.' She said those last five words in a dark, husky whisper. 'How about that?'

'Sounds good.'

'Now, what about this one?' She unhooked a suit off the rail and held it up against him.

They finished the reports in about an hour, sitting in the CID office in Lancaster.

It was four o'clock. Henry was having trouble keeping awake. The week had shattered him anyway, but now his sore body and soul was the icing on the cake.

He yawned and slouched back in the chair, glancing very quickly through the statement he'd concocted.

'You look whacked, Henry,' Siobhan said softly. She was sitting on the other side of the desk, gazing at him.

'I admit it. Been a long week.'

Yes, it had.

Beginning with kneeing Shane Mulcahy in the nuts last Saturday evening and ending here, almost a full week later, having been shot. And in between, what had there been? The murders in the newsagents. The dead girl on the beach. Boris the gorilla – Christ, he'd forgotten about the gorilla. The chase with Dundaven after Nina had been shot (Christ, he'd almost forgotten about her too). McNamara. Degsy dying. Long hours. Meeting John Rider for the first time. Virtually no sleep. Dead cops, injured primates. Gun finds and fights. Helicopters. Arguments with Kate. The NWOCS. Being teamed up with Siobhan Robson. That kiss . . . which seemed to make it all worthwhile.

Henry's back was to the door. Siobhan looked past him and nodded at someone entering the office.

It was Gallagher, having completed the first interview with Anderson, who was being represented by a duty solicitor. Not surprisingly he'd said nothing. The interview sessions with him were going to be long and drawn-out, like pulling teeth, only much more painful. Henry was glad now that it was someone else's problem. He enjoyed interviewing suspects but all his energy had drained out.

Gallagher told them how difficult Anderson was being, but he wasn't worried. 'He'll be well stitched-up by the time we've finished,' he said. It transpired that a search of Anderson's flat had produced a Dolce & Gabbana T-shirt, a pair of two-tone shoes and a white pork-pie hat. Exactly the gear the gang had been wearing on the robberies.

The term 'stitched-up' left Henry somewhat cold. It had ominous overtones and wasn't a world away from 'fitting-up'. Falsifying evidence and other such illegal practices was a road that Henry would never go down. He believed it was his job to find evidence, root it out, even if the way he found it was occasionally off-centre. He had never resorted to anything underhand. He was just too straight.

Maybe 'stitched-up' was simply one of Gallagher's favoured phrases and meant nothing. Henry let it pass. It would soon come back to haunt him.

'Right, Henry, time to go home now,' said Gallagher. He swapped a quick glance with Siobhan which Henry caught but did not comprehend. A furrowed brow, a questioning look, a brief nod to each other, then the DI said, 'Oh, I forgot. That surveillance van needs to go back to Blackburn. Siobhan, do you mind? Henry – sorry, pal. The other team'll need it tonight. Pick up one of the other cars to get you home.'

'Sure, boss,' she said.

'Henry?'

'No problem,' he said wearily. However, the prospect of a trip all the way to Blackburn before heading home to Blackpool was fairly daunting. It would add at least ninety minutes to the journey time – on a good day – and this was a Friday, rush hour. Yuk! He was beginning to need his bed desperately.

'I like that one, I really do,' she said admiringly, a thoughtful finger on her chin, pretty head tilted to one side. 'It makes you look sexy.'

Munrow said, 'Good, let's get it.'

It was a nice suit and fitted him perfectly. He liked it. At two hundred quid, he loved it.

'Yes, let's,' she said gleefully, but grabbed another one from the display, 'and try this one too. It's lovely.'

She handed it over to him.

He turned the beginning of a scowl into a smile of acceptance and reluctantly took the suit. 'Then we go – and fuck,' he said. *And you give me plenty money*.

Her eyes sparkled. 'Yes, darling.'

Munrow went back into the fitting room and reversed into a cubicle, drawing the curtain behind him.

He tugged the jacket off and dropped it deliberately onto the floor in a little display of petulance. He unzipped his trousers and let them slither down his legs and kicked them off over his shoes.

The curtain was yanked back.

He was about to tell whoever it was to fuck off out of it and maybe give the bastard a push in the chest for invading his privacy, but he didn't get the opportunity to do either.

'No, John,' he gasped instead, terrified. He stepped backwards against the wall and raised his hands defensively. 'No, don't.'

They were the last words he spoke.

The gun in John Rider's hand roared twice and deafeningly in the confined space of Debenham's men's fitting rooms.

The first of the .357-calibre bullets left the barrel of the revolver and flashed its short way through the air, entering Munrow's face by way of his top lip, blowing a huge hole below his nose, destroying the upper set of teeth, tearing through the back of his throat and exiting through the base of his skull.

The next one whacked into his cranium, above and to the right of his left eye. This one did not exit, but remained inside the skull, ripping his brain to shreds with the glee of an angry bull in Debenham's china shop.

Rider was gone before Munrow's twitching body shimmied to the floor. A mass of blood, deep red, almost black blood, full of oxygen, and particles of bone were smeared down the cubicle wall. A fine haze of pink spray hung in the air, mixing with the smoke from the gun.

His new suits were ruined.

Chapter Eighteen

Henry was never completely sure how it started. He didn't think he was responsible, nor did he think he did anything to further it. There was a blur, then he found himself almost at the point of no return before his senses clicked into gear.

Siobhan drove from Lancaster, all the way to the NWOCS offices in King Street. It was a fairly uncomfortable journey in the high-seated Transit but Henry, well strapped in, dozed off quickly. His head rolled and jerked with the motion of the van and his partly opened mouth allowed spittle to dribble down his chin and jacket. He was away with the fairies and would have been no use in an emergency.

Before he knew it, they were in Blackburn, pulling into the secure yard.

Siobhan parked in one corner whilst Henry shook himself into wakefulness and rubbed the dried saliva from his face with a sheepish glint at Siobhan to see if she had noticed. She had.

'Ole sleepy head,' she said with a soft chuckle.

He had a painful crick in his neck from his sleeping position and a heavy sensation behind his eyelids, as if grains of sand had been surgically implanted. His eyes were gritty and sore, his chest was throbbing and his ear screaming.

He was not in good shape.

Siobhan unbuckled her seat belt and dropped lightly out of the van. Henry duly followed suit. His movements were like an old man's. His injuries had tightened him up and the pain in his chest on moving was initially like a heart attack until he straightened up. He was also beginning to appreciate how hard Anderson had punched him in the face during their fight.

A couple of minutes later, having negotiated the alarm system, they entered the deserted offices and signed their guns and equipment back in. Henry was switched on enough to see that Morton had not countersigned the firearms log-sheet. Siobhan told him not to worry. It was something that often happened. He would do it later.

Henry was holding his bulletproof vest in his hand. He proffered it to Siobhan, who was holding hers.

'Come on, I'll show you where we keep stuff like this.'

'I thought the other team would be on duty,' Henry remarked.

Siobhan just shrugged.

They went back downstairs and walked across the car park to a door to the right of the garage doors. She keyed in a number on the pad and opened it. They entered a small vestibule. The main garage was through a door to the left. A staircase was dead ahead. Siobhan went straight up in front of Henry. He glanced into the garage which housed three saloon cars. He assumed they belonged to the unit. Then he was right behind her, with her compact bum at his face level, her flesh packed into the tight jeans she'd been wearing all day. Henry attempted not to notice. And failed.

Upstairs there were two offices. The larger was a store-room-cum-equipment room with shelving and large metal cabinets lining the walls. An old settee and table were also in the room, probably remnants from previous occupants, Henry guessed.

Siobhan unlocked one of the cabinets and hung up the body armour.

Henry stifled a yawn.

'Am I boring you?'

'Far from it.'

A wave of *déjà vu* skittered through him as once again he found himself within inches of her face. Inexplicably he became weak and open for offers.

'Henry,' she said hesitantly, 'I was terrified today – when Anderson opened up and Dave got shot right next to me. I thought I'd be next.' The words tumbled out, becoming increasingly shaky. 'I've never experienced anything like that. It happened so fast, too. I mean, suddenly I was on the ground and Anderson was firing. It was all so unreal, yet so utterly frightening. I can't find the words to describe it.'

'I know.'

'You've been through it before.'

'Doesn't get any easier. I was frightened too. There's nothing wrong admitting it. If you bottle it up, it'll do your head in.'

'Henry.'

'Yes?'

'Will you hold me? I need some . . . comfort. I feel all dithery.'

He nodded.

She fell into him, crushing herself against his chest. Very painful for him, actually. He steeled himself and took it like a man, without complaint. Her breasts pushed up against him and her warm body clung desperately to him, wanting to find some reassurance from him that she was safe now. He closed his eyes and tilted his head back, his arms wrapping around her shoulders and gently squeezing.

He wasn't sure how long they stayed like that. Probably only seconds.

Then he became aware that she was looking up at him. She drew back slightly and said, 'That was nice, Henry. I needed that.'

'So did I.'

'And I still want to kiss you.'

There was a pause between them when time stood still. And from that moment on, things became very mixed-up and confused for Henry.

He lowered his head, she went up onto her toes, and their lips came into soft contact. An electric shock pulsated through him. Initially they tentatively explored each other's lips. Then their mouths forced themselves hard onto each other. Hard and passionate. A whimper of pleasure escaped from somewhere deep inside Siobhan's throat. Her tongue slithered into his mouth. He took it. Bit it. Bit her lips. Sinking his teeth firmly into the soft wet flesh, driving her into a frenzy.

Her fingers gripped his hair. He grew hard quickly. She felt it and responded by spreading her legs around his thighs and grinding herself urgently against him. Her breath came in short pants. Through the denim of her jeans Henry could feel the pulsating heat of her sex.

She threw her head back and Henry's mouth moved down to her beautiful throat, where he could see her jugular throbbing wildly.

She forced his jacket off his shoulders. He drew his arms out of the sleeves. The garment dropped to the floor with a sigh of air. Her fingers went to his shirt, fumbling impatiently with the buttons, eventually ripping the last one off. She tugged the shirt out of his jeans and her face went to his injured chest. She softly licked the deep purple bruising over his breastbone and she unbuckled his belt.

The pain ebbed away from Henry's damaged body, replaced by a wave of energy.

'Oh God, Henry, we need to do it,' she said.

No. Say no, Henry, you complete fucking imbecile. Think of Kate. The girls. Think about what happened last time.

'Yes,' he said hoarsely.

He eased her out of her zip-up jacket and pulled her tracksuit top over her head. She released her grip on his fly and lifted up her arms obligingly to facilitate the movement. He tossed the top to one side and his arms quickly carried out a pincer movement to her back, his fingers meeting in the middle at her bra strap. It was a smooth manoeuvre and the clasp was breached in a second and the bra dropped to the floor.

He could feel her easing his jeans off, which ended up around his ankles, then she pulled down the front of his Y-fronts.

Another of those deep throaty groans broke from her lips when she grabbed his hard, swaying cock and slid back the foreskin.

'Aaah,' he heard himself say. His hands went to her breasts, her nipples erect against the palms. He looked down at them. They were sweet, deep pink, long and excited.

'Come over here,' she urged him.

They shifted to the settee like practising dance partners, allowing Henry the chance to step out of his jeans and trainers. He sat down quickly, removing his underpants and socks as he did so. Siobhan stood over him, bending forwards, those beautiful breasts hanging near his face. In a second she was out of her jeans and knickers. Both of them were completely naked.

He had only a few seconds to appreciate her body before she pushed him back onto the settee. He lay there without a fight. She went on him immediately, devouring him in her mouth and he surprised himself by not ejaculating there and then. She worked on him with wonderful lips and a wet, wet tongue, constantly looking up at him, judging his pleasure, until he could stand it no longer – at which juncture he took hold of her and drew her up.

He sat up. She sat next to him. He dropped to his knees and twisted round between her legs.

God, she smelled intoxicating.

For a moment they stared into each other's eyes. Her mouth was open and wet and hot as he clamped his over it and kissed her fiercely. His fingers slid from her breasts and down between her legs, searching for and finding her. She was soaking.

'I get very wet,' she said.

'Apparently.'

She lay back, opening herself to him. His head went down, his mouth working over her, tongue probing deftly, darting in, out, around. She squirmed and moaned, rotating her hips as everything built inside her. 'Beautiful,' she murmured appreciatively. 'Henry, come on, do it, fuck me. Come on, let's fuck now.'

What? Maybe he was an old-fashioned fuddy-duddy, but somehow the word seemed so . . . inappropriate. OK, it is what they were about to do. But *fuck*? This wasn't going to be a *fuck*, was it? Kate would never use such terminology . . . yeah, Kate.

He shrugged off the brief unease and helped Siobhan to lie full-length on the settee. He clambered over her, holding himself aloft, his elbow joints locked. She drew up her knees and Henry, keeping his balance with one shaky hand, reached down and aimed his prick towards her, knowing that within a matter of seconds he would be in deep.

In deep . . . all of a sudden he caught an image of himself in his mind.

He saw his jeans and underpants, socks and trainers, out of the corner of his eye.

Then he visualised Kate and remembered the look on her face the last time. The hurt, the pain. The despair, the tears. The anger. Kate, the only woman he had truly loved since the age of sixteen. Who he never wanted to hurt and who he had betrayed in the worst way imaginable. He had done it once, and every day since it had been with him. The guilt. Always ready to pop up at the most inappropriate moments and niggle away at him like a cancer.

Yet here he was again. Once more with a younger woman. His penis touching the fat wet lips of her vagina, ready to plunge in, and fuck the consequences.

But this time there would be no consequences.

In that moment, when it could have gone either way, he made the decision, with a little whimper.

'I'm sorry,' he said, kneeling up, his penis curved up out of his bush, touching his belly, swaying between them like an innocent bystander. He reversed off the settee like a crab, leaving Siobhan lying there stunned and unsatisfied, still wanting. 'I can't. It's lovely. It's been really lovely. And I really would like to do it.' He gulped for air. 'But I can't. I'm sorry. Just won't work.' He scooped his clothes together and danced an impressive jig as he got into his Y's. The bulge of his penis remained highly prominent.

Siobhan lay there for a few seconds in total, gobsmacked disbelief. This was replaced by a look of scorn and hatred which turned Henry's soul cold. 'You can't do this, Henry. Starting something and then leaving me in mid-fucking air.' It was as if another character had taken over her, someone slightly deranged. Or maybe just completely pissed off, Henry couldn't be sure. 'So, come on, fuck me. I want it. I want you. You can't leave me in the air like this.'

'Look, I'm really sorry, but I can't go through with it.' He was struggling to get into his shirt and fasten it, finding one of the buttons missing and a tear in the fabric where it had once been. 'It was a silly thing to contemplate. We're colleagues, I'm a supervisor and I'm married. It'd all go horribly wrong.'

She rolled off the settee and stood proudly before him, seething anger hissing from every pore. Henry wasn't so far gone that he couldn't appreciate what a wonderful body she had and he was already regretting not completing the act.

'Is it me?' she demanded. 'Am I not good enough for you?'

'No, it's not you. I mean – oh damn! You're great, brilliant. I couldn't think of anything better than making love to you. God, it's me. Definitely me.'

He was slightly off-balance, hopping about on one foot whilst pulling a trainer on.

The hard, open-handed, perfectly-aimed slap which sent him winging across the room, crashing into the cabinets, caught him completely by surprise. It jarred everything that was hurting and made the punch Anderson had laid on him pale by comparison.

'Jesus,' he yelped, in a pathetic heap on the floor. 'There was no need for that.'

Still naked, quivering with resentment, she stood over him, her eyes ablaze.

'I'll tell you one thing you are right about, Henry fucking Christie, you out-and-out bastard. It *has* all gone horribly wrong. For you, that is.'

She stooped down, picked up her clothes and strutted into the other office to get dressed.

* * *

206

They met, as ever, at the Country Club, all arriving at different times. This, however, was purely a business meeting and no time was spent in the pool. They had use of a small conference room which had been swept for listening devices prior to their arrival.

Drinks and sandwiches were laid on. All very civilised.

Morton. McNamara. Conroy.

The three men who had met many years before, when each had been at the beginning of their chosen career, and since then their lives and fates had intertwined.

Morton and Conroy went back to 1960s Manchester. They had met when Morton had been a Salford city beat bobby and Conroy was running a couple of streetwalkers and a very iffy protection racket on a few Pakistani shopkeepers. Each assisted the other to mutual benefit. Morton made things easy for Conroy by feeding him information about police activities which might impinge on his business interests; in return Conroy offered up one or two sacrificial lambs by way of good quality prisoners which enhanced Morton's professional standing.

Both had prospered.

Conroy grew as a criminal. Morton was promoted as a detective.

Now Morton was close to retirement. At fifty-four he had thirty-five years' service, having been rotten for thirty-four of them. At his rank he could have stayed until he was sixty, but mid-fifties had always been his aim.

And fifty-five it would be.

When he said goodbye to the job next year he would step into a world of secretly acquired wealth, amassed cautiously over the years, in particular the last ten or so during the life of the NWOCS when he became virtually autonomous, being able to operate how he saw fit. And also Conroy had become much more profitable over these years, mainly due to Morton's protection.

Now Morton owned a villa in Spain, an apartment in Barbados and a holiday cabin in Eire. The Spanish home came with a pool, Porsche and maid; the Caribbean one with a Mini-moke, the Irish one with a small lough, brimful of trout. All had been bought covertly through third parties.

When he retired he intended to split his time between the three, pretending they were rented if anyone should ask. His life would be financed – on the face of it – from his police pension and savings, and some legitimate stock-market dealings. This, in fact, would only be pin money, the icing on the cake of a career of corruption: his association with Conroy had placed £2.2 million in Channel Island and Cayman Island bank accounts. He reckoned this would provide him with about one hundred and fifty grand a year in interest.

Life would be very sweet.

All he needed to do was see the next twelve months through.

Multi-millionaire Sir Harry McNamara had come into the equation in the 1970s during a shady land deal associated with Conroy, which was fortunately being investigated by Morton who was then on the Fraud Squad. By some wily manoeuvring, Morton prosecuted some of the tiddlers and allowed the fat fish to swim away. Craftily Morton made this appear to be a successful operation through police eyes.

The land deal had been ratified by a certain local councillor called McNamara, as he then was. All three men benefited from the sale of the land which was purchased for an inflated fee by a national company who built a multi-storey car park on it. The spin-off in terms of building contracts were enormous. All from a piece of scrubland that Conroy had bought for next to nothing from an old bloke who needed to have a gun shoved into his mouth before he signed the contract.

From that inauspicious start an empire grew.

Soon afterwards, Conroy started supplying McNamara with women in payment for certain favours. A couple of these women mysteriously disappeared. Conroy asked no questions, but warned McNamara. No more disappeared – until Marie Cullen.

When McNamara became an MP and, for a short time, a big noise in the Foreign Office, it wasn't long before Conroy urged him to look into the possibilities of dealing in guns. Towards the end of the 1980s Conroy, who had always dabbled in the British underworld scene of arms dealing, had a flourishing trade based on selling arms stolen in America or bought in Eastern Europe to warring African countries. He'd made a real killing selling to Ethiopian warlords. They always seemed to have enough money to buy guns and whisky.

In essence, McNamara used his position of influence whilst in the Foreign Office to bring about arms deals, usually right under the nose of the PM, who had a soft spot for him. There were many photographs of the Premier shaking hands with overseas dignitaries – usually African – whilst in the background McNamara could be seen standing next to a government official, smiling, chatting, arranging deals.

In his own constituency McNamara was a staunch proponent of law and order and policing issues. When gang warfare came to Lancashire and Manchester in the mid-1980s, it was McNamara's pressure and his mouth to the PM's ear, that the Home Office should fund a regionalised unit, an extension of the Crime Squads, to tackle the problem head on.

And who better to run it, McNamara recommended, than that excellent detective with a wealth of experience in dealing with gangsters – Tony Morton, then a Detective Superintendent.

Fully dressed, Henry said, 'Which car are we going to Blackpool in?'

'I don't give a shit. Use which you want. They've all got their keys in the ignition. I'm not coming with you.'

'Yeah . . . Look, I'm sorry, Siobhan. Nothing personal.'

'Fuck off, Henry,' she said sourly.

He nodded. Tight-lipped, hot and flustered, he went swiftly down the stairs to the garage below. He opened the electrically controlled doors and got in the first car he came to. There was a piece of material in the driver's seat which reminded him of a bikini bottom. He tossed it into the passenger footwell and then adjusted the driver's seat which was pulled forwards for a short person. Then he reached for the ignition key. It wasn't there. He checked the sun visors. Not there either.

Siobhan rapped her knuckles on the window.

'Not this one,' she said in a tone which made him feel stupid. 'It's a stolen car, been seized for evidence.'

'Oh, right,' he said. How was he supposed to know? Where was the property label that should be prominently displayed on it?

'Use that one,' she said, pointing to the next one along, a Vauxhall Vectra.

He got out, sidled past the stolen one, wondering how he could ever have mistaken an Alfa Romeo for a police car.

Minutes later he was on the road, heading west out of Blackburn. Away from Siobhan and a big mistake that might have been.

'Right about now he should be getting his end away, if it's all going to plan,' Detective Chief Superintendent Tony Morton declared after checking his watch. 'And,' he added with aplomb, 'I have no doubt it *is* going to plan.'

'I'll believe it when I know it for sure,' said McNamara. 'He's not stupid,' he went on, referring to Henry Christie. 'He might just suss what's going on.'

'Naah.' Morton shook his head. 'My woman detective is very good. She'll fuck his brains out before he knows what's hit him. She's done it before.'

'At least he's getting sorted,' Conroy said. 'Make sure you do a proper job, that's all, Tony.'

'Worry not. By tomorrow night he won't know his arse from his tit.'

'Hm,' McNamara muttered through closed lips. 'What's happening with Marie Cullen's murder, that's what I want to know.'

'It's going nowhere, rest assured. Particularly now that Saltash is out of the picture, as it were.'

'Very funny,' said the MP, not appreciating the play on words relating to the pimp's demise underneath a portable TV set. 'What about that Gillian, the one who did it? Where is she? She's the one I had at our last meeting, if you recall.'

'Is she?' Morton hadn't realised that. 'Does that cause you a problem? The cops wanted to talk to Saltash and he was a link to Cullen. Now he's gone, what's the fuss?'

The look on McNamara's face made Morton ask, 'What's the fuss?' again, this time firmly.

McNamara opened his mouth to say something. He quickly clamped it shut.

'Spit it out, Harry,' Morton commanded.

'Shit . . . if the police catch her and interview her, she might tell them about me.'

'Why should she? Her killing Saltash, and her clients are two different things.'

'I said something stupid, I think, when I was with her. Something incriminating. She might use it.'

'What did you say?'

Conroy, listening, closed his eyes despairingly.

McNamara shrugged as though it were nothing. 'I made reference to Marie.'

A long, pissed-off sigh exhaled from Morton's lungs.

Conroy exploded. 'Are you a complete fucking nutcase? You must be short of something up here.' He tapped his head. 'What the hell happens to you when you get an erection? Does all the blood come out of your brain, or something, because it's fucking obvious it goes into neutral.'

Morton rubbed his eyes wearily. 'You are really going to have to get yourself sorted out. You're becoming a weak link.'

'What can we do about her?' McNamara insisted on knowing.

'Ronnie?' Morton turned to Conroy, eyebrows raised.

'I'll sort her out,' he said angrily, through gritted teeth. 'I'll get some Salford low-life to blow her away – if we can find her, that is.'

'Good,' said Morton. 'Now, some better news for you both. Munrow's been killed.'

The change in Conroy was visible. One moment he was hard-faced, the next bright and happy on hearing of the death. 'Hoo-fucking-ray,' he cheered. 'Rider?'

'We can only presume so,' Morton said. 'Unidentified male blew his head off in a Debenham's changing room. Could be Rider from the description.'

'Looks like my little ruse worked. *Yes!*' He punched the air. 'What the hell was he doing in Debenham's?'

'Buying clothes presumably,' Morton answered.

'And what about Rider?' Conroy asked. 'He could do with stitching up for that. Any chance? If he was out of the game, we could have his club.'

Morton gave a noncommittal shrug. 'I'll see what I can do.'

In his mind he was already formulating a course of action which involved the newest detective on his unit.

The sharp knock on the door made them jump.

Conroy opened it.

Scott Hamilton walked in.

Henry parked the NWOCS car at Blackpool and dropped into the station to see if there had been any developments in the investigations he had so happily left behind for a quick move onto a new squad. A move which had already got him shot and into a compromising position. All in one day. Not bad going by any standards.

Nothing seemed to be moving on anything.

Particularly in respect of Marie Cullen; the case seemed to have come to a standstill with the death of the man supposed to be her pimp.

Working on the assumption that his short secondment to the NWOCS was virtually over, Henry decided that he'd do a few things with it next week. Maybe if there was a push, it might lead them properly to McNamara, millionaire bastard – and friend of Tony Morton . . .

Henry frowned.

He recalled the photos on Morton's wall. Him and McNamara looked pretty close buddies. One of those horrible queasy churnings moved through him like a bad case of wind.

Surely not . . .? He banished the thought.

A note had been scribbled out and left on his desk asking him to call round and see Annie, Derek's widow. She had something for him, apparently. Henry pulled his nose up at the thought of revisiting her. Then his sense of responsibility overpowered this. He would call in for five minutes on his way home.

At least it would delay seeing Kate. It was going to be difficult to face her and act normal, knowing that he had as good as committed adultery for the second time in their marriage.

Was it technically adultery when another woman sucked your cock? Or if you went down on her? Surely it had to be full intercourse?

It was a fine line, to be sure. But he knew one thing for certain; Kate would be blind to the semantics. If she ever found out.

'I am trying to understand the situation,' Hamilton was saying. 'We all have difficulties from time to time. In fact, I recently had a couple of FBI agents snooping around the Jacaranda. One was eliminated by two good friends who were staying with me at the time; they made it look like a drunken accident.'

'And the other?' Morton enquired.

'Beaten to within an inch of his life,' he boasted. Not quite true, but these three didn't have to know that.

'Who are your friends?' That was Conroy.

'Professionals. And should you ever need their services, contact me. They are very, very good. One hundred per cent track record. As messy or as clean as you like. Don't mind killing cops . . . but we digress. The problem we now have is that the agent acting on behalf of the buyer is arriving soon and we have no goods to display because they are in the hands of the police.'

'That's about the long and short of it,' McNamara said.

'Do we know where these guns are at the moment? Are they accessible?'

'Yes and no,' said Morton firmly. 'We're not busting them out of the police store.'

'Who said bust them out?' Hamilton said.

The three waited.

'Why not borrow them and then return them – and no one is any the wiser? It solves the problem of me having to arrange to bring more into the country from Madeira. Simply borrow them for a couple of hours.'

Morton sat back and clasped his hands behind his head. Now why hadn't he thought of that one? 'Possible,' he said, chewing it over. 'Just possible.'

Chapter Nineteen

Police Sergeant Eric Taylor's financial trouble could be traced back over twelve years – to the 1984 miners strike, actually. One of the longest and most bitter strikes ever to hit the UK, lasting for over a year, it had a major spin-off for the police officers who were required to police it: by working the excessive amounts of overtime needed, they made plenty of extra money. This particularly applied to officers who had to travel from their own force areas to the trouble spots to support their colleagues. These travelling officers often found themselves working away from home for weeks on end, and their pay packets reflected this, with up to double their usual earnings.

Some officers, it was said, taunted the striking miners by waving their hefty pay cheques at the picket lines. Others sent postcards from far-flung places around the globe to the miners' leader Arthur Scargill, thanking him for the money which had paid for the holiday of a lifetime.

Another downside to the money was that some officers found themselves in debt when the strike ended and the wage slips returned to normal.

Eric Taylor had made a great deal of money out of the strike.

He was one of those who was always available to go, and over the year he spent about seventeen weeks away from home, policing the miners, earning a relative fortune.

But, like so many others, he failed to plan ahead and the end of the strike caught him by surprise.

A new car, conservatory, new three-piece suite, a couple of holidays abroad – all still needed to be paid off once the strike was over.

And he was still feeling the ramifications to this day.

He had had to borrow to service his borrowings – and then borrow to service *those* borrowings. At least a third of his salary went out to pay for loans taken on board twelve years earlier.

And he was a bitter man.

His wife left him, taking their two children and a large percentage of his remaining salary in maintenance payments.

A long-term woman friend also took him to the cleaners.

Now he lived in a rented terraced house, alone, unhappy and ripe for corrupting.

These people were always easy targets.

He was the first of two to be visited that evening.

Whilst Henry was shuffling around Blackpool police station, DI Gallagher and DS Tattersall knocked on the front door of Taylor's house, knowing he was off-duty and fully aware of his severe financial problems. He was unlikely to be out gallivanting.

Perfect.

A sour-faced man opened the door.

Gallagher and Tattersall held up their warrant cards and introduced themselves. Gallagher was carrying a briefcase.

Taylor recognised them. He'd seen them knocking about the station throughout the week, but he did not know who they were.

'Sergeant Taylor, is it?'

Taylor nodded suspiciously. He did not like being visited at home by anyone. He was always slightly embarrassed by his inferior surroundings, having once lived in a detached house with a double garage. He had really come down in the world, in his own estimation. And he was particularly wary of two detectives from NWOCS.

'Yeah,' he answered shortly. 'What can I do for you?'

'Could we possibly come in and have a chat?' Gallagher asked affably enough. Tattersall remained silent, as he was to do for the remainder of the visit. He was a brooding, unsettling presence, hovering behind Gallagher. The DI noted Taylor's look of wariness. 'Nothing to worry about, honestly.'

Taylor accepted the words of comfort grudgingly. Not completely happy, but nevertheless, he was intrigued.

He allowed them into the threadbare lounge which was furnished like some 1970s throwback. Typical of cheap rented and furnished accommodation.

'Sit down.'

Gallagher sat. Tattersall shook his head and stood next to his boss.

Taylor settled himself on the settee and waited.

Gallagher coughed and attempted to come across as fairly uncomfortable, though inside he was completely at ease.

'First of all,' Gallagher began, 'I want to reassure you that what we say from now on is completely confidential. Nothing will go beyond these walls.'

'I'm not sure I can give you that reassurance,' Taylor said. 'Mainly because I don't know why the hell you're here or what you're gonna say.'

'I appreciate that . . . but I do ask you to keep it confidential.'

Taylor gave a non-committal twitch of the head.

'I'll come to the point quickly, Sarge. We're here on behalf of Henry Christie. He's asked us to come and speak to you to ask for a favour.'

Taylor perked up. He was listening now. His eyes narrowed slightly. 'Go on,' he said.

'You were the Custody Sergeant last Saturday evening when DS

Christie allegedly assaulted a youth then stupidly forgot to enter it up on the record.'

Taylor said nothing.

'Well, Henry's looked through the custody record and noticed that you were the last person to make any entries on it up to and including the point where this youth was taken to hospital. There are no entries after that because he was subsequently released from custody and reported for summons for the offence he had committed.'

Taylor watched Gallagher closely, hardly able to believe what was being said.

'Henry wondered if you'd do him a favour. See, he's in a lot of trouble over this – or could be – and it's hanging over his head and, well, the thing is, without an independent witness to back him up, it looks like he could be in for some rough times ahead.'

'Tough. And I'm not sure I like what I'm hearing,' Taylor said stonily.

'OK . . . but let me finish, please. Henry wondered if you'd be willing to . . . how shall we say? . . . amend the custody record in his favour to say you witnessed the whole thing.'

Taylor's heart, by now, was ramming against his ribs. He almost expected it to break them and splurge out. His face tightened up. 'How dare you?' he demanded.

Gallagher held his hands up, palms out, defensively. 'We understand your initial reaction, Sarge.'

'Look, you bastards, are you setting me up or something? Are you wired up? I'm an honest cop and this is completely out of order.' His voice rose as he began to rant. 'I don't know what you're trying to pull, but as far as I'm concerned you can fuck right off out of my house. I'm going to complain about you both – and Henry Christie! Though I can hardly credit he would have sent you. It's not like him. For a start, he'd do his own dirty work.'

'He's in trouble, Eric,' Gallagher said earnestly. 'A colleague in trouble and he's asking a friend to do him a favour, that's all.'

Taylor remained steadfast. 'No.'

'And that's your final word on the matter?'

'Yes.'

'I believe you have some money problems, Eric.'

'And that's fuck-all to do with you, pal.'

'We are prepared to help you, if you help Henry in return. No, don't say anything.' Gallagher reached for the briefcase which he had put down by the chair. He placed it on his knees and flicked the catches, opening it so Taylor could not see into it. He took out an A4 sheet of paper which the Sergeant instantly recognised as a custody record. Gallagher laid this on the smoked-glass coffee table which was between them.

Eric's anger bubbled. It was the custody record he had filled in last Saturday, one of over fifty that day, but one he remembered well. The name on the top was Shane Mulcahy.

He glared at Gallagher.

'Get out,' he spat.

Gallagher held a finger up. 'One second,' he said.

He placed the open briefcase on the coffee table next to the custody record and slowly swivelled it round so Taylor could see what it contained.

On top of the contents was a note, printed in capital letters. It read: THERE IS £10,000 IN USED BANK OF ENGLAND NOTES IN HERE. YOU MAY COUNT IT IF YOU WISH. ALL YOU HAVE TO DO TO RECEIVE THIS MONEY IS TO ALTER THE CUSTODY RECORD AND HELP A FRIEND IN NEED. ERIC, PLEASE HELP ME. The signature could have belonged to Henry Christie. Taylor wasn't sure.

He looked at the note and the money underneath it.

Then his eyes met Gallagher's over the lid of the briefcase.

Gallagher gave him a quirky smile.

It was a lot of money, for not much effort.

'You've made me leave, John,' Isa said. Glassy tears were twinkling in her eyes. 'I wanted to love you . . . I do love you . . . but you've spoilt it.'

She bent down and picked up her suitcase.

'There was absolutely no need to do what you did. No rhyme, no reason, no excuse. Cold-blooded murder.' She shook as she said the words.

'I didn't have a choice, Isa,' Rider said simply. They were standing in the lounge area of his basement flat, the bedsits above. There was a huge crash from the room above which juddered the whole ceiling. Probably the couple in the ground-floor flat having one of their usual domestics. Rider was not bothered by what was happening above. It was his own, fairly subdued domestic dispute which was his problem at the moment. He was very tired now. The action of the day had sapped everything, including his resolve to keep Isa. He was too weary to put up much of a fight, although he knew what was happening was very important. He wished it could be put off until tomorrow when he was feeling stronger.

'Everybody has a choice. You made yours without even thinking about me – and after what we said, promised each other, only hours before.'

'He killed innocent people. They burned to death on my property. I was responsible for them.'

'Did he kill them? How the hell d'you know that for sure? Where's your evidence? It could just as easily have been one of your crack-crazed residents out of his tiny mind. Those idiots are capable of anything.'

As if to confirm what she said, there was another crash from upstairs. They both looked at the ceiling, then at each other.

'Why didn't you tell the police? You had the opportunity.'

'Because they're useless, corrupt bastards. Munrow would have paid them off, like Conroy does. You know what I think about cops.'

'John, you are a fool,' she said sadly.

'So is this it?'

'Yes.' It was a quiet, almost inaudible word. One she did not wish to utter.

She walked to the door, opened it and went through without looking back. Rider made no attempt to stop her, even though something inside him was willing him to do so. He knew he was being pig-headed and stupid.

He heard the front door close softly and saw Isa walk up the steps past the net-curtained window.

Maybe tomorrow.

Another crash from upstairs.

Rider's nostrils flared. Noisy bastards. He was going to throw them out on their arses right now if they couldn't damn well behave.

He stormed out of the room to the door in the short hallway which gave him access up a flight of stairs to the flats above without having to go outside. He unlocked the several bolts and chains and opened the door, treading carefully onto the darkened and narrow stairway.

They burst into the flat before he knew what was happening.

Two men. Blue boiler suits. Heavy boots. Hoods with eye and mouth slits.

One had a straight, extendable baton.

The other had a gun.

At the moment Shane Mulcahy opened his door, the one with the baton rammed it into his stomach, causing him to bend double; the baton was then expertly smacked across Shane's face, breaking his nose with a sickening crunch of bone.

Shane was bundled back into the flat and his thin spidery body was slammed face down onto the bare floor where the red gush from his nose flooded out. The one with the gun knelt on Shane's back, one knee planted firmly on his spine just between the shoulder-blades, the gun thrust into his cheek.

Jodie, Shane's much-abused girlfriend, had been trying her best to breast-feed the baby which was cradled in her arms. One poor-looking breast and nipple were exposed. She reacted instinctively, drawing her arms around the baby and cowering in a chair for protection.

The one with the baton said to her, 'If you speak or scream I'll whack this across your head and then the baby's.'

Jodie did not speak because, although not having experienced this type of scenario before, she was sufficiently street-wise to know when to shut up. She had immediately assumed these people were drugs dealers come to collect an unpaid debt. It was the culture she inhabited and she knew her best chance of survival was acquiescence.

She nodded nervously.

The baby, deprived of its meagre supply of milk, sucked air desperately.

'Now then, Shane, old bean,' the man with the gun said, lowering his mouth near to Shane's ear. 'You've been a naughty, naughty lad, haven't you?'

The young skinhead could hardly breathe, let alone speak. Blood had gagged in his throat. He coughed and choked, spitting a fine spray of red saliva.

'I don't owe you owt,' he gurgled.

'Oh yes you do, you owe us a great deal.'

Despite herself, Jodie let out a wail of anguish. The stupid idiot had obviously neglected to pay his drugs debts and from the sound of it they had amounted to a tidy sum. Now collection time had come and if they could not find the money, Shane's brains might be joining his nasal blood on the floor.

The baton arced through the air towards Jodie's head. She saw it coming, braced herself for the impact. It stopped a millimetre from her left temple. Her eyes focused on the end of it.

'Next time,' the man warned, 'I take your fucking head off. Now, shut it, bitch.'

She bit her lips and hugged her child which whimpered pathetically, picking up on the tension in her body. She rocked it.

The man holding the gun ground the muzzle into Shane's cheek. He thumbed the hammer back. Shane closed his eyes tightly and lay there paralysed with fear. Tears formed in his eyes.

The man with the baton walked over to the TV set which was perched on a small table. He tapped the screen with the tip, lined himself up like a golfer before a tee shot and swung it into the screen, which exploded.

Jodie let out a gasp.

The baby in her arms jumped and started to cry.

Their TV had been destroyed. The TV set Jodie was tied to for all her entertainment. It had been her lifeline.

The man then kicked it off the table. It crashed to the floor.

Shane's eyes strained in their sockets to look up at what had happened. He watched the man with the baton take a couple of steps over to him. The man with the gun, keeping it firmly implanted in his cheek, stood up, relieving the pressure on Shane's spine.

It was a short-lived relief. Shane was then given much the same treatment as the TV set with about a dozen well-aimed, hard blows across his back and ribs.

When he's finished, Shane lay curled up on the floor, emitting horrible grunting noises.

The gun was still in his ear. The man holding it said, 'You may wonder what this is about, Shane.'

The baton man then demolished the stereo with a series of expertly wielded strikes, destroying a cheap but perfectly acceptable system which, again, Jodie relied on for her sanity. Her whole pathetic world was being decimated and she was unable to do anything to save it. As with the TV set, the stereo was kicked to the floor where it landed with a loud crash, the plastic parts splintering all around the room.

The man returned to Shane and tapped him gently a few times on the knee-caps and shins. Shane's thin legs would have been very easily broken and probably damaged for ever. The baton man let the tip rest against a shin whilst the gunman spoke.

'Now then, Shane,' he said reasonably. 'Listen very carefully. All you have to do is this: tomorrow morning, you go into Blackpool police station and present yourself very smartly at the front desk, with your solicitor if you like . . . with me so far? . . . and be very nice and pleasant and say that you wish to retract the complaint you made against me, Detective Sergeant Christie. Now that's all you have to do Shane, pal, old buddy, old mate. And don't even think of mentioning this little get-together here, because if you do . . .' His voice sank to a terrifying whisper. 'Do you understand?'

Shane nodded.

'Good.'

The baton man gave Shane a loving tap on his shin.

The gunman stood up.

Both crossed to the baby's cot, picked it up and between them and threw it against the wall where it disintegrated into matchsticks.

Then they left.

In the hallway outside the flat, they turned right and ran for the rear exit, pulling their hoods off as they went.

Neither one of them saw the figure of John Rider ascending the darkened staircase which led up from the basement flat below.

Chapter Twenty

There was an air of jubilation in the murder incident room next day when Tony Morton announced that all three men arrested yesterday were going to be charged with the murder of Geoff Driffield and the other people in the newsagents. The one they had failed to arrest would be circulated as wanted.

In just one week they had a major result, and all the detectives and uniformed police officers involved in the case were invited to a celebration that evening in the club upstairs. 5 p.m. start. It would be a long, boozy evening.

Henry experienced a certain degree of satisfaction. He had been instrumental in the arrest of the gang leader, Anderson, and had nearly died for his trouble.

As the officers cleared the room, Henry caught sight of Siobhan talking earnestly to Tony Morton, occasionally glancing across at him. She looked upset, on the verge of tears. Henry wondered if she'd had some distressing news or something. He did not even begin to think she could be upset about last night and the coitus interruptus. He had reflected on her behaviour and concluded he did not really blame her . . . but on the other hand she had said some nasty things. Threats, almost.

She and Morton walked out of the incident room towards the office he had been allocated for the duration of the investigation.

Henry went to the CID office and sat at his desk where he re-read a photocopy of the post-it note Derek had left for him on the night of his brutal murder. What the hell did he want to see me for? Henry asked himself. Was it the reason why he was murdered? Henry could only speculate. The note was bare and said little . . .

His mind wandered back to the previous evening when he had called in to see Annie Luton on his way home. She had given him a whole package of work-related stuff that Derek had taken home over a period of time. It was all in a carrier bag.

'There's everything there he ever brought home in relation to work,' Annie said. 'I've been round the house from top to bottom, gathering all this together. It was all over the show . . . he was so untidy. I even found some under our bed.' Her eyes moistened as she talked.

Henry glanced casually at the contents. None of it seemed to be of major importance. Copies of reports, statements . . . the type of bumf most young officers probably had at home. Henry had been like that years ago. Taking work home. Feeling the need to write up reports off-duty so he could spend more time out on the streets when on-duty. Yeah, he could relate to that.

These days he took nothing home.

He had spent about half an hour with Annie. She was very rational and together, though a desperate and tragic figure. Henry saw resilience in her and guessed that sooner rather than later her life would be back on track.

He left with a hopeful, positive feeling inside him. The carrier bag she had given him was dumped on the back seat of his car, forgotten.

Then he went home to Kate.

He could hardly bring himself to look at her, so ashamed was he of his actions with Siobhan. Did Kate pick up his body language? Could she see right through him? Did she intuitively know that not long before, he had literally been on the verge of making love to another woman?

Henry would not have been surprised.

Wives were so perceptive about their husbands' every little transgression.

Thankfully she seemed far more concerned with his injuries and getting him into a hot, soothing Radox bath and subsequently to bed. She fussed around him like a mother hen, or at least someone who cared very deeply for him and to whom his wellbeing was her main concern. Inside, he boiled angrily with himself whilst on the outside he revelled in the blue water and the glass of Jack Daniel's which Kate placed in his hand as he lay back and soaked his soul.

He was beginning to think he had the makings of a serial adulterer, but maybe he was exaggerating the problem.

His daughters, Jenny and Leanne, were another reason for this self-loathing. With the soap bubbles covering his rude parts, they sat on their knees next to the bath, whilst Kate took a back seat on the lid of the loo, and listened wide-eyed at the story of his day, culminating in him being shot and the fight in the clothing displays of M & S. He proudly displayed his chest-wound for them to see. It had turned the colour of black grapes. He also carefully removed the bandage on his ear to show them how chewed it was.

He was their hero and although he knew the truth – he had been completely terrified most of the time – he never revealed it to them.

Their dad. The hero.

The serial adulterer.

Kate ushered them out of the bathroom after the story.

She sat back on the loo, looked him straight in the eye and said, 'I think you've got something to tell me.'

The words hit Henry harder than the bullet.

'How did you know?'

Were there claw-marks down his back he hadn't realised Siobhan had inflicted on him? Teeth-marks around his foreskin?

'The fact you were in Lancaster for one thing. Then you had a gun. And you were arresting people for that multiple killing job. You've already moved onto, what's it called, North-West Crime something or other?'

'North-West Organised Crime Squad,' he corrected her, trying to cover the relief in his voice. 'No, I've just been helping them out, that's all, so they can look at me and I can look at them. See if we like each other.' He went on to explain the possibility of a six-month secondment, followed possibly by a full transfer, and how right he thought the job was for him.

He didn't mention Siobhan at all.

'OK,' Kate said, tilting her head. 'If that's what you want – chasing criminals with guns all over the place, fine by me. If you're happy at your work, I'll be behind you. Just please don't let it get in the way of us this time, Henry. That's all I ask.'

'I won't,' he promised meekly.

And once again, Kate, his wonderful, beautiful wife, had surprised him with her generosity. And through no fault of her own, made him feel like an absolute bastard.

Maybe that's my lot in life, he'd reasoned.

Henry was brought bang into the present as the phone went, interrupting his recall. It was Karl Donaldson.

'Karl, how you doin'?'

'OK, buddy,' Donaldson said, but Henry picked up a bum note in the American's voice. 'I need to see you pretty urgently, Henry.'

'About what?'

'Not over the phone. Face to face. I'm gonna travel up, bring Karen along too. Settin' off shortly. Looking at four-five hours maybe with traffic and weather. Can you accommodate us?'

'Sure, sounds important. Nothing over the phone?'

'No clues, bud.'

'I'll see you at home then.'

The phone went dead. Henry hung up, mystified and slightly worried. He had no time to ruminate, however. The phone warbled again.

'DS Christie – get up into my office now.'

Rather like Siobhan's open-handed slap last night, Henry was caught unawares by what happened next.

He meandered down the corridor towards Morton's office. When he was a few feet away from the door, it opened dramatically and Siobhan burst out, virtually into his arms. Tears were streaked down her face and she was heaving with loud, gut-wrenching sobs. She looked up at Henry and reacted instantly as though she had walked into the monster from hell.

'Get off me, get off me!' she screamed, making a great show of disentangling herself from him. She was not entangled by any stretch of the imagination. She drew back, slapping the air like she was trying to free herself from Spiderman's web. 'Leave me alone. You've done enough damage.'

'Siobhan!' Henry was wrong-footed completely. 'What d'you mean?'

'You bastard! Don't come near me again.'

With that she ducked to one side, swept past him and scurried off down the corridor towards the ladies toilets. Henry watched her retreating back with shock. He turned. Tony Morton was standing in the doorway of his temporary office.

'What was all that about?' Henry asked, nonplussed.

Morton said nothing for a moment, but surveyed Henry with a calculating look which made him shiver.

'Come in and sit down.'

Morton stayed by the door. Henry slid by him into the office. He sat down, intertwining his fingers on his lap in a gesture of submission.

Morton closed the door softly and walked to his seat behind the desk, putting a large space between him and the Detective Sergeant and peering down at him from a greater height. Henry could not help but be awed by the old-fashioned power psychology. It always worked on him.

What the hell was going on?

Morton did not speak for a few moments, but allowed Henry to savour the atmosphere.

Then he dropped the bomb.

'DC Robson claims that you have sexually harassed her and this has culminated in a serious sexual assault. Namely rape.'

Three items appeared on Karl Donaldson's desk just as he was in the process of packing his briefcase.

The first was from Madeira and had come by DHL. It was the sample of human tissue taken from under Sam Dawber's fingernails. It was in an airtight container, with Santana's signature across the seal as well as the doctor's who had performed the post mortem.

The next item was a statement from an FBI scientist which contained the DNA profile resulting from the sample taken from under Sam's nails at the second autopsy. There was a computer print-out attached which meant nothing to Donaldson. It went on to say that the FBI DNA database had been searched, but no match had been made.

He assumed that if he got the police here to DNA test the sample from Madeira, the result would match up with the one from the States.

He slid both items into his desk drawer and locked it.

They would have to wait.

He wanted to get on the road to see Henry, ASAP.

However, the next item caught and held his attention.

It was the photograph of Wayne and Tiger Mayfair taken on their arrival at Madrid Airport a couple of days before. Donaldson had already received a brief written report about the arrival from a field agent out there. They were good quality photographs and Donaldson was pleased by the high resolution. But it was the report which accompanied it that made him sit up. Again, from the same field agent, a guy named Moody, who had been doing a bit of digging. It briefly said that, under assumed names, the Mayfairs had now left Spain en route by air to Paris. The agent had also discovered that they had flown into Madrid from Lisbon.

And into Lisbon from Madeira.

Donaldson looked at the photograph again. Something odd about Tiger Mayfair.

He rooted around his stationery drawer and found a magnifying glass which he held over Tiger's head.

Yes, there was no mistaking it.

Donaldson laid the photo down and breathed deeply.

Scratch-marks down his left cheek.

Henry stumbled out of Morton's office with a face of granite and all-pervading waves of cold fear gripping his intestines.

Allegations of sexual harassment, followed by indecent assault and then, possibly, rape, were dreadful to be levelled at anyone. Especially when they were untrue.

And that is what Siobhan had alleged against him.

She had said that from the first moment they'd met, he had constantly made lewd comments to her, sexual jokes and innuendo and he had leered at her virtually all the time. 'Active mental groping' was the term used.

She had gone on to tell Morton she had become physically sick as a result of his behaviour, but she felt powerless to do anything about it. After all, he was a Sergeant, she was only a Constable. But above all he was a man.

To Morton she said that Henry had forced her to kiss him at the NWOCS office in King Street when they had been there alone, collecting equipment. He had rubbed his body up against hers but she'd managed to struggle free and tell him not to touch her again. That night, she claimed, she'd gone to bed and cried herself to sleep, petrified at the thought of doing observations with him the following morning in Lancaster.

Things got worse after the shooting incident when, in the casualty department of all places, he had enticed her into the cubicle where he was receiving treatment and exposed himself to her.

It all culminated at King Street, again when they were alone. This time, she alleged, Henry forced her to undress and tried to rape her. He failed to penetrate her and ejaculate because he could not maintain an erection.

She had been terrified. Put through an horrendous ordeal by a man with power.

And now she wanted some action taken against him.

As the story was revealed to Henry, he simply sat there open-mouthed, unable to believe what was being said. It was all nonsense, of course. Both had been willing participants in the engagement until Henry's head had cleared and he realised how foolish he was being – which was at the point where his *very erect* penis had brushed up against the lips of WDS Robson's vagina.

Henry ran quickly through the legal definition of rape in his mind. Only the slightest degree of penetration needed to be proved, neither did the emission of seed have to take place. The other main thread to the offence was the question of consent. Was there true consent to the act of intercourse, or was it obtained by fear, force or fraud? Henry had dealt with enough rapes to know the pitfalls of proving it to a court; Siobhan would struggle to convince a jury she had been raped.

It was the others elements of her allegation which worried him.

Sexual harassment.

Indecent assault.

The former was strongly condemned by the police service and many male officers had lost their jobs because of it; the latter was a serious criminal offence which was often used in place of rape because it was easier to prove. It could lose him his job too – especially if he was in prison.

And I stopped myself from shagging her just to prevent future repercussions, he thought. Now I wish I'd carried on. What the hell was behind this?

Henry calmly relayed his side of the story.

'Whatever the truth of the matter,' Morton said when Henry had concluded, 'and I don't suppose we'll get to it anyway, this is a very serious matter, Henry. Very, very serious.'

'I realise that.'

'It affects so many others, directly or indirectly – the job, the squad, your wife, kids . . . God, the effect it could have on them beggars the imagination,' Morton emphasised, making Henry squirm. 'Your friends, colleagues. Mud sticks, old lad, even if these allegations prove to be unfounded.'

And wives divorce you.

And friends snub you.

Oh, shit.

'But at the moment,' Morton explained, 'no one but we three know about this. Maybe there is a solution. Let me have a think about it.'

His mind reeling, Henry made his way back to the comfort zone of his desk and slumped heavily down in the chair. His first reaction had been to find Siobhan and demand of her what the hell she was playing at, but he'd been severely warned against this course of action. Anything which smelled of intimidation or victimisation would be dealt with harshly, Morton had said.

Henry's thoughts were bleak. He had never considered himself to be a

225

sexual harasser. The notion made his skin crawl. Maybe he always had been, but hadn't recognised it. Maybe he was so immersed in the sexist white heterosexual culture, he couldn't see when he was harassing a woman. Could he be one of those men who made his blood boil? Those who constantly touched women, patted their arses, brushed against their tits? Perhaps he was.

Kate!

She would go ballistic. His eyes closed in a shudder of despair.

Two years of getting his marriage back on the straight and narrow. Working hard at it. Putting family first. It had taken a lot of dedication and love.

Once again through his own foolishness it was very likely to come tumbling down around his ears.

How the hell could he keep this quiet?

Just then, his day took a further turn for the worse. In stalked Superintendent Guthrie from the Discipline and Complaints branch.

Henry suddenly felt weaker than alcohol-free lager.

For the second time that day, Henry came out from an interaction with a higher-ranking officer with his head in a spin. Again he had difficulty taking in what was told him. This time things were in his favour, but even so it did not feel like a victory. It simply added to his overall confusion.

Shane Mulcahy had been into the police station earlier and retracted his complaint of assault, saying that everything was his fault. He'd pulled a hidden knife on the detective and the officer had acted in reasonable self-defence. In other words, Shane admitted he deserved what he got – a knee in the bollocks.

And to add weight to the retraction, Superintendent Guthrie said he had checked the custody record and found it backed up Henry's description of the fight in the cell corridor.

'What?' Henry had said, totally perplexed. 'You mean the custody record says . . . ?'

'That you acted in self-defence, yes.' The Superintendent winked at Henry. 'I knew things would work out for you. They always do when it's a flimsy allegation. So, all I need to do is tie the loose ends up and write the whole unpleasant incident off. And I hope you learn something from the experience.'

'I'm sure I shall.'

On leaving the room Henry made his way quickly to the custody office where he looked up the relevant custody record.

It was true.

Eric Taylor had written that he'd observed the tussle between him and Shane, and had entered it onto the custody record.

Except it wasn't the original entry, as Henry well knew. Because he'd checked the custody record last week and been in despair that firstly he'd

226

forgotten to make an entry himself, and secondly that Eric Taylor did not leave him any space to write something in later.

Henry knew that Taylor was a good custody officer. Very fair in his dealings with prisoners and police officers alike. So why had he changed the entry in Henry's favour?

Not something Taylor would have done in a million years.

He replaced the custody record binder on the shelf and sauntered back up to the CID office, trying desperately to get a grip on what had happened. He found it impossible and very disturbing.

'We need to judge this just right,' Morton was saying. His audience consisted of Gallagher, Tattersall and Siobhan Robson. 'Henry's a dangerous individual because, basically, he's honest. He might bend the rules to get a conviction, but you can bet it'll be watertight in the end and will survive even the most ruthless scrutiny. So, people, how do we proceed?'

Gallagher replied, 'He might be honest, but he's not stupid. He'll know when the cards are stacked against him and I'm sure he'll hold his hands up.' He laughed.

'Siobhan?' Morton raised his eyebrows to her.

'Go straight for him,' she said in a brittle tone. 'Lay it on the line. He'll realise he hasn't any choice and he'll stick with us. He's not stupid, as Gallie says.' She nodded towards the DI. 'He doesn't want to lose his job and his wife.'

There was a knock on the door. 'Come,' said Morton.

Superintendent Guthrie, Discipline and Complaints, poked his head through the door. He held up a finger. 'Done and dusted,' he said.

'Thanks, Will,' Morton said. 'See you later about it.'

Guthrie closed the door.

Morton clamped his fist tight triumphantly. 'Right! This will be a difficult time, for us *and* him. His first reaction may be to go running to someone else and blurt everything out. If he does that, we need to be watertight. Are we?'

'I am,' said Siobhan.

'Me too.' Gallagher.

The laconic Tattersall merely nodded.

'Right. Let's wheel him in, drop a few more bombshells on him, then see where we stand.'

Henry tapped without confidence on Tony Morton's door. He had been summoned once more, probably, he guessed, to receive an update on the Siobhan affair. 'Come,' he heard Morton call out.

Henry pushed the door open, expecting to see only Morton. It knocked him sideways when he firstly saw Siobhan, then Gallagher, then Tattersall, sitting in there too. They were in a semi-circle facing Morton's desk. At the open end of the semi-circle was an empty chair.

Henry had a quick look round for The Four Horses of the Apocalypse.

Overcoming an urge to run away and hide in a toilet, he entered the room. If he'd had a tail it would have been between his legs. His eyes avoided contact with Siobhan's; his mouth was arid extra dry.

Tattersall stood up and approached Henry. 'Let me search you.'

'Eh?'

'You heard.'

Gallagher rose from his seat and without warning he and Tattersall hurled Henry against the wall.

'What the fuck's going on here?' Henry demanded. He flicked around and tried to pull himself out of their grasp.

Gallagher punched him hard in the chest with the base of his hand.

Henry bent double as the pain from the bullet-wound corkscrewed out through his heart and lungs.

Gallagher and Tattersall hoisted him up against the wall and searched him quickly and expertly. They then manhandled him to the chair and threw him onto it. His arms crossed over his breast and nursed the pain. He looked up at Morton, unable to speak for the moment.

Gallagher seized a handful of Henry's fine hair and pulled his head back. He looked down at him and said, 'That is to show you we are not pissing about, Christie.'

The two detectives sat down.

'What the fuck's going on here?' Henry struggled to say.

Morton took a deep sigh and stared coldly at him before he began sombrely. 'There are a few things that have been brought to my attention since this morning's complaint from DC Robson here.'

There was a sheet of paper on the desk top. Morton held it up for Henry to see. His watery eyes found it hard to focus. 'This a photocopy of the firearms authorisation sheet used by the NWOCS. It clearly shows you booked a firearm out without my signature to authorise it.' Morton indicated the offending blank space on the form.

'But she said,' he turned hopelessly to face Siobhan, 'it was OK to do that. That you'd automatically sign the form later.' He looked at Morton again. Then back to Siobhan. 'Come on, tell him. I did what you said.'

A warm trickle ran down Henry's neck. He wiped it and saw blood on his hand. His ear had started bleeding again.

She remained silent, her eyes as cold as ice cubes.

'This is fucking outrageous,' Henry spat, and got to his feet. 'What the hell is this?'

Tattersall moved quickly, followed by Gallagher. A well-aimed blow to the kidneys from the DS brought Henry to his knees in front of Morton's desk. Gallagher forced his head onto the desk, holding his cheek to the wooden surface, squelching his features, but allowing him to look up at Morton.

228

'A very serious discipline offence,' he heard the Chief Superintendent say. Morton's eyes lifted and looked at Gallagher. 'Put him back on the chair.'

Two pairs of hands lifted him bodily back and deposited him like dumping a sack of rubbish.

'I don't know what's going on here, but as soon as I get out of this room every one of you is in deep shit.'

Morton laughed. 'Henry, you're splitting my sides. If you do anything like that, I promise you'll face a charge of rape as well as a civil litigation suit for harassment. Both will stick. That's a promise too.'

Henry had lost all sense of comprehension. His mind was being blown, like he was on some kind of hallucinogenic drug, and he was adrift on the Sea of Unreality.

'How did your D & C interview go?'

'What's that gotta do with anything?' As he was speaking he analysed the question. 'You!' he said.

'No, not quite,' Morton said affably. 'In essence, yes. But in reality – no. You did it, Henry. It was all your work. Bribing that poor custody officer to change the record so it read in your favour. You beat the living shit out of that defenceless young man – what's he called – Shane. Just so he would retract his statement. All in all, you've been a very busy and naughty boy, Henry. What do they call it? Perverting the course of justice.'

'I deny it.'

'Well, you would, wouldn't you? But that's neither here nor there. The point is that we' – here Morton indicated everyone in the room, including himself – 'could, if necessary, prove you did. And that's all that matters, isn't it? So all in all you're well and truly stitched up, as they say.

'Let's look at it. Firstly there's sexual harassment. Then there's rape, or indecent assault at the very least. And we can find the necessary witnesses if we have to. Then there's the discipline offence re the firearm. That in itself could lose you your job. Then there's perverting the course of justice and, of course, planting evidence.'

'What the hell are you talking about?'

'Those guns found in Anderson's Shogun. You were left alone with the car for a few short minutes and lo and behold, guns appear. Very neat, wouldn't you say?'

Henry thought back to the incident. How Siobhan had gone to the toilet, leaving him to start the search of Anderson's vehicle. And then him finding the guns.

'Fucking bad news all this,' Morton said. 'Individually they're horrendous. Put them all together, pal, they're devastating. You are a very corrupt and perverted individual, and we have done well to unmask you, wouldn't you say? You will never recover from these allegations professionally or personally, once they start being investigated. What d'you say, Henry? Cat got your tongue?'

'I'm not guilty of any of those allegations,' Henry replied stubbornly to Morton's prodding.

'Doesn't matter whether you are or not. I mean, I know you're the cleanest cop in the world. Bet you don't even have skid-marks on your undies, do you? What matters is that we will make sure that, at the very least, you will lose your job and your private life will go to rat-shit.' The matter-of-fact way in which Morton spoke the words hit Henry like a hodful of bricks.

A hush descended on the room.

Henry stared past Morton's left shoulder out of the window where he could see Blackpool Tower, now painted a garish blue colour to promote a fizzy drink. It was raining hard, driving against the glass, obscuring the view, distorting the Tower.

He blinked, brought his vision back to focus and said, 'Why?'

'If you haven't sussed that out by now,' said Morton, sounding a little exasperated with him, 'you're not the great detective I thought you were.'

'Dundaven and Marie Cullen,' he stated. His brain cells shuffled through the incidents of the last week. 'Marie Cullen I can see. You have some connection with Harry McNamara and I suppose you're protecting him because he's as guilty as fuck. I can only speculate about Dundaven. Must have something to do with the guns. Presumably you're protecting somebody else and I was getting too close to them, and they – or you – didn't like it.'

'By Jove I think he's got it,' Morton chortled patronisingly. 'But that's enough of the speculation. You don't need to know anything further, other than you were beginning to worry some people and they needed to be . . . reassured. Remember when you said a little dickie bird would tell you when you'd gone as far as you could with those enquiries? Chirpy chirpy cheep cheep. It's me. I am that bird.'

'You bastard!' Henry had a sense of being trapped in a cage.

'You should know that certain people want you dead, Henry. I saved your life. You should be thankful to me, not call me names.'

'Big deal. What's to stop me walking out of that door, going straight to my Chief Constable and blowing the whistle on you?'

'You still don't get it, do you? Your life will be worse than hell. We will drag you through the mire. We'll come up smelling of roses and you'll just smell like cowshit. You'll lose. We won't. Simple as that. We've had problems like this before and dealt with them accordingly.'

Henry stood up without warning.

Morton drew back defensively. Gallagher braced himself and Tattersall was half off his seat.

He walked to the window and stared out blankly through the rain.

He had nothing on these people. They had everything on him, twisted

230

and perverse though it was. And they were prepared to use it, should Henry make a stand.

They had power and organisation. He could not even begin to guess the scope of their activities.

Standing there he was isolated – and beaten.

He turned slowly from the window, a look of defeat on his face. 'So what's the score?'

'I'll lay it on the line, Henry, then you know exactly what is required of you. Firstly, you must ensure that to the best of your abilities those two investigations get nowhere.'

'That may not be within my power. Other people work on them.'

'In which case you must keep me informed of any progress, you must destroy or contaminate evidence without drawing attention to yourself, and you must pull your weight in terms of making enquiries hit dead ends. Otherwise you'll suffer.'

'And secondly?'

'Keep a watching brief on the Derek Luton case and let me know how that goes.'

'Why?'

'Because I'm interested. And thirdly, before you go back to your normal duties, we may have something else for you to do.'

'And what's that?'

'All in good time, Henry.'

'So you've got me by the bollocks.'

'Only if you value your life and how you lead it.'

'Is that it?'

'No,' said Gallagher sharply. 'You were given some documents by Annie Luton last night, I believe.'

'How do you know?'

'Telephone. Hand them over to us now.'

'I left them at home,' Henry said quickly. 'I'll bring them in this afternoon.'

'Make sure you do.'

'Can I go now?'

'Yes, you can. Go away and reflect on things. Consider your position very carefully, but realise one thing: you now belong to us and basically you've no way out of that.'

Tight-lipped, Henry strode angrily to the door and wrenched it open. He stopped for an instant, turned quickly and uttered the word 'Cunts!' before storming out, slamming the door behind him with a ferocity which nearly brought it off its hinges.

Morton regarded the other three with raised eyebrows.

'I don't trust him,' Siobhan said.

'Nor do I,' Gallagher agreed.

Tattersall said nothing.

'Me neither. Make sure he's followed. We really don't want him to do anything stupid, do we? Jim?' Morton looked towards Tattersall.

'I'll see to it, boss.'

Chapter Twenty-One

T he weather over the whole of the country was appalling.

Karl Donaldson, with Karen sitting by his side, drove their Jeep Cherokee through driving snow around London, sleet and icy hailstones all the way up the M1, five minutes of clear weather around Birmingham on the M6, then bucketing rain the rest of the way up to Blackpool.

The journey took nearly five hours at an average speed of 50 m.p.h., headlights blazing all the way.

As ever they made the trip more pleasurable by singing along with each other. A Beatles session, followed by Motown, a little opera and finally some good ole country music onto which Donaldson had successfully weaned Karen. Dwight Yoakam, the O'Kanes and Lacy J. Dalton were no longer a mystery to the girl who'd been born in Oswaldtwistle, Lancashire, not Nashville, Tennessee.

It made the time fly and helped Donaldson concentrate.

They arrived at Henry's house about twenty minutes before he did.

Kate greeted them warmly. They had become good friends and often made excuses out of nothing to visit each other, even if it meant a two-hundred-mile hike. The two women had an extra dimension to their relationship now and talk turned immediately to babies, pregnancy and childbirth. Kate began to feel broody again.

When Henry came in like a bull with a wasp stinging its arse, it was immediately obvious to all three that he was fuming with anger.

He refused to say anything about what was bugging him, but his body language put them all on tenterhooks.

Kate coerced him into the kitchen and said sternly, 'Henry, they've come all the way from London to see you, you could try to be just a little bit polite.'

He nodded and breathed down his nose. 'You're right.'

They had a light, but hot lunch, and Henry made an effort. They exchanged stories about their injuries – Henry's chest and ear, Donaldson's face. Over coffee Henry said to Karl, 'What can I do for you, pal? I know this is a work-related visit first and foremost.'

'Henry!' Kate said in a warning way, 'Don't be so rude.' She looked apologetically at the other couple. 'He's had a long week.'

'Kate – you don't know the damned half of it.' Henry's voice was hard and unyielding. 'And don't talk about me like I'm not here.'

He stood up without a further word and left them. Donaldson found him in the conservatory, sitting on the bamboo sofa. Rain streamed down the windows. The garden was waterlogged and there seemed nowhere for it to drain away.

'Mind if I join you?'

'Help yourself.'

Karl placed himself next to Henry and gave a little shiver. 'That's the trouble with these places. They look darned good, but they're too cold in winter, too damned hot in summer.'

'Mmm.'

'Can you talk to me, H.? Kate's really upset in there.'

Henry leaned back. He stared up at the glass roof and shook his head. 'Big problems, Karl. But mine at the moment. I need to think them through.'

'OK.'

Henry sat up. 'What've you come up for, Karl? It's a hell of a day to travel. Must be pretty important.'

'That occurrence in Madeira with Sam – I think she was murdered by a guy she'd seen out there, name of Scott Hamilton, or at least murdered on his orders. I have an idea on that score, but that's another story. Anyway, the cops in Madeira were eventually interested enough to put a tail on this guy. He hopped on a plane to Manchester yesterday.'

'And you want some help tracking him up here?'

'Naw. I got on to MI5 to help me out. They're so under-employed these days they'll jump at the chance to do anything. So I asked 'em to pick up Hamilton's tail in Manchester, stick with him, take some mug-shots and stay within eyeball until he got back on the plane home. Which is what they did. Real pros, they are. Pity they don't know what the hell their role is any longer. I got the surveillance photos pushed through my door late last night – and that's why I'm here. Take a look at these.'

Donaldson had brought a briefcase with him which he placed on his knees and opened. 'I had problems identifying the man Hamilton met – until Karen looked over my shoulder and said, "Ooh, I know him. He was in one of my classes once".'

Henry looked sharply at his FBI colleague.

Donaldson handed him an eight-by-ten black and white photograph taken on the steps of some grand-looking house. The time and date were imprinted in the bottom right-hand corner.

It showed four men standing, talking to each other. Their faces were clearly visible, even though it was apparent the camera was some distance away.

'This is the only one of them all together and the photographer had to be darn quick to get this. They appeared literally for an instant and then split, as if they didn't want to be seen together.'

234

Donaldson pointed to one of the men. 'Scott Hamilton.' His finger moved to another man. 'He's—'

'Detective Chief Superintendent Tony Morton, Head of the North-West Organised Crime Squad.'

'Hey, you know him?'

'You could say that. The guy next to him is Sir Harry McNamara, ex-MP.'

'But we can't get a make on the last one of the group.'

'I know who he is. He's called Ronnie Conroy. Into everything that makes money illegally. Once ran a surveillance on him about four years ago when I was on RCS . . . it got nowhere. Just seemed he knew everything we were going to do.'

Henry looked up, his eyes suddenly alert.

'He was suspected of dealing in guns, selling them to the London underworld and also out of the country – to Africa, I think. Now I know why we got no result!' His eyes met Donaldson's. 'Corruption. The best fucking police unit in the country is corrupt and it does deals with criminals. It protects them with information about police operations, and fuck knows what else it gets up to. Karl, I have something to tell you which may go some way to explaining why I've been such a bad-tempered git.'

'What about Kate? Perhaps you should tell her.' That was Donaldson's suggestion after he had listened to Henry's story – which included everything that had happened – and they had discussed it for a while. The American was clearly shocked by what he had heard.

It was an idea that did not go down well with Henry.

'No. It'd be the final straw for her. I just feel that I need to fight this without her knowing.'

'Does she have to be told all the gory details?' Karl said delicately. 'You may need her support with this. She's not a fool, Henry. It might be a rough ride, but you'd make it. You two are very strong now.'

'No.' Henry was adamant.

'Fine . . . but what do we do now?'

'We?'

Donaldson nodded. 'Yes, we. I'm involved in this from the Sam Dawber point of view. Karen can help out, too. She won't tell Kate anything – it'd be cop business. But I do know something, Henry old pal – you can't handle this alone. No way. You need help if you're going to fight it.'

Henry gazed at his fingernails, wondering where he should begin.

'Hang on a sec!' he said to Donaldson, remembering something. He leapt from the sofa and rushed through the house and out to his car, from which he grabbed the package Annie Luton had given him. He ran back to Donaldson.

'They want this lot for some reason,' he told the American. 'They even

235

went as far as searching Derek Luton's house but failed to find it. Maybe there's something useful here.' He wasn't particularly hopeful but nevertheless tipped the contents out onto the coffee table.

There was a lot of dross which he quickly sorted through and discarded. 'Degsy left me a note the night he was murdered, asking me to come and see him. I didn't get it till too late. I wonder if . . .' He found four statements which had been crumpled up and straightened out. They were photocopies, not originals. Henry ran his hand over them to flatten them. 'These are recent,' he said, noticing the dates. 'Last Sunday.'

There were yellow highlight lines over certain areas in all the statements. A quick glance confirmed to Henry that they were all statements taken in connection with the armed robbery in Fleetwood which had preceded the massacre in the newsagents. The highlighted areas included the time of the robbery, and descriptions of the people involved. Question marks, also in highlighter, had been placed in the margins. Henry noted that the officer taking the statement was DS Tattersall, accompanied by DC Luton.

The two detectives perused the statements.

'Henry, I don't know what this means,' the American admitted.

The Detective Sergeant's brow was deeply furrowed. 'Nor me. These are photocopies of the original handwritten statements. They would have been subsequently typed up.' Henry was thinking out loud. His eyes went to the statements again. Then something clicked. 'When I was at the scene of the murder last Saturday night, Derek told me that the gang had pulled an earlier robbery in Fleetwood. He mentioned a time.' Henry willed himself to recall the conversation. It came to him. 'Seven-ten, seven-fifteen.'

'And these statements highlight those times,' Donaldson observed.

'Yeah, but why?'

Donaldson shrugged and pursed his lips.

'And why the question marks in the margins?' Henry nagged.

'Maybe your dead pal found something out,' Karl suggested. 'Such as these statements having been altered at some stage. These are probably his highlights, marking the areas which've been changed.'

'And Derek got caught finding this out.'

'And it worried someone bad enough to put a bullet through his head.'

'No,' said Henry firmly. 'I can't believe this. I don't want to believe it.'

'Henry, buddy, from what you've told me, and from what I can gather, we are dealing with ruthless people here. They will do anything to stop those who get in their way.'

'Even murder a cop?'

'What about the cop in the newsagents? How come he died?'

'Rogue. Loner. Guy thought he was Dirty Harry . . .' Henry's thoughts turned to Siobhan and her assertion that Geoff Driffield had come on duty alone and disappeared alone. Yet the books he had seen at the NWOCS –

the duty states, the radio book and the firearms book – showed he had come on with four other people. The four Henry had encountered not very long ago.

'Or did he get set up too?' Donaldson said presciently.

Silence. The words hung in the conservatory air.

'Let's apply some creative thinking here, Henry,' the FBI man said assertively. 'I know it could be well off the mark, but have a listen to this: Geoff Driffield thought he was going on a stake-out to catch a gang of armed robbers. He found himself alone in a shop, having been told that the gang would strike there that night. He was kitted out and tooled up. Maybe it wasn't unusual for him to be alone, and so he suspected nothing. Meanwhile, his four colleagues dress up as this gang and hit the shop and kill Geoff Driffield and any other poor son of a bitch who happens to be there. What they don't plan for is the real gang robbing a shop in Fleetwood ten miles north, and they've gotta do some real fancy footwork to make it look like the gang did both jobs. It was their intention to frame this gang anyway, to blame them for Driffield's murder . . . I'm just thinking out loud, you understand.'

'No, can't be.'

'Sit back, think it through. Even on the night of the shootings, as you told me, you were sceptical about the two crimes having been committed by the same gang. Even then, you had doubts. Now does it seem that, maybe, just maybe, your first reaction was the right one?'

Henry acknowledged this with a reluctant, 'Yes.'

'You're dealing with a very violent, nasty cabal here who have gone out of control and who will do anything necessary to achieve their own aims.'

Henry stared into space. 'And not only that,' he said, 'I think that Fanshaw-Bayley and Guthrie are involved too.' Henry couldn't shake the memory of FB and Morton together, colluding, conspiring to set him up. He felt physically sick. 'Which means that the top detective in this force is corrupt. Where does it end, Karl?' he asked plaintively. 'Where do I go from here?'

'I have an idea,' Donaldson said.

Chapter Twenty-Two

It was approaching 3.30 p.m. by the time Henry returned to work. Technically his lunch-break should have been only three-quarters of an hour long, but he couldn't care less about that. Being caught out for taking a long lunch was way down on his worry list.

He found a tight space for his car in the almost overflowing car park at the rear of the police station.

Hoping that none of the NWOCS spotted him, he jogged down the rear yard with the carrier bag Annie Luton had given him in his hand. Once inside he opted for the stairs in preference to the lift and climbed them slowly, emerging on the floor where the murder incident room was situated.

This was the problem area.

He needed to get into the incident room unseen, find the typed statements and photocopy them. He also had to make copies of the written statements in the carrier bag.

He pushed the stairs door open wide enough to allow him to peep through the crack into the corridor.

Empty.

He stuck his head out and looked both ways. Clear.

All the while he expected Gallagher or Morton to appear. If they caught him before he completed his task, he was finished.

He stepped into the corridor.

Morton's office was around the corner. The door to the incident room was directly ahead. Three strides saw him inside.

Two HOLMES operators were working at their computers. Neither looked up. No one else was in the room.

First things first.

Whistling tunelessly, he walked confidently to the copier. He almost screamed when it sensed his approach, clicked on and the message on the control panel told him he had to wait five minutes for the warm-up. A wave of frustration jittered through him. Five minutes is a long time to stand next to a machine, looking guilty.

Better fill the time constructively.

He slid across to the statement reader's desk where there were three big fat ring-binders bursting with statements. He grabbed one of the

238

folders marked *Fleetwood* and went back to the copier.

Please wait 4 minutes. Warming up.

Henry snarled at the machine then set to work scanning through the folder. He found one of the statements very quickly and removed all four pages.

Please wait 3 minutes.

'Bastard,' he hissed. He continued to flick through the pages, knowing that each passing second put him in greater jeopardy. He found another, three pages long, and yanked it roughly out of the binder.

2 minutes, the copier taunted.

Henry twitched. Somebody walked past the door.

He found the third and fourth statements he was looking for.

Ready, the copier declared with a prim beep.

'At last,' he breathed.

He stacked the four statements to one side and picked up the plastic bag, pulling out the creased photocopied originals. Because they had been screwed-up and flattened out, Henry did not dare feed them into the copier for fear of causing a jam. He would have to do each sheet one at a time. A slow process, especially when there was a total of nine one-sided and four double-sided sheets.

When the paper tray ran out halfway through the third statement, Henry nearly sank to his knees and cried.

He looked around wildly for more paper and saw a stack of it in one corner of the room, behind a flip-chart stand.

As he was unwrapping a ream, Gallagher appeared at the door.

Henry quickly leaned sideways, putting the flip-chart stand between him and his tormentor, became still and prayed.

Gallagher called something to one of the HOLMES operators, who laughed.

Then he was gone.

Shaking, Henry ripped the wrapping paper away from the A4 sheets, returned to the copier and stacked the paper in the relevant tray, which he slammed back into place.

'C'mon, y'bastard – work,' he hissed at the machine.

Moments later it was ready to restart.

Henry fed the remaining sheets through.

He placed the new copies into the carrier bag, slotting them in amongst all the other papers.

He had originally intended to photocopy the typewritten statements too, but decided to steal them from the binder and hope they would not be missed. He slid them and Derek's highlighted copies into an A4 envelope, together with a batch of blank statement forms.

As he turned out of the room, Gallagher was coming towards him.

'Henry. I thought I saw you come in. What've you been up to?'

'When – now? Or over lunch? If you mean over lunch I've been crying in my soup, if you must know. Just now I've been to the accounts department to drop my expense sheet off for last month. It's overdue, you see, and they've been on my back to get it in as soon as poss. Life goes on even when you're corrupt, you know.'

'Let's hope you're not screwing the system. I'd hate for you to make false claims about anything.'

'Gallagher, why don't you just shove it. You've got me by the balls, I accept that, but unless I have to, I don't really want to have to talk to you.'

'You ain't got much choice, pal.'

Henry eyed him. He wanted to hit him very hard. Instead he shoved the plastic bag into his chest and said, 'Here, I believe you wanted this stuff?'

Gallagher took it from him.

'Have you been through it?'

Henry took a deep breath. 'If there's anything in there that tells me more about your squalid little set-up, then I don't want to read it. I know more than enough now, thanks.'

'Hey, this is just the beginning, Henry,' the DI sneered. 'You're on board now, one of us. You'll get to like it. Then you'll start reaping the benefits. It's not all bad.'

'Yes it is,' said Henry. 'I hate bent cops.'

'Then you must really despise yourself. I mean, all those nasty things you've done in the last few days. Makes me look like a beginner.' Gallagher snorted.

Henry had had enough. 'Finished?'

'Tony Morton wants to see you. Got a little job for you.'

'He'll have to wait.'

Henry shouldered his way angrily past the smirking DI and made his way to the stairs. Gallagher was delving in the carrier bag, not watching Henry, who twisted into the stairwell, then ran down to the public enquiry counter. He opened the security door and handed the envelope through to Karen who was waiting on the other side. She gave him a forced smile, deep concern visible behind her eyes, then left.

With an empty feeling, Henry turned back into the police station and dragged himself unwillingly up to the murder incident room, dreading what might be in store for him next.

'Something odd happening, boss.' It was the voice of an NWOCS detective called Hunt who had been told to keep Henry under surveillance. He had trailed Henry home and then back to work after lunch. He was now parked up outside the police station, talking on a mobile phone to Morton, who was in his temporary office.

'What do you mean, odd?'

'I followed him home and waited for him to reappear. There was another car in his drive when he arrived. Later he came out with two other people, a man and a woman – not Christie's wife. Christie got into his own car, they got into the other and followed him back to the nick. The guy stayed in the car. The woman went to the enquiry desk and reappeared after about ten minutes with a large envelope in her hand. Whoa, the car's just moving off now . . . What d'ya want me to do?'

'Could be nothing. Stick with them. Let me know what they're up to.'

The call ended at the exact moment Henry knocked on the door and entered the office.

Morton clicked off his mobile.

'You wanted to see me?'

'Yes, got a good job for you, Henry.'

John Rider stood on the Promenade at South Shore. He wasn't dressed for the weather, being in jeans, trainers and a flimsy blouson. The rain was plastering his hair flat on his head and rolling down his face, intermingling with the tears he had thought himself incapable of crying.

He had fucked up everything.

The chance of a settled, normal life, with a woman who loved him and had done so for years. And he had been unaware of it, so obsessed had he been with his macho gangster image, his drink, drugs and other women.

In the space of a couple of days he'd been given the opportunity of a real life, but instead he'd reacted to a difficult situation like the Rider of old, which Isa could not handle.

Straight to Violence. Do not pass Go.

A wave crashed against the sea wall and broke over him, drenching his soul with its icy, salty blobs.

He hardly noticed.

He wanted to drown. To throw himself into the dangerous water.

But he didn't have the courage even to do that.

'It's good to be working with you again, Henry – honestly.'

Siobhan was sitting in the passenger seat whilst Henry drove the NWOCS Vectra. His face was stony and unresponsive. He couldn't believe that Morton was making him work with her again. Humiliating him, rubbing it in.

'I was really disappointed when you didn't fuck me, you know. I was really looking forward to it. I'd have come as soon as you got your dick in me, then lots of times after that. You missed a real treat. I'm so easy to satisfy.' She shook her head sadly. 'All these problems and you didn't even get a jump for your trouble. Poor Henry.'

They had reached their destination. Henry drew the car into the side of the road, stopped and kept the engine running. The windscreen wipers were on double speed to cope with the downpour. He kept his hands firmly on the steering wheel, rotated his head slowly and glared down his nose at her.

'I'd just like you to know that the decision not to screw you was made because I'm a married man and your supervisor. There is another reason why I didn't even entertain shoving my clean cock into you. I was frightened of catching something nasty.'

She slapped him very hard across the face.

Or at least she tried to. This time he saw it coming. His hand whipped up and grabbed her wrist before she connected. His face displayed all the anger and repulsion he felt towards this woman.

She whimpered, 'Let go, you bastard.'

He flung her arm away from him.

'Don't ever tempt me to hit you, Siobhan. I don't feel like I've got very much more to lose at the moment, and it'd give me a great deal of pleasure. A charge of assault on top of everything else wouldn't matter a rat's fart to me.'

He glanced into the rearview mirror. A double-crewed police car pulled up behind. Their assistance was here.

It was time to make an arrest.

Donaldson drove north up the Promenade towards Fleetwood. Karen had slipped the statements out of the envelope. On one knee she balanced Luton's photocopies and on the other the typed statements Henry had appropriated. She read them all carefully and compared them.

'This is incredible, Karl,' she said nervously. 'The statements have been changed, but it's fairly subtle and well done. I'd say that this DS Tattersall knew what he was going to do when he took the statement initially, so that the subsequent changes wouldn't be easily apparent. When these come to be presented at court in six, eight, ten months' time, whoever made them won't know any different. They'll just go along with what has been written. Particularly if the prosecutor is on the payroll. This really worries me. If they've done it for this one, how many more times have they done it? How many more people have been wrongly convicted?'

'How many more people have been killed?'

'Do you think they killed Sergeant Driffield?'

'It all points to it, from what Henry says.'

'We need to tell someone.'

'The problem, as I see it, darlin', is that we don't know who to tell. How far does this cancer spread? If we talk to the wrong people, we put ourselves in jeopardy and Henry too. Let's just take it step by step and see what happens. Now, get that street map out, babe. I don't know my way around Fleetwood.'

He checked his rearview and his eyes narrowed.

Hands thrust into his jacket pocket, thumbs overhanging, a very wet and bedraggled John Rider came round the corner. He had been walking against the driving rain, head down, not looking ahead. As he turned into the road where his flat was situated, the force of the rain lessened and the wind dropped because of the high buildings on either side.

He looked up.

Two uniformed cops, Henry Christie and a woman cop (he assumed) were standing in a huddle on the pavement.

Their faces lifted simultaneously and saw Rider. Christie pointed at him and shouted something that was lost in the rain. Rider did not hesitate. His finely honed survival skills clicked into place.

He ran.

Three of the four officers gave chase.

Henry let them go. He climbed back into the car and flicked the heater fan onto full blast. Normally he would have been quite happy to join the chase – but nothing was normal any more. He decided to do it from the comfort of a vehicle. No point getting too wet. After all, it was only an NWOCS job.

He executed a leisurely three-point turn and went in the general direction of the disappearing officers.

It soon became apparent they had lost Rider.

Other patrols were being called to the area to assist in the search.

Over the radio, Siobhan called Henry and asked to be picked up.

Henry guffawed. Some hope. Maybe when the bitch was thoroughly wet through and completely pissed off. He switched his radio off.

Revenge of some sort and quite sweet in a childish way.

Yet even though he had a desire in him not to make any effort, it was an interesting scenario.

John Rider, Henry had been told by Morton, was suspected of putting two bullets into the brain of a no-hoper gangster called Munrow who had died whilst getting a new suit in Debenham's, Preston. This interested Henry because of his previous dealings with Rider – whom he did not like very much. The man might have been involved in the gorilla-shooting in the zoo and the wounding of a man in the leg – and these things kicked Henry's arse into gear. Even if Rider had not popped Munrow it would give Henry a chance to speak to him at length about these other matters.

Fuck! Henry cursed his conscientiousness. Once a detective, always a detective.

He combed the streets for John Rider . . .

. . . Who had panicked when he saw the cops outside his flat.

He sprinted into an alley, skidded on the cobblestones and pushed himself as hard as he had ever done, with only one thought in mind: evasion.

He concentrated on putting distance between him and his pursuers, knowing that the first couple of minutes were usually the critical ones. If they hadn't caught you by then, your chances were pretty good.

His other problem was that he didn't have the fitness or stamina to sustain himself over more than two minutes of hard running. Within the first hundred metres he started to feel a tightness in his chest as his lungs worked at a pace not experienced for probably twenty years.

Now he was over forty, unfit, with too much charcoal in his lungs and alcohol deposits in his veins.

He emerged out of the alley, did a right down the next street, crossed over and zigged out of sight into another alleyway. A quick look over his shoulder before he disappeared told him no cops in sight.

This alley ran behind a series of guest-houses, emerging into Waterloo Road, the main shopping street in South Shore, running at right-angles to the Promenade.

Dodging the cars, he crossed over and took the next right onto Bond Street. Still no cops behind.

He began to feel confident, though his body was sending out warning signals, such as: 'Please stop, you're hurting me!' and : 'Knackered body, can't run any further.'

He tried to ignore them and jogged as far as the junction with Dean Street into which he turned left, then left again into Bright Street where he had to stop. He leaned on the gable end of a guest-house, gasping for air, his lungs desperate for a rest. He was about to heave up and vomit, he was sure. His head throbbed with the exertion and pain shot through it like a lightning bolt. His vision swam.

He bent forwards and put the palms of his hand on his knees.

He vomited.

A rush of stomach contents, mostly bile, surged through his mouth and erupted onto the wet pavement below.

He wiped his mouth, aware vaguely of a car drawing up nearby.

Hands still on his thighs he looked up, spitting the last remnants of sick out of his mouth. His face grimaced in disgust as he watched the figure of Henry Christie saunter up to him. A pair of rigid handcuffs were swinging tauntingly on the index finger of the cop's right hand.

Rider tried to run again. His legs refused to carry him.

Without a word, Henry clamped the first cuff onto Rider's right wrist. He twisted the cuffs in a well-practised movement. Rider screamed but was powerless to resist Henry who wrenched his right arm up behind his back, flattened the luckless Rider against the wall, grabbed his other arm and well and truly handcuffed him, his hands 'stacked' behind his back, one above the other. Rider's cheek was pressed against the stone wall. A trickle of sick ran out of the corner of his mouth.

Rider eyed Henry, who smiled, gave a short nod and said, 'You're under arrest. Suspicion of murder.' He tried to recite the caution, but made a hash of the wording despite the practise. Rider understood its sense and made no reply.

After a cursory body search, Henry directed Rider into the back of the Vectra, after ensuring the child locks were operative. He climbed into the driver's seat.

'Bit of a wet one,' he commented.

Rider did not respond, but slumped sideways across the seat, panting. Henry shrugged and reached for his PR.

Siobhan stood waiting on a street corner as wet as any person could be.

She pulled the passenger door open and shouted, 'Where the fuck did you go to, you bastard!' On the last word she saw Rider in the back seat.

Meekly she got in. 'Where did you find him?'

'Coupla streets away.'

'How did you know where to look?'

'I'm a detective. It's my job.'

From that moment on, all the way back to the police station, not another word was spoken in the car.

'I did my bit. You've got him, now it's down to you.'

'Not quite so fast, Henry.' Morton grabbed his sleeve.

'Look, you asked me to assist in the arrest. I did. Now leave me out of anything else. Take him to Preston and let them deal with it.'

'Preston aren't dealing with him. We are, and I want you to interview him.'

'Why me? I know nothing about the incident and, to be truthful, I don't even know why he's been arrested. What evidence is there against him?'

'There is none – just reasonable suspicion. That's all you need for an arrest, isn't it?'

'Where's the reasonable suspicion then?'

'He was tied up with Munrow in some sort of underworld deal. They are believed to have fallen out and bang bang, Munrow's dead. Rider is prime suspect. And you're dealing with it.'

Morton waved a file of papers in front of Henry's face. 'Here's all the details of the crime itself, including ballistic reports. What I want you to do is interview him and then charge him with murder.'

'Simple, eh? Just like that. Where's the fucking evidence?'

'That's down to you, Henry.'

'Meaning?'

'If you can't find real evidence, then stitch him up. Fabricate evidence, get a conviction. Do whatever is needed to get this man a life sentence. This will show us that you are one hundred per cent with us now. Do this for me, do it well, and I'll consider letting you off the hook. If you don't do it properly, then the first thing that'll happen is that your darling wife will get a phone call – anonymously – to say you've raped a female officer. That female officer will then lodge a formal complaint against you. Then all that other shit will hit the fan. It's your choice, Henry, but it would probably be in your best interests to fit Rider up. Then you have my word we'll part amicably.'

Henry went slowly down to the custody office. It was a painful journey, not only because of the soreness of his body (his chest and ear were hurting dreadfully) – but because of the dead weight on his shoulders.

How had they done this in such a short space of time?

How had he fallen for it so easily?

Fool.

Yet, in retrospect, there had been nothing tangible to suspect. Odd twinges, niggles, some bad feelings, yes. Other than that, nothing. A bit like a bogus gas official knocking on your door. You're not completely happy, but you let him in, he leaves and then you find your life savings have gone.

Happens all the time. People get conned. Even the ones who would never imagine in a million years they could be a victim of such a crime.

And all because he had rattled a few cages without even realising there were tigers inside them. The NWOCS – and Tony Morton in particular – had close ties going back many years with Harry McNamara. It was obvious that he was being protected. And now the 'Conroy connection' had been revealed by Karl Donaldson and those photographs taken by MI5. A proper little triumvirate. Conroy, McNamara and Morton. All protecting one another, no doubt. All in each other's pockets.

And FB too.

Henry shivered at the thought.

Frightening.

He reached the custody office and booked himself a set of tapes out for the interview. Eric Taylor walked into the room from the cell corridor.

'Why?' whispered Henry.

'To help you, of course.' Taylor moved in close to Henry so they were within earshot only of each other.

'How much did they pay you?'

'Don't know what you mean.'

'How much did they fucking well bribe you to alter that custody record, Eric?'

'Don't you mean – how much did YOU bribe me?'

A PC walked in, whistling. The two men drew apart from each other, a look of loathing on Henry's face. 'I want to interview Rider,' he said, now businesslike. 'I've booked a set of tapes out.'

Taylor flicked open the current custody record binder and went to Rider's.

'He says he wants someone telling he's here and he wants to make a phone call.'

'He can have what the hell he wants,' Henry said.

'Sign here.' Taylor's forefinger pointed to the space in Rider's record where Henry had to sign to take responsibility for the prisoner. 'Last time I gave a prisoner to you, you kicked him in the balls,' Taylor said.

'Allegedly.'

* * *

246

They found the first address in Fleetwood. Donaldson parked outside the house, which was a semi-detached council house.

'What've we got here, honey?'

She had the relevant statements on her knees. 'This man witnessed the robbery. He was in the shop when the gunmen burst in and fired the shotgun into the ceiling. He gave a pretty good account and some detailed descriptions which have been watered down on the amended statement.'

'How are we gonna approach him? He ain't gonna like it a whole bunch when he finds out his statement's been tampered with.'

'Let's just play it by ear.'

She kissed him on the cheek and alighted from the Jeep.

Rider sat up straight when he heard the key in the lock of his cell door. The gaoler, a young PC with less than two years' service, beckoned him. 'You're going to be interviewed now.'

Rider half-thought of being awkward. The idea of a few hairy-assed coppers laying into him with feet and fists, however, did not appeal to him. Ten, fifteen years before, they would have had to drag him from the cell screaming and kicking and he would have taken great delight in whacking a few of the boys in blue in the process. Times had changed. He wasn't the hard man he once was and the events of the last few days had proved that, even though he had killed a man. It hadn't been easy to do and as soon as the trigger had been pulled he had regretted it.

Not that he was about to bare his soul to whoever interviewed him. They would get nothing from him.

Rider stood up wearily.

The PC stepped to one side, allowed him past and followed him down the cell corridor.

He was taken to an interview room where Henry Christie was waiting for him.

Rider sat down on the chair on the opposite side of the table to Henry. At one end of the table, next to the wall, was the double tape machine. Stuck to the wall above it was the mike. The sealed tapes and various documents were on the table.

The gaoler left the room on a nod from Henry.

Henry opened his mouth to speak, but closed it when the door reopened and Siobhan Robson entered the room. She sat down next to Henry with a smile. 'Just want to see how a professional operates,' she whispered to him.

Henry sighed. He unpacked the tapes and slotted them into the machine. Obviously they were going to make sure he did as he was told.

The witness was good.

Karen began by showing him a copy of the 'amended' statement and asked him to read it carefully. He obliged. When he had finished he looked up at them and said, 'It might be my bloody name on top, but I didn't say that.' He was very precise and pointed out the discrepancies.

She showed him Degsy's copy then. He glanced through it quickly and declared, 'That one's mine.'

She and Donaldson exchanged a glance of quiet triumph.

'What's this all about? Why has it been changed?' the witness asked.

'We're not sure,' Karen answered. 'But would you mind making a further statement, telling what's just gone on now? I know it's a real imposition and it'll take a while to do, but we think it's very important.'

She looked at the witness with her big wide eyes and a smile which could have melted granite. He immediately said, 'Yes, no problem.'

Hunt keyed in Tony Morton's mobile number into his own and pressed the send button.

'They've just come out of the house, boss,' he said. He gave the address to Morton and said, 'What d'you want me to do?'

'Stick with 'em,' ordered his Chief Superintendent. 'I want to know what the fuck's going on – if anything.'

'Will do.'

Donaldson's Cherokee pulled away from the kerb. Hunt dropped the mobile onto the passenger seat and followed.

Morton looked at the address given by Hunt with a puzzled expression. It meant nothing to him and he wondered if the two people were simply making house-calls to friends.

Hunt had also given him the registered number of the car he was following. Morton tapped the number for a second or two before picking up the internal phone and dialling down to the communications room where there was a PNC terminal.

The first interview was concluded. Rider had declined the offer of a solicitor, waiting until he knew what sort of evidence the cops had on him.

Henry, of course, was pissing in the dark against a pretty strong wind because he knew next to nothing about the case and would need to know an awful lot more about it, Rider, Munrow and their antecedents before he really began to probe.

Throughout, Rider had been non-committal. He was not exactly obstructive, but he wasn't helpful and the interview achieved nothing.

After Rider had been taken back to his cell, Siobhan dragged Henry back into the confines of the interview room. Once behind the closed door, she cut into him. 'You'll have to do a damned sight better than that, Henry, if you want to keep your nose clean.'

'I'm new to this game. I might've been known to bend the rules in the past, but I've never actually fitted anyone up before. I'm just learning,' he said sarcastically. 'You're the fucking expert.'

'And here's some tips, baby,' she snarled. 'Let's begin with the arrest.'

'I'm listening.'

'Verbal him up.'

'What? "It's a fair cop, guv, you're too good for me" kinda thing?'

She nodded. 'Something like that. I'll back you up.'

'You weren't even there.'

'So?' she shrugged. 'And what about the journey back to the nick?'

'He didn't say a word.'

'Yes, he did – he kept blabbing about how sorry he was, how he'd set Munrow up, how he'd shot him. Didn't you hear him, Henry?'

'No,' he said bleakly.

'I think you did . . . and what I suggest you do is go away and write your arrest statement to include these things. Then let me have a look at it. Then you can really start to get into the bastard's ribs. He really did it, y'know?'

'He may well have done – but there's no evidence against him.'

'There will be, Henry,' she reassured him. 'You just need to get creative.'

'How the hell do you sleep at night? Christ! How many times have you done this?'

'A few, Henry . . . and very well, actually.'

'What's this all about, Siobhan?' he pleaded. 'How far does it go?'

'You don't need to know, Henry. Not yet, anyway. Maybe when you've settled into your role, accepted the inevitable, shown you can be trusted. Maybe then, but for now, all you need to worry about is getting Rider charged with murder – and making it stick.'

They had problems finding the next house. The map didn't seem to make sense and they drove down a few wrong turns before they eventually pulled up outside.

'Men don't listen . . .'

' . . . and women can't read maps.'

They laughed. It was one of their favourite personal jokes, often quoted to each other after they had attended a seminar of the same name. Today it seemed totally appropriate.

The night was drawing in quickly. Lights were coming on. The rain made it darker than ever.

'At least it's confirmed something to me, all this chasing our tails up and down the mean streets of Fleetwood.'

'Oh – what?'

'That we're being followed.'

'Can't seem to work out the number of the house they've gone into,' Hunt was saying to Morton via the mobile. He told him it was on Douglas Place. Morton wrote it down at his end.

He looked at what he'd written. Next to it was the result of the PNC check which told him that the vehicle was a Jeep Cherokee, owned by someone called Donaldson who lived in Hartley Witney in Hampshire. The owner's name meant nothing to him, but he knew exactly where Hartley Witney was – not five minutes away from the Police Staff College at Bramshill where he had attended several courses for high-ranking officers. And from where he had extended his business interests with like-minded detectives who were happy to feather their nests for comfortable retirements by supplying Morton with details of police operations which might affect him and Conroy.

'Donaldson, Donaldson . . .' He worked the name through his mind. Nothing came to mind, other than the Bramshill connection.

The cell door opened.

Rider had been dozing on the plastic mattress, a very hairy blanket drawn up to his chin. He sat up and scratched his head. There was something very flea-like about the cell which made him itch all the time.

It was the custody officer, Sergeant Taylor, who had been most fair with him during his stay.

'I know you said you didn't want one,' Taylor said apologetically, 'but a solicitor has turned up saying that he is acting for you. If you don't want him, I'll tell him to sling his hook. But, to be honest, mate, if I was in your position, I'd have one. You need all the help you can get.'

Rider rubbed his eyes.

He hadn't been banged up for long, but already he was aware of his own bodily odours. As much to escape them, the cell and his solitude, he stood up and said, 'I'll see him.'

The solicitor's interview room was bare, functional and not a place in which to linger. There was a table (screwed to the floor) and two chairs.

Rider entered the room and the solicitor got to his feet. He proffered a hand and introduced himself as Pratt.

When the custody officer had reversed out and closed the door, Pratt said, 'You're probably very surprised to see me.'

'Considering I hadn't asked for a brief yet – yes,' admitted Rider. 'Amazed would be more accurate.'

'I've been asked to represent you by a third party, on the proviso that you do something for that third party first.'

'I'm intrigued. Who is this third party?' He expected to be told it was Isa or Jacko and he had to vow to go straight, or something ridiculous. The name he heard made his flesh creep.

'A Mr Conroy. I believe you know him?' Pratt took a second or two to compose himself and the words he was about to say. 'Firstly, I can promise you that if you do this one thing for Mr Conroy, you will be released from custody immediately.'

'And that is?'

'Sign the ownership of your club over to him.'

The hairs on the back of Rider's neck bristled.

'If you do this, I guarantee this allegation against you will go no further.'

'And how can this guarantee be given?'

'It can, believe me. Mr Conroy has influence.'

'How do I know he'll stick to his word, once I've signed whatever I need to sign?'

'You don't,' Pratt said blandly. 'Having said that, if you refuse to sign, Mr Conroy guarantees that you will serve a life sentence for murder.'

'Does he now?'

For Pratt, the next second or so happened in very slow motion. Rider's tightly bunched and very large, hairy right fist drove through the air towards his nose like a piston. It began at normal size, but as it homed in grew very quickly to ginormous. Then it connected with an almighty crunch. Pratt's nose broke. The energy from the blow was transferred from fist to nose and reverberated right through to the back of his skull.

He went backwards over his chair, legs shooting upwards into the air like a massive 'V' sign to Rider. He crashed onto the floor and rolled to one side, both hands clutching a nose from which blood torrented.

Rider came round to him and bent down to speak into his ear.

'Just tell Mr Conroy that if I get out of here, he's a dead man.'

Karen and Donaldson were admitted into the house by a pretty young lady about thirteen years old. She was the witness.

She showed them into the living room where her parents were glued to the TV, watching one of those early Saturday evening knock-about shows which always foxed Donaldson. It was something to do with embarrassing the fuck out of the general public. Very popular, apparently.

Grudgingly the girl's father went into the dining room with them. His presence was required because of her age.

Donaldson interrupted proceedings after a few moments and asked if he could go into the back garden and take some air; foul night though it was, he explained, he had to get some fresh air into his lungs. He was feeling nauseous.

Karen was puzzled. It showed on her face.

He winked at her.

Five minutes later, wet and bedraggled, he was back in the house, saying he was feeling much better. There was a wide smile across his countenance.

Karen's eyes slitted briefly, then she returned to her task.

The cell door slammed shut behind him. He paced the confined space like a tiger, his thoughts in mayhem, much of his anger directed at himself.

251

Isa's words flooded back to him.

'How can you be sure that Munrow is responsible for killing those people?' she had wanted him to ask himself. Where was the proof?

He had then acted recklessly and killed a man who probably had not set fire to the flats. Or, at least, killed the wrong man. The one who should be dead now was called Ronnie Conroy and Rider had fallen for it. Typical of Conroy. Sneaky, deceitful and, of course, brilliant.

He wanted Munrow out of the way because he was being a pain in the arse, yet he, Conroy, didn't have the bottle to do it himself. So why not prey on John Rider's paranoia and make him think that Munrow was out to get him.

Yeah, get John Stupid Rider to do your dirty work for you, then set him up with the cops.

It was all so simple.

And it was obvious they were tame cops too.

Tame cops like Henry Christie who were on Conroy's payroll.

He continued to pace the cell and each time he reached the door he slammed the side of his fist against it.

Trapped and doomed.

The young girl had a good memory. When she read 'her' statement, she was shocked at the changes. She quickly made a further statement and promised to keep quiet about the matter. Karen laid it on thick for the father, who looked the type to be bragging it around the local pub later, that this was top secret and not a word of it should leak. This was a very sensitive matter and if things got out, lives could be at risk.

Back in the Jeep, Donaldson said, 'Two down.'

'They've taken dozens of statements in this investigation. How many more have been tampered with? In the end everyone will have to be revisited.'

'Yup.' He started the engine.

'And where the hell did you disappear to?'

'Couldn't resist,' he admitted with a big grin. He held up his pocket knife with a gleeful smile.

'They're moving away, boss,' Hunt said into the mobile. He gave Morton the second address, then ended the call. He allowed Donaldson enough time to move off before he slipped his car into first and followed.

After only a few metres he realised that the car would be going no further. It was limping sadly along like a cripple. He drew in and raced round the back where he saw that the two rear tyres were as flat as two-day-old beer.

He swore and pulled his jacket up around his neck.

'Bastards!'

* * *

252

Henry Christie faced John Rider across the interview-room table for the second time that day.

Siobhan sat frostily to one side.

The tapes were running.

'When you were arrested, you said to me, "What the fuck am I meant to have done?"' Henry said levelly to Rider, referring to his notes. The interview had been going forty minutes. Henry had given Rider the opportunity to admit the killing, but the prisoner was not forthcoming. Henry had therefore switched gear and gone into 'verbal-up' mode. 'I then told you and you replied, "Yeah, you're fucking right. I shot the bastard. He well deserved it". What do you say to that, John?'

Henry's voice was affable, unflustered, but underneath he was churning. His stomach felt like someone was dragging a rake around inside it. His hands, though visibly calm, were on the verge of trembling. His nerve-ends tingled at the lies he was putting to Rider.

Rider made no reply, but folded his arms and glowered contemptuously at his captor. So this is it, he thought. The beginning of the fit-up. The opening salvos in what would probably be his downfall. Rider had been confident there was no evidence against him and now they were resorting to these tactics.

'Both myself and DC Robson here heard you. Do you deny you said those words?'

No reply. No response.

'During the journey back to the police station, I reminded you that you were still under caution and that it was in your interests to be quiet until we reached the police station where an interview would be conducted formally. However, you continued to talk throughout the journey, though we did not invite you to do so. You said, and I quote – because DC Robson made notes of the unsolicited remarks – "I had to kill the bastard. He would have done me in otherwise. It were him or me and I made fucking sure it were him. I blasted him in those changing rooms and he didn't have a chance in hell. Bang fucking bang! Dead Munrow". Any comment John?'

As if.

Henry persisted with this for thirty further minutes, having to change the tapes partway through. Not surprisingly he got nothing out of Rider, who at the end of the interview declared he wanted a solicitor for the next one and refused to sign the tape seal when he was invited to do so.

They led him back to the custody office and handed him back to Sergeant Taylor. Henry said, 'Interviewed in accordance with PACE and the Codes of Practice. No admissions made.'

Rider was taken back to his cell.

Siobhan linked her arm with Henry's and drew him to one side. 'Well done, Henry. I'll tell the boss you're trying.'

'I feel like dirt.' He pulled his arm away.

She smiled. 'You'd better start thinking about finding some evidence at his place now. Like a ski mask, or something, maybe splattered with blood.' She left the custody office.

Henry walked back to the charge desk where Taylor was scribbling in a custody record.

'Eric?'

Taylor looked up defiantly. He placed his pen down.

'How much did they give you?'

'You should know, Henry.'

'Don't talk shit. You know I never sent that money. I just don't operate like that. I'd rather get convicted of assault than pervert justice.' Which he knew was rich coming from someone who was in the process of doing just that to another person.

'Five grand in a briefcase.'

'And where would I get that sort of money from? I haven't got five hundred in the bank.'

'How do I know?'

'Have you still got it?'

Taylor nodded.

'I suggest you keep it very, very safe, Eric, while I think of how we can both get out of this mess and still be in employment. Understand?'

Henry was astounded by the level of threat in his voice. It frightened him a little as he said, 'Because if it disappears, I'll throw you off the Tower, Eric, and I'll enjoy watching you fall and splat onto the shops below. And I mean it.'

Their faces had got closer as if they were hypnotising each other.

The gaoler came back from the cell corridor and broke the spell. 'Rider says he wants to see you, Sarge,' he said to Henry.

'Right,' Henry nodded, eyes on Taylor. 'Put it down in his custody record that I visited him and spoke to him through the cell hatch on an unrelated matter.'

Rider's face was pressed into the hole in the door.

'Henry fuckin' Christie.'

'My middle name's James, actually.'

'I wouldn't mind, Henry, but I don't even speak like that! I mean: "It were me or him, I made sure it were him"! I might be a toe-rag to you, but my English grammar is just as good as yours.'

'So? What're you getting at?'

'You'll have to do better than that if you want to stitch me up.'

'I haven't finished yet,' Henry said coldly.

'I thought not, but I'll tell you something.' Rider changed the position of his face. 'I'm surprised at you. I don't like you and I've only known you a week, but I'd thought to myself, "Here's an honest cop. A bastard, but honest". And I respected that – but you've let me down. Big style. What does it feel like to be someone's puppet, doing someone else's bidding? How does it feel to be out of control?'

*   *   *

They met at midnight in the conservatory. Kate had gone to bed, leaving Henry, Karen and Donaldson.

'Two out of four ain't bad for a first strike,' Donaldson said quietly. He took a sip from a cool can of Colt 45. He was referring to the fact that the other two witnesses had been out. 'We'll get 'em tomorrow.'

Henry was tired. His chest was sore and he had made his ear bleed again by fiddling with the dressing. He sat back in the bamboo chair and took a sip of the malt whisky he only brought out on special occasions. It flowed silkily down his throat and put up a temporary barrier against the pain.

'We were followed,' Donaldson told him. He recited the registered number of the car and the make.

'Tch,' Henry uttered. 'Sounds like an NWOCS car.'

'It means they're onto us, Henry,' Karen said quietly. There was a note of warning in her voice. 'They might have figured out what we've been doing.'

'And it means you'd better watch your step, Henry, because if they've put it together, they may act on it . . . which could mean you might be in real danger.'

'Don't make it sound so dramatic, Karl,' Henry said in an attempt to shrug it off. However, Donaldson's words were not to be ignored. Two cops had been wasted already. A third wouldn't make much difference.

'You might be targets, too,' Henry said bleakly.

'So in that case we'd all better be careful and we better make sure we get that evidence together tomorrow. Quick.'

Chapter Twenty-Three

Conroy, Morton and McNamara assembled the morning after – Sunday – at their usual place. The time – 8 a.m. – was pretty *un*usual.

It was a business breakfast. They were served with eggs, bacon, tomato, mushrooms, toast, orange juice and fresh coffee.

Two of Conroy's men sat outside the room, having been provided with coffee and bacon sandwiches.

The three men were dressed casually. Conroy and McNamara intended to play nine holes of golf after the meeting, using Conroy's men as caddies.

'How do things stand?' Conroy enquired.

'Christie's been well and truly done over and he knows there's no way out for him but to give in,' Morton said. 'Having said that, I don't think we'll keep him down without a fight. Something's going on, but I'm not sure what. I'll follow it up later.'

'Expand,' McNamara said.

Morton shook his head. 'Just a funny feeling. If there is anything, I'll let you know.'

'If there is anything,' said Conroy, opening his mouth and dropping a rasher of bacon into it, chomping as he spoke, 'Henry Christie should be iced. We've spent enough time farting around with him and we shouldn't spend any more. At least if he's dead he won't be able to tell tales.'

'He might say more dead than alive,' Morton retorted. 'If there's a way of dealing with things which means people don't get killed, we should do it that way, even if it means a bit of dancing on our feet. Killing's easy, as we've shown already. The repercussions are difficult. That's why we're working so damned hard in Blackpool, covering our backs.'

'Fair enough – for the time being.' Conroy took a swig of coffee. 'But if he gets difficult, don't hesitate: do him.'

'Have you found that prostitute yet?' McNamara said.

'Still looking,' said Conroy. 'She's gone to ground but we'll find her. I got someone on it. Bit of a loon, like, but reliable. She's a different problem to Christie. No one'll miss her and the cops won't bust a gut to find her killers.'

They ate in silence for a while.

Conroy cleared his plate and covered some toast thickly with butter and Tiptree Lime Marmalade. McNamara pushed his food around, eating little.

He wasn't hungry. Morton ate most of his, but it was coffee he craved. He had drunk three large cups of it so far.

'And the other matter?' asked Morton.

'Hamilton meets the buyer's agent today in Lisbon. He'll be with us to view the goods tomorrow. He'll buy, I'm sure of it . . . then we can arrange payment details and transportation.' That was McNamara.

Morton: 'Where will they be displayed? I'll fix up to get them out of the police store, but where are they going to? I believe Rider was rather obstructive to your offer, Ronnie?'

'Well, he had his fucking chance. I'll have that club in my hands tonight – in a physical sense. Then I'll exert some more pressure on John and I'm sure he'll sign everything over to me . . . and then get convicted.' He guffawed. 'Then there'll be no one in my hair to bug me. Munrow gone for good, Rider gone for life. If you do your job, that is.'

He looked at Morton.

'That's just what Henry Christie is doing for you.'

Rider's breakfast appeared on a blue plastic plate with a white plastic spoon and red plastic mug of tea. The food was lukewarm, having come all the way down from the canteen. It consisted of congealed beans, a sausage and a rubbery fried egg and one piece of toast which had looked at a grill from about six metres. The tea was hot and sweet, tasted wonderful and he devoured it.

He munched his sausage and took a few measly bites of the toast.

His night's sleep had been interrupted by the consistent banging of other cell doors and the shouting and bawling of drunks. Being a suspected murderer he was given a cell to himself, for which he was grateful. Had a drunk been thrown in with him, he would have murdered him too.

He was allowed a quick shower and a shave before being banged up again.

A cop pushed a copy of the *People* through his hatch and Rider thanked him genuinely. Any short escape from boredom was welcome.

He settled down, deciding to read every word.

When the cell door opened a few minutes later he was deep into an article about a show-jumper and a tart.

'You've got a visitor,' the gaoler informed Rider.

Breakfast in the Christie household was a chaotic affair. The two girls rushed around as if the house was an obstacle course, both seemingly hyperactive after a good night's sleep. They were getting ready for riding lessons and moved around in various stages of undress, finally emerging in jodhpurs, boots, whips and hats, ready to go. Kate and Karen volunteered to take them. They went in Donaldson's Cherokee and the girls were delighted that, at last, they were in a car which complemented their hobby.

257

The men sighed and stretched out.

'Great kids,' commented Donaldson.

'Sell 'em to you,' Henry offered. 'Nahh, they're brilliant. Not long for you now?'

A smile of satisfaction spread slowly across the American's face. Fatherhood beckoned and he was a willing participant.

Henry drank the last of his tea and the two men finalised their plans for the day ahead with an agreement to meet or contact each other at 6 p.m.

They shook hands before parting.

'Watch your ass,' Donaldson said. 'Don't trust any of the fuckers an inch.'

'I won't.'

They weren't allowed to touch one another. It was a closed visit. Rider sat on one side of the room with a wall and glass panel in front of him. Isa sat on the other side. A speaker in one corner of the glass allowed them to communicate.

She looked forlorn and helpless and he had a need to reach out and hold her very tightly.

'Jacko told me,' she said in answer to his question.

Rider nodded. 'I told him not to tell anyone.'

'He thought I should know.'

'I don't deserve you,' Rider said simply.

Her eyes misted over. She tilted her head back but could not prevent a tear rolling down her cheek. 'I love you, John. I can't stop loving you because of what you've done. I just want you to know that I'm here for you and I'll wait. Corny, but true. You're all I've wanted for years and I'm not going to let you go.'

He looked away from her quickly. His eyes were unable to level with hers.

'I'm sorry, I'm sorry,' he babbled. 'I really screwed up, didn't I?'

She forced the glimmer of a smile. 'Yeah, so what's new?' she said, but not unkindly. 'What's going to happen, John?'

'They're trying to fit me up, but there's no evidence. I should walk, but you were right. I don't think Munrow did light that fire.'

'Who did?'

'Conroy. I was conned by Ron the Con. Munrow didn't do it; it wasn't his style. I should've realised that. He would have met me face to face. I should've listened to you, then maybe we'd still be in bed, reading the Sunday papers . . . naked.'

'Don't, John,' she said quietly. 'I don't want to think about it. All I want to do now is help you. How can I do that? How?'

'Just do what you said you would. Be there for me. That's all I need. You'll pull me through that way.'

* * *

258

Henry walked past Isa as she was leaving the custody office, not knowing who she was, of course. Siobhan was waiting for him, reading through Rider's custody record.

'Ready?'

He nodded. 'Yeah. I've got the Duty Inspector to authorise a search of Rider's flat. We'll see if we can find the gun there and some authentic evidence. Maybe then there won't be a need for this charade.'

Siobhan had already booked out a set of sealed tapes.

'Interview first,' she said.

The morning custody officer walked into the office. 'The duty solicitor rang in about ten minutes ago to say she would be delayed about an hour.'

'Thanks, Jim.'

'In that case, we might as well have a brew together, Henry,' Siobhan suggested.

'I think not,' he replied.

Henry took the opportunity to approach the Patrol Sergeant who, amazingly, rustled up four bobbies to help him search Rider's flat. Henry knew it would be a waste of time, because if Rider did have a gun, or a ski mask, or bloodstained clothing, it would be gone by now. Rider was no fool. But the motions had to be gone through.

Prior to setting off, Henry went to his desk and found his extendable baton which he fixed on his belt in its plastic, quick-draw pouch. Just in case there was any resistance at the Rider household.

The little team set off in a personnel carrier, with Henry sat in the back together with two of the Constables. The other two were upfront, one driving.

Siobhan ran out of the back door of the station to see the van drawing away. She shouted something which Henry could not hear, but his lip-reading skills were advanced enough to know that she was questioning his parentage. He gave her a little wave.

They were at the basement flat within minutes and went *en masse* to the door at the front of the steps. Henry knocked. He was looking forward to breaking the door down, just to vent some of his suppressed anger.

There were footsteps inside.

The door opened.

Henry immediately recognised the woman as being the one he'd walked past in the custody office not many minutes before.

'Yes?' she said suspiciously.

Henry dangled an A5-size form in front of her eyes. 'I'm DS Christie from Blackpool police station. This is an authority to search these premises – by force if necessary.'

She peered closely at the form, then closed the door.

Henry was about to exclaim, 'Yes!' in anticipation, and reach for his baton – which he had yet to use – when the chain slid back and the door opened fully.

'Come in,' she said wearily. 'You won't find anything.'

Henry stood by to let the PCs pass him and commence the search.

'You his wife or something?'

'Some hope,' Isa said. 'Do you want a brew? I've just boiled the kettle.'

Surprised by the hospitality, Henry said yes. House searches were usually met with resistance, not acquiescence. They were often battles and quite good sport.

She led him into the kitchen and flicked the kettle switch again.

'And you are?' he asked.

'Why?'

'I need to make a record of people present during the search.' It was true, he did.

'Isa Hart.'

He scribbled her name down on a piece of paper.

She turned to the worktop and began the tea-making process, facing away from Henry. She was leaning on the surface with both hands taking her weight. Henry thought she was watching the kettle boil. Then he saw that her shoulders were shaking. Her head dropped, chin onto chest, and she sobbed.

'You all right?' he asked.

She tried to pull herself together, wiping her eyes with the sleeve of her blouse and tilting her head back as though to get the tears to roll back into her eyes. They would not stop coming.

Henry reached for the kitchen stool and placed it to one side of her.

'Hey, sit down before you fall down. C'mon,' he said gently.

She lowered herself onto the stool and blinked despairingly up at him. Her eyes were pools of clear water and streams of tears ran down her cheeks. She wiped them irritably away. 'I'm sorry. This isn't getting the tea made.'

'That's OK,' he said, not bothered about tea. He was more aware that quite often, valuable information, sometimes good evidence, could be gained from emotional friends, relatives, lovers. His pleasant bedside manner was a bit of a con trick really. 'D'you want to talk? I may be able to help, you never know.'

'No, no, it's all right.' She heaved a huge sigh. 'It's just . . . Oh God, he promised . . .' She shook her head. 'I'm lying, he didn't promise a damned thing, but he said he loved me and suddenly we had a future, then in the next breath it's gone.'

'Why did he do it?' Henry asked.

Isa was worldly enough not to get taken in by that one, even in her turmoil. 'I didn't say he did it . . . but I know that he's been set up and now he's told me you lot are going to make certain he gets sent down. He doesn't have a chance. We don't have a chance. Oh God, I don't know who I feel more sorry for, him or me.'

'You said he was set up?' Henry's ears (at least the unbitten one)

260

had picked up gold dust from the emotional dross.

'Bastard Conroy!' she wailed. 'And now you're working for him, aren't you? Just like all the other cops on his payroll.' The expression on her face taunted him. 'I hope you're proud of yourself. Guilty or not, you're going to get him, aren't you?'

She buried her face in her hands. 'He'll be an old man when he comes out, *if* he comes out, and I'll have had a completely wasted life.' Suddenly she flared up without warning, anger bubbling over. She propelled herself at Henry and attacked him, pounding her fists into his chest.

He grabbed her hands and bent them roughly back. She screamed. He tossed her away from him. She skittered across the floor and landed in a heap next to the washer where she continued to cry.

Henry rubbed his chest. Too many people were hitting it.

'Y'allreet, Sarge?' A couple of the PCs had abandoned the search on hearing the commotion in the kitchen.

Henry nodded. 'One of you make sure she's OK and the other one take me back to the nick. Then come back and finish the search.'

Before leaving, Henry wrote his home number down on a scrap of paper and left it on a work surface. 'If you feel like talking,' he told Isa, 'bell me.'

Henry ensured he was dropped off at the front of the station. Siobhan, if she was waiting, would probably expect him to come back via the rear yard, one floor below. He wanted to avoid her at all costs. He dashed in through the public enquiry area and was buzzed into the building. He dropped down a flight of steps into the custody office.

No sign of Siobhan. Good.

'Duty solicitor arrived yet?' he asked the Custody Sergeant, who was dealing with a couple of juveniles.

'Nope.'

'I want to speak to Rider, about a matter not concerned with his arrest, not a criminal matter.' Not strictly true, Henry had to admit to himself, but probably the only way he'd get to see Rider alone now.

Two minutes later they were face to face again.

'I won't speak to you without a solicitor present.'

'I think you will. I've been to search your flat.'

'You won't find anything unless you put it there.'

'I found a woman called Isa. She told me something very interesting.' Rider sniffed indifference.

'You're being well and truly shafted here, aren't you?'

'You should know.'

'You'd be surprised how little I know. The name Conroy was mentioned.' Rider bit the inside of his mouth with a squelch.

'Get to the point, Sergeant.'

'I may be able to help you, but in return you have to help me first.'

'Look – you're out to get me, come hell or high water, and probably at

261

Conroy's bidding, so why should I help you? I mean, this whole thing' – Rider waved his hands at the room – 'could be a set-up, just to get me to admit something. How do I know there isn't a hidden mike somewhere?'

'You have my word.'

Rider nearly fell off his seat. 'The word of a man who has already verballed me up? What's that worth in real terms?'

Henry pushed himself to his feet. He walked to a corner of the small room and lounged there.

'I need a fag,' Rider complained.

'Sorry, no smoking. Force policy.'

'Fuck force policy!' Rider leaned his forearms on the table and intertwined his fingers. He twiddled his thumbs, rotating them against each other.

'You've got something together with Isa, haven't you?'

'Did have.'

'She's devastated, you being in here. Really fucked up.'

'Did have, I said.'

'You still could have, John – if you'd trust me. At the very least, what you'll get out of this is a fair and honest investigation. If there is evidence of murder against you, you'll get charged. If not, you'll be released. But I promise there will be no evidence fabricated against you.'

'Sounds fucking great,' he said cynically. 'The devil and the deep blue sea.'

'It's better than what you've got at the moment,' Henry said pragmatically.

'What's going on, Sergeant?' Rider looked across at Henry with eyebrows raised. Henry strode back and sat down opposite Rider again.

His voice was earnest. 'Isa says she believes you've been set up for this murder by a man called Conroy. Is that what you think?'

'You, him – and others, probably.' Rider spoke guardedly, not wanting to say anything which might go against him.

Henry saw the look. 'I'll tell you why you can trust me.'

'Go on, astound me.'

'Do you think I'm doing this shite willingly? Well, I'll tell you, I'm not. I'm doing it because if I don't, I lose my job, my wife, my pension, my reputation, everything – and may even end up in prison. Yeah, it's true. I've been set up too. In a different way, for a different reason – or maybe the same reason, I dunno. Maybe there's some connection between us two. But there's something I do know. If I convict you on false evidence I'll be trapped for ever and I'll be a bent copper for ever, unless I do something about it . . . and you'll be in prison for the rest of your life. We could be the key to saving each other.'

Henry had been leaning forwards, becoming more and more intense as the words torrented out. 'But if you're not interested, let's go down the road to hell together.'

The next official interview was over fairly quickly, much to Siobhan's disgust. They presented Rider back to the custody officer and he was returned to the cells.

'Speaks,' Siobhan demanded.

They adjourned to the interview room and closed the door.

'That was a poor performance, Henry. You didn't seem to be trying very hard.'

'Just feeling my way, getting used to the situation.'

'Find anything useful at the flat?'

'Don't know yet. Going to go back and check. Then we'll move onto his club and do that.'

'Leave the club!' Siobhan said sharply.

'Why?'

'Just leave it, that's all. It's an order. We're not interested in the club.'

'Sure, fine,' he said. 'Who am I to argue?'

'Exactly. Who are you?'

Henry left her in the custody office, telling her he was going for a dump, which might take some time.

Instead of going into the station, he turned right out of the custody office, after checking Siobhan didn't see him, and sprinted down the rear yard to get into a CID Metro for which he had the keys in his pocket. He gunned the small car out of the garage and into Blackpool town centre where he whizzed up and down a few streets, including going the wrong way down a one-way street. He wanted to know if he was being followed and was fairly satisfied he wasn't.

He pointed the car in the direction of Lytham.

Behind him, Jim Tattersall tapped Tony Morton's mobile number into his own, hardly able to suppress a laugh at Henry's anti-surveillance tactics.

Morton told Tattersall to stick with him.

Morton ended the call and placed his mobile on the desk. He drummed his fingers agitatedly and asked himself what the significance could be of Henry's departure from the police station without Siobhan, his chaperone.

The internal phone rang.

'Morton.'

'Siobhan, boss. Just seen the custody record. Henry's had an unscheduled conversation with Rider before I got here. It says on the record it was in connection with a matter unrelated to the investigation.'

'Do you know where he is now?'

'Having a shit.'

'Wrong, you stupid bitch! He's in a car and he's heading out of town, for fuck's sake. I thought you were supposed to be keeping an eye on him?'

Morton slammed the phone down.

Morton had ordered a two-car tail on Donaldson. And Mr Donaldson, FBI employee, didn't spot it until quite late because they were good. By the time he saw them, he and Karen had visited the other two witnesses and taken statements.

He swore when he realised, but there was nothing more to be done about it – other than to lose them for the fun of it.

But by then, both addresses were on a piece of paper in front of Tony Morton.

Morton asked Siobhan to check the voters' register to put names to them. He was beginning to feel very uncomfortable; also that he had been too generous with Henry Christie by allowing him to live. The challenge of corrupting an incorruptible officer was proving to be a headache of epic proportions.

It would have been far easier to have had him whacked straight away.

Henry drove quickly, pushing the Metro hard through the mid-morning traffic which, due to the season and the weather, was fairly light.

He picked up the coast road and was soon in Lytham. He had a vague idea of where he was going because a few years ago he had delivered a message there, about what he could not recall. He did not know the town well, but it was only a small place and he trusted his memory and sense of direction.

He found the road in about ten minutes. Thirty seconds later he stopped outside the house, a large, bow-windowed semi.

He looked at the building for a while just to make sure he wasn't mistaken.

Yep. It was the right one.

He got out of the Metro and went through the garden gate, failing to see the car which had drawn up two hundred metres behind him.

Tattersall was quickly on the blower.

'Boss . . . we could have problems here.'

Morton paced his temporary office. Siobhan was sitting watching him with a fearful expression.

He had four names and addresses on his desk which still meant nothing to him.

And Henry Christie had spoken to Rider alone for about twenty minutes. And now he was at an address which sent goose bumps down his spine.

'I don't like this one little bit.' He rubbed his chin.

'He's wriggling,' Siobhan said. 'That's all.'

'He should've been killed like the two others. I regret not having him done now. I protected him and he could well be causing me problems.'

Gallagher came in bearing the statements which had been amongst Luton's other paperwork in the plastic bag.

264

'Got the statements back,' he said triumphantly.

He handed them to Morton who glanced at the top one and tossed them onto his desk. Then his neck craned down as he saw the name on the top one. He fanned all four out, his face turning ashen.

'These are the people that Donaldson guy has just been to see. He's been visiting the witnesses again on Henry's behalf.'

'What?' asked Gallagher, who had not been privy to these developments. He'd been making a show of running the murder enquiry.

'Some guy called Donaldson and a woman have been visiting our witnesses again. Where have you been for the last twenty-four hours, numb-nuts?'

'Somebody has to make it look like we do policework occasionally,' he griped.

'Yeah, yeah.'

'Did you say Donaldson?'

'Yeah, why?'

'Name rings a bell.' Gallagher was thoughtful for a moment whilst he wracked his brains, the tip of his tongue resting on his lower lip. 'Got it! FBI agent linked to that big trial Christie was involved in about eighteen months, two years ago. The mafia guy, remember? Yeah, I'm sure Donaldson was the name of the FBI agent who was a major witness.'

'So an FBI agent and a female who we don't know are going round visiting witnesses?' Siobhan wanted this to be cleared up.

'Probably his wife. She's a policewoman, ex-Lancashire now in the Met. Works at Bramshill these days, I think.'

'I know her,' Morton declared. 'She was one of my course tutors on the senior command course.'

Morton looked at the statements again. His mouth sagged as something else dawned on him. 'These are photocopies of photocopies.'

Gallagher's brow creased.

'Luton screwed his copies up when I caught him. These should be creased, for God's sake! Look, look at them. You can see that the ones they've been copied from were creased. I am surrounded by imbeciles.'

'Let me look.' Gallagher took them from his boss. It was true. They were photocopies of creased statements. Gallagher's despair showed on his face. 'So they've still got the copies Luton made?'

'It fucking well looks that way, doesn't it?' screamed Morton. He took in a deep breath. 'Seems we'll have to sort Henry Christie out properly this time.'

Chapter Twenty-Four

'I don't suppose for one moment you'll remember me, sir...'
Before he had a chance to finish, the older man said, 'Course I bloody do, you're Henry Christie. I don't forget faces like yours in a hurry.'

The former ACC of Lancashire Constabulary, Roger Willocks, stood to one side and allowed Henry into the house. He pointed to the lounge and Henry went in.

Henry could not fail to see the large number of sympathy cards around the room, filling every available flat surface.

'I'm sorry, Mr Willocks. If I've come at a bad time...'

'No, no, no, nothing of the sort. My wife died nearly a month ago – cancer. Just haven't got round to taking the cards down yet. Seems such a final thing to do.'

He smiled sadly at Henry.

'It's good to have a serving cop round. Most of my friends are retired now and I don't have any particular connection with the Top Team now. Coffee?'

They chatted briefly about the good old days – which Henry was glad to see the back of, actually – and Henry told him of the sweeping changes which were taking place today in the job.

Willocks was not impressed. 'Glad I got out,' he said. He put his coffee down. 'So, my lad, to what do I owe this honour? I don't suppose you've dropped by just to delve into the past, have you?'

'Yes and no.' Henry paused and gathered his thoughts together. 'A few years ago you headed an enquiry into the North-West Organised Crime Squad.'

Willocks' face blackened over. 'I'm not sure I want to talk about it,' he said stiffly.

'I need your help,' Henry begged him. 'Two police officers have died within the last week, another has been shot, and another is having his balls squeezed – and the thread through them all is that squad. The more I find out about it, the less I like – and my testicles are starting to hurt quite badly.'

Willocks' gaze drifted around the cards in the room, all sent in sympathy for his departed wife.

He laughed to himself and said, 'Don't suppose it matters now she's gone.' He turned to Henry.

'You've only scratched the surface,' Willocks commented, when fifteen minutes later he had listened to Henry's very edited version of events. 'Come with me, Henry, let's go to my thinking shed.'

He led the detective through the house and out into the garden at the rear. The rain had stopped and the cloud had thinned considerably. They walked down a path to the garage and entered it by means of a door at the back. Inside it was dark and Willocks pulled a light switch. A series of three spots came on, revealing a workshop with lots of pieces of furniture scattered about the place in different stages of renovation. A workbench was covered in tools of all descriptions. Fumes which Henry assumed were paint-remover or turps pervaded everything.

'Don't light up, whatever you do,' warned Willocks with a laugh. 'Leave the door open, it'll clear. This is where I spend my spare time. Buy crap, make it look good, sell at car boot sales. My hobby,' he said proudly.

Henry, to whom anything in the sphere of DIY was an anathema, tried to look impressed. He sat on a newly renovated chair, while Willocks perched on a stool.

'The NWOCS is a police unit which is out of control,' the former senior officer declared. 'It's like a private army and its little Adolf Hitler is Tony Morton. It was a badly conceived set-up in the first place, one of those knee-jerk reactions to a particular problem which existed at that time in the mid-1980s. You know the sort of thing – let's set up a squad.'

Henry nodded. The police service's answer to everything: set up a squad.

'It has no parameters, no terms of reference, no rules by which to work, and most importantly of all, no control. It stood alone, ostensibly an offshoot of the Regional Crime Squad, but in reality it declared UDI. There was no one to oversee it, probably because no one thought it belonged to them. It did what it wanted to do, and still does. It continues to have good results against organised crime, but in reality those results mask something that is very, very bad. This is because the man who championed its formation and the man who runs it are corrupt and in co-hoots with organised crime.'

Henry found himself becoming angry. 'Well, why didn't you do something about it? It was your job, wasn't it?'

Willocks smiled at Henry. He understood the detective's annoyance.

'I was asked to investigate when some doubt was cast about unsafe convictions. I looked at a handful of people the squad were responsible for convicting, and each claimed they had been framed. Some lied, of course, but some told tales which began to hold water. I delved. I was devious. I bugged places and people . . . and the more I did so, the more I uncovered – until I began to realise that here was a group of police officers who were

267

controlled by, acted with and protected criminals – particularly Ronnie Conroy.'

'What, everyone on the squad?'

'No. Most of them are pure, honest, good cops. But there is a nucleus of officers who are corrupt. They all circulate around Tony Morton. Never more than ten officers, I suspect, but because they're backed by Morton they carry the weight and control and monitor what the clean officers do.'

'So, again, why didn't you do anything?' Henry accused him.

'What did they do to you, Henry?' Willocks asked, looking directly at him, evading the question.

'What d'you mean?'

'You said they had you by the balls. You weren't very specific. What was it? Did they con you into taking a bribe? Set you up with a woman and film it, then threaten to tell your wife?' Henry coloured up and the wily old man knew he had hit a nerve. 'Does that begin to answer your question, Henry? I fell foul of them. I was naive enough to think I could pull a woman who was almost three times younger than I was. In fact, she was only fifteen. Looked nineteen. Acted thirty. And I did it, God, I did it . . . then I saw the still photos, then I saw the video footage, and then I saw the written statement complaining of rape and the doctor's testimony to go with it . . . And then I saw Tony Morton's face and thought about my wife. I caved in immediately.'

'They know how to intimidate, lie, cheat, cover their tracks. They are very dangerous, completely ruthless.'

'Do you think they'd murder?'

They were back in the living room, chatting over a cup of tea.

'Maybe, though I never uncovered it,' said Willocks. 'Wouldn't surprise me to learn that they'd murdered people to silence them. Usually they're a bit more subtle, like they were with you and me. Put people into impossible situations, or pay them off, or frighten or harass people, do whatever suits their circumstance – and don't forget the double-edged sword. They've got cops and criminals doing the work for them. It's bad enough being leaned on by a cop. Having a criminal do it as well . . .'

'So that's what I'm up against.'

'No, it's more than that. There's the political angle too with McNamara. He's very influential and can bring pressure to bear in other ways.'

Henry blew out his cheeks. 'You've blitzed me.'

'I thought I might.'

'How do they operate?'

'They facilitate crime. They allow Conroy – who is probably one of the biggest and wealthiest criminals in the country – to operate unmolested. In return they get paid big money from his gun and drug dealing and all other sorts of criminal activities. And Conroy gives them a succession of sacrificial lambs – sometimes spectacular busts which boost the standing of the squad. Which is why it has been allowed to continue for all this time. It gets results but they are not as a consequence of police work, they're as a result of corruption.'

'I'm going to get them,' Henry said firmly. 'I'm not going to allow them to beat me.'

Willocks looked sadly at Henry. 'Don't put yourself in peril, lad. These men will not give up and they can destroy you far easier than you them. You tell me two cops are dead, so if you make a mistake and they find out what you're doing, you could be dead too. In the name of justice these people need to be stopped . . . but for God's sake don't do it at the expense of your life.'

Chapter Twenty-Five

The sky was very dark. Out across the Irish Sea, forks of jagged lightning scorched down into the water. Henry drove back slowly along the Promenade. Big spats of rain splodged onto the windscreen, slowly and almost thoughtfully at first, then grew heavier. Henry flicked on the wipers and headlights.

It was 2 p.m. He had eaten no lunch and his empty stomach gurgled noisily in accompaniment to the thunder which suddenly roared overhead.

He drew into the kerb opposite the Big One on the Pleasure Beach and sat there with the engine idling. The car which pulled in seventy metres behind him went unnoticed by Henry, for his thoughts, black as the sky, dominated his whole being. They were in a whirl of conflict and disbelief.

A police department out of control. Working alongside criminals and bent politicians for financial gain, apparently capable of killing people who got in their way. Or so it seemed.

Yet what about the trigger to this last week's events, the murder of Geoff Driffield and others in the newsagents? What had Driffield done to incur their wrath? Had he uncovered something and had he told anyone else, or had they got to him before that and silenced him?

Henry realised he might never know.

The thunder overhead seemed to rock the small car. The rain was so dense, Henry could hardly see.

And now he was in the middle of all this corruption. *He* had been corrupted. Fallen hook, line and stupidity.

He explored his options.

The first was to carry on with what he was doing and involve the Donaldsons in a game which might get them hurt. Or perhaps he should just accept his lot, concentrate on getting Rider convicted and then plead to be freed from his obligation to them.

He rubbed his temple with forefinger and thumb. In his mind's eye he saw Morton, Conroy and McNamara looking pityingly down at him as he made his plea. They would never willingly let him go. He was too much of a prize. Another bent cop in their pocket.

Yet Henry did not want to be a bent cop, was not a bent cop and never would be . . . He slammed the gearbox into first and accelerated out into the stream of traffic. There was no way he could allow his life to be compromised and dominated by people who had an illegal hold on him.

He would fight them.

But he knew he could not do it alone.

Five minutes later he was parking in the rear yard and walking towards the police station. He dashed up to his office and took a piece of equipment from a drawer in his desk, and after checking it worked, he went down to the custody office, avoiding any meetings with his friends from the NWOCS.

It was unusually peaceful in the charge office. The afternoon Custody Sergeant lounged in a chair behind the custody desk. Henry knew the Sergeant well, but she seemed distant and slightly wary of him.

'You OK, Sal?'

'*I'm* OK, Henry,' she said, emphasising the 'I'm'.

Henry shrugged off her attitude; he couldn't be bothered. He asked to see Rider.

She made an entry in the custody record. 'Use interview room two, will you?'

'Sure.'

Henry waited in the room until a tired-looking, slightly bedraggled Rider was steered sleepily in.

'I'll lay it on the line, John,' Henry began without preamble. 'I want to know everything you know about Ron Conroy's criminal activities and corrupt connections with the North-West Organised Crime Squad, and anything else you've got on him. The more I know, the more evidence I gather, the more chance we both have of getting out of this by the skin of our teeth.'

'You're asking a lot, mate. What do I get in return? Charged with murder, then iced by Conroy at some non-specific time in the future?'

'No – you won't get charged.' Henry shook his head. 'I've decided that if you do what I ask, tell me what I want to know, then I'll stick my neck out for you. I promise that you will not be prosecuted for the murder of Charlie Munrow.'

'Do you have the authority to make that promise?'

'Probably not – but believe me, John, if I have the power to fabricate evidence to convict you of a crime, then I also have the power to get you off a charge. But I believe that if you come across, I'll be supported one hundred per cent by the people I go to with the information.'

'Who will that be?'

'Probably my Chief Constable.'

Rider sat back. 'That's not enough. These are dangerous people. They kill.'

'I know.' Henry marshalled his thoughts for a few seconds. 'I'll guarantee that, if you want, you'll get put on a witness protection scheme. Isa too, if you like. New identities, new locations, some cash, new job . . . whatever we can do. That is my second promise to you.'

271

Rider nodded thoughtfully. His eyes locked into Henry's. 'And what about you? Just 'cos you're a cop doesn't mean you're not a target.'

'I imagine,' said the detective, 'that we'll probably both end up stacking shelves in Asda in Newcastle in our new lives.' He grinned. 'So what about it? It's a lot to ask.'

'Fucked if I do, fucked if I don't,' Rider said pragmatically. 'Having said that, I'm not sure how much help I'll be to you. Ten years ago I knew everything. A lot of what I know now is third-hand.'

'Just start blabbing. I'll be the judge of what's useful and what's not.' Henry produced the hand-held tape recorder out of his pocket and placed it on the table. 'Let's have a quick preliminary chat here . . . just to get going.'

And the tiny radio mike which had been secretly fitted underneath the wall microphone of the official tape machine picked up everything that was said and relayed it to the speaker and tape recorder in Tony Morton's temporary office.

He was expecting it, but when the knock came Eric Taylor nearly jumped out of his skin. He trailed reluctantly to the door and opened it. He recognised Karen Donaldson immediately from her Lancashire days.

'Ma'am,' he said nervously. 'Come in.'

She stepped across the threshold accompanied by her husband who nodded curtly at Taylor.

'This is my husband, Karl Donaldson. He's with the FBI in London. He's assisting with this matter.'

Glumly Taylor nodded.

'Where's the money?' Donaldson asked.

Taylor picked up the briefcase he'd been given and opened it.

'Sit down, Sarge,' Karen said.

All three sat. Taylor alone in the middle of the settee, the others on chairs.

'What we need to do here, Eric, is come at this from a different perspective than you simply taking a bribe, even though that's the bottom line, isn't it?'

Taylor remained tight-lipped. He wriggled his shoulders pathetically.

'In order to clear your good name,' her voice was sweet and hypnotic in its rhythm, 'we need to apply some creative thinking, don't we? I suggest we go from the premise that you simply played along with these people who "bribed" you, because, in fact, you were acting on our behalf by gathering evidence of corrupt and improper practice. Do you get my general drift?'

'You mean I was sort of acting for you?'

'Spot on. You're a bright boy,' Donaldson said impatiently.

'Henry won't suffer, will he?' Taylor said. 'I feel really bad about that.'

'No, because he's doing the same thing – working to expose corruption at high level. Now, all you need to do is make a detailed written statement outlining your role in this investigation and then what happened and who gave you the money. Simple.'

'What if I don't do it?' His eyes narrowed as he tested the waters.

'You're fucked,' Donaldson rasped darkly.

Henry knew he was taking a risk by spending so much time talking to Rider. Siobhan could come down at any time. Still, he reasoned, the time for inaction had gone. If he wanted to get out of this thing, then a risk it would have to be.

Rider told a good story. It covered his early years and association with Conroy and Munrow which blossomed in the late 1970s, early 1980s, based on drugs and guns. By 1982 they had a big, lucrative empire which was growing in all directions, legit and otherwise. But when the gangland territorial wars started, catching the attention of the forces of law and order, the empire began to crumble.

Rider left.

Munrow got busted.

And Conroy saw it as an opportunity to expand even further, this time protected properly by his police and political friends who he had been nurturing and working alongside for years. Rider named names.

'I hadn't seen Conroy for a good while,' he explained, 'though I kept tabs on what was happening. I never wanted to go back to that life, so Ronnie and his activities didn't bother me one way or the other – until last weekend, when he contacted me and asked for a meet. He wanted to get a toehold into my club – for drugs, I thought. I told him to piss off.'

'He wanted to sell drugs through your place?'

'That's what I thought originally... then I saw that thing about Dundaven in the paper the other day and put two and two together.'

'Whoa, hold on,' said Henry. A light dawned. 'You mean Conroy and Dundaven are connected?'

'Yes – I thought you'd know that.'

'Only sort of.'

'And instead of drugs, I think he wanted to store those weapons at the club, probably as far away from himself as possible.'

Henry shook his head in disbelief.

'That meeting between me and Conroy took place at the zoo, incidentally.'

'When?' Henry blurted. 'Last Sunday? When Boris got shot?'

'Yeah ... proper sad, that.'

After twenty minutes Henry had enough to be going on with. He switched the tape recorder off.

'Now what?' asked Rider.

'We go to the Custody Sergeant and I'll tell her that there's no evidence against you, and you are to be released immediately. Then we'll get out of here as quickly as possible. Pick up Isa, my wife and kids, then we run to the Chief Constable – hopefully before we get a bullet each in the brain.'

Chapter Twenty-Six

De la Garde had developed a speciality which ensured that, occasionally, just to supplement his drug-derived income, he made a nice bonus.

His specialism was drive-by shootings.

He was a gun for hire.

A plague in the States, but a rarity in Britain until recently, the DBS – as it has become affectionately known – is now a fairly common feature of the inner cities. Liverpool has experienced its fair share, as have Manchester and Leeds. Lancashire, trailing behind these urban areas in terms of violent crime, had never had one – yet.

The DBS was often used as a tool to frighten and intimidate, the message often being more important than the injury.

But De la Garde had been given specific instructions: this time there was no message to deliver, just sudden death. 'Ensure that your target dies,' he had been told in no uncertain terms.

He had not even blinked or asked why. He was paid two and a half grand up-front and promised the same amount on completion. Not much, but well above the going rate for most of the killers who roamed the streets of north-west England. It would pay for a pleasant holiday to Jamaica he had planned for next week.

His target was the prostitute called Gillian, the one causing so much anguish to McNamara.

It had taken De la Garde some time to hunt her down.

He had been patient and let it be known he was seeking her through his contacts. She had gone to ground since killing her pimp, Saltash, but De la Garde knew she would reappear soon. People like her couldn't hide for ever, nor could they run. They were trapped on a hamster wheel and had to make a living the only way they knew how.

So patience, shaking down a few hookers and petty drugs dealers eventually put De la Garde on the right track and led him, unusually, to a pub on the main road between Preston and Blackburn.

De la Garde had been waiting in a strategic position on the council estate in Shadsworth where Gillian lived, and the information he had obtained proved correct. The fucking cheek of the bitch. She was still driving around in Saltash's car, though she'd had the brains to change the plates.

Eventually, as he knew she would, she drove past his observation point. He followed her to the pub, waiting for a chance to kill her, but she managed to park up and get inside before he could move in.

Not that he cared. Sooner or later she would come out and he would make his money. He sighed at his driver, his usual one – another black man who called himself Rufus T. He was the best in the business at present, constantly in demand for shootings and blaggings. De la Garde had negotiated fifteen hundred for him – less ten per cent commission.

They were in an extremely hot Jaguar XJS in the pub car park, tucked away in one corner, listening to the owner's Abba collection on CD.

On his knees De la Garde had laid his instrument of death.

In this case an HK MP5.

Lovely. Light. Accurate.

Morton's head was in his hands. The cassette player on his desk clicked off, ending the recorded conversation between Henry Christie and John Rider, in which Rider had blabbed everything he knew about Conroy, his organisation and contacts, and naming a few names including Tony Morton and Harry McNamara.

Across the room, Gallagher and Siobhan sat quietly, waiting for instructions.

Morton looked up. 'Get down to the custody office now and do something before they both walk out of here!' he shouted. 'If Conroy falls, we fall too. I don't need to tell you what that means.'

'What shall we do?' cried Siobhan.

'Fucking think of something.'

Henry and Rider had to queue up at the custody desk. Four other prisoners and their arresting officers were ahead of them.

'Just what we don't need,' Henry moaned, looking at the queue. He was feeling jumpy and very, very vulnerable. They had to get out of here as soon as possible.

One of the prisoners ahead began to complain loudly to the Custody Sergeant about how badly he was being treated.

Eric Taylor read his statement through very carefully. He placed a firm full-stop at the end, signed his name and initialled one or two corrected errors.

'That's it then,' Karen said. 'For your own sake don't tell anyone else you've made this statement – not yet, anyway. These are very dangerous people we're dealing with here, and we need to keep this under wraps until the rest of the operation bears fruit – which might be a couple of days yet.' She spoke to give the impression there was an organised investigation on-going.

'I understand.' He pushed the money-filled briefcase across the coffee

276

table towards them. 'Take it. I'm sick of looking at it.'

'We need to count it and give you a receipt.'

'Fair enough. But I can assure you it's all there – all five thousand pounds of it.' Taylor didn't bat an eyelid when he said this, but a trickle of sweat ran down the middle of his back and made him cringe a little inside.

There was only one prisoner ahead of them now.

Siobhan strolled casually into the custody office.

Henry stiffened and suddenly felt like a schoolboy who'd been caught smoking by the cycle sheds. He actually blushed.

'What's going on, Henry?' she asked.

'Just about to take his fingerprints,' he replied quickly. 'That is all right, isn't it?'

She surveyed him through slitty eyes. Her mouth hardened. But even so, there was no doubt about it. She was totally desirable. Once again Henry experienced regret at not having gone all the way.

'You can forget them. He has to be taken to Preston.'

'Why?'

'Because the officer in charge of the investigation is screaming at Tony Morton to bring him over,' she lied crisply. 'That's where he should be lodged anyway, as you well know. The crime happened there.'

'Doesn't usually bother you that procedures aren't followed,' Henry pointed out.

She gazed blandly at him. 'We've borrowed a section van – so get him booked out and we'll meet you out back. Make sure he's handcuffed.'

'It's a uniform job, transferring prisoners.'

'We're going to do it this time, so stop messing about and be ready to roll in five minutes.'

She spun on her heels and exited.

'At the first opportunity in Preston I'll get you released,' Henry said quickly to Rider. 'We'll go along with them for the time being. Don't want to make them suspicious.'

The prisoner in front had been dealt with. Henry presented Rider to the custody officer, who firmly believed, because the NWOCS had told her, that Henry was suspected of corruption in a big way. That was why it had been necessary to bug the interview room. But just act natural. Don't let him see you suspect him of anything, they had instructed her.

Gillian laid a hand on the shoulder of the other woman in a consoling gesture.

They made an unusual pair, one which attracted inquisitive glances from the other customers in the pub. The young black girl, dressed provocatively in a cheap, bust-revealing blouse, micro skirt and long leather boots contrasted with the slim, anxious white woman in her mid-thirties dressed conservatively, but expensively, in a black suit by Dior.

'I'm really, really sorry,' Gillian said inadequately. And she meant it. Never in a million years would she, as a prostitute, contact the wife of one of her clients, no matter how sick and depraved the man was. And she'd met some real weirdos in her time who would probably have been perfect gentlemen with their wives. Sickos she could handle. But this was completely different. Here was a man who, she was certain, had murdered her friend and it would only be a matter of time before he killed again.

'I didn't know what to do, but I had to do something. I couldn't go to the police because . . .' Gillian broke the sentence and paused hesitantly. *Because I've killed my pimp and the cops're after me*, was what she almost said. 'For certain reasons,' she eventually said. 'It's been going around and around my head for days, ever since he . . . stuck a knife next to my cunt.'

The other woman squirmed with distaste at the last word. Even Gillian winced, but it was a word she used every day and she couldn't think of anything less offensive. She was what she was.

The other woman's head was bowed in shame. She was trembling all over. Tears poured out. She looked up. 'Don't apologise,' she said. 'I've suspected for so long . . . prostitutes . . . but murder?'

'He told me Marie was going to go public about their relationship unless he paid her big bucks. He didn't actually say he'd killed her, but said he'd made her suffer. Like he'd make me suffer if I told anyone. That was when he did his demonstration with the knife. I'm sorry, Mrs McNamara. I didn't know what else to do.'

Rider held out his hands. Henry snapped on the rigid cuffs, not too tightly, letting them be as comfortable as handcuffs could be.

The Custody Sergeant gave Henry Rider's custody record, having made a copy for filing. The original always went with the body.

Donaldson's bleeper informed him to phone the Legat in London, which he did as soon as he and Karen returned to Henry's house after taking the statement from Eric Taylor. He was told to ring an international number. He dialled it immediately after clearing it with Kate.

His heart leapt as he recognised the language spoken at the other end – Portuguese. He falteringly told the woman his name. He was reconnected successfully.

'Santana,' came the gruff voice.

'George, Karl Donaldson here. What's happening?'

'Your friend Hamilton . . . we have been sticking to him like glue since he returned to Madeira. He spent little time here and then boarded a plane to Lisbon where we were able to keep up with him. He met a man there at an hotel. Our men have watched them carefully.' Santana sounded proud of his achievement. 'They are both booked onto a flight to Manchester tonight.'

'Who is the man?'

'We don't know, but we have taken photographs of him. They are good quality. Maybe I could send them to you?'

'Yeah, sure, hold on . . .' Donaldson clamped a hand over the receiver and said to Karen, 'Honey, can we use one of the fax machines at a police station hereabouts?'

'Yes, shouldn't be a problem. We'll need to find a number, obviously.'

'You can send a fax to this number,' Kate interjected. 'Not to that actual phone, but to the one that's plugged in upstairs. Henry bought it for some reason and never used the thing, but it works.'

'Great.' Down the phone he said to Santana, 'You can fax the photos to this number and send the real ones by DHL to the Legat in London. Gotta pen?' Donaldson recited the number. 'Put the flight details on it, willya?'

Santana said he would. 'There is something more. While Hamilton was in Madeira, we followed him to the docks in Funchal, to the container depot. He checked the contents of a container which was resealed. I swore out a warrant and broke the seal.' Santana laughed.

'George, you have something to tell me, I feel sure.'

'It was full of guns of all descriptions, as well as hand-held missile launchers. Many, many weapons.'

'What did you do?'

'Resealed the container and arrested a Customs official whom we suspected of being involved. He is singing like a baby. Mr Hamilton is a very bad man.'

The fax came through fifteen agonising minutes later. They were good, clear photos of the man who had met Hamilton in Lisbon. When he saw the face, Donaldson blew a sweet kiss to Sam Dawber, because without her, he would never have been able to identify the man. Thanks to her memory games with mug-shots, Donaldson recognised him immediately as Raymond de Vere – a man wanted by several police forces throughout Europe. He made his living buying weaponry for terrorist organisations worldwide.

Karl let out a long, satisfied sigh. 'Kate, d'ya mind if I make another call?'

The van, one of the smaller Sherpa models which Lancashire police used as general purpose vehicles, had been reversed as close to the rear door of the station as was geographically possible.

Henry and his handcuffed prisoner came out of the custody office.

Siobhan opened the rear doors of the van and then the inner cage.

Rider walked ahead of Henry, ducked, and climbed in. He sat placidly down on the bench seat.

Siobhan remained at the open door. 'You go in with him, Henry.'

'I'd rather sit up front.'

'Not enough room.'

Henry got in with Rider.

279

The cage door slammed shut behind him with a loud crash and the spring-loaded locking bar jerked into place. Henry sat opposite his prisoner. Rider gave him a wan smile, leaned back and rested his head against the side of the van.

Siobhan climbed in the front passenger seat and said something to the driver that Henry could not make out.

The driver turned and peered backwards, giving Henry a quick salute. It was Gallagher.

Siobhan's door opened again. She budged up and allowed space for a further person to sit next to her on the double seat.

This was Tattersall.

'Have you got the keys for these cuffs?' Rider asked.

'Yeah, why?'

Coolly, as though he was simply passing the time of day with idle chatter: 'Because I think we could have a problem here. That guy' – he cocked a thumb at Gallagher's back – 'is one of the two who visited Shane Mulcahy and left him with little option but to retract a complaint against you. I'll lay odds the other guy was his running mate.'

Henry's mouth dropped open. 'You sure?'

'Saw him leave Shane's flat and pull his ski-mask off.'

The van moved off slowly.

'Made a real mess of the lad.'

Donaldson and Karen moved to the dining room and spread everything out on the table.

They had four statements from witnesses to the robbery in Fleetwood. All clearly confirmed that their original statements had been tampered with.

Then there was Eric Taylor's statement and five grand, and the MI5 photographs of Conroy, McNamara, Morton and Hamilton.

Finally there was the faxed photo which had recently come up the line from Santana.

'Several threads here,' mused Donaldson, 'all interlinked by the North-West Organised Crime Squad. I think there's enough here for Henry to breathe a sigh of relief, although he still might have some explanations to make to Kate.

'The bottom line is that these bastards in this squad are up to their necks in criminal activity and we've got enough to lay it on the table and say to them, "Answer that, assholes!".'

'What do you know about this guy?' Karen pointed to the newest face on file.

'He's an agent and simply brings buyers and sellers together and takes his percentage. Raymond de Vere, he's called. French background, Irish upbringing. Hence the fact that the IRA are one of his biggest clients.'

Donaldson checked his watch.

'I think it's time Henry came in and we told him this. Then I think we need to decide what to do. My feeling is that he should take all this to his Chief Constable and then he should go into hiding, because his life will be in real danger from that point on . . . if it isn't already.'

De la Garde and Rufus T were patient men. Waiting was not a problem. They listened to more of the Jaguar owner's collection of middle-of-the-road music without complaint.

Then she came out of the side door of the pub, accompanied by another woman.

De la Garde tapped Rufus T on the leg. The driver came to attention and his hands took hold of the wheel.

De la Garde cocked the weapon.

The two women walked arm in arm across the car park. They had reached the prostitute's car.

'What about the other woman?' Rufus T enquired. The music had been switched off.

'Fuck her,' growled the gunman. 'GO!'

The Jag slewed out of its parking spot. De la Garde had the MP5 resting out of the open window. The car accelerated at an alarming rate.

The women looked in the direction of the approaching car. The prostitute screamed something and grabbed the other woman's elbow to drag her out of the way.

The Jag drew level and the MP5, in its understated way, crackled a spray of bullets across the two women.

The prostitute went down as six splattered across her chest. She was dead before she hit the hard ground.

The other woman got four across her midriff. She went down onto her backside where she sat upright for a few moments, looking with disbelief at the spreading redness over her stomach and feeling a terrible, nauseating pain. This was followed by complete blackness.

Only feet separated the women in death.

A chasm had divided them in life.

But the activities of one man had drawn them together for this final, fatal encounter.

The Jaguar was long gone, racing towards Preston, then cutting left onto the M6. Twenty minutes later it was found abandoned and burned out in Wigan.

Chapter Twenty-Seven

Daylight had gone. The blackness of evening came swiftly, and with it more torrential rain which, as they travelled eastwards, turned to relentless driving sleet. Typical horrendous northern weather which looked set to continue.

In the back of the police van it was extra dark. The light which illuminated the cage was controlled from a switch on the dash, but Gallagher steadfastly ignored Henry's shouts to turn it on.

Henry glared across at Rider who sat there with his eyes closed, his face visible only in brief flashes of fluorescent orange when they passed under street lamps.

Fuming, Henry sat back, unable to do anything but brood and wait until they reached Preston before he told the DI what a cunt he thought he was. He folded his arms and tapped his feet, aware he was powerless to do anything other than bide his time.

The van reached Marton Circle outside Blackpool and picked up the A583 towards Preston.

Still restless, Henry shuffled along the bench seat until he was directly behind Tattersall and Siobhan who were squashed up on the double passenger seat. Henry peered through the toughened glass window, shading his eyes with his hands, watching the journey unfold through the poor headlights which struggled ineptly against the weather. Although the wipers worked at double speed, they were fighting a losing battle. Gallagher was forced to lean forwards constantly as though the extra inches would give him some sort of visual advantage.

They stuck on the A583, with the town of Kirkham to their left, eventually reaching the traffic lights at Three Nooks – and the junction with the A584 – where only a week before, Henry and Dave Seymour had made a decision to go towards Preston instead of turning back to Blackpool, and then found themselves in a life-and-death car chase with Dundaven. It felt like a year ago, not seven short days.

Half a mile later they bore left onto the dual carriageway which would take them into Preston. The River Ribble and the old docks were on their right.

Just a few minutes from the police station now. Then Henry could voice his feelings to Gallagher. He was relishing the prospect.

At the first set of traffic lights, Gallagher filtered into the offside lane and then into the right-hand lane specifically for vehicles turning right into Nelson Way. The lights were on red and he stopped.

Henry could see the indicator flashing a right.

'What the fuck's going on?' he demanded suspiciously, alerting Rider who shook himself out of his reverie, opening his eyes at the sound of Henry's utterance.

The lights went to green. Gallagher let out the clutch and turned the wheel.

'We should be going straight on here,' Henry said. He rapped the window with his knuckles and shouted, 'What's happening?'

He was ignored.

He looked quickly at his travelling companion.

'This takes us onto the shit end of an industrial estate.'

Rider leaned forwards, concern on his face.

Gallagher gunned the van down the road which was lit for about a hundred metres. Then nothing. It was like driving into a coal mine. Open fields were on either side.

'Get me out of these, Henry,' Rider said urgently. He pushed his hands forwards, presenting his cuffed wrists.

Henry looked at him, but Rider's face was only shadow on shadow.

'Come on,' the other man hissed. 'If this diversion is legit, then put 'em back on. If not, I think I'd be better hands free.'

Henry did not hesitate. Within seconds Rider was massaging the blood-flow back into his hands.

The van slowed down and turned. The beam from the headlights swept across the outer wall of an old factory. The van stopped about four feet from, and pointing into, the wall.

Henry knocked on the glass again.

'Hey, what's happening, folks?' he shouted, trying to sound jovial and unconcerned. The reality was that he was shitting bricks.

The interior light came on in the front cab. Siobhan handed something across to Gallagher. Something metallic. A gun.

Rider had seen it too.

Something inside Henry twisted like colic. He wanted to burst into tears.

Gallagher flicked a switch and the light in the cage came on.

With the engine still running and lights on, the three detectives stepped out of the van.

Henry caught Rider's expression. He was just as petrified.

The back doors of the van opened. A burst of cold air whooshed in, making Henry shiver and feel weak.

Gallagher, Tattersall and Siobhan pushed their faces up to the metal grill.

Gallagher's face, in the light given out by the interior bulb, looked evil. He smiled.

'End of the road, Henry.'

'What do you mean?'

'Exactly what I say. It's been decided to whack you, pal – and you, mate.' He indicated Rider and rested the muzzle of his pistol on the cage door. 'Sorry an' all that, but you should have taken the hint and done what you were told. Your life would have been good, with all sorts of perks, not least shafting Siobhan here as and when you liked.'

'I'd rather fuck a rusty drainpipe,' Henry said.

'So you're gonna shoot us, is that what you're sayin'?' Rider cut in.

'Yup.'

'And how you gonna explain that?' he asked incredulously.

Gallagher jerked a finger at Henry. 'He knows enough about us to answer that one, don't you, Henry?'

'Creatively, I suppose,' Henry conceded.

'Spot on,' Gallagher said. He shrugged. 'Just thinkin' off the top of my head . . . you're overpowered by the prisoner in the back of the van who has secreted a knife on him. We . . . ahh . . . realise that unless we accede to his demands he'll kill you and so we play it safe. Drive down here as he tells us and open the back door. He's got the knife to your throat . . . demands our guns . . . he shoots you in the back of the head. We overpower him and in the struggle he gets shot dead too. Something like that. And we'll be heroes.'

Siobhan said, 'Whatever the circumstances, we'll fit a story to answer the evidence. What it boils down to is that both of you are due to die.' She spoke with glee and a sneer.

'Like all the others?' Henry demanded.

'Exactly like the others,' she confirmed.

'Derek Luton had you sussed, altering those statements. Which one of you killed him?'

Tattersall gave Henry a friendly wave and a smile through the cage door.

A lurching sensation went through Henry.

'And Geoff Driffield? What about him?'

'Team effort,' Gallagher said. 'He thought we were going to catch that gang of gypos, poor sucker. We turned up instead. Just unfortunate they hit that shop up the road at more or less the same time as we hit dear old Geoff.'

'And what had he done to you? Looked at you wrong?'

'Got caught collecting evidence against us. He had to go.'

'You know other people are involved with me – people like the FBI?'

'We'll deal with them as and when we need to. Anyway, I'm sick of talking now,' said Gallagher, 'getting pissed wet through. What I want you both to do is climb out of here nice and slowly, walk up to that factory wall and put your noses up to it, OK? I see you've taken his cuffs off, Henry, but it makes no odds. If you piss about, we'll shoot you anyway, so it's as broad as it's long. If you want it over quick and clean, just follow orders.'

Henry and Rider exchanged glances.

'Is that FBI shit true?' Rider asked.

'Yeah,' Henry squeaked.

'Well, that makes me feel a whole lot better.'

Henry's throat felt like his windpipe had been constricted by a boa and despite the cold, a clammy sweat had formed under his armpits.

Siobhan smacked the release catch and the locking bar sprang open.

The three armed detectives took a few paces back and covered Henry and Rider as they slowly descended out of the van. Henry saw Siobhan was holding some kind of machine pistol and looked very confident with it.

'Up to the wall,' Gallagher reiterated.

Henry's heart-rate was incredible. He thought it had reached his limit. A myocardial infarction was more likely to be the cause of death than a bullet.

He and Rider walked side by side to the wall. By the time they reached it they were both drenched.

'Right up to it,' snapped Gallagher.

Henry stood with his nose pressed up to the bricks. His hands hung loose and weak. He closed his eyes despairingly and let his forehead drop onto the wall.

'Who'd like to be first?' Gallagher offered the choice.

Rider said, 'Kill the cop first. At least it'll give me some pleasure before I die.'

'But you're both in this together,' Siobhan argued. 'We've listened to your little chats.'

'Just shoot the cop first,' Rider insisted. 'He's still a cop, isn't he?'

'Thanks,' breathed Henry.

Gallagher stepped forwards and placed the muzzle of the revolver at the back of Henry's head at the point where vertebrae and cranium met.

'Don't worry, Henry, you won't feel a thing.'

Terror welled up inside him and made him want to shit and vomit and scream and cry and wake up from this fucking nightmare of nightmares.

Rider looked at Henry. 'Always wanted to see a cop get blasted away. I'll die happy now . . .' and on the *H* of *Happy* his open-palmed left hand shot out with the intention of smacking the revolver away from Henry's head before Gallagher fired.

Except Gallagher was ready for this manoeuvre. He stepped smartly back a stride, pulling the gun away.

Rider slapped thin air and found himself staring down the barrel of the revolver.

'You idiot,' Gallagher laughed. 'I was hoping you'd try that, because I wanted to kill you first anyway.'

Henry's mind clicked into gear at that moment. His right hand swung to the leather pouch on his belt which held his extendable baton. He thumbed up the catch and drew it out, making his movements smooth and unhurried.

'You're too slow,' Gallagher taunted Rider. 'Do you want to see if you can bat it out of my hand now, before I blow your head off?'

Hoping Gallagher wasn't too far behind him, Henry swivelled at the hips and in one flowing motion pirouetted and released the catch on the baton which extended with a whoosh and a click. He turned 180 degrees with the baton swishing through the air like a sword and slammed it against Gallagher's right forearm with all the force he could muster. Had it been a blade, Gallagher's hand would have been sliced off.

Gallagher screamed. The gun jumped out of his grip, skittering away into the darkness.

Coming back round for a second time, Henry whacked the baton against the side of Gallagher's head; it connected against his eye-socket with a satisfying jolt.

Neither Siobhan nor Tattersall, standing behind their DI, were able to shoot for fear of drilling holes into his back.

In that moment of confusion, Rider grabbed Henry's jacket and dragged him bodily into the van's headlights, shouting '*Run!*' For a second both men were completely exposed. Two shots were hurriedly fired . . . then they were beyond the headlight beams and had launched themselves into the total wet blackness of the night.

Siobhan was in time to glimpse Henry's disappearing back. She flicked the safety off the machine pistol and riddled the night with bullets.

Blindly, Henry pitched himself headlong onto the ground, landing clumsily and jarring his sore chest and dropping the baton. He ignored the pain and forced himself to roll along the hard ground for about twenty metres, feeling the spray of bullets passing only inches overhead.

He righted himself onto one knee, aware fleetingly that his clothing was now in an abominable state. His trousers were torn, jacket sleeves ripped.

And besides hurting his chest, he had also caught his ear, which felt as if it had been ripped away from the stitches. The pain was dreadful. But Henry pushed himself on. Where was Rider? Had he been hit?

Henry scrambled up and ran into the further darkness, not knowing what sort of terrain lay ahead. Next thing he tripped. He went head over heels down a steep grassy bank, expecting to roll and tumble into something awful. He came to an unexpected stop. More bullets cracked above.

Henry stopped breathing. Tried to listen. The heavy sleet deadened everything.

Voices. They were searching. Can't make out the words, but there's annoyance there.

Keep still. Don't move. Odds are against them finding you. My ear, my fucking ear!

The engine revving, the beam of headlights lighting up the land to his left . . . getting closer, the van crawling closer. More voices – Siobhan's – and some shouts.

The headlights swept to the spot where Henry lay.

He knew they would see him. He was briefly reminded of those World War II POW escape films. He knew that if they saw him, he was dead.

The lights passed over him. The engine grew fainter.

Henry breathed out cautiously, but didn't move. It could be a ploy to flush him out. He was wet and cold, but fuck that. Hypothermia was better than lead poisoning. He gritted his teeth at the pain in his ear.

Ten minutes passed.

A hand clasped his shoulder. 'You OK?' It was Rider. He had been lying up only feet away.

'No, not really.'

'They'll bring other cops in to search. We need to make some progress, Henry.'

'Let 'em,' said an exhausted detective. 'We can give ourselves up.'

'Are you fucking thick, or what?' Rider was incredulous. 'You'll be an accomplice to me. You'll get convicted of that and all the other shit, and probably end up murdered in prison. We can't give ourselves up yet anyway, not until it's safe – not until we've decided on a way out of this crap.'

'So what do you propose?' Henry couldn't have given a toss at that moment. Everything was too much for him.

'First things first. Let's get out of here and stay free.'

The plane touched down at Manchester Airport at nine o'clock. The pilot handled the atrocious weather conditions with aplomb. The passengers gave him a round of applause and were glad to be alive. They disembarked and having collected their luggage, made their way through Customs. Only a couple were stopped, their cases searched perfunctorily. Scott Hamilton and his companion, Raymond de Vere, sailed through unchecked, were met by a driver at the meeting point and led immediately to a waiting Mercedes.

Behind, in front, and around them, a team of expert watchers, military and police trained so they understood all aspects of the game, slotted unobtrusively into place.

The two men didn't have a clue.

'Henry should have been in contact by now,' Donaldson announced to Kate and Karen. He looked at his watch. 9.30 p.m. He eyed his wife worriedly.

'What's going on?' asked Kate. She knew that when her two guests and husband had got into their secretive scrums the evening before, something exceptional was taking place, but she couldn't begin to guess what it was. She wasn't that interested, actually. Policework bored her rigid.

Karen took a deep sigh. 'I think you need to know that Henry's become involved in a police corruption enquiry, and there's just the remotest possibility he could be in some sort of danger. God, it sounds corny even saying it, but it is remote,' she tried to stress. 'We're involved in it too, and just waiting to get updated by Henry. He should have spoken to us by now.'

Kate's mind homed in on the word 'danger'. 'Does it involve Derek Luton?'

Karen nodded.

Kate closed her eyes. 'Christ!'

'Kate, does Henry normally phone in when he's working late?' Donaldson asked.

'No, not really. Sometimes . . . I mean, I usually see him when I see him.'

'So we're probably making a mountain out of a molehill,' Donaldson said. 'But just to put my mind at rest, will you phone in and ask to speak to him, honey?'

She did. At the end of the conversation she put the phone down slowly, a crease of puzzlement on her face. 'They said he's taken a prisoner to Preston, but they sounded strange. Almost as if they didn't want to talk to me.'

On being alerted by the NWOCS, every available police officer in the Preston area had descended on the industrial estate and a search began. The officers were told they were hunting a suspected murderer and the police officer who had engineered his unlawful escape from custody. Both were considered to be very dangerous men.

Raymond de Vere settled comfortably into his room at Conroy's country club where wine, sandwiches, fruit and coffee were provided, followed by a high-class hooker who demonstrated an imaginative use for a banana. De Vere gratefully devoured it *in situ*.

In a ground-floor seminar room, Conroy, McNamara, Morton and Hamilton met up.

'Before we begin, Rider and Christie have escaped from custody,' Morton announced with some trepidation. 'And knowing what they know, leaves us with a problem. Rider has decided to grass on us.'

'I thought you were going to kill them,' whined Conroy. He tugged his pony tail agitatedly. He was heartily sick of Rider and that damned detective who should have been wasted long ago instead of all this pussy-footing around.

'They got away. It wasn't my fault. I wasn't there.'

'You should have been more ruthless in the first place,' said McNamara,

288

entering the bickering which looked set to spiral out of control. All three men were on edge.

Hamilton stepped in, stroking his goatee thoughtfully. 'These two guys causing you heartache?'

'Heartache?' muttered Conroy. He turned to Morton. 'You've made a complete balls of this.'

'Whoa, gentlemen,' Hamilton interjected, raising his hands to pacify. 'What you need is a professional solution. If you recall, I mentioned two friends of mine who specialise in such matters. They work quickly, efficiently and cheaply. And they have a one hundred per cent track record. They are very very high class – exactly the type you require to deal with these two people, I would suggest.'

'But we need them now,' said Conroy.

'Would tomorrow morning do? They're in Paris as we speak. An hour from Manchester by air.'

They all nodded.

'I'll contact them,' Hamilton said. 'All you need to do is use your resources to pinpoint the position of these individuals and let my friends do the rest.'

An air of relief seeped through the room.

'That leaves us with the question of where the goods are going to be displayed.' Morton looked at Conroy.

'By midnight, Rider's club will be staffed by my people.'

Not having received any instructions to the contrary, Jacko kept the club up and running. Unusually, even for a Saturday night, the place was packed, doing a roaring trade.

Weekends were the only times doormen were employed – four bruisers not renowned for their interpersonal skills. Two kept door, two drifted around inside. They changed their roles on a regular basis.

Conroy's men swaggered up to the front door – six of them – and confronted the two lounging by the till. There was an exchange of words and gestures and Rider's employees acknowledged defeat. They slunk away from the doors and disappeared into the wet night, now unemployed.

The other two were located in a strategic position overlooking the dance floor. They had no qualms about joining their pals.

A bloodless coup – so far.

Jacko was a different proposition. He was bundled into the manager's office and beaten into a messy pulp.

Almost a bloodless coup.

Now Conroy ran Rider's club, practically if not legally. Maybe the latter would follow.

The man who had led the assault used the phone in the manager's office to convey the good news.

Chapter Twenty-Eight

They were out of the immediate area within minutes, working their way cautiously through the industrial estate towards the retail end which was nearer to the town centre.

Henry held his left hand over his ear which was bleeding profusely through his fingers.

They skirted past a drive-thru McDonald's and scurried through the dark car parks of Texas Homecare and Morrisons, with what used to be the docks on their right. They stayed in the blackest shadow, ducking when a car approached, rising slowly when it passed.

Henry Christie, fugitive. Unreal, surreal. He was floating through a different world and was struggling to remind himself that this was reality.

A few minutes later they were in the car park of the Ribble Pilot, a modern pub right on the dockside. Rider crouched down, pulling Henry with him. They worked their way around the parked vehicles and Rider tested every door.

One opened.

It was an old Ford Granada.

'I loved these motors,' Rider whispered. He slid in and fumbled around in the wires underneath the steering wheel, until his hands expertly found the ignition wires. He ripped them out, yanked two apart to expose their metal ends, touched them and they sparked and – *voilâ!* – the engine started first time.

Henry remained on his haunches outside the car.

'Get in.' Rider reached across and flicked the catch on the passenger door.

'We're gonna steal a car?' He could not believe it. This was getting all too much.

'Yep, and if you don't get in, I'm going to drive off without you.'

'Oh my Christing God!' Henry chunnered. He went round to the other side of the car and got in.

It was an automatic. Rider slotted it into Drive. Moments later they were back on the A583, heading towards Blackpool. Henry cowered down in the passenger seat. Aiding and abetting the unlawful taking of a conveyance. He was having grave problems coming to terms with this additional responsibility, on top of everything else. His brain was due for implosion.

'Let's just hope the owner's set in there for the night . . . give us a head start,' Rider was saying.

Henry made a feeble attempt to pull himself together. He sat up, tugged down the sun visor, flicked on the interior light and inspected his ear. What he saw made him whimper.

It was hanging on by a thread of gristly skin, swinging like a sign outside a pub. He moaned. Blood flowed onto his left shoulder and dribbled down his chest.

'It's a fucking mess,' he blurted out, almost crying.

'It'll be all right,' Rider comforted him. 'So long as you get some medical treatment fairly soon. Better than a bullet in your brain at any rate.'

'I don't mean that,' Henry said churlishly. 'I mean everything – the whole fucking shooting match. What the hell are we running for? I've done nothing wrong.' He was rambling a bit as he tried to unscramble his brain. 'Let's just give ourselves up, John. We've nothing to fear.'

Rider took a left at Three Nooks and headed towards Lytham.

'They've just tried to kill us, mate – that's what we've got to fear. What we need is some breathing space so we can reorganise ourselves and plan ahead. Presenting ourselves at a police station isn't the answer, not to my way of thinking. If we do that, they'll simply say we escaped from custody and we'll be fucked again.'

Christ, the pain.

'Right, OK,' said Henry in an attempt to be positive. He was thinking now . . . slowly, but at least he was thinking. 'We need to get our act together, get the evidence together and then hit the bastards with it. We could go to my house—'

'Like fuck we could. They'll be watching and waiting, just like they'll be watching and waiting at my flat. I have a better idea – somewhere we can crash out for the night, then see how things look in the morning.'

Henry slumped back in the big comfy seat. 'Whatever,' he said dejectedly.

They did more than watch Henry's house. On the stroke of midnight they raided it.

A mean-tempered Gallagher with a bandage wrapped around his right arm and an ugly-looking swelling by his right eye, banged angrily on the front door.

Tattersall and Siobhan were directly behind him. Three other NWOCS detectives hovered behind them, looking hard and uncompromising, like they'd never smiled since joining the cops.

Kate raced to the door. She and the Donaldsons had been sitting in the lounge, tense, awaiting any developments. Karl stood with her at the threshold.

'Is Henry Christie here?' Gallagher demanded.

'No, I—'

Before Kate could say anything more, Gallagher interrupted. 'He's wanted for assault, allowing a prisoner to escape and other corrupt practices, including rape and sexual assault. We're gonna search the house.'

Donaldson stepped forwards. 'Now hold on a moment, buddy.'

'By force if necessary,' Gallagher warned him.

'Where's the warrant?'

'Under English law we don't need one. Now step aside and let us in, or we'll gladly kick the fuck out of you.'

The officers poured in to the house. They pushed past Kate and one went straight through to the back door which he opened to allow three more detectives in. They had been watching the rear to prevent Henry escaping out back.

'What do you mean, rape and sexual assault?' Kate cried. She was confused and on the edge of tears.

Gallagher sneered evilly at her. 'Your husband can't keep his hands off other women, can he?' he said with extreme cruelty.

'Shut it, asshole,' Donaldson warned him, and stepped forwards menacingly. Gallagher and he were much of the same height and build. It would have been an interesting conflict.

'Go on, do it,' Gallagher invited.

Donaldson gritted his teeth and held back.

The moment past.

'Now I suggest you get everyone in the house assembled in the living room,' said Gallagher.

They parked the Granada in a badly-lit street in South Shore, and sat there hoping not to draw attention to themselves.

Henry found an oily cloth in the glove-box and pressed it to his ear. The bleeding had lessened. Coagulation was taking place.

They had another brief argument about presenting themselves at a police station. Henry's instinct told him this was the way forwards. Rider laughed at him.

'That's what comes of never having been on the wrong side of the law,' he sneered. 'You wanna look at it from a crim's perspective occasionally. When a cop's out to get you, it's a godawful feeling when you know you can't trust anyone. And for some, that's what it's like. A police station can be a place where everything you do or say is twisted.'

Which was hard for Henry to perceive. He had always – truly – believed that if he was in trouble he could go to the law and be dealt with fairly and justly. In a matter of days his world had been up-ended. Now he didn't know who to trust, who to turn to, where to go. The badness of this squad seemed limitless, its influence phenomenal. Who could he go to who wasn't touched by it?

Sitting there with a bleeding ear, a thumping head, in soaking wet

292

clothes, he felt very much alone. He knew he could trust Karl Donaldson – but how could he get to him? And he knew he *had* to trust John Rider.

There was a silence between the men, filled by the engine ticking over. Warm air blew out of the vents.

'So did you kill Munrow?'

Rider turned his whole body in his seat to look at Henry. A slash of yellow light fell across his eyes. The rest of his face was in darkness. He said nothing.

'I thought so,' Henry concluded.

The search had been thorough. An hour after starting, the police withdrew, taking nothing away with them despite having visited every nook and cranny.

Gallagher looked cheated.

'What did you expect to find?' Donaldson asked him. 'He ain't done nothin' wrong, bud – unlike some people I could mention.' He looked knowingly at Gallagher then gladly closed the front door behind him.

Donaldson returned to the lounge where the two exhausted daughters had crashed out on the settee and the two weary women, hollow-eyed, looked tiredly at him.

Kate had gone beyond crying.

'Is it true?' she begged desperately. 'Can Henry really have helped a murderer to escape? And rape? What does it mean?'

'You can take it from me that Henry has not raped anyone, nor has he helped a murderer to escape,' Karl hissed quietly, one eye on the two girls. This was a conversation they didn't need to overhear. 'Henry's as straight as an arrow; he's just become involved with people who aren't.'

'What do we do now, Karl?' Karen asked.

'Wait,' said Donaldson. 'I'm sure he'll contact us when he can. In the meantime, let's have a cup of tea and get these little ladies back to their beds.' He winked at Karen and gestured for her to follow him into the kitchen.

'They were after those statements as much as anything,' Donaldson said quietly to her. 'What did you do with 'em, babe?'

'They're down my knickers – almost. As soon as I heard them at the door I grabbed the paperwork and folded it down the front of my jeans.'

Donaldson's face turned into a wide smile. 'Now I know why I love you,' he said. 'Any chance of me removing them with my teeth?'

She punched him gently on the arm. 'Every chance.'

Henry was wet and shivering again, the dryness of the car having been left behind ten minutes ago.

He and Rider were, once more, in dark shadow. This time they were fifty metres down the road from the front of Rider's club, watching the last of the stragglers stagger away from the doors.

At last the place closed up and the lights went out.

The street was quiet. Nothing moved.

Ten minutes later the door opened again and the staff left *en masse*, a small posse of people probably on their way to a curry house.

The door closed.

'Jacko should be leaving soon, then we'll have the place to ourselves.'

Ten more minutes.

No Jacko.

'I don't like this.'

'Perhaps he's robbing the till.'

Rider ignored the remark. 'I didn't see the bouncers, either. They usually leave with everyone else.'

He nudged Henry. Both of them trotted across the road and into a high-walled alley which ran down one side and the rear of the club. They stuck to the building line and at the point where the alley took a right-angled turn, Rider pressed Henry and himself into a doorway.

'Two minutes here, just in case,' Rider whispered into Henry's good ear.

The rain continued to fall, straight down, like thin steel rods. Unrelenting. Cold.

For Henry the wait was interminable. He needed to lie down. Here would do, but preferably in a hospital bed with lots of nurses fawning over him.

Rider tugged his sleeve.

They stepped out of the doorway and almost immediately there was a scuffling noise and a cough behind them. Rider flattened himself against the wall, dragging the slow-witted Henry with him.

A man walked down the alley, back-lit by street lights. He had that peculiar stagger which denotes someone pissed out of their heads who firmly believes himself to be sober.

The man paused unsteadily in mid-step, looking in their direction, peering towards them in the gloom. He was ten feet away. Henry could smell the beer and spirits on the man's breath.

The man unzipped his flies, turned to face the wall. With both hands he directed his urination up and down the wall, making fancy patterns. He belched, broke wind, then vomited through the arc of piss. He spat the remnants of the Chinese meal out and finished his bodily function. He shook the drops off and slid the member away.

Henry's stomach turned.

The man wiped his mouth on his sleeve, turned and wandered happily back out of the alley, muttering something.

They let him go before moving again.

Rider located the gate which led into the back yard of the club. It was locked.

'We'll have to go over.'

'Fine, fine,' acceded Henry.

'Give me a leg up,' said Rider, seeing Henry did not seem able. 'I'll open the gate from the other side.'

Henry nodded. He intertwined his fingers, crouched low with his back to the wall, braced himself and hoped Rider hadn't stepped into any dog muck.

Rider put his right foot into Henry's hands, counted softly and on 'Three!' Henry heaved up, propelling Rider who got his left foot onto Henry's shoulder and a moment later was lying astride the top of the wall. He shuffled his legs over and dropped into the yard.

Uncaringly, Henry wiped his hands down the sides of his trousers, dog shit or not.

The gate opened. Rider beckoned him through into the yard, which was not particularly big and was full of empty beer barrels and all the paraphernalia associated with the waste from licensed premises.

The back door to the club was a huge steel panel, riveted to the brickwork.

Henry studied it despairingly. 'How the hell do we get in here? We'll need bloody cutting gear.'

'We don't – we get in up there.' Rider pointed up to a window at first-floor level. 'We'll stack up some barrels and climb up. It should open OK. This place is about as secure as Buckingham Palace.'

'I'm surprised you haven't had it screwed.'

'We have. Security's crap on the outside, but the bar area's pretty tight.'

Together they manoeuvred two barrels on top of three others and Rider climbed cautiously onto the top one to find his head and shoulders more or less on a level with the window. He heaved at the window. Nothing gave. He tried to lap his fingers underneath the frame, which was rotten, and he started to ease it away. With great effort and persistence there was some movement. But the window remained firmly shut.

Using the initiative which seemed to have deserted his recent actions, Henry scoured the yard to find some kind of implement to assist.

More by luck than judgement he kicked against a rusty hand-trowel of the type used by builders. He handed it up to Rider who jammed it between window and frame and applied leverage.

With painful slowness the window moved. Eventually it was wide enough for him to get his fingertips in properly, and he completed the task with a loud, splintering crack, nearly overbalancing off the barrels at the same time.

Seconds later he was inside the club.

Henry followed, dropping down behind Rider into what was a long disused lavatory.

'Thank God for—'

'Shh!' Rider warned him hoarsely. 'You never know – cops could be at the bar, waiting for us to show. Let's take it one step at a time.'

Chastened, Henry nodded silently. He followed Rider out of the toilet and into a dark corridor. With soft footfalls, they made their way along.

'What we can do,' Rider whispered over his shoulder, 'is get some sleep up here. We won't be disturbed. Then tomorrow . . .' His words drifted.

'Yeah, tomorrow,' said Henry sourly.

They stopped at the first door they came to. There was a bolt on the outside which Rider slid back. He placed his hand on the doorknob and suddenly the door seemed to have a life of its own and exploded open.

A huge form careered out of the blackness, brandishing a chunk of wood which was about the size, weight and length of a pick-axe handle.

The wood swished down into thin air, slicing through the point where a split-second before Rider's head had been.

Rider crimped himself out of the way and the blow was completely ineffective. In a continuation of the same movement, Rider swung back, and landed an iron-hard punch into the guts of the attacker. The wooden weapon dropped out of his hands and bounced on the floor as the impact of the fist whooshed the wind out of the man, who sank down to his knees, clutching his stomach.

Rider stepped behind the figure, clamped his right hand across the man's mouth, yanked him upright and growled, 'Jacko, you dumb stupid bastard, it's me!'

From what they could see of him in the darkness, Jacko looked a mess. Conroy's men had not been nice to him. His nose was knocked out of shape, and one eye was cut, swelling and oozing some sort of unpleasant-looking greasy substance. A tooth was loose and his ribs and stomach were a welter of bruises and grazes.

The three of them were in the room in which Jacko had been imprisoned. Henry stood on guard at the door, cocking his head down the corridor and half-listening to Jacko who was giving Rider the lowdown.

Rider listened without interruption.

'Six of them, you say?' he asked finally.

'That's all I saw. Could be more.'

'They came in, took the place and they're still here. I wondered why we didn't see our door staff leaving. What d'you make of it, Henry?'

'Conroy . . . the guns?'

'Yeah, makes sense, taking the place over. But why, tonight, unless he needs the place now, or later today for something. Jacko, did they mention anything that could give us a clue?'

He wracked his brains. Couldn't think of anything.

'What're they doing now?' Rider asked.

'Just hanging about, I think. I got dumped here and haven't seen any of 'em since. I couldn't hear anything because we're so far away from the front of the club here.'

Rider looked up at Henry again. 'They're here for a reason and it's nothing to do with selling drugs, because there ain't no one here to sell 'em to. I think you're right, it's connected with the guns. Let's go and have a look what they're up to.'

Exhausted, Henry's heart dropped.

'Jacko – you leg it out of the window and stay low. We'll lock this door and if they check up on you it'll look like you're still in here.'

'Anything you want me to do?' Jacko asked.

'Yeah – gimme your fags and matches and don't get involved. Henry . . . let's go looksee.'

'This place used to be a casino, closed early sixties. When I bought it, though it was being run as a club, it was in a pretty dangerous condition once you got beyond the public areas. So were some of the public areas, come to that. The ceiling over the dance floor is not the most secure in the world. I keep expecting the rotating silver ball to crash to the floor and kill some poor bastard underneath.'

'Any electric up here?'

'No, only on ground level.'

Rider was leading Henry along an endless maze of dark, dusty corridors populated by spiders' webs, dust, planks and other miscellaneous pieces of rubbish which made quiet progress difficult and walking hazardous. The lack of lighting made it all much worse.

'What you see downstairs is only a fraction of what there is,' Rider continued. 'There's two floors over that. Lots of rooms have been bricked off for whatever reason. It's just incredible, really. You don't appreciate what there is until you start looking.'

Rider struck a match which flared briefly, lighting up his face and also what he wanted to see – a door.

'I think we're here.' He extinguished the match, but before he threw it down ensured its tip was cold. 'It's so dry in some places, wet in others, don't want to chance a match anywhere. The place could go sky high. Fire hazard, really.'

'Sounds a peach of a building.'

'It will be, it will be,' Rider said, seeing his dreams for a moment. 'We need to be real quiet now. If I'm right we should be over the main part of the club once we go through the door. I think the floor's . . . not good, shall we say?'

'So I could drop through.'

'Distinct possibility.'

Henry thought about two broken legs. It would round things off nicely.

'Why are we going in here?'

'I'll show you. Tread carefully.'

Rider pushed the door open and edged into the room. It was large and expansive. There were windows but all were boarded up and blocked out any light. Henry stuck behind him but found that he could see quite well;

his eyes were taking advantage of all available light.

Rider went down onto his hands and knees in a movement so swift that Henry thought he'd gone through the floor.

'Look at this.' He had found a trapdoor which he hauled open.

Henry bent down onto one knee and peered into the hole.

'This room is directly above where the main part of the casino used to be. There's a few of these trapdoors in this room. I think the management used them to keep tabs on the tables below, using oneway glass.'

'Bit primitive.'

'Before the days of CCTV.'

Henry looked into the void. It was black. 'Can't see anything.'

'No, you won't be able to. That's a false ceiling you're looking at, and below that there's another suspended ceiling. If we're careful, we could remove a panel from this ceiling and try to move a panel from the suspended one, then maybe we could see down into the club, find out what's going on.'

'Risky, but what the fuck.'

Rider reached into the space and fumbled about. 'Got it.'

Henry fully expected Rider to come back with a ceiling panel in his hand, but he got the shock of his life when the other man produced a revolver which had been hidden in the space between floor and false ceiling.

'We may need this.'

'I suppose you shot Munrow with that, did you?'

A beat passed between the two men which sent a tingle of apprehension down each one's spine.

'Thought so,' said Henry, feeling sick.

'There's two bullets left . . .'

After a whispered debate they decided that the best time to do any messing with the ceiling would be round about 4 to 5 a.m. From Henry's experience, this was when people were at their lowest ebb. In the meantime, they tried to get some sleep – after Henry had set the alarm on his Casio wrist-watch.

Completely drained though he was, Henry could not sleep on the dusty, uncomfortable floor. His mind whizzed and banged as it thought through his predicament from every angle.

He made one incontrovertible decision. In the morning he would seek out Karl Donaldson and with his protection he and Rider would go to Police Headquarters and demand to speak to the Chief Constable. She was his only hope of salvation and fairness. Karl was his only hope of staying alive.

He knew he could not go on the run. No doubt Rider would be able to guide him through the low-ways and by-ways of the underworld, but it wasn't for Henry.

He believed in justice. Old-fashioned though that belief was, it had seen him through twenty-one years as a frontline cop and he wasn't about to have those values shattered by a corrupt squad which believed itself to be beyond the law. At whatever cost he would fight. Even if it meant becoming a protected witness, a change of name and address and that job in Asda stacking shelves. He would win . . . because they had made him angry. He almost laughed at the triteness of it: 'They have made me angry.' Talk about a fucking understatement.

As for Rider – he could do whatever he wanted.

'Henry . . . time?' Rider asked.

In the darkness Henry could see the tip of a burning cigarette brighten as Rider sucked.

He checked his watch. 'Four-fifteen.'

'I take it you can't sleep?'

'You guessed.'

'Ten minutes, then we'll do some joinery.'

Chapter Twenty-Nine

Breakfast was conducted at a leisurely pace. Champagne, strawberries and then a choice of full English or continental. Coffee or tea to finish off with.

Morton had departed early, leaving Conroy to entertain Hamilton and de Vere. McNamara was scheduled to arrive shortly.

At 9.45 a.m. Conroy said, 'We need to be moving now.' He was annoyed that McNamara had not yet appeared, because part of the deal would be that his haulage company would deliver the weapons to any point in Europe requested by the client. Conroy was also dying to tell McNamara the good news about the prostitute, which he'd only just heard himself.

But there could be no further delay. De Vere wanted to see what was on offer. His customers were pressing.

On the steps outside the country club, Conroy's Mercedes drew up, ready to take passengers. A second car drew up behind, two bodyguards on board.

De Vere and Hamilton settled in the rear seat. Conroy was about to drop into the passenger seat when his attention was drawn to a car speeding up the driveway towards the club.

The car skidded to an ostentatious stop and two good-looking young men dressed in jeans and trainers bounced out, all smiles and teeth – appearances which belied their chosen profession.

Hamilton got out of the Mercedes. 'These are the gentlemen I told you about – the professionals: Wayne and Tiger Mayfair. Old friends of mine.'

'Hi,' they said in unison and with a wave.

'Glad to meet you,' Conroy said. He looked closely at Tiger and saw four scratches down his cheek. 'Problem with a lion or something?'

Tiger chuckled. 'You could say that.' He exchanged a knowing glance with Hamilton.

'I want these wankers out of here now,' Morton said to Gallagher, eyeing the motley assortment of men who had made the bridgehead into Rider's club. 'Fucking shite.'

'Right, lads, you've done your bit. Now you can fuck off. You'll get your dosh later, as arranged.'

They trooped out of the place with fierce looks of contempt on their faces at being ordered around by cops.

300

'A car stolen from Preston last night has been found in Blackpool, boss. It was nicked at the same time we were searching for Christie and Rider.'

'So?'

'Could be they're here in Blackpool, lying low. There was blood on the passenger seat. We might've shot one of them.'

'You should've shot 'em both – in the back of the head,' Morton said sarcastically. 'How hard can it be?'

'Just bad luck.' Gallagher pointed to his swollen eye and held up his bandaged wrist. 'We'll get them. It's Donaldson who worries me now. Where did he hide those statements?'

'I presume you searched everybody in the house?'

The look on Gallagher's face gave the game away. 'In view of the fact we were searching for a wanted man, I think it would have been OTT to start strip-searching folk, don't you?'

'No, I fucking don't. You stupid, stupid bastard. How can I soar like an eagle when I'm surrounded by donkeys?' he wanted to know. He took a deep sigh, but try as he might, he could not shake his sense of foreboding. Henry Christie was proving to be hard to handle.

'Right,' he said, consulting a piece of paper in his hand, 'we've got thirty different weapons to show, so I suggest we set up about fifteen of the tables on the dance floor and put two on each with boxes of ammo. Then de Vere can wander about to his heart's content. You do that, and I'll go and help the others bring the gear across from the station.'

He left, fuming.

Twenty minutes later he returned with Siobhan and Tattersall. They were each carrying heavy holdalls which contained the guns. They had been removed openly from the armoury at the station because openly aroused less suspicion.

Morton directed their distribution.

Ten minutes later he walked round the tables, checking the merchandise. At one point he stood on some grit on the highly polished surface. He scuffed his shoes in it, gave it a moment's attention, then forgot it. His mind was consumed with other matters.

Thirty feet above, Rider and Henry peered down through the two-inch crack they had engineered in the ceiling to give them a restricted view down to the room below.

'What are they doing?' Rider said more to himself than anything.

'Haven't a clue.'

From their position, laid out side by side in the old casino office, chins hanging over the edge of the trapdoor, squinting down through the minute gap, they could see a couple of the tables Gallagher had dragged onto the dance floor.

'Rearranging the furniture,' Henry said.

The top of Tattersall's head came into view. He placed something on a table with a clatter of metal. His shoulders hunched over his task, obscuring the view. A minute later he moved away, revealing two guns lying on the table. One was a semi-automatic pistol, the other a big revolver. Boxes of ammunition stood by them.

Tattersall moved to the next table within their view and left two more weapons on it. One could have been an Uzi, the other was a semi-automatic pistol. And ammunition to go.

'A gun bazaar, I'd say,' Rider murmured. 'Marketing their goods.'

'They've got police property tags on them too,' Henry noted. 'I think they're the ones we found in the back of Dundaven's Range Rover. The cheeky swines.'

They drove in convoy to Blackpool, the Mercedes followed by the Mayfairs and then a Mondeo driven by Conroy's minders. They arrived outside the club at 10.30 a.m.

Morton met them at the door, then led them inside to the dance floor and main bar area. Gallagher and Siobhan were left to guard the entrance. De Vere sniffed the atmosphere huffily but said nothing. He began to browse through the display, lifting up and examining the goods closely. He was impressed.

Hamilton introduced the Mayfairs to Morton as the men who would be killing Henry Christie and John Rider.

'I don't think you'll have to look far. I reckon they're in Blackpool somewhere. That should make things easier for you.'

After ten minutes amongst the tables, de Vere turned to Conroy. 'We need to talk money now.'

Which is exactly what Conroy wanted to hear, but he also needed McNamara's presence because of the transport arrangements which were an integral part of the deal. 'Just give me a second,' Conroy said. He went to Morton. 'Where the fuck is Harry?'

At which exact moment the man himself walked hurriedly in through the door. His face was a mask of controlled grief, though none of the men in the room picked that up. They wanted him for his contacts, not his face.

'Ahh,' Conroy announced with relief. 'We wondered where you'd been hiding. Come over here. We're talking business.'

Kate picked up the phone on the first ring. 'It's for you. Somebody called Kevin Summers.' She handed it across to Donaldson, then sat down again. Her eyes were sunken and surrounded by dark circles. Karen placed an arm around her shoulder and gave her a hug.

There were only the three of them in the house. The girls had been taken to school without any explanations about what was going on.

Donaldson asked a few muted questions and hung up.

He turned to the women. 'Developments,' he said. Before he could expand, there was a knock on the front door. 'I'll get it,' he said.

It was Detective Chief Superintendent Fanshaw-Bayley.

Ten yards above the dance floor, two escaped prisoners watched and listened as intently as possible. Only the occasional word could be made out.

Henry adjusted his position ever so slightly to relieve the pain he was feeling.

Rider's stomach gurgled obscenely, reminding Henry how hungry he was himself. It had been a long time since both men had eaten or drunk anything warm and they were both close to starvation and exhaustion.

Donaldson and FB burst out of the front door and sprinted down the driveway to FB's car, a Ford Probe.

FB was shouting into his personal radio, ordering all the ARV patrols to go onto channel 71, the secure radio channel to which only firearms officers had access.

'How many teams are in Blackpool at this moment?' Donaldson asked.

'Three. That means six officers, all armed and dangerous.' FB slammed the Probe into first and accelerated away from the kerb. 'All ARVs to meet me, as a matter of urgency, on the Promenade, near to the pleasure beach, opposite the Big One. Do not use two-tones, or blues,' he said into his radio, then repeated the message and asked for acknowledgements. He then instructed them all to prepare their weapons and don their body armour.

When FB had finished speaking, Donaldson said, 'Henry thinks you're one of them.'

'Henry's an arsehole,' FB muttered, negotiating a blind bend and slewing the back wheels across the tarmac.

'And he's been used by you, hasn't he?'

FB slotted Donaldson a sidelong squint of contempt, then concentrated on his driving, choosing to make no reply to what was a very leading question.

After discussing the planned demise of Christie and Rider with Morton, the Mayfairs sauntered between the tables of weaponry, watched closely by Morton who did not like, or trust them very much.

They strolled until they were – accidentally – directly under the aperture in the ceiling through which the two escapees were peering. A table displaying two AK 47s was next to Tiger.

Tiger's trainer scuffed the dusty grit on the dance floor. He bent down, dipped his fingers into it, frowned and looked up at Wayne.

The ARVs responded brilliantly. Within five minutes, each car had converged beneath the shadow of the Big One. The officers, all kitted out in their body armour, Glock pistols and MP5s, waited expectantly for FB who screeched to a halt a minute later.

There was also another car present. The nondescript occupant got out of it and approached Donaldson. They shook hands. Donaldson then introduced the man to FB. 'I'd like you to meet Kevin Summers, FB. Kevin's with the MI5 Surveillance Branch. He's been doing some superb work for me.'

Coolly Summers said, 'I think we've got a situation here and we should move as soon as possible with it.'

McNamara, de Vere and Conroy paused at one of the tables which was displaying .357 Ruger revolvers.

McNamara nonchalantly picked up one of the empty guns in his left hand and flicked the cylinder release whilst continuing to discuss matters of transport and money with the other two. He held a speed-loader in his right hand which was fitted with six wad-cutter bullets.

'Yes, yes, I think so. We can arrange all that,' he said, continuing with the conversation. 'No problem. I'll arrange for my company to distribute them however you require.' He smiled, slotted the bullets into the chamber and twisted the release mechanism on the speed-loader.

Summers was succinct. His team of twelve had been tasked to pick up Hamilton and de Vere at the airport. They did so and followed them with ease to the country club where they met up with Conroy, Morton and McNamara. The team of watchers settled in for the night, even though the weather was atrociously wet, cold and slushy.

McNamara was the only one to leave the club that night. Summers took the decision not to have him followed.

In the morning, though, when Morton left early, Summers directed four of his operatives to tag him. This left eight to deal with the remaining gang. Easily enough to cope with people who were not expecting to be followed.

A good set of Polaroids taken through a long lens recorded the departure of the men from the club – and the arrival of two more players.

Summers handed the photos to Donaldson, who immediately recognised the Mayfairs. His face went white. And again he saw the scratch-marks on Tiger's face and wondered whether it was his tissue underneath Sam's fingernails.

Perhaps he would soon find out.

The MI5 team followed them, Conroy, Hamilton, de Vere and the Mayfairs to Blackpool, where they liaised with the four who had tailed Tony Morton and recorded his activities for posterity that morning. The four produced photographs of Morton, Tattersall and WDS Robson removing weapons from the armoury.

FB looked at the photographs and began to boil.

'They took all these guns to a club,' Summers said. He handed over the final shots of Conroy, de Vere and Hamilton entering Rider's club.

'The place is under observation by my team and they've told me that McNamara has just turned up.'

'You have done some excellent work here,' FB said genuinely. 'Can you tune your radios onto our frequency?'

'They already are—' Summers began, but was interrupted when the airwaves crackled to life and one of the MI5 watchers reported hearing the sound of gunfire from inside the club.

'You did a good job with the prostitute,' McNamara said suddenly and savagely to Conroy. The conversation about financial arrangements was brought to an abrupt close.

'You know, then?' Ronnie asked, slightly bemused. 'I was going to tell you later. How did you find out?'

'The police were waiting for me when I got home last night,' McNamara said. 'You also shot my wife, or at least the tosser you hired did. I had to go and identify her body last night, for God's sake.'

Conroy had heard another woman had been hit alongside the prostitute named Gillian, but he'd assumed it was just another hooker.

He was stunned.

'Philippa was with her. I don't know why, but my wife was with that piece of filth.'

McNamara closed the cylinder and pointed the Ruger at Conroy's throat.

Rider shifted uncomfortably, not realising that when he did so, more dust and grit were dislodged. They fell in a tiny cloud of particles onto Wayne Mayfair's shoulder.

He turned slowly and casually lifted an AK47 from the table and eased a magazine into the breech. Tiger reached for a Sig 9mm on another table.

Morton approached them.

'You got someone watching from up there?' Tiger asked. He raised his eyebrows to the ceiling. 'Don't look up,' he added with a hiss.

Morton caught on. He shook his head and thought: Rider and Christie.

'In that case, you won't mind if I test this gun, will you?' Wayne announced. He stepped back, knocked the safety off and swung the barrel of the gun up.

He pulled the trigger back at the same time that McNamara shot Conroy in the throat.

The bullet from the Ruger slashed into Conroy's Adam's apple and exited through the back of his neck, creating a huge hole. Conroy stood where he had been shot, astounded – it seemed – that someone should have the effrontery to even point a gun at him, let alone fire the thing.

For a moment, McNamara could see daylight through the wound, but he didn't peer through it. Instead he put another couple into Conroy's chest. These two went right through him, leaving a swathe of organ destruction behind them.

Henry saw – sensed – something was wrong below, then glimpsed the AK swinging upwards.

He shouted something which stuck in his dry craw and rolled away from their viewing aperture as a spray of armour-piercing bullets exploded through the ceiling.

Rider had not moved. He took two full in the face and as the shells came up through the floor, took another seven down the whole length of his chest and stomach, making his body twitch like it was being given a series of massive electric shocks.

Wayne continued to hold down the trigger and kept firing through the ceiling in no particular pattern. The magazine was empty within two seconds, some thirty bullets having been discharged.

Henry rolled and scrambled across the unsafe floor to the edge of the room where he curled into a ball, hands covering his head, as if this protective gesture would fend off bullets.

The sound of the shooting died away.

On the dance floor Conroy's body lay twitching, floundering in a pool of blood like a stranded fish on a deck.

McNamara stood impassively over him.

Wayne stared at the ceiling and smiled when a gob of blood blobbed down through the gap. He glanced triumphantly at Tiger, grabbed another magazine, discarded the empty original and slammed the new one home.

Morton stared, transfixed by the sight of Conroy and McNamara's smoking gun and the pool of blood.

Everyone else in the room was petrified, as in stone, trying to make sense of what had just taken place.

Wayne raised the AK again and gleefully pulled the trigger.

It was as though intercontinental ballistic missiles were coming through the wooden floor as the deadly shells forced their way all around Henry.

He stayed rigid; one tore through the boards perilously close to his head.

Then they stopped again.

The gun was empty.

'We're going hunting,' Wayne said to Morton.

He threw the AK down, grabbed another Sig and the two brothers ran to the door at the back of the ballroom and disappeared through it.

'I love her . . . I loved her,' McNamara wept over Conroy's body. 'I treated her badly, but I loved her. I did.' He sank to his knees.

'Get these fucking guns together and let's get out of here,' Morton screamed at his officers, shaking himself and them out of their trances. They reacted instantaneously.

Hamilton grabbed de Vere's arm.

They walked quickly towards the door but were stopped in their tracks by the sight of Gallagher, Siobhan and Tattersall accompanied, and covered by, two firearms officers, guns drawn and pointed with menace.

Four more officers sprinted into the club, followed by FB and Donaldson, then Summers and six of his team.

'Where the fuck d'you think you're going?' Donaldson said, standing in Hamilton's path. Hamilton took a swing and gave the FBI agent the most pleasure he'd had in ages when he decked the other man with a perfectly weighted right which sent him staggering back over the tables.

Henry breathed out, removed his hands from his head and looked across to Rider's unmoving body. Henry struggled to see the damage. He dragged himself silently and unwillingly towards him. When he was only inches away, he gasped. Rider's head looked as though he'd been chewing a grenade.

Henry needed to vomit. He retched.

Then he heard the sound of footsteps running down the corridor.

They came to a halt. 'Come out, come out, wherever you are,' he heard a man sing out playfully – Jack Nicolson style.

'Wherever you are, you're fucking dead,' came another voice. Less tuneful, less playful.

Two voices. Two men. Two killers.

Only one Henry.

Henry had the advantage. He had been in the dark for several hours. He could see everything very clearly in the room. The broken furniture. Planks of wood. An old desk. Rider's body . . .

He also had a blood-soaked gun which he had prised out of Rider's clammy, dead hand which didn't seem to want to let go.

And, supposedly, there were two bullets in the gun.

So, yeah, technically, he had the advantage.

Except he was a crap shot. His hand was shaking like mad. They were probably armed to the back teeth and no doubt ex-SAS members, with the ability to kill with deadly efficiency in a darkened, smoke-filled room whilst fighting off Dobermans at the same time.

So if he didn't make the bullets count, he was dead.

If he missed, he would have betrayed his position.

And he would be dead.

He lay on the floor, desperately trying to remember the intricacies of the prone firing position. Flat out on your stomach, legs together, gun in right hand (of course), supported by the left, forefinger on trigger – just the tip of it – breathing, watch the breathing, for fuck's sake . . .

I can hear them outside the door. They've gone quiet.

Sweat drips down the forehead, collects in the eyebrows, then dinks onto the eyelids . . .

And not two feet away lies a bullet-riddled body . . .

Fuck, the door is opening!

And suddenly Henry is very calm.

Wayne came in first, low, rolling across the room to the left. Tiger second, the opposite way.

As Wayne came up into a shooting position, Henry fired, remembering everything in that split second: don't anticipate the kick, don't snatch, aim up, slightly right, just below the chin . . . He didn't even wait to see if he'd hit the man – he knew he had – and he turned his attention to the second man, who had disappeared . . .

The calmness inside began to evaporate.

There was an old desk over there – the only cover he could be using. Henry focused on the desk. Yes, he must be behind it.

Silence.

Then, to Henry's right, there was a groan and a movement as Wayne rolled in his final death-throe.

Tiger roared something incomprehensible in anguish and stood up from behind the desk, Sig in hand and fired repeatedly in the direction of his already-dead brother.

Henry got a bead on him immediately and fired the last bullet.

Click.

A dud.

Tiger laughed uproariously.

Henry dropped the gun and lay there with his head on the floorboards hoping death would be quick, painless and a better place than where he was at that point of time.

After several light-years of uncertainty, Henry decided to face his attacker. He pushed himself onto his knees and watched the dark figure of Tiger Mayfair step menacingly towards him – and then disappear through the floorboards with a screech, plummeting thirty feet onto the dance floor below, half-landing on one of the tables, smashing his hip and crushing his right arm.

Henry stared open-mouthed at the hole in the floor.

He was still staring when Donaldson found him.

Epilogue

Henry was out of it for two whole days. He spent these hours as if in his perfect dream: in bed, being tended to by a series of concerned and beautiful nurses.

He woke with a start on the third day, feeling almost normal after a fifteen-hour mammoth session of drug-induced sleep.

He blinked, then had a slight regression when he saw FB parked on a chair next to his bed.

'Am I dead?' Henry asked. His mouth was parched dry and the words came out croakily.

FB smiled. 'Hello, Henry. How are you feeling, mate?' he asked quietly.

Henry shook his head and yawned. He rubbed his caked-up eyes and felt groggily for his ear. There was a big bandage on the side of his head.

'They've refitted it,' FB informed him. 'Eighteen stitches this time.'

Henry nodded. He sat up stiffly. 'What's happening then? Last thing I remember is shooting someone.'

'And killing him.'

'Shit. You've come to arrest me for murder.'

'Hardly,' FB said with a snort. 'I've come to pat you on the back, and explain one or two things.' The Chief Super's eyes dropped awkwardly. 'And I've come to apologise to you.'

Henry frowned. His head was still hurting.

FB sighed deeply. 'I've got to admit – I used you. I'm not happy about it, but,' he shrugged, 'needs must.'

Henry waited.

Uncomfortably FB said, 'Me and a Detective Superintendent from Northumbria have been investigating the NWOCS for about two years now. Not overtly, but discreetly. We knew they were all as bent as nine-bob notes, but we were struggling to prove anything because they were so tight. It was a major coup for us to get Geoff Driffield on, because they only usually choose who they think will fit. So we made Geoff look like the ideal candidate.'

'Bent, you mean?'

'Exactly. Anyway, he was working undercover for us. He was a success initially, but then Morton cottoned on and Geoff got careless and they caught him. Which is why he ended up dead.'

'Why kill everyone else in the shop, though?'

FB shrugged. 'I think the rationale was that a dead witness is better than a chatty one.'

'And they were going to pin it on Terry Anderson and his motley crew.'

'That was their idea. Obviously it would have been far easier if Anderson hadn't robbed the shop in Fleetwood. That was very inconvenient. It meant they had to put in extra work and fix the statements. Sadly for Derek Luton, he discovered their scam . . . to his cost. Tattersall killed him on Morton's orders.'

There was a pause.

'I was back to Square One and, I'll be honest, Henry,' FB admitted, 'when Morton asked for you specifically, it seemed too good a chance to miss. I went along with him. I didn't exactly know why he wanted you, but I suspected something was bubbling. So I used you, hoping you'd come up trumps. Sorry.'

'And you didn't even brief me,' Henry sputtered. 'You didn't give me an inkling. I could've been killed – I nearly was!'

'You might have refused – then where would I have been? I was just doing a bit of risk management, that's all.'

'Risk management is about taking risks with finance and paperwork – not lives. You know what? I think you are a complete bastard, FB.'

Once Henry had given more free and frank feedback to FB, he felt much better. FB took it all on the chin because he recognised how badly he had acted. No words could adequately describe how guilty he was feeling. However, given the same circumstances, he would have done it all again.

Henry was right. He *was* a complete bastard.

Morton could not shut up. He blabbed for England and incriminated just about everyone he could think of. He openly admitted his last thirty odd years of corruption, readily talked about Conroy and McNamara and their criminal dealings, all driven by greed.

McNamara was a brooding, angry man, difficult to interview. He gave little away at first, but as time passed and the officers skilfully persisted, he cracked. He admitted his part in the gun running as well as the murder of Marie Cullen.

Henry's ears pricked up. FB related to him how McNamara had confessed to trailing Marie to Blackpool late one evening, where she had fled following a violent argument in which she had threatened to reveal their relationship to the press. McNamara had tracked her down to a grubby bed-sit in South Shore, enticed her into his car then driven her to the sea front 'to talk things over'. They had argued again and she had demanded money from him to keep quiet. That was when he dragged her onto the beach and murdered her.

Hamilton and de Vere were different. They said nothing. However, the police in Madeira raided the Jacaranda and seized everything they could lay their hands on. Long study of the documents revealed a money laundering operation achieved by creative accounting: selling and re-selling non-existent timeshare apartments. Something like four million pounds a year was coming through Hamilton's books on behalf of Conroy, McNamara and their illicit drugs and gun-selling businesses. That was the beauty of accountants. They found it impossible not to keep records.

These records also showed that Hamilton had arranged a massive burglary at a gun warehouse in Florida; the guns were transported across the Atlantic to Madeira using McNamara's haulage company. A small proportion of the weapons had apparently been sent by ship to England so that they could be used as samples to impress buyers.

De Vere was hard to pin down. Very little could be proved against him. But with Morton's testimony, the cops threw conspiracy at him. It stuck.

Siobhan was easy to deal with. She confessed all, from being the driver of the getaway car after the murder of Geoff Driffield right to the false allegations she made against Henry Christie.

Gallagher and Tattersall tried to kick against the pricks, but in the end it didn't matter how tough they wanted to be. There was enough evidence against them to sink a bloody battleship.

Tattersall was charged with Derek Luton's murder, and he and Gallagher were both charged, alongside Morton and Siobhan, with Geoff Driffield's murder and the unlawful killing of the people in the newsagents.

Henry listened to FB talk whilst he consumed a hospital meal.

'Which brings us to the dead people,' said FB. 'The Mayfair brothers – Tiger, the one who fell through the roof – died of an embolism in hospital a day later, by the way. They won't be missed, couple of bastards. They've been killing people around the globe for years. A DNA sample ties him into the death of that FBI agent in Funchal.'

'Sam,' Henry said.

'We'll never know what she discovered. Hamilton won't tell us, but whatever it was, it was enough to get her killed.'

'Conroy?'

FB shrugged. 'We've raided all his drug-supply houses and scored a few good hits, but the fight goes on. Some other sod will take his place. Drugs don't stop coming in just because a major player dies.'

'John Rider?'

'Cremated next Monday.'

'And how is Nina?'

'Still hangin' in there. She's a bit of a tough nut. I think she'll make it.'

They met at the zoo.

Isa looked across the wall at the Silverback gorilla sitting proudly on the tree with a mass of bandages around his left shoulder area.

Henry stood next to her, gazing at Boris, wondering why she had asked him to meet her there.

'Do you think John knew he was going to die?'

'It's always a possibility,' Henry said, 'but I don't think he wanted to. He had a life ahead of him.'

Henry looked sideways at Isa, who was crying. Down by her feet was a carrier bag.

'I think he knew he'd die. That's why he came to the zoo after getting out of hospital and donated all that money specifically to Boris here. Ten thousand pounds. Like one last, grand gesture.'

'He said he hated animals to suffer.'

'He blamed himself for Boris getting shot.'

'He looks all right now,' said Henry, eyeballing the beast who stared back at him with a look of contempt.

Isa bent down and rooted in the carrier bag, then stood upright with an urn in her hand.

And Henry nearly died of embarrassment when she began to scatter John Rider's ashes in Boris the gorilla's enclosure.

At the same time as this ceremony was taking place, a lady was walking her Golden Retriever down a country lane in Heysham, near to Morecambe, in the north of Lancashire.

In comparison to the rest of the county, little snow had fallen in that area. Instead, the weather had been horrendously wet.

On either side of the lane were drainage ditches about three feet deep which caught the water from the lane and the fields.

Ollie, big, healthy, and full of bounce, enjoyed getting dirty and rooting through the undergrowth, even in the worst of weather. And it was pretty filthy that morning.

He and his owner walked down the lane. She avoided the puddles, but Ollie splashed heartily through them, regardless. It was not unusual for him to disappear over the edge of the lane into the drainage ditches and he did that about fifty metres ahead of his owner.

When he started barking in a strange, unnatural, slightly hysterical pitch, his owner immediately raced up to him.

He was belly-deep in the dirty water at the bottom of the channel. His tail twitched unsurely. He emitted that rather disturbing sound through bared teeth. His ears were pinned back and his eyes were showing their white edges. His attention was focused on something in the water ahead of him.

The owner put her hand to her mouth to stifle a scream.

In the water, half-submerged, was a body, face down.

Suddenly Ollie lurched and grabbed at the body's clothing before the owner could stop him. His teeth snagged in the shirt the body was wearing and the dog pulled. The body of a young man slurped round in the water,

312

an arm swinging in an arc, terrifying Ollie who, with a shriek, leapt out of the ditch and tried to jump into his owner's arms.

As Henry had predicted, Jonno's body had turned up in a ditch.